I0693990

DESTINY
THE GAUL FOREST

VANESSA MARI

For all the Destined yet to come.
May your courage guide you, and may you find the strength
to shape your own path.

PROLOGUE

Written by Margo Lear, Cataloger of the Destined at Raster Library

Clara Lildar is among millions living in Raster, the capital of Ebony, where being chosen by Destiny is rare. Destiny, an ancient and powerful magic, creates an unbreakable bond between humans and elves, a partnership essential for maintaining the magical balance across the nations of Pagos, Ebony, and Polent. Those chosen by Destiny undergo a transformation through the magic of the Gaul Forest, becoming stewards of this fragile balance.

The Gaul Forest is the lifeline of civilization. From its depths, all three nations harvest magic, a force that sustains their cities, nurtures their crops, and fortifies their borders. Those chosen by Destiny gain abilities closely connected to protecting the forest and advancing their nations. However, Destiny's magic is unpredictable. The bond it creates between a human and an elf is the most profound connection imaginable. It extends beyond partnership to intertwine their very essences, forming a single, inseparable Destiny.

So much about Destiny remains hidden. Beyond the few chosen, little is truly known about the bond's nature, the powers it grants, or the sacrifices it requires. This book, my modest effort as a cataloger of these nations, aims to uncover some of those secrets through the perspective of one of the newest Destined: Clara Lildar.

Magic is the lifeblood of these nations, flowing through every part of life. In Ebony, it makes sure that Raster's nearly constant rain is used effectively. Tall aqueducts, sculpted like large arches in the sky, carry water to protect the city from floods and provide clean water to all citizens.

In Pagos, a land shaped by its harsh desert landscape, magic breathes life into the arid soil. It turns barren sand into fertile farmland, allowing crops to grow. Without magic, Pagos would face starvation; its people would be forced to wander the scorching sands in search of food. In this country, magic is not just a tool but a vital means of survival.

Meanwhile, in Polent, magic is the backbone of military power. The basilisks, massive serpentine creatures with steel-like scales and red eyes, are among the deadliest guardians known. Only a few of these wild beasts can be captured and tamed. Polent's Royal Guard uses their strength to patrol the skies and defend its borders. These formidable creatures, featured on Polent's coat of arms, serve as a reminder of the kingdom's strength and resilience.

Yet magic does more than sustain these lands; it binds them together in a fragile peace. The Treaty of Destiny, born from centuries of conflict over the Gaul Forest's resources, ensures that no nation takes more magic than is allowed. Magic acts as a bridge, uniting humans and elves in a shared purpose, with each Destined pair using their abilities to keep harmony.

Among the Destined, some share similar powers, their bonds amplifying the magic between them. Others are paired with opposing abilities, creating a strong union that can change a nation's fate. The most famous Destined pair in history was Queen Alondra of Polent, a human, and King Arisen of Ebony, an elf. Over five centuries ago, they challenged the deep rivalry between their peoples, establishing policies that shared magic fairly between humans and elves. Their bond ushered in an era of balance and peace that lasted for centuries.

However, as history often proves, peace is never permanent.

Despite the harmony Queen Alondra and King Arisen had built, resentment simmered beneath the surface. Humans envied the elves' greater mastery of magic, accusing them of hoarding its power. At the same time, elves, who had long held the majority in all three nations, viewed humanity's growing influence with suspicion. For nearly two centuries after Queen Alondra and King Arisen's reign, these tensions remained subdued. However, once their bond faded, the fragile peace they had established began to fracture.

Even as unity unraveled, the legends of the Destined persisted, filled with stories of bravery, magic, and bonds that crossed time. Clara's favorite was the tale of a human and an elf whose Destiny allowed them to extend human lifespans. This story resonated deeply with her and quietly wove itself into her own journey.

This book chronicles Clara's unique encounter with Destiny and her transformation from a woman living in Raster to a guardian of the Gaul Forest. Her newfound powers and responsibilities would not only alter her life forever but also determine the fate of three nations.

Cataloger's Note: The events chronicled in this book are drawn from

Clara's diaries, notes from her friends, and historical accounts. For further exploration of her Destiny, refer to *Destiny: The Heir* by King Arisen, located in the Pagos Library, 2nd floor, section 1.6.

CHAPTER 1

From Clara's Diary

The alarm had been ringing for the past five minutes, and I still couldn't find a way to get out of bed. Those twelve-hour workdays were draining, but I wanted to get up to help my niece, Hale, and her dad, Kent. Her little feet pattered around the house, and her loud yet sweet voice sounded outside my door.

"I'll be there soon, Hale!" I called out to her as she opened the door.

She ran in with her arms wide open, ready to hug me. That was enough to give me the energy I needed to get prepared for the day. Kent had styled her white-blonde curly hair into two short, bouncy pigtails that bobbed with each step she took. She was taller than my knee, and I loved it when she hugged my leg. Hale had just turned two, and this toddler stage was my favorite.

I picked her up, set her on my bed, and tickled her until her giggles filled the room. Her laughter was contagious and hearing it made me happy. We played for a while until Kent called us downstairs. She wrapped her little legs around my waist and rested her arms over my shoulders as we went to meet her dad.

We were welcomed by the smell of fresh rain blending with the aroma of breakfast that Kent had made. He waited at the dining table and greeted us with a warm hug. I sat beside him and eyed the cinnamon oatmeal with appreciation. It was a perfect meal for another rainy day. I noticed the pile of unopened mail I had grabbed on my way in last night and slowly sifted through it between bites.

"Anything interesting?" Kent asked as he placed Hale in her high-chair and helped her with her food.

"Just the usual, although I can't believe we keep getting invitations to King Arisen's wedding. This is the third invite he has sent out. At this point, who cares? Isn't this his twenty-eighth wedding?" I mused, extracting the green envelope from the pile addressed to *Ms. Clara Lildar*.

"It is his thirtieth," he corrected with a chuckle, dabbing at Hale's chin smeared with oats.

I scoffed at the extravagance. "Don't you think it's excessive that everyone in Raster is invited? How can he muster enthusiasm for a thirtieth wedding?"

"He's over six hundred years old, and the elves hold him in the highest regard. Inviting us humans is just a political gesture to present a unified front. It's all about appearances, really."

There was excitement surrounding the upcoming wedding. Everyone seemed captivated by the story of Commander Vasa being "the one" for the King. After all, it was a story of love at first sight, and it captured the hearts and imaginations of all. It was the kind of romance people dreamed about, the kind that sparked whispers of hope and wonder.

But to me, it felt far-fetched. Having been single for over three years, I knew love wasn't a lightning strike but a slow burn, something nurtured over time. My own experiences showed me that true love arises from trust, understanding, and connection, not from a single, fleeting moment.

That was my favorite type of love and the one I wanted to find.

Truthfully, King Arisen had known Vasa through his last six marriages, which made this idea of love at first sight an overstatement.

In human culture, marriage usually happens only once in a lifetime, while elves, known for their immortality, often had multiple spouses over the centuries. I couldn't blame them for that. Spending hundreds of years with the same person seemed impossible to me. Even my parents, who shared a strong and loving bond, were married for ninety-eight years (a full human lifetime) before they passed away.

Elves, on the other hand, had a different approach. Take King Arisen, for example. He had been married thirty times in the span of less than two hundred years, averaging a new wife every six to seven years. By comparison, human marriages were monogamous and lifelong. The King's pattern raised eyebrows among many, though it wasn't entirely unheard of in elvish culture.

As for Vasa, this would be her first marriage, making her King Arisen's thirtieth wife. Having served as the head of the Royal Guard for over fifty years, she had earned a reputation for her strength and leadership. Many credited her with managing tensions with Pagos, the northern nation hostile to us, and maintaining peace in Ebony. Despite her public accolades, Vasa remained private, rarely speaking about her personal life.

Amid everything, I hoped the city would become less crowded once the wedding was over. We were packed with visitors coming for the event. I was used to being able to move around easily, but walking or riding a gondola meant weaving through rows of elves and navigating much more crowded waterfronts.

"So, will you be attending the wedding?" Kent interrupted my thoughts. He took the invitation from me to read it himself. "It could be entertaining. He's hosting it at the Royal Gardens, after all. That place is rarely open to the public."

"That's true, but I don't think so. I'd rather stay here with you and Hale. I rarely have days off from work, and I do have one on that day. It might be fun to stay in, rest, and go out as a family. I heard there will be fireworks; Hale might like that."

Hearing her name, Hale enthusiastically bounced in her chair. I smiled at her and leaned over to kiss her cheeks. She giggled and returned to eating her oatmeal with her bare hands, making the high-chair even messier.

I loved this little girl so much.

"Hmm, even Hale thinks it's a great idea. However, the fireworks aren't until the next day. It would be best if you did both. I insist because you need a life outside of just us. Trust me, I appreciate you, but you should go out and have fun."

Ever since Kent became a single dad, he's been living in my home with his daughter. I loved having them here, though I could tell he was worried. I'd repeatedly told him, "I hope you know you're not imposing," but he never seemed convinced.

If only he realized how much joy having them close brought me. I'd grown so used to the quiet, sometimes too quiet, but now the space was filled with laughter and energy. Hale's tiny footsteps echoed through the halls, making me realize how lonely I'd been.

"I'll consider it," I replied as I sifted through the remaining mail. King Arisen's invitation to the royal wedding remained there, but my eyes skimmed past it, landing instead on a long-awaited package. The waterfall painting I'd ordered had arrived. Hale had spotted it in a storefront window weeks ago, her face lighting up at the colors.

Of course, I couldn't resist.

"Is that the painting?" Kent asked, standing now by the doorway with his arms folded. He wasn't one for decorations, but even he had to admit it had caught Hale's attention in a way most things didn't. "Looks nice."

"It's for her," I said, smiling, setting the mail down, and walking over to hang the painting in the living room. Hale was still busy with her toys, but her eyes drifted toward the painting as soon as it went up. She smiled, a quiet, content kind of smile that Lorraine used to have.

It was uncanny how much Hale resembled her late mother. She had the same blonde hair, fair skin, and delicate, rosy lips that always seemed ready to smile. But Hale had our eyes, those round, black eyes with long lashes that brushed our brows.

I glanced at the only picture of Lorraine hanging beside the new painting. Hale's gaze followed mine.

"That's your mom," I said softly, my voice catching slightly. "She would've loved the painting too."

I hadn't known Lorraine for very long, just the one meeting before everything happened. But she had been kind and warm during that short time, becoming someone I could easily see as a sister. Kent had met her on one of her trips to Raster, and she had talked about raising Hale in both Raster and Hertm. Lorraine had big dreams for their daughter.

Dreams she never got to see come true.

"I wish I could've known her better," I whispered under my breath, more to myself than to Hale. Kent must've overheard because he stepped in with a quiet sigh.

"I wish that too," he said, his voice heavy with the grief that hadn't yet faded. He had spent months mourning her after the accident, lost in the pain.

A snowstorm took Lorraine from us—an unrelenting storm that swept over Hertm just weeks after she'd given birth to Hale. Months later, we received her ashes, and Kent kept them in a small silver box in his room. It was a box Lorraine had given him before she left, telling him it held great value to her and urging him to always keep it close. True to her word, he never let it out of his sight.

I felt the pain of that loss, not just for Lorraine, but for Kent, Hale, and the life they could have shared. Watching Kent grieve was difficult, but while he fell apart, I held things together. I cared for Hale, provided her stability and love—everything Lorraine would have given her if she'd had the chance.

Hale's hand reached for mine, pulling me out of my thoughts.

"Look!" Hale's excited voice snapped me back to the moment as she bounced on her toes, clutching a colorful block in her small hands. Her eyes flashed with pure happiness as she handed it to me, signaling for help.

I smiled, sitting on the floor with her and carefully stacking the blocks into a tower. Every time the structure wobbled and toppled, her contagious, lighthearted giggles filled the room. Moments like these made everything feel right.

As we worked together to build the tallest tower possible, Kent walked in, his expression softening when he saw us. He held out my parestine with a small smile. "Someone's trying to reach you."

With that, he went back to the kitchen, leaving me to grab the parestine. It hummed softly in my hands—a magical device powered by the magic of the Gaul Forest. I marveled at its simplicity—like paper that displayed messages, which faded after being read. Originally designed for diplomatic communication, it had become common everywhere as a way to connect regardless of distance.

Marcos's familiar handwriting greeted me as soon as I unfolded it, and I smiled. He never let me fall too far behind on anything important. The message was about the upcoming wedding, of course. Marcos had a way of being everywhere; his work, helping humans and elves alike, had made him well-connected. Despite his busy life, he always found time to check on me.

I read the message, and by the third one, I knew I had to respond before he started teasing me.

Hey, friend! Sorry, I was playing with Hale. How are you?

Marcos's reply came in quickly, his words scribbled like he'd written in a hurry: *Did you get the invite?*

I smirked, knowing precisely which invite he meant. *Yes, I did. A thirtieth wedding. What a joke.*

Everyone agrees with that. But listen, we're going, and Jastop got us prime seats.

I couldn't help but smile wider at that. Jastop, Marcos's elvish boyfriend, always used his connections to get us into the best spots. He was an event coordinator, and somehow, no matter what, Marcos always ended up with the best arrangements.

Kent insisted I go. You know how easy I am to convince, I wrote back, laughing.

Marcos and I had shared countless adventures in the past. He liked to remind me of those wild nights, even though things had changed since Hale came into my life.

His next message read, *We'll relive those memories and make new ones at this wedding.* I could almost hear his laughter and see his signature wink.

I paused for a moment, realizing how much I missed him. I also missed that part of myself—the part that used to go out, have fun, and live a little more recklessly. Hale had shifted my priorities in the best way possible, but maybe... just maybe, one night wouldn't hurt.

Count me in, I finally replied, grinning. *I'll see you in two days. And please tell me what you're wearing; we should match.*

As the last words appeared and vanished from my parestine, I felt a toy block hit my lap. Hale was staring at me expectantly, her eyes wide with mischief.

Out of the corner of my eye, I caught a glimpse of the message: *Don't worry, I'll take care of it.* It vanished the moment I finished reading it.

"All right, all right," I laughed, scooping her up and tickling her as she squealed with delight. I only had an hour before work and aimed to make every second count. Hale wiggled in my arms, her giggles filling the room.

"You win," I said, setting her back down to continue building our tower. One night to myself wouldn't hurt, but right now, my time belonged to her.

CHAPTER 2

From the archives of the Raster Library
Edited by Margo Lear
History of Raster

By now, you've glimpsed into Clara Lildar's life through her own words, showing what it was like before she became a Destined. However, to truly understand Clara's journey, it's important to put her story into context by examining the world she lived in and how life during her time differed from today. This chapter will provide the background needed to fully appreciate Clara's experiences, struggles, and victories.

Life in Raster, where Clara's story started, was different. Hidden in the southern part of Ebony and next to Polent's lands, Raster was a large city home to millions. Though the city was lively and full of energy, not a single person in the city had been chosen by Destiny. *Not one.*

Power and influence primarily rested with the elves, whose long lives gave them a natural advantage. Humans, on the other hand, had shorter lifespans and often occupied the lower levels of society, their voices quieter in the grand chorus of the kingdom.

Imagine, if you will, a city where rain is a constant presence. Dark clouds cover Raster's skies, and rain pours for hours every day. But the city has learned to adapt and uses it to its advantage. The magic granted to Ebony is used to build tall aqueducts, with arches rising above the streets, carrying rainwater to every home. Gondolas move along waterways, gliding silently through the rain-soaked streets and serving as a common way to get around. This magic isn't just about convenience; it's crucial because it helps prevent flooding in the city.

The country was named Ebony to symbolize the constant darkness and rain that cover its capital, Raster, a city often shrouded in perpetual twilight. But beyond Raster, Ebony's landscape is as diverse as its population. To the west lay the Gaul Forest, an ancient area bordered by the Sierra Mountains. This forest is the source of magic for the three nations, yet it remains a region few dare approach. Its magic is too powerful and unpredictable. People live far from its edges because living near the Gaul Forest involves certain risks to both body and mind.

Two small towns, Pitores and Hertm, perched on the highest peaks of the Sierra Mountains, were the closest settlements to the forest. Pitores, with its large population of elves, endured winters so bitter that a human couldn't survive more than a few minutes outside. Yet the elves thrived, their bodies adapted to the extreme cold. The magic of the Gaul Forest didn't touch Pitores; its high altitude kept the town beyond the forest's reach.

Just a few miles from Pitores, nestled in a valley that trapped warmth, was the human town of Hertm. Here, humans lived comfortably, though always aware of the forest looming just beyond the mountains. Hertm was shielded from the worst of the elements, making it a far more hospitable place for humans to settle.

Getting to these towns was difficult, and travel was often impossible without the Destiny gates. These portals, known only to a few in the Royal Court, allowed the Destined to travel instantly between places. However, they were protected by magic, and their existence was kept secret from everyone except those trusted with their knowledge.

And what about the Gaul Forest itself? It served as a sanctuary for both the ordinary and the extraordinary. It was home to creatures as common as squirrels and as dangerous as the mythical beasts born from the magic that surged through its veins. The public knew little about the forest's inner workings, but everyone understood its significance. Magic flowed from the Gaul Forest into the three nations, and the Destined were the guardians of that balance.

Pagos lay to the north, east, and west of Ebony, vast enough to nearly surround it like a predator circling its prey. Ruled by elves and far more populous, Pagos had long been at odds with Ebony. Those tensions only grew worse after the Gaul Forest began to fade.

The forest once stretched deep into Pagos, saturating the land with magic. Long before the age of Destiny, however, the Pagostonians had consumed most of that power. Now, only a fraction of the forest remains, confined within Ebony's borders. The loss of that magic and the forest's slow shift southward shattered whatever little peace was left between the two nations.

Queen Franes, a cold and unyielding leader with little patience for diplomacy, ruled Pagos. Her policies shut Ebony out, tightening the borders and refusing to engage with King Arisen. The people of Pagos, the Pagostonians, had delved too deeply into the Gaul Forest's magic when it was still part of their country, and that excess altered them.

The Pagostonians stood taller, their ears elongated further than any other elves, their pale skin almost translucent, and their eyes—red as blood—looked painful and swollen.

In stark contrast, King Arisen of Ebony had worked tirelessly to mend these fractured relationships. During his reign, he pushed for alliances that transcended racial divides. While his efforts bore fruit in some quarters, his overtures to Queen Franes and Pagos were repeatedly rejected, deepening the rift between the two nations.

To the south of Ebony lay the more welcoming lands of Polent. Ruled by King Llorent, a human whose family had reigned for nearly two centuries, Polent was an ally of Ebony. Its population was split almost evenly between humans and elves, and they used their share of magic to train the most dangerous creatures from the Gaul Forest. These beasts, with their impenetrable scales and piercing red eyes, were the pride of Polent and a constant reminder of the dangers that lurked within the forest.

King Llorent and his people held tightly to their traditions. They wore their hair long, often to the waist, as a symbol of endurance in the face of hardship. Their coat of arms featured a red ruby that represented a basilisk's eye. Both these symbols and the magic of Polent would play a pivotal role in Clara's journey.

The three nations, Ebony, Pagos, and Polent, were bound together through magic, politics, and history. Each of their leaders shaped Clara's path as she embraced her Destiny. In the chapters ahead, you will follow Clara as she navigates the complexities of love, the intrigues of royalty, and the perils of her world while stepping into her role as one of the Destined.

Cataloger's Note: This will be my second-to-last entry as the cataloger of this tale. The rest will be told by those who knew Clara most intimately.

CHAPTER 3

From Clara's Diary

I was looking forward to it now that I had agreed to attend the wedding. Over the past few months, there had been more cases of injuries in the healing ward, and long nights had become almost routine. The last human couple I cared for lived only a few houses down from mine, and I knew them well. They reported that one of our towering aqueducts had malfunctioned, causing a flood in their home that resulted in injuries.

The water had gushed through their bathroom so forcefully that it created a hole in their roof. Reports of similar incidents continued to pour into the healing ward, and I stayed late to see them through. Just a few days ago, an elderly elf slipped on the wet pavement near her house and fractured her arm. Since it rained almost daily in our city, damp pavement was a common sight. However, the streets usually dried quickly with magic. Fortunately, I was there to assist her, and her wounds were relatively easy to treat.

Elves typically didn't need treatment, and if they did, they sought it from another elf. This healing ward was designed to serve both humans and elves, but I mainly worked with the former, especially since humans couldn't heal as fast. The ward was filled with similar stories each night: people slipping, falling, and injuring themselves. And each time, the injuries seemed worse than the last.

Enjoying the wedding with Marcos was the one bright spot in an otherwise exhausting week. I was eager to take a break and focus on other things. It had been a while since I'd had elvish wine, and I missed how it made me feel… relaxed and disconnected.

By the end of the day, the simple makeup I had applied was smudged, and my ponytail was a tangle of flyaway strands. After my shift, I walked home in the rain, careful not to step in any puddles that magic hadn't dried yet. Why was it taking so long for them to dry? As I approached my house, I saw the familiar sight of Hale's face pressed against the window. I smiled brightly as I stepped inside to greet her.

Kent was sitting at the kitchen table, his expression worried. He looked up as I entered. "Another long night?"

I nodded, slipping off my wet coat and hanging it by the door. "Something is going on with the aqueducts. We had three more cases of injuries tonight."

"I heard about those. I wonder if anything is being done about it."

I shrugged, not wanting to dive into another discussion. "Maybe. Either way, it's keeping me busy."

He smiled sympathetically. "Well, at least you have the night out with Marcos to look forward to. A chance to unwind."

"Yes, I suppose I do. And I need it now more than ever."

I spent the rest of the evening doing what I loved most, cuddling with Hale as we read a book about the magical creatures of the Gaul Forest. It was widely known that a basilisk's breath could wilt plants and scorch the earth, but this story painted a different picture. It described how basilisks also carried a magical energy capable of making flowers bloom and healing wounds. And, according to the tale, in the rarest of moments, a basilisk could even sacrifice itself, releasing the last of its life force to give life to another.

I couldn't help but smile at how children's books always found a way to put a positive spin on even the most feared creatures.

After putting Hale to bed, I treated myself to a long, relaxing bath.

I was ready, more than ready, for elvish wine and a good time with Marcos.

Yes, please. Tomorrow couldn't come quickly enough.

CHAPTER 4

I admired the coral-pink gown Marcos had chosen for me. It hugged my waist and flared gently from the hips, the sweetheart neckline resting softly against my collarbones. The color warmed my skin, and the fabric caught the light with a subtle, starlike shimmer. Marcos had even picked long gold gloves to match, adding a graceful finish. I slipped into one of the few pairs of stilettos I owned, surprisingly comfortable and just high enough to make me feel confident.

I brushed my hands along the gown, admiring its beauty. Marcos always had an eye for style, and I was immensely grateful that he took shopping for a gown off my already overwhelming list of responsibilities.

I gathered my auburn hair into a neat bun, leaving a few wavy strands to frame my face. Since my hair fell to my waist, I usually kept it in a bun or braids to make it easier to manage. Tonight, the loose waves that spilled onto my upper back helped make the gown's low back feel a bit more modest for a wedding. I pinned a hair clip with red and silver rhinestones to the side of the bun, then fastened the final touch around my neck: a necklace with a deep red stone that Marcos had given me some time ago.

I finished getting ready with light makeup, darkly lined eyes, and red lipstick. The last big event I had attended was over a year ago, when Marcos surprised me with a celebration for my thirtieth birthday. I had enjoyed that night, and I hoped this one would be even better.

For this event, Marcos had offered to pick me up in his gondola. I glanced out the window to check the weather. The clouds were dark, but a few rays of sunlight peeked over the horizon. My parestine glowed as new words appeared, letting me know he was on his way.

Before leaving, I went to kiss Hale goodnight. She was already in bed, but I slipped into her room and pressed a kiss to her forehead. Her eyelids fluttered open for a moment, a sleepy smile forming before she drifted back to sleep. I lingered, brushing a strand of hair from her face, then slipped out and closed the door softly behind me.

Outside, Marcos was already waiting by his floating gondola.

"Hey, friend!" I called, waving as I walked over.

Marcos beamed as he took me in. "You look great, Clara!" he said, opening the door for me. "Wow, I have good taste. I'm confident Jastop will think so too," he added, his voice dripping with pride.

Marcos wore a fitted gray suit, and, as always, his eye for detail shone through. His coral-pink handkerchief matched the hue of my gown perfectly. The colors complemented his deep brown skin, and his slicked-back dark hair made him look effortlessly polished. A long silver earring dangled from his left ear, catching the light as he gestured for me to step inside.

I smiled at his enthusiasm. "Thank you. You look great too. Now that I'm dressed and out of the house, I'm glad you thought of me for this event."

"Of course! I love these opportunities to relive our earlier years. I miss going out with you."

As I settled into my seat, Marcos gave me a once-over and smirked. "You know, if it weren't for your ears and shorter stature, I wouldn't be able to tell you weren't an elf," he teased.

I nudged him lightly with my elbow and rolled my eyes. "Ha-ha, very funny."

It wasn't the first time someone had pointed it out, especially now that I was dressed more like an elf. Humans tended to favor practicality in their clothing, while elves chose elegance and extravagance. Their robes were embroidered with fine silver thread that shimmered, and their tunics carried intricate patterns that reflected their long traditions. Their fabrics were light and fluid, moving like water and giving them an almost timeless presence.

Humans, in contrast, wore sturdier materials, favoring earthy tones, strong stitching, and layers made for travel and work. Even our formal wear, though refined, leaned toward structure rather than display.

I had never minded. I liked the reliability of human clothing. But tonight, wrapped in flowing silk and delicate embroidery, I finally understood why elves dressed the way they did; it was impossible not to feel different in an outfit so effortlessly beautiful.

The gondola drifted away from the dock, gliding toward our destination. The Royal Gardens were only a few minutes from my house, but the waterways were crowded. Gondolas jostled for space as more guests arrived, and some attendees had chosen to walk along the narrow sidewalks instead. We could hear their footsteps above us, their laughter and conversations carrying over the water.

Not far away, a bottle—probably elvish wine—shattered against the stone. Part of me was content to remain in the gondola with Marcos. Another part longed to be out there among the crowds, a glass of my favorite elvish wine in hand.

"Should we walk? We're almost halfway there," I asked.

Just as Marcos pulled the small gray curtain from the glass window, a few raindrops hit the wooden top of our gondola.

"Okay, never mind," I said, laughing.

With the threat of rain looming, people and gondolas moved quickly.

Marcos reached under his seat and retrieved a slender bottle of elvish wine, its deep amber glass shimmering subtly in the dim light. As he uncorked it, a sweet, earthy aroma filled the air, blending the scents of wild berries and forest herbs. I couldn't help but giggle at the hidden bottle. He poured us two glasses, and we softly clinked them together in a quiet cheer.

"To one of those nights we'll never forget," I said as I took a sip.

"Yes, and most importantly, to King Arisen and soon-to-be Queen Vasa. May their love last more than six years."

It was hard not to spit out some of the wine as we laughed. But we were able to compose ourselves and let the warmth of the drink ease us into the night ahead.

Soon, Marcos opened the door for me, and I stepped out. I wrapped my arm around his, and he led the way. We were just outside the Royal Gardens, the closest I had ever been to this place, and the sight of it left me unexpectedly speechless.

The entrance was stunning, framed by an archway of luminescent vines. As we passed through the gate, tall trees with thick leaves formed a natural canopy, shielding us from the rain. Their trunks were carved with images of past Destined and intricate elvish designs representing the Gaul Forest.

The marble path looked like a single, unbroken stone, softly lit along its edges. In the distance, ponds shimmered with each raindrop, the ripples reflecting the light in a way that made the entire garden seem magical. Its beauty was undeniable, yet I felt a mix of awe and frustration knowing that such a place was rarely open to the public except for exclusive events.

The air buzzed with excited chatter, so loud that it was hard to hear what Marcos was saying. He pointed to the left, toward a door tucked out of sight. We pushed through the crowd and made our way toward the amphitheater, where the wedding would be projected for everyone. He opened the door, and we stepped into a small, dark room.

"Wait here," he said and rushed down a narrow corridor.

I started to protest, but he was already gone before I could speak. I stood in the darkness for a moment, confused, until Jastop appeared from the same corridor, Marcos's hand in his.

Jastop was a shorter elf with strikingly blue hair that matched his bright eyes. His warm, golden-toned skin seemed to catch and reflect the light around him. He wore a tailored green suit accented with touches of gold, colors that represented both the elves and Ebony. The suit fit him perfectly, and the vivid contrast made him stand out. I doubted that was accidental, given his role at such a high-profile event.

Jastop and Marcos were among the few elf-and-human couples I knew, rare in a world where our two peoples still struggled to coexist. Yet they had defied those odds. Jastop's long, graceful fingers often rested on Marcos's shoulder in a quiet, protective gesture, and Marcos was always quick to speak up when others questioned their relationship.

Their bond gave me hope that someday elves and humans could see past their differences. Selfishly, it also made me long for a partner who understood me as profoundly as they understood each other. I wanted someone who knew me without needing constant explanations, someone whose presence alone could bring comfort and clarity. Watching them together reminded me how much I yearned for that kind of connection, where silence could speak louder than words.

"I'm so happy you're here, Clara. It's been so long! Thank you for keeping Marcos company while I work on this event," Jastop said, pulling me from my thoughts and giving me the warmest hug.

I laughed and hugged him back. I missed them so much and vowed not to let another year pass without seeing them.

"Here are your entry passes to the atrium. Have fun, and please have drinks for me, though I can see you've already started enjoying yourselves." Jastop's gaze dropped to the empty glass in my hand, a playful smile tugging at his lips. We laughed and said our goodbyes. He kissed Marcos, gave my hand a quick squeeze, and hurried back down the corridor.

My eyes widened as his words sank in. My stomach dropped. "We are going to the atrium?"

Marcos took my arm and tucked it through his. "Why do you think I invited you? I told you it would be fun."

"You didn't tell me we would be that close. We will be in the same room as every member of the Royal Court. Don't you think they will immediately see that we don't belong? We are not elves, Marcos."

"Not with these passes," he said, lifting them with a grin. "Besides, you look incredible. Together, we will blend in just fine. No one will be paying attention to us. We can pretend we belong." He slipped the passes into his pocket. "Come on. Let us get back to the crowd and head to the atrium."

"All right, but we will be the only humans in there. You really do not think they will mind?" I asked, feeling silly for how nervous I sounded. "I know Jastop has connections, but still."

"Yes, we probably will be. And who cares? It is time the elves socialized with us. Let us go before the event starts. We would not want to miss their wedded bliss," he added with a wink.

I smiled and nodded. This could be a fun night.

We stepped back into the flow of people heading toward the amphitheater. The rain had picked up, but the trees kept us dry. Servers moved through the crowd with trays of drinks, and before I realized it, Marcos had placed another glass in my hand.

We followed the beautiful path, and as we went farther, the crowd began to thin. Most people veered left toward the amphitheater, while the entrance to the atrium waited ahead, slightly off to the right.

Before we could reach it, two large, dark shapes emerged in the distance. At first, they were little more than shadows, massive and still, with a presence that made the hairs on the back of my neck rise. I slowed, narrowing my eyes to get a better look.

Their outlines sharpened. Long, serpentine bodies lay coiled in guarded stillness, thick with muscle and covered in glinting, scale-like armor.

"Those are basilisks," Marcos said quietly, his voice edged with awe.

I turned to him, my eyes wide. Basilisks here in Raster, and on the ground? These creatures usually soared high above the clouds, their massive forms blending into the sky until they were little more than rumors and distant growls that could be mistaken for thunder. Seeing them here, grounded and tethered, was beyond anything I had imagined.

As we drew closer to the entrance, I saw them clearly. There were two of them, each restrained by thick ropes looped around their necks. Heavy black bands covered their eyes, likely to neutralize their lethal gaze and lessen the immediate danger they posed. Even so, an overwhelming sense of threat radiated from them.

Instinctively, I held my breath. Could they sense us? Could they hear the faint crunch of our footsteps on the gravel?

"Looks like King Llorent of Polent is here. Rumor has it he has the kind of face that makes people stare," Marcos said with a smirk.

I froze for a moment, my thoughts spinning. King Llorent, here? I had heard rumors about him before, whispered among both elves and humans. His striking appearance was common knowledge, but I never imagined I would see him in person. The idea sent a jolt through me, part curiosity, part disbelief.

From what little I knew of his policies, he was considered a fair and just ruler, someone genuinely liked by his people. And now I was about to be in the same room as him. It felt unreal.

"Oh, wow," was all I managed to say before walking as far from the basilisks as possible. Fear crawled through me, mingling with a growing sense of anticipation, and I had to fight the cold sweat threatening to break out.

When we finally stepped inside, the atrium opened before us. The glass walls gleamed, and more than twenty golden lanterns hung from the ceiling, casting a soft, dappled light across the floor. Beneath the glass under our feet, clear streams of rainwater flowed through narrow channels, glowing faintly as they moved.

The seating areas were carved from natural stone, while the chairs reserved for King Arisen and Commander Vasa were woven from living vines and lined with soft cushions. The beauty of it all left me breathless.

A tap on my shoulder pulled me out of my trance. An elvish woman, whom I recognized as Eliza, needed to pass. I could not believe I was this close to a Destined. Her dark gown and red eyes made her look mysterious, almost untouchable. Even in my heels, she still stood a full head taller than I did.

As she moved, the fabric of her dress shifted, revealing glimpses of the intricate forest-green Destined mark curling over her shoulders and tracing down her back. The swirling lines glowed faintly in the dim light, like delicate branches etched into her skin, a quiet reminder of the power she carried.

I quickly stepped aside and then squeezed Marcos's arm, moving closer to him. We followed the ushered flow of guests to our seats. Bells rang out, signaling that the wedding would begin in just a few minutes.

"We have excellent seats," I told Marcos. I glanced around and saw everyone settling onto the stone chairs. From our place near the center of the semicircle, we would have a clear view of the backs of King Arisen and Commander Vasa.

I recognized most of the elves of the Royal Court, including Rijor, King Arisen's right hand. He looked calm and at ease as he chatted with other guests who were clearly members of the court. His short white-blond hair made him instantly recognizable, as did the oak-tree pin on his chest. His ears were slightly more rounded at the tips than most elves, a subtle but distinct feature that set him apart.

Nearby, I noticed another group of elves and humans with long hair, clearly part of a different royal court.

"That is King Llorent of Polent," Marcos whispered.

As if sensing that his name had been spoken, King Llorent's gaze swept the crowd and found mine. His eyes stayed locked with mine for several long seconds. His black hair cascaded down his back in two perfectly braided strands, adorned with tiny red beads and sparkling jewels. My gaze remained fixed on his freshly trimmed beard and striking green eyes. Marcos had not exaggerated; the king was undeniably handsome.

He wore a long black tunic embroidered with the red symbols of Polent, including a basilisk embroidered across his back. Even from across the room, his presence was magnetic, and he was easily one of the most beautiful men I had ever seen.

I became suddenly aware of the ruby necklace resting against my collarbone, the one Marcos had given me. It matched the rubies worn by King Llorent and his court, the national stone of Polent that represented the basilisk's eye. I caught myself twirling the ruby between my fingers and quickly stopped, self-conscious under the memory of his lingering gaze.

The second bell rang, its sound rolling through the atrium as the crowd settled into a hush. In that brief stillness, I took in the gathering. I could still feel the sensation of King Llorent's earlier attention, but I forced myself to focus on the others.

I noticed a distinct group among the guests: the Destined. They stood out in all black, each pair marked by the unmistakable symbol of their bond, three gold circles intertwined and embroidered over the left side of the chest. Three elven Destined and three human Destined stood together.

Their expressions did not match the festive atmosphere. With furrowed brows and tight mouths, they looked tense and uncomfortable, as if they had been obligated to attend rather than invited. A heavy stillness seemed to surround them. Their eyes remained fixed on the two empty vine-woven chairs at the front, reserved for King Arisen and the future Queen Vasa. Their unease felt deeper than simple disinterest.

Beside those seats, another chair remained empty, set aside for Queen Franes, who had yet to appear.

Marcos leaned in and lowered his voice. "I highly doubt Queen Franes is coming. Everyone knows how much she dislikes Ebony."

I nodded, still surprised. Her resentment toward Ebony and its rulers was well known, but I had assumed that for an event of this magnitude, she might set aside her grievances. This wasn't a routine political gathering; it was the wedding and crowning of a queen. Still, it seemed that not even this was enough to bring her here.

A group of workers, dressed in green and gold uniforms like Jastop's, walked by, carrying silver trays filled with drinks. Marcos reached for two glasses, delicate crystal with long, slender stems and wide, shallow bowls that caught the light beautifully. He refilled my wine with practiced ease, handing it back to me with a grin.

"Hey! I wasn't done with that!"

"You must try this. An insider told me it has a dusting of magic to make you feel at ease."

At this point in the night, I felt like I needed to relax. Call it sensory overload, but I was on high alert. I was here to have fun, so I grabbed a glass of wine. It tasted like elderflower and rosemary. Just from the first sip, I felt instantly relaxed, the tension in my shoulders disappearing.

"Thanks for the tip," I said with a smile. Immediately afterward, soft music played, the last signal that the wedding was about to begin.

The music swelled, harps welcoming the king as he entered and walked down the long aisle.

This was the first time I had seen King Arisen in person. I had seen his image before, but nothing could have prepared me for the force of his presence. He stood more than a foot taller than me, his lean, muscular build unmistakable even beneath his tailored clothes. His green hair, slicked back to his shoulders, caught the light beneath a bronze headpiece shaped with long pointed ears that echoed his own.

He wore a deep gold tunic trimmed in green, the Destiny emblem stitched proudly over his chest. Dark brown pants contrasted with his honey-toned skin, which seemed to glow under the lanterns. He moved with effortless confidence, his sharp gaze fixed straight ahead as he approached the altar.

When he reached it, the music softened into a lilting elvish melody, signaling the bride's entrance.

She was breathtaking.

Her strapless white gown swept across the floor, and her dark hair was styled in an elegant bun beneath a sheer veil. A wave of admiration passed through the crowd as every eye turned to her while she walked down the aisle.

Except his.

King Arisen turned to face the crowd instead. His honey-colored eyes scanned the sea of faces, pausing only for brief moments, until they met mine.

Time seemed to slow.

My breath caught, my heart pounding so hard it felt like it might burst from my chest. I could not look away. For that suspended instant, it felt like he could not either.

From where I sat, I noticed tiny flecks of blue in his otherwise golden eyes, like stars buried in sunlight. The moment our gazes locked, that blue seemed to flare. Heat rushed through me, wild and unrelenting, a pull I could not explain.

Then the pain hit.

A sharp, searing burn tore through my left arm. I gasped and clutched it instinctively as the world tilted. Invisible fire raced through my veins. My fingers dug into my skin, desperate to stop the rising agony. It felt as though my blood had turned to molten metal.

Through the haze, I saw King Arisen move. His hand flew to his neck, his brows knitting in confusion and discomfort. He winced, as if sharing my pain. His gaze darkened and his posture shifted. There was something new in his expression, something that looked a lot like recognition. Maybe even fear.

Beside me, Marcos placed a steadying hand on my back.

"What is happening? Are you all right?" he asked, his voice tight with worry.

Only a few seconds had passed, but it felt like hours stretched between the king and me.

"I… I do not know," I whispered, my voice shaking. My pulse thundered in my ears, and my body burned from the inside out.

I could not stay. I had to move. I had to get out. I muttered a quick apology to the elves beside me and bolted down the aisle, each step making the pain sharper. I kicked off my stilettos and ran barefoot toward the exit. Behind me, the music faltered, and voices rose in confusion.

At the doors, I glanced back one last time.

The Destined stood alert, wide-eyed, their gaze locked on me. But it was King Arisen who held me in place, scanning the crowd and searching intently.

Before his gaze could find me again, I pushed through the doors and vanished into the night.

I had to stop the burn.

I had to go home.

CHAPTER 5

As I ran, faint whispers reached me that King Arisen had left the atrium. I could not focus; the pain was too intense, disorienting me completely. I had no idea where I was going. I only knew I needed to escape. With each step, the burning in my arm grew fiercer, searing through my body in relentless pulses. Marcos called my name from somewhere behind me, but I was too consumed by the fire inside me to stop.

I passed the two tethered basilisks outside and heard a deep rumble rise from their chests. One lifted its head and unfurled its wings, the leathery spans catching the twilight. I hurried past them and kept running.

I burst through a set of doors and spotted the nearest building: the amphitheater. My bare feet slapped against the cold wooden floor as I stumbled inside, driven by heat and pain.

Somehow, I ended up on the second floor, looking down at the crowd below. The amphitheater was larger than the atrium and far more crowded, with a high glass ceiling and tall windows that cast the space in muted light. I could not really see any of it; everything blurred as the pain clouded my vision, turning my surroundings into a distant haze.

When I reached an empty corridor, I collapsed against the cool stone wall, gasping for air. The chill of the stone brought a brief, fragile relief. Within seconds, Marcos was at my side, his eyes wide with concern.

Ahead of me, a large glass window looked out over the seated crowd. People were slowly rising, glancing around in confusion. The music still played, masking the sound of my ragged breaths. I barely had time to steady myself before the armed Royal Guard entered below.

I shrank back from the window, trying to make myself as small as possible. From where I stood, I watched the guards move through the rows, their eyes sweeping over every face. Sweat beaded along my hairline, and the pain in my arm was so intense it was hard to stand without shaking.

Marcos wrapped his hands gently around my left arm to steady me. The contact sent a jolt of white-hot agony through me. My knees buckled, and I dropped to the floor, biting my lip hard to keep from screaming.

"What is happening?" Marcos whispered urgently as he tried to help me up.

"My arm," I gasped, tears filling my eyes. "It feels like it is on fire."

Marcos's face tightened with worry as he examined my arm, but there was nothing to see.

"Clara, your arm looks fine. It has to be the wine. I did not think it would affect you like this."

"It cannot be just the wine," I said, my voice shaking. "It feels like my skin is burning."

Before Marcos could respond, a guard's shout cut through the noise outside. "No one moves! This is a direct order from the Royal Guard."

The amphitheater fell silent. The soft rustle of shifting feet was the only sound.

Jastop appeared suddenly from one of the doors behind us and motioned frantically. "Come this way," he whispered, pulling a nearby door open.

Marcos grabbed my hand and led me into a small, dimly lit room. Jastop slipped in after us and shut the door, his brow furrowed.

"Why are you two here? You are supposed to be in the atrium."

Marcos ignored the question. "What is happening out there?"

Jastop glanced around the room, then leaned closer. "I overheard a few members of the Royal Guard. They said a mark appeared on King Arisen's neck. It looked like a Destined mark."

I gasped and met Marcos's eyes. A Destined mark? That was impossible. King Arisen had already been Destined to Queen Alondra. How could he be chosen again?

"The Destined have gathered with the Royal Guard," Jastop said urgently. "They are trying to figure out who his new Destiny is. The Destined can sense each other. It is only a matter of time before they find out."

A wave of nausea rolled through me, and I dropped to my knees, clutching my arm.

"Are you all right?" Jastop and Marcos asked simultaneously, panic in their voices.

Summoning what little strength I had left, I whispered, "Jastop, can you get us out of here? I need to go home."

Marcos did not hesitate. "The gondola is just outside. I will take you to the healing ward."

"No," I said through gritted teeth. "Do not take me there."

He faltered. "Clara, forgive me, but you look terrible. We have to at least try to get you help."

"No," I repeated, shaking my head weakly.

The thought of the crowded healing ward made my stomach twist. If I did not understand what was happening to me, the other healers would not either. More than that, a feeling deep inside me insisted that I needed to be home.

"Please… just take me home."

Jastop grabbed a small lantern and led us through the dark corridors, his hurried steps making barely a sound. The candles above us twinkled to life as we passed, momentarily brightening our path.

After minutes of walking and tripping over rocks, I felt the pain in my feet become almost as unbearable as the burning sensation in my arm.

"Exit through this door," Jastop directed, swinging it open. "Move through the bushes and avoid being seen. They are sending out more guards. You were right to leave; this does not look like it will end soon." He closed the door behind us with a final goodbye, leaving us to navigate the night.

We moved swiftly, ducking at the sound of footsteps and hiding in the bushes. With every step I took, a sharp pain shot up my legs, but the overwhelming need to go home kept me moving. Finally, we reached the bay, where Marcos's gondola floated among hundreds of others.

He reached it first, making sure no one was watching. When he opened the door, he signaled for me to follow. As soon as we were both inside, the magic pushed the other boats aside to make a clear path. The gentle rocking eased some of the tension in my body as the gondola glided toward the exit.

"Are you feeling better?"

My arm still pulsed, but the pain had eased. "I think so. Please remind me to never drink that wine again," I replied, exhaling in relief. Strangely enough, the further we moved away from the Royal Gardens, the better I felt.

Marcos gently clasped both my hands in his. "Clara, what just happened was strange. Take off your gloves. We need to see why your arm was bothering you so much."

Drawing a deep breath, I followed his instructions, easily slipping the glove off my right arm. As I moved my fingers, relief flooded over me; almost no discomfort remained. "I need help with this other glove," I admitted, gesturing to my left arm, where a faint edge of pain still lingered.

Carefully, Marcos placed his fingers on the top rim of the glove. He pulled it down slowly, and a fresh wave of pain shot through me. "Please stop," I begged.

Marcos wiped the tears from my eyes with his thumb, gently cradling my chin. "Clara, something is happening with your arm, and we have to find out what it is."

"Remove the glove quickly," I said, finally giving in. I closed my eyes and braced myself for the inevitable pain. "Just do it," I muttered through gritted teeth.

Marcos gripped the top of the glove and tugged it down in one motion. I screamed so loudly I startled myself. When I opened my eyes, the color had drained from Marcos's face, and a golden light from my arm illuminated his features.

"What is it?" I asked. Then I saw it. Gold lines wrapped around my skin. "What is this?"

Marcos stared at me in stunned silence. His mouth moved, but no sound emerged.

"Marcos, what is this?" I repeated, my voice rising.

"You have been Destined, Clara," he finally managed, his voice thick with shock.

Notes from Marcos

I watched Clara, her face drained of color except for the vivid red of her lipstick. Anguish and pain carved lines across her features. She was struggling to breathe, and the fitted dress seemed to squeeze every last bit of air out of her. I did not hesitate. I reached for the bows at the back and slowly loosened them. The fabric slipped from her shoulders, and her rib cage finally expanded with a long, desperate breath.

That was when I saw it.

The marks on her arm extended from her hand to her elbow, intricate and otherworldly. Thin golden lines intertwined like veins of liquid fire, forming delicate symbols that shimmered against her skin. They pulsed softly, the glow brightening and dimming in a steady, unnatural rhythm, almost as if they were alive. The light quivered like candle flames and cast a warm hue over the small space inside the gondola.

I tried to study the symbols, but she kept shifting her arm. Every movement sent ripples of golden light across her skin, the markings responding to her distress.

"I do not understand, Marcos," she said, her voice trembling. The glow flared for an instant, then settled into a steady radiance. "Why me? It does not make sense if this is what we think it is."

I took her hands in mine. Heat radiated from the markings, as if magic itself had been woven into her body. I drew a deep breath and gently squeezed, guiding her to match her breathing to mine. Gradually, she did. Her breaths slowed, and the tears in her eyes stopped falling.

"We both know this happens on its own," I said quietly. "We have never seen it with our own eyes, but these are the signs of the Destined. You have been marked."

The truth was hard to accept. Meeting someone Destined or being chosen by Destiny was something from myths and history books, not our everyday life. Destiny had become a story grandparents told at night, a tale of power and sacrifice from a long time ago. But here it was, happening right in front of me. My childhood friend, someone I had grown up with, had been chosen. It was almost impossible to believe.

The last Destined had been chosen long ago: Eliza and Rogers. Everyone believed they were the final ones, the last echoes of the magic. People had assumed the forest was done granting these powers, that whatever consciousness guided Destiny had gone silent. Our nations had moved on and adapted to that silence. So why now? Why disturb the balance after so many years? And why my friend Clara, of all people?

A chill ran down my spine. If the Gaul Forest were to choose again, it meant something had changed. And it had to be strong enough to call Destiny back.

I searched her wide, fearful eyes for answers, but I knew she had none. Neither of us did.

"When did you first feel the burning in your arm?" I asked. "Did you feel anything else?"

Clara stared at me, her lips trembling as she reached back into her memories. "I felt it as soon as King Arisen turned to face the guests at the wedding. We made brief eye contact."

I squeezed her hands again, offering what little comfort I could. She shifted closer and rested her head on my shoulder.

"I do not know what to do," she whispered.

"We will figure it out together," I told her, although doubt pressed heavily at the back of my mind. I took another slow breath and let her rest for the last few minutes of the ride. When her eyes drifted shut, I gently tilted her chin up so she would look at me.

"We are here," I said softly. "Let us start by going inside."

I stepped out first and offered her my hand. Clara lifted the hem of her pink gown and stepped out of the gondola. I followed close behind. The faint golden hue of her mark lit up the dark, wet pavement, its glow reflecting on the rain-slick stone. Her bare, bruised feet touched the cold ground, and the shimmer of the markings made the moment feel even more unreal.

At the door, she brought a finger to her lips and motioned for me to keep quiet. Even now, in this chaos, she thought of Hale first.

"Kent and Hale are sleeping," she whispered as we entered the dark living room.

I lit the candle by the door, and the rest of the candles in the room flickered to life. Even so, the candlelight seemed weak. The golden glow from Clara's arm was brighter than all of them.

I asked her to sit on the couch and went to the kitchen to get a bowl of water to wash her face. When I came back, she was staring at her arm, tracing the golden lines with trembling fingers. Her eyes were swollen and bloodshot. The markings shimmered on her skin, their glow reflected in the wet shine of her tears.

I placed the bowl beside me and sat down. She lay her head on my lap, and I carefully loosened the bun in her hair. With a damp towel, I wiped away the streaks of makeup on her cheeks.

"Did you notice any details in the markings?" I asked.

"It is the mark of the Destined," Clara said quietly. "You were right. I cannot tell what it means, but the elvish markings of the Gaul Forest are there. I do not recognize the other symbols."

The markings were truly beautiful, as if they had been designed specifically for her arm. The golden elvish script of the Gaul Forest appeared like real gold embedded into her skin. The rest of the symbols intertwined in intricate patterns, like a puzzle written in a language only Destiny understood. I had a feeling King Arisen might hold at least part of the answer.

Clara eventually drifted into sleep on the couch. A final tear slipped from the corner of her eye as her breathing evened out. She was utterly spent. Her body needed rest, whether Destiny allowed it or not. I stayed where I was, stroking her hair, letting the steady rhythm of her breaths calm my own racing thoughts.

I was close to falling asleep myself when the sound of footsteps startled me. Kent emerged from the dark archway, his outline cut sharply by the golden light still leaking from Clara's arm.

"Is everything all right?" he asked.

"Help me carry her upstairs," I said. "It is a long story."

He crossed the room in a few strides. The moment his gaze fell on his sister's arm, his eyes widened.

"What happened?"

Clara stirred at the sound of his voice. Her mark brightened for a heartbeat, casting long, dancing shadows across the walls, then dimmed again.

"I will explain once we get her to bed," I replied. "She is exhausted."

Kent gently lifted Clara into his arms, holding her carefully while I hurried ahead to set up the bed. As he laid her down, a golden glow spread across every surface in the room. It felt as if the magic itself wanted to hold onto her.

I pulled the blanket over her, and slowly the light faded beneath the covers. The room darkened, leaving only the soft glow of the candle in the corner.

I felt Kent's eyes on me.

"What happened?" he asked again, his voice quieter this time.

So I told him everything. I described what happened at the Royal Gardens, from when the pain started to when we saw the mark in the gondola. I left nothing out. When I mentioned King Arisen and his new mark, Kent shifted uncomfortably, his jaw tightening. We both knew that whatever was coming for Clara wouldn't be easy.

When I finally left their house, my heart felt heavy. The night air was cool against my skin, but it did little to clear the dread that had settled over me. I knew, with a certainty that scared me, that my friend's life had just changed forever.

CHAPTER 6

Iwoke up disoriented, greeted by a throbbing headache that intensified with each passing minute. I shifted in bed, tempted to fall back asleep, but the house was eerily quiet. Too quiet. Where were Hale's playful footsteps, her cries, her joyful giggles?

Panic gripped me as I rushed to the living room, only to find Kent watching the morning news while Hale quietly played with her toys. Relief washed over me, and for a brief moment, last night felt like a distant nightmare I had finally escaped.

"Good morning," Kent said, his gaze dropping immediately to my arm. His eyes lingered, and the memories of last night rushed back: the warmth, the magic, the overwhelming realization of what I had become.

I followed his gaze and looked down, startled to see the faint golden markings still glowing softly in the morning light. I had forgotten about them. Instinctively, I hid my arm behind my back.

"Morning," I muttered, my voice uneven as I tried to compose myself, my heart pounding harder than I wanted to admit.

"We need to talk," he said quietly, "but first, you should bathe and change out of those clothes."

Only then did I realize I was still wearing my pink gown, now hanging loosely off my shoulders. A glimpse of my reflection in the window made me cringe. My hair was a tangled mess, the dress stained with rain and dirt, and sweat clung to my skin, leaving an unpleasant, sour smell.

I glanced at Hale, who was now staring at me with her arms outstretched. She wanted to be held, and I wanted nothing more than to scoop her up and wrap her in my arms.

"I'll be back soon, Hale. Just give me a minute," I said hastily, darting toward the bathroom. The rain outside meant the water would not be warm enough to soothe my aching body, but I filled the tub and bathed quickly.

Once I was done, I slipped on the warm mauve long-sleeved bathrobe that hung on the door. After brushing out my tangled hair, I returned to the room. Hale's face lit up with the most adorable smile when she saw me. I hurried over and settled her on my lap.

"Marcos told me what happened last night, but I need to hear it from you."

"I am sure what he told you is accurate. I do not know what to do, and that is the problem," I replied, brushing Hale's curls away from her face.

"How are you feeling now?" Kent asked. He fiddled with the temple tip of his eyeglasses, his brows drawn together in concern.

I exhaled slowly, my fingers tracing the golden markings on my arm as if hoping they would disappear. "I am feeling better, but it all happened so fast," I admitted. A tremor ran through me that I could not entirely suppress. "Kent, I do not know what I should do. If Destiny chose me, I do not even know what that means for me or for us."

The words tasted bitter as they left my mouth. Being chosen by Destiny meant everything in my life would change forever, and I did not want that. I did not want anything pulling me away from the life I had built—my home, Hale's world, watching Kent grow into the father he was becoming. Even if I had been chosen for some higher purpose, I wasn't sure the sacrifices were worth it. I already had a purpose: I helped people through my work, and that fulfillment had always felt enough.

Kent's expression darkened, and he let out a heavy sigh. "Clara, you cannot escape it. The Royal Guard is actively searching for King Arisen's Destined."

I swallowed hard. "Do you think they will find me?"

Kent rubbed his hand over his face, the weariness in his posture twisting my stomach. "Marcos said there were only a few humans there. Just the two of you and the three other guests who were Destined. You and Marcos were the only ones who could have been chosen."

Oh. No.

I opened my mouth, then closed it again. What was I supposed to say to that? That I was scared? That I wanted nothing to do with this? That even though Destiny had clearly chosen me, I tried to pretend it hadn't?

Instead, I forced a weak smile. "Okay, I think we should get ready to go to the fireworks show," I said, my voice strained as I tried to change the subject. I bounced Hale lightly on my knees, hoping the movement would ground me. "We planned to go," I added quickly. "You want to go, right?" I asked her. She answered with a delighted giggle.

"I do not think that is a good idea. People are upset, and the Royal Guard is on high alert. According to the news, there were stampedes of humans and elves trying to leave the Royal Gardens. The guards kept people there for hours, searching for you." Kent shook his head immediately.

"Really?" I asked, incredulous. "It must have calmed down by now."

Kent gave me a sharp look. "I heard they plan to make it up to the attendees with a fireworks show, but I still do not think it is safe to go, especially with Hale."

Oh.

I looked down at Hale, my fingers instinctively brushing through her soft hair. She was still blissfully unaware of what was happening. For now.

"Kent, I need you to tell me what to do. I am nervous, and I am worried." The pounding in my head grew stronger, matching the erratic rhythm of my heart. This was the first time in my thirty-one years of life that I felt completely lost.

Kent's gaze lingered on the silver box on the table. He seemed to be considering his words, as if he understood that whatever he said next would set something irreversible into motion. Just as he parted his lips to speak, a firm knock sounded at the door.

My heart lurched.

"That might be Marcos," I said quickly, placing Hale gently onto Kent's lap before hurrying to answer.

The moment I opened the door, I was met with the sight of a tall, broad-shouldered figure. His frame filled the doorway, and despite the crisp cut of his uniform, there was an effortless strength in the way he held himself: rigid, unwavering, and unmistakably authoritative.

"Good morning, Ms. Clara Lildar," a deep voice greeted me.

And in that instant, my entire world shifted again.

CHAPTER 7

It wasn't Marcos.

My eyes traveled upward, taking in the figure before me. I hadn't expected to recognize him so quickly, but he was hard to miss, especially with the large oak tree pin on his chest. Rijor, the right-hand man of King Arisen, stood in my doorway.

My first instinct was to slam the door, but I stayed frozen. How did he know my name? How did he know where I lived?

"It is good manners to invite me in. After all, it is raining," Rijor remarked, glancing over my shoulder into the house.

I stepped back to give him space. His chest brushed lightly against mine as he entered, the scent of cedarwood filling the room. I closed the door and saw at least ten Royal Guards outside, arranging themselves around their armored gondolas.

Rijor loomed over me. His short, white-blond hair was neatly styled to the side, with a few strands falling into his deep green eyes and slightly rounded elvish ears. His tall leather boots clicked against the floor, drawing my gaze downward.

Oh. No.

Heat flooded my cheeks as the realization hit me. I was standing in front of a member of the Royal Court wearing nothing but a bathrobe. At least it hid most of my marked arm. I pushed my hands into my robe pockets, trying to hide any signs of the markings.

"Please sit," Kent said, bowing slightly.

Oh. No.

I had forgotten to bow, so I hurried to follow his lead. "Yes, please sit. How can I help you?" I asked, forcing a polite smile and clinging to the hope that acting naïve might somehow help.

"I think you know why I am here, Ms. Clara Lildar." Rijor's gaze swept across the room as he moved into the living area, taking everything in. His eyes lingered on the silver box resting on the mantel, and he stepped closer, his expression unreadable.

"What can we help you with?" Kent asked, his voice tight, as Rijor slowly ran his fingers along the top of the box.

"I am looking for the owner of these," Rijor said, pulling my stilettos from a duffel bag. "I believe they belong to you."

His gaze dropped to my feet, where tiny bruises dotted my skin. "Such a shame you do not take better care of yourself," he added with a widening grin.

Oh. No.

Mortified, I snatched the shoes from his hand. "Thank you," I muttered.

"Oh, there they are," he said, eyes narrowing as he focused on the hand I had used to grab the shoes. "The markings of the Destined."

Oh. No.

My flimsy attempt to keep the mark hidden had failed immediately. His sharp eyes locked onto the faint glow at the edge of my sleeve. He reached out without hesitation and pushed the fabric higher, revealing the golden designs etched from my wrist up to my elbow.

His smile grew, revealing perfectly white teeth. An unsettling amusement flickered in his expression. "You intrigue me, Ms. Clara Lildar," he said, his tone almost pleasant. "I came to inform you that you must join me at the Royal Palace to discuss this with the king."

"I can't go today. We plan to see the fireworks," I lied, desperate for even a little more time.

"Oh, I see. Well, Ms. Clara Lildar, you don't have a choice," he replied, stepping closer. The lightness vanished from his voice. "What you might not realize is that the king barely survived being Destined a second time, something no one believed could happen. For his safety, and yours, you must come with me."

His words stunned me. "Barely survived?" I repeated, my voice just above a whisper. The memories of last night's pain flooded back. How close had I come to dying?

"Yes. Destiny has never chosen someone twice. It is a phenomenon we cannot afford to take lightly. And you, Ms. Clara Lildar, are the newest Destined." He gestured to my arm. "That mark binds you to the king. Refusal is not an option."

I glanced at Kent and Hale. My brother stared at me, waiting, while Hale wriggled in his arms, eager to be put down.

"Let me speak with my brother first," I said, motioning for Kent to join me in the kitchen with Hale.

Rijor nodded and turned away, pretending to give us privacy as he continued to study the room.

"What am I supposed to do?" I whispered. "I don't want to go, and I definitely do not want to drag you both into this."

"Clara, you can't refuse to be Destined. Destiny has called you," Kent said. Hale twisted in his arms again, so he set her down. She immediately toddled back into the living room, drawn to her toys and, unfortunately, to Rijor.

"Hale, come back," I called softly. I turned back to Kent. "You are right, but I cannot leave you both behind." Tears pricked my eyes.

"You will not. We will go with you."

When we returned to the living room, Rijor was handing Hale one of her toys. Their similar shades of blond hair caught the light. Hale beamed at me, blissfully unaware of the storm closing in around us.

A few guards had stepped inside, their attention drawn to the waterfall painting in the corner. The silver box with Lorraine's ashes glowed faintly, making the water in the painting appear to shimmer.

"Okay, we will come. Where should we meet you?" I asked, my voice unsteady.

"Oh, Ms. Clara Lildar, we are not letting you out of our sight again. The Royal Guard will escort us there," Rijor replied smoothly.

My instinct was to argue, but I knew it would be pointless. "Fine. I just need a minute to change."

"Yes, you do." His eyes lingered for a moment before I turned and hurried upstairs, heat rising up my neck.

I tied my hair into a high ponytail and slipped into a cream tunic dress made of thick woven fabric. I paired it with my most comfortable maroon leather boots, scuffed at the toes but perfectly broken in. To cover the mark, I grabbed the only gloves I owned: the gold, elbow-length pair from the night before. They did not match the outfit's practicality, but they would have to do. It was not as if I kept spare elbow-length gloves around for emergencies.

When I came back downstairs, Rijor was waiting by the door.

"Shall we?" he asked, holding it open as the gondolas waited outside.

CHAPTER 8

From Clara's Diary

Reluctantly, we followed Rijor into the rain.

This was not how I thought today would go, being escorted to the Royal Palace with my family under the watchful eye of Rijor and the Royal Guard.

The journey was silent, rain drumming steadily against the gondola windows. Kent sat beside me, his hand resting on my shoulder in quiet reassurance, while Hale played with her toys. Rijor sat across from us, his sharp gaze occasionally flicking toward Hale, lingering just long enough to unsettle me.

Before long, we arrived at the entrance. The gentle waves made by the gondola sent ripples through the water, reflecting the bioluminescent creatures below. Their vibrant glow shimmered across the surface, creating a mesmerizing display of color that only appeared near the castle. For a moment, I lost myself in their beauty until Rijor reached for my hand.

I hesitated before taking it. His grip was firm as he helped me disembark. He lifted Hale easily, setting her down before turning to Kent. With the Royal Guard following us, we entered the palace.

Tall columns greeted us, water softly flowing down their sides. The air carried a subtle scent of damp stone and aged parchment.

"This way," Rijor said, leading us toward a large central door.

A tingling sensation spread through my left arm, subtle yet undeniable. My fingers instinctively brushed over the spot, feeling a quiet pulse beneath my skin.

Rijor pushed open the heavy wooden door. Its surface was carved with intricate patterns, eerily similar to the ancient symbols etched into the trees of the Royal Gardens. As the door groaned open, two figures stood waiting inside.

Then I heard his voice.

"Those are the eyes I have been searching for."

The smooth cadence of King Arisen's words sent a shiver down my spine.

I had seen countless portraits of him, but none captured the sheer presence he commanded. The crown, nestled between his sharp elvish ears, was almost an afterthought compared to the golden markings adorning his skin. They wrapped around his neck and climbed his jawline, glowing faintly against his bronze complexion, the unmistakable mark of our shared Destiny.

Beside him, Vasa stood poised, her icy gaze sweeping over every inch of me. Her expression was unreadable, but beneath her restraint I sensed something sharper, something far more dangerous than simple scrutiny.

I barely had time to react before Rijor's hand pressed firmly against my lower back, urging me forward.

"Sit, Ms. Clara Lildar," he said.

Before I could move, King Arisen stepped toward us.

He did not hesitate. He crossed the room in a few long strides, closing the distance between us in seconds. Up close, his height was impossible to ignore, and my eyes fixed on his broad chest before I forced myself to look up.

"Ms. Lildar, sit here." He gestured to the chair closest to him.

My pulse quickened under his attention. It felt as though he could see through every wall I had tried to build around myself before coming here.

Up close, I noticed even more detail in his eyes. The honey-colored irises, so striking from a distance, held subtle flecks of deep blue beneath the gold, flickering in the dim light like the candles around us.

I held my breath, pinned in place by his stare.

"Sit," he repeated, and this time my body obeyed before my mind could protest.

This was not how I had imagined meeting the King of Ebony.

In truth, I had never imagined meeting him at all. Very few people did. He was reserved, and everyone knew it. His public appearances in Raster were rare, and his weddings were among the only times people caught even a glimpse of him.

Yet here I was, face to face with him. A man tied to me by forces neither of us had chosen, bound by a power greater than I could fully understand.

King Arisen spoke again, his voice shifting, gaining a quieter, almost intimate tone.

"Now, Ms. Lildar," he murmured, leaning forward slightly, "let us discuss our Destiny."

I sat rigid in the chair, every nerve on high alert. Destiny, which I had once dismissed as a distant myth, was now real, etched into my skin.

"We are connected by a magic greater than anything we have ever known," he said. "Our marks… they are a testament to that bond, one that can only be broken by death."

My mouth went dry as I fought to steady my breathing. Heat radiated from his body, his gaze lingering with an intensity that pressed against the fragile boundaries of this newfound connection.

Was this the man Rijor claimed had nearly died? He seemed perfectly fine now. Stronger, even.

But I felt it too. The same pain. How could I ever forget?

"I did not ask for this," I said, though I was not sure if I was telling him or reminding myself.

"No one asks for Destiny," he replied softly. His gaze softened briefly, and in that moment I saw emotions—perhaps regret or acceptance. I knew I was not his first Destiny. That was Queen Alondra's. Yet here he was, facing this fate again, this time with me instead of a royal.

"What do you expect from me?" I asked, my voice trembling slightly despite my efforts to stay composed.

"I expect your loyalty and obedience."

Loyalty. Obedience. Was that really what he expected from me? I had never been the type to offer either freely, especially to someone I did not know.

As I tried to process his words, my gaze shifted to Vasa. Her eyes met mine, just as guarded as the king's, perhaps even more so. She offered no reassurance, only a silent, watchful intensity.

I furrowed my brow, trying to hide my unease. I searched behind me for Kent and Hale, needing their steady presence. They stood a few feet away, just as confused as I was. I shifted in my seat, desperate for something to steady me, but nothing felt stable under his gaze.

"Take off your gloves. I need to see your markings."

My hand clenched into a fist. I stood and took two sharp steps toward him, my lips parting as I prepared to protest. My eyes locked with his, and I found myself caught between defiance and obedience.

"Here," Rijor said, cutting through the moment. He stepped forward, his calm demeanor a sharp contrast to the intensity radiating from King Arisen. His hand hovered near mine, urging me without words.

I swallowed hard, my hands trembling as I hesitated. I felt the king's eyes on me, watching every movement. My chest tightened. With a deep breath, I reluctantly peeled off my gloves, one finger at a time.

As the fabric fell away, the markings on my skin shimmered in the light, glowing faintly. King Arisen's gaze darkened as his eyes traced the golden lines, following every curve.

"Loyalty and obedience are not given lightly," I said softly, meeting his stare. "Especially to someone I do not know."

The moment the words left my lips, I surprised myself. Not only for speaking that way to a king, but for the sudden awareness of how close we were. The room was full of people, yet it felt as if only the two of us existed.

His expression flattened. "Then I suppose we will have to work on that, will we not?"

He took my hand from Rijor's, his grip firm but not harsh, and examined the markings closely. When his thumb brushed the glowing lines, warmth spread through my body. It was not the searing burn from before. It was deeper, as if the markings recognized who was touching them.

I glanced around the room. Every pair of eyes was fixed on us, unblinking. King Arisen's lips pressed into a thin line.

"You are, indeed, my Destiny," he murmured, releasing my hand, as if his words alone were enough to seal the bond between us. The warmth vanished the moment his touch left my skin, leaving me cold and disoriented. His eyes met mine for an instant, and my heart slammed against my ribs before he turned away and walked back to Vasa, who stood stoic at his side.

Hearing it from his lips, those five simple words, felt different. It felt final. Real.

"What should we do about this, King Arisen?" Rijor asked.

My voice caught in my throat. I wanted to scream that this was not what I wanted. I had not asked for this. I was not ready to be tied to anyone, much less a king. But the words stayed locked inside me, and I stood there, lips parted, unable to speak.

"We need to meet with the other Destined immediately," the king said. "Let them know we are here. This meeting is for Destined only."

Rijor shifted uncomfortably. Vasa's expression tightened, as if she were about to object, but King Arisen cut her off before she could speak.

"No exceptions."

I was done being quiet. "I am not staying here without Kent or Hale," I said, my voice firm. Did he truly think I would sit in a room with strangers while my family was left alone?

"This meeting will be private. Kent and Hale can wait outside," he replied.

"I said I am not staying here without them," I repeated, planting my feet. I knew I sounded stubborn, even childish, but I did not care. They needed to understand that I would not abandon my family.

Kent stepped closer, resting a hand on my shoulder. "Clara, I do not think you have a choice. We can wait outside," he said gently, though I heard the unease in his voice.

"We do not know this place. I do not want to leave you both alone," I muttered, though my stance softened just a little. This was not how I imagined any of this. This was not what I wanted.

"I will take care of them," Rijor said smoothly, his hand brushing my shoulder. "Perhaps they can wait by the balcony and see the fireworks you mentioned."

"That sounds safe, Clara. Hale would like that. Remember, you said how much she would enjoy it," Kent added, trying to reassure me. My stomach churned.

I was running out of options.

Slowly, I placed my marked hand on Hale's back, trying to comfort her. She flinched away, startled by the golden glow. The rejection was small, but it broke me inside.

"I love you so much," I whispered into her ear, my voice shaking.

"I assure you, Ms. Clara Lildar, they will be safe," Rijor said calmly, taking his hand from my shoulder.

Commander Vasa brushed past me without a word, her expression unchanged. My eyes stayed fixed on my family as Rijor led them out of the room. I watched until they disappeared down the corridor. The silence that followed felt heavy, pressing against my chest. It was not only their absence that made it hard to breathe.

I felt his presence behind me before I heard his voice.

"Good. We are alone now."

King Arisen's deep voice filled the room. I turned slowly, and he stepped closer, his eyes locked on mine.

"Come closer."

I swallowed hard. His nearness was impossible to ignore. The connection between us, the pull of Destiny, was undeniable, an invisible force that made it feel as though the very air was drawing us together.

There was no resisting it. No controlling it.
And I could not bear it.

CHAPTER 9

He moved closer. I felt the warmth of his breath on my skin, faintly scented of mint and cider. My eyes remained fixed on his neck, on the patterns of gold running across his skin. I felt his gaze burning into me, searching for my eyes, and I refused to look up.

"Ms. Lildar." King Arisen's voice was a deep, deliberate rumble. "You are a human I have never heard of. I need to know how you ended up Destined to me."

His tone was not curious; it was accusing, as if I had somehow engineered this. A challenge flickered in his gaze, and heat tightened in my chest. Did he truly think I had a say in any of this? He knew how Destiny worked. It chose us, not the other way around.

I wanted to snap, to throw his words back at him, but I swallowed the anger simmering in my throat and forced my voice to stay even.

"You tell me. I was just trying to enjoy the wedding."

His lips twitched not out of kindness but with amusement, as if my frustration amused him. As if the mention of the wedding was oddly funny. I clenched my jaw, but the smirk quickly vanished, replaced by something quieter, almost regretful.

"You must understand. No one has been chosen for centuries. The magic of the Gaul Forest is too weak, too fractured. For you and me to be marked now, it is nearly impossible."

Centuries. The word froze in my chest.

"You think I do not find this improbable too?" I muttered. "I did not ask for any of this."

"Neither did I," he said, his voice softening. "Yet here we are, bound by a power greater than both of us. And now we have six months to train, until our bond fully awakens."

Six months.

I blinked, trying to catch up. "Six months? My entire life is here. I have responsibilities. I have a family."

"And they will be in danger if you stay," he said flatly.

I drew a breath. "Where does this training happen? Somewhere nearby?"

He shook his head. "Pitores."

My heart dropped.

"No," I said, the word escaping before I could think. "That place is not safe for humans. I will not survive the cold. I will not even be able to go outside."

"You will manage," he replied, unmoved.

"Manage? So, I am just going to freeze for half a year?"

"That is the first test for every Destined human. The cold or the magic. One of them always breaks you first."

His words felt colder than any Sierra air. My mouth went dry.

"Breaks me?" I repeated sharply. "That is not a test. That is a death sentence."

He did not flinch. "It is reality. Surviving it proves you are strong enough to wield the magic that binds us."

"I am not going to Pitores." My arms crossed before I realized it. "I will not leave my family. And I will not die for a magic I did not choose."

"You do not understand the danger. Destined pairs attract attention and threats. Others will come for you. If they cannot reach you, they will go after your family."

My stomach twisted.

"I am still not leaving them behind."

He stepped toward me, the pull between us flaring like the tension in the air before a storm, but just as he was about to speak, the door burst open.

Rijor entered, followed by the other six Destined.

King Arisen stepped back, giving me space, though the tension did not ease.

"Good. Everyone is here," he said, his voice sliding back into cold authority. "Rijor, arrange for Ms. Lildar's family to be relocated to Polent. King Llorent has agreed to provide protection."

I blinked. So did Rijor.

Polent. That was not just safety. That was politics. Power games wrapped in good intentions.

"Oh no," I whispered, a knot of dread tightening in my chest. I did not know what this was turning into, but I knew one thing with certainty. Destiny was not only a bond.

It was a tether, pulling two lives together whether they were ready or not.

CHAPTER 10

The mention of my family being sent away stunned me. What did King Arisen have in mind? And why did they need to be taken to Polent? We had never traveled outside Ebony, and now they were being sent away… without me?

Rijor hesitated. His brow twitched for just a moment, almost too quickly to notice, but then he gave a short nod. "Of course. I'll see to the arrangements promptly."

There was tension behind his words, as if he were forcing them out.

In just a few minutes, King Arisen had managed to infuriate me. Was this how he communicated? Ordering people around and making decisions without a word of warning? Frustration bubbled in my chest, and I pushed past the gathered Destined, barely noticing their curious stares.

The hallway stretched endlessly before me as my footsteps echoed down the marble floor. Some people moved aside while others watched with confusion, but I didn't care.

"Kent! Hale!" I shouted, my voice bouncing off the stone walls. Panic rose alongside my anger. "Where are you?"

"They won't hear you," Rijor said from behind me. He followed at his usual, measured pace, but something about him felt more guarded.

"What do you mean they won't hear me?" I snapped, spinning around. "What did you do to them?"

His brow furrowed. "They're on the balcony, watching the fireworks. There's music out there." His tone was calm, but there was a faint irritation behind his eyes, as though the situation had blindsided him, too.

"Take me to them," I said, arms crossed, glaring.

He gestured coolly toward a staircase. "This way."

Reluctantly, I followed. As we passed a room framed by long, white curtains, I caught a glimpse through the glass. Kent and Hale stood on the balcony, bathed in the glow of fireworks. Hale's laughter rose above the soft music as Kent held her close.

I stopped in my tracks. For a moment, the noise in my head quieted.

"They seem happy," I said softly.

"They are," Rijor replied, continuing ahead without looking back. "Would you prefer to let them enjoy the show?"

I hesitated. I wanted to run to them, to hold them and make sure everything was okay, but I didn't want to shatter their joy. I nodded slowly, the fight leaving me.

"Why wasn't the show canceled?" I asked, trailing behind him.

Rijor finally glanced back. "We wanted this to be the focus, not the fact that King Arisen left Commander Vasa standing at the altar to chase after you."

A lump formed in my throat. "And you think the fireworks will distract them?"

"We're counting on it."

I stopped again. "I'm not going," I said, arms folding tightly over my chest. I wanted him to know I meant it, that this wasn't fear or uncertainty. I was standing my ground.

Rijor turned to face me. This time, he stepped closer, his expression less guarded than before. He gently took my hands in his, his touch warm.

"They'll be taken care of," he said softly. "King Llorent will watch over them. Basilisks surround his kingdom; it's the safest place they could be."

There was something beneath his calm, something practiced, yet not insincere. I studied him for a long moment, then said, "There's only one way I'll agree to this."

"Name it," he replied.

"I need to be able to visit them. I'm not spending six months apart from Kent and Hale. If I can't see them, I'm not going anywhere."

He nodded slowly, his grip loosening. "That can likely be arranged," he said after a pause. His eyes searched mine carefully. "Anything else?"

I exhaled, finally letting my arms drop. "This is a logistical nightmare. What about my house? My job? I can't just disappear."

"We'll handle it," Rijor said, as if the answer had already been prepared. "Your home and belongings will be watched. Your job isn't your concern anymore. Your Destiny and your family's safety take priority now."

His tone was steady, but I could feel the wall tightening around me. He was right. It all made sense, but it didn't make it easier.

"Are Kent and Hale really in danger?"

Rijor's expression softened. His composure faltered just slightly. And then, in the most genuine tone I'd heard from him yet, he said, "Hale will never be in danger while she's with me. I promise you that."

The words struck hard. I took a deep breath and nodded, tension draining from my shoulders.

"Fine," I said quietly. "Take me back to the Destined meeting."

He nodded and turned. I followed him, my eyes drifting to the dark walls around us. This castle was beautiful, but cold, vast, and hollow.

And I couldn't help but wonder if it mirrored what lived inside the king.

CHAPTER 11

From Clara's Diary

I reentered the room to find all the other Destined waiting, their eyes turning toward me the moment I stepped inside. The room fell silent. Everyone was seated around a large wooden table, a detailed map of the continent stretched across its surface. The relief map raised the land into ridges and valleys, a tactile rendering of the world we were meant to protect.

My gaze drifted straight to the Gaul Forest, which looked impossibly far from where we stood. Then I found Pitores, a tiny glowing dot perched on an enormous mountain. The sheer isolation of it made my chest tighten.

"Glad you could join us, Ms. Lildar." King Arisen's voice cut through the quiet. His eyes, already hard to read, narrowed slightly. He was not pleased with my abrupt exit.

Ignoring the heat in my cheeks, I moved toward the farthest seat from him, determined to keep as much distance between us as the table allowed. I felt his gaze following me as I sat.

"We have much to discuss. But first, introductions."

The other Destined exchanged glances before turning their attention to me. I did not belong at this table, where everyone else seemed to understand what was happening.

As I settled into my seat, Rogers, a human from Polent, offered me a polite smile.

"Hello, I am Rogers, and this is Eliza. We have been Destined as aldarons. We work to understand the forest's ecosystem," he said, extending his hand.

I shook it, trying to focus on his words instead of the pressure building in my chest. Rogers had a quiet strength, his blue eyes sharp and assessing. His lean frame made him seem approachable, but something about him suggested he was used to fighting. His fair skin and neatly cut black hair gave him a clean, composed appearance. There was a calmness to him that, for some reason, helped ease my nerves.

Eliza, on the other hand, was striking. As an elf from Pagos, she had blood-red eyes that contrasted sharply with her dark, wavy hair that fell to her shoulders. Her skin was pale, almost see-through, and her long ears reached the top of her head. She didn't smile, but her gaze was steady and observant. I saw her at the wedding, but she looked even more intimidating here. Her posture was flawless, every movement precise, like someone who had faced more battles than conversations.

"And we are Matry and Reato," the next couple said. "We are lorethils, magic harvesters."

Matry, an elvish woman with long white hair, wore a kind but reserved expression. Fine lines framed her eyes and mouth, deepening when she smiled, the marks of a long life shaped by wisdom and hardship.

Reato, a human, appeared to be the oldest in the room. Deep wrinkles carved across his forehead and cheeks, the kind that come only from years of labor and lived experience. He leaned on a wooden cane as if it were part of him, his gnarled hands resting on it with practiced familiarity. His long white hair matched Matry's, and together they looked almost like siblings. The exhaustion in his eyes hinted at burdens long carried, yet his gaze held a steady resolve that told me he could still wield his magic with purpose, even if his body resisted him.

They carried a quiet dignity, not through power or presence, but through the endurance of a bond that had weathered decades.

Finally, the last pair introduced themselves.

"Karlos and Victor," Karlos said, his deep voice surprisingly rich for his small frame. "We are Morgotherns."

Morgotherns were rare, their mastery of dark magic almost legendary, but seeing one in person was very different from the stories.

Karlos, a human from the small town of Hertm in Ebony, stood just five feet tall. His sharp brown eyes, each circled by a delicate ring of gold, shimmered with intelligence. There was a clarity in them that set him apart, a stillness that made me feel as though he saw more than he said. Of everyone in the room, his eyes were the most striking, not only for their unusual coloring, but for the quiet truths they seemed to hold. Despite his small stature, there was a steady confidence in the way he carried himself.

Victor, in contrast, was an imposing presence, a Black elf from Polent towering close to seven feet tall, his muscles pressing against finely tailored clothes. Yet his warm smile softened his features as he extended a hand to me, his greeting far gentler than his size suggested.

I shook their hands, but my thoughts drifted back to the glowing dot on the map. Pitores. The idea of going there, of spending months in the cold and isolation with the king, made my stomach twist.

As the introductions concluded, King Arisen's gaze returned to me. "Now, Ms. Lildar," he began, his voice easily commanding the room, "we must discuss our plans for Pitores and the Gaul Forest."

I swallowed hard and met his eyes. I knew he was not only talking about our shared Destiny. There was something in the way he watched me that felt uncomfortably personal.

The moment Eliza spoke, her voice was sharp and direct. "We know that finding your Destiny means you must go to Pitores for the next six months, but we do not have that time. We cannot afford to wait."

A ripple of agreement moved through the room as the other Destined couples nodded in unison. It was clear they shared an understanding that I did not. Everyone seemed to grasp Eliza's words; everyone except me. I was still trying to piece things together, feeling like an outsider in a conversation I was supposed to be part of.

"The last remnants of magic in the Gaul Forest are critical," Eliza pressed, her voice tight with urgency. "Your proposed six-month absence is impractical."

The last remnants of magic. My heart skipped a beat, confusion tightening in my chest. The Gaul Forest was the lifeblood of all three nations, the source of our power and balance. If something was wrong with it, why was this not common knowledge? Why was no one speaking of it beyond these walls?

"You know it is protocol," Rogers said, his calm voice trying to steady the room. "Leaving for six months is part of the process. It is what has always been done."

"Yes, but time is running out," Eliza shot back, her eyes narrowing. "Every minute we lose without addressing the problem brings us closer to war."

The word war echoed in my mind. The Destined began talking over one another again, voices rising and overlapping. Their arguments were layered with meanings that kept slipping through my grasp. The more they spoke, the more I realized how little I understood.

What was happening to the Gaul Forest? Why had no one said anything? Was this why Destiny had suddenly reawakened and chosen me after centuries of silence?

King Arisen stood at the head of the table, his hands braced on the edges as he leaned over the raised relief map. Candlelight cast shifting shadows across his face. While the room buzzed around him, he remained quiet, his attention fixed on the contours of the land.

I could not hold back any longer. "Why is the magic disappearing again?" I asked.

My voice cut through the noise. The room fell silent, and every eye turned toward me. My chest tightened under their attention.

Eliza glanced at Arisen before answering, her voice softer. "There are several theories, but nothing definitive. We will need to work together to uncover the truth."

We all waited.

She hesitated, then continued. "Rogers and I have discussed this at length. Our knowledge leads us to believe there are only two real possibilities. The first is that the Gaul Forest is being poisoned. Not in a traditional way, but through magic. A slow, insidious corruption spreading through its roots and weakening it over time. If that is true, we need to find the source before it is too late."

She looked to Rogers. He nodded grimly.

"The second," she said carefully, "is that we are witnessing the end of the Gaul Forest itself. Its magic may simply be running out."

"And what happens if it runs out?" I asked, bracing myself.

The room shifted uneasily. No one looked surprised. They only looked afraid.

Eliza's face tightened. "It would be catastrophic. To begin with, Raster would flood. Without the magic sustaining the aqueducts, there would be no way to control the rainfall."

My stomach dropped. Rain was part of daily life here. The idea of it becoming unstoppable did not feel real.

"How long do we have?" I asked.

King Arisen's voice cut through the tension. "Less than a year."

A collective gasp rippled through the room. Faces that had been composed moments before now showed open fear. Even those who had been arguing just moments ago were silent.

Victor, the imposing elf from Polent, scoffed. "The Gaul Forest does not play by our rules. It has already claimed too much."

Arisen's gaze slid to Victor. The quiet that followed felt heavy, and Victor shifted under the king's stare.

I forced myself to speak again. "If this is urgent, why go to Pitores for six months? We should be at the Gaul Forest now, trying to fix this."

King Arisen's eyes snapped to mine. The intensity of his focus sent a shiver through me, but his tone remained calm and measured. "You do not yet understand the danger, Ms. Lildar. Without training, without learning how to wield the magic you were given, you would not last a day in the Gaul Forest."

"But—" I began.

He cut me off, his voice firm and final. "We go to Pitores. Protocol exists for a reason. We will shorten the process, but you must be prepared. Otherwise, entering the Gaul Forest would be your death sentence."

His words landed like a physical blow.

The meeting ended as abruptly as it had begun. Chairs scraped softly as the other Destined rose, their voices dropping into low murmurs as they filed out. A few gave me nods of understanding or faint approval, but none of it comforted me.

I remained seated, thoughts spiraling. I was not done with this conversation, especially not with him. Too much was at stake, and too much of it now lived between my skin and his.

As the last couple neared the door, I caught King Arisen's eye. Heat pricked my cheeks. "We are not done," I said.

He raised a brow, a hint of challenge tightening his gaze. "No. We are not," he agreed quietly. His eyes lingered on me a heartbeat too long. "But you will need to decide if you are ready to listen."

The door shut behind the others, and the room felt larger and smaller at the same time. The silence wrapped around us, making the space between us feel charged rather than empty.

"I will do this," I said, pushing to my feet. My voice was steady, even as my hands shook. "But I cannot go six months without seeing my family. I need to visit them in Polent."

He didn't answer immediately. His gaze shifted from my face to my marked hand, then back to my eyes. Frustration flickered there, but something else surfaced too, making my pulse race. His lips pressed into a thin line before he finally spoke. "You are difficult, Ms. Lildar."

The words should have stung; instead, I felt a strange pull at the sound of my name in his mouth.

For a moment, I thought he would refuse. The tension stretched between us, taut and humming. Then, with a sharp exhale, he relented.

"There are Destiny gates in Pitores. I will grant you access to visit them once, on one condition. You must travel with my escort."

I took a small step closer without meaning to, drawn in by the quiet roughness in his voice. "Destiny gates?" I asked.

The term felt unfamiliar on my tongue. He seemed to notice my confusion, and his gaze softened slightly as it dropped to my lips, then lifted again.

"They are portals that allow us to travel instantly from one place to another," he said. "They are reserved for the Destined."

The idea was both thrilling and terrifying. One visit every six months still seemed too infrequent. A lump formed in my throat. I opened my mouth to protest.

He took a half step toward me, closing some of the distance. I felt the faint warmth of his body, the familiar hum in my mark answering his. Before I could speak, his eyes hardened and his voice lowered, almost daring me to push further. "You are excused."

He turned away without waiting for my response. His green cape swept behind him as he left the room, his departure as controlled and final as his words. Only when he reached the door did I realize I had been holding my breath.

I stood alone, feeling small and dismissed, with the echo of his nearness still burning along my skin.

At the doorway, Commander Vasa lingered. She did not follow him immediately. She simply waited, her expression unreadable, as if she needed a moment separate from him before moving on.

They were engaged, yet there was no warmth between them. No shared look, no unspoken understanding. They seemed like two pieces placed side by side rather than halves of a whole. That realization settled uncomfortably in my chest.

I pushed the thought away and left the room. The corridors felt tight and airless, pressing in on me as my mind spun.

Outside, the crisp night air cooled my skin. The stars glittered above the palace, their light soft and distant. I breathed in slowly, yet the questions in my mind did not quiet.

If the decay of magic was already causing problems in Raster, how much worse could it become? I pictured the city drowned in endless rain, streets and homes swallowed by water. Knowing that Destiny had chosen me to help prevent that felt crushing.

Why me? Out of everyone, why was I chosen? If even the king seemed uncertain, how was I supposed to trust my own ability to succeed?

I stared up at the stars, searching for answers in their cold light. None came.

I shook my head, forcing the doubts aside. There was no room for uncertainty when the fate of three nations rested on the magic we were trying to save.

I could only hope that working closely with King Arisen would be better than my first impression of him.

Because if it were not, this would be impossible.

CHAPTER 12

Rijor joined me outside, walking silently at my side as he escorted me back to my family. I was grateful for the quiet; my mind was already racing with too much to process. I did not need small talk. I needed to see Kent and Hale. I needed something to ground me.

The fireworks had ended, leaving the night eerily still. As we approached the balcony, I saw Kent sitting with Hale in his lap. The moment she spotted me, she slid down from his lap and ran toward me, her tiny feet pattering against the floor. I bent down and scooped her up, holding her tight. Her weight in my arms was the first real comfort I had felt all night.

"Come on, let's go home. We need to talk," I said softly, my voice betraying how drained I felt.

If I had not gone to that wedding, my life would have stayed on its quiet, predictable path. Now everything was different. I was tangled in a Destiny I had not chosen, bound to a man I barely knew, and my family was being dragged along with me.

Rijor's voice cut through my thoughts. "Ms. Clara Lildar, I will leave you to discuss things with your family. But after tonight, there will be little time left. You will be leaving for Pitores soon."

Kent's eyes widened, confusion and worry flashing across his face. He looked from me to Rijor, waiting for an explanation. Before I could ask why everything was moving so quickly, Rijor disappeared down the corridor.

"Kent, we need to talk," I repeated, gesturing for him to sit with me. His expression tightened, but he followed me to a quieter corner of the balcony where we could have a moment of privacy.

I told him everything: the Destiny, the move, the danger. With each new piece, his jaw clenched tighter, his hands gripping the edge of his chair. He was not angry at me but at the situation. Uprooting his life to move to Polent had never been part of his plan. It was not part of mine either, but this was our reality. He had only just begun to feel like life was settling again.

"This is the safest option," I said, trying to reassure him, even as the words felt hollow in my mouth.

"The safest option?" he repeated, his voice tight. "Clara, you are asking me to leave everything we have ever known. To take Hale away from her home. From you."

"I know," I whispered. My eyes stung. I glanced at Hale, who was happily entertaining herself with the curtains and teacups nearby. Her innocence made everything harder and made my heart ache more.

"You really think this is the right thing to do?" Kent asked again, softer this time.

"I think it is the only thing we can do," I replied, barely able to meet his gaze.

He exhaled, his shoulders sagging as he looked over at Hale. He knew we did not have much of a choice. So did I.

"I will visit," I promised.

Kent nodded, his face tight with worry. "Hale's safety matters, but I cannot help worrying about you too," he said, his voice cracking on the last word.

I squeezed his hand. "I will write often. I will keep you updated on everything."

Tears blurred my vision as I looked at him. He had already lost Lorraine, and now the little stability we had built since her death was being ripped away. I wanted to take his pain, to make this easier, but there was nothing I could do.

"I love you, Clara," he said quietly, pulling me into a tight embrace. "You are the best sister."

I held him close, my tears soaking his shirt, as Hale ran over and wrapped her tiny arms around our legs. I hugged her, kissing the top of her head and breathing in her scent, trying to memorize it. I was going to miss her more than anything.

Before I could say more, a knock at the door cut through the moment. I wiped my face, expecting to see Rijor again, but when I opened it, it was the king.

His tall frame filled the doorway, his eyes glinting in the dim hallway light. "Let us gather your things. Kent and Hale leave at first light, and we depart tonight."

With her usual bold innocence, Hale ran straight to him, wrapping her arms around his leg. King Arisen stiffened, clearly unaccustomed to such affection, but after a moment he rested a hesitant hand on her head. A faint smile tugged at his lips. It was the first smile I had seen from him.

"Sorry about that—" I started, moving to retrieve Hale, but King Arisen cut me off.

"Let us go."

And so, we moved.

The four of us walked down to where the vessels waited. The sleek wooden craft floated on the water, its polished surface reflecting the soft glow of lanterns lining the dock.

As we settled inside, I felt relief. King Arisen chose the farthest seat from us. His presence still pulsed through the mark on my arm, but at least, for now, he was out of sight.

I leaned my head against the window, watching the castle fade behind us as the familiar waterfront rose into view.

After a few minutes, we reached the dock in front of my house. By the main door, Marcos paced anxiously, his shoulders tense, his gaze flicking toward the canal with every step. The rigid lines on his face softened only when he finally spotted me waving.

As soon as the gondola stopped, I stepped out.

"Marcos! I'm so glad to see you." I rushed to him, throwing my arms around his neck. He hugged me tightly, holding me as if he could anchor me in place.

"I can't say much, but I'll be reaching out to you soon," I said, my voice trembling. "I'll be leaving Raster for a while. Just know that I love you so much and appreciate you more than I can say. I've loved the time we've spent together, and I'm grateful for everything." A tear slipped from the corner of my eye.

"I love you too, my friend. You know you can always count on me." His voice was steady, but I could feel the confusion under it. I only hoped I'd be able to explain things one day. Marcos was well-connected; he might be able to help.

We held each other for a few moments until a stern voice cut in.

"We need to move now," one of the Royal Guard barked, his eyes darting between us.

I blew Marcos a quick kiss and hurried inside to gather my belongings. When I turned back, King Arisen stood a few feet away, silently watching us.

The Royal Guard filed into the house, some taking positions by the doors while others moved to help with the packing. I glanced toward the entryway, hoping to catch another glimpse of the king, but he had vanished, likely overseeing the operation. I focused on what needed to be done.

I started with the essentials. The necklace Marcos had given me was a small but deeply sentimental token. My worn running shoes had carried me through countless walks to and from work. My few hygiene items were necessities I couldn't leave behind. And finally, my parestine, the magical device that now felt like my only link to the world I was being pulled away from.

Despite the size of my modest house, I was surprised by how quickly the packing went. Within an hour, everything was neatly stacked and ready to be loaded onto the gondola outside. Realizing what came next made my stomach twist: saying goodbye to Kent and Hale.

I found them in the living room, surrounded by the remnants of our life. The waterfall painting, Hale's favorite, lay shattered on the floor. My heart squeezed at the sight. It had been ruined in an instant.

Carefully, I stepped over the broken pieces, the faint crunch beneath my boots a cruel reminder of how fragile everything had become.

Hale had fallen asleep in Kent's arms, her tiny body curled against his chest. In his other hand, he held the small silver box containing Lorraine's ashes. My throat tightened. He could not leave her behind. He still grieved and holding that box must have cut him open again. His glasses hid some of it, but I could still see the shine of tears at the corners of his eyes.

"I don't want to leave you," I whispered as the first tears slipped down my cheeks.

Goodbyes had never been easy for me, but saying goodbye to Hale was the hardest thing I had ever done. I knelt beside her and leaned close to her ear.

"I love you," I murmured. "I'll love you forever, and I'll love you every single day we're apart."

When I looked up and met Kent's gaze, the strength I'd been clinging to crumbled. I fell into his arms, my tears soaking his shirt as he patted my back in the same steady rhythm he always used to calm me. We held each other, neither willing to let go, as if holding on a little longer could somehow change what was coming.

"You know you're the best sister, right?" he said quietly.

I tried to smile, though my face was wet and my nose clogged. My heart felt unbearably heavy, but his words pushed a small warmth through the ache.

"I'll see you soon," I promised, my voice thick. "I'll be counting down the days."

He squeezed my hand. "Me too," he murmured.

During our brief embrace, the Royal Guard finished loading our belongings onto the larger gondola. Outside, a smaller vessel waited, carrying only King Arisen's things and mine. I wiped the last of the tears from my face and noticed, for the first time in hours, that my mark was faintly glowing again, though it no longer hurt.

I hated it. Its presence reminded me of the life I hadn't chosen, of the burden I hadn't asked for. It drew eyes and questions and expectations. Now, it glimmered softly, almost taunting, a reminder that my life was no longer my own.

"Let's go, Ms. Lildar," King Arisen said. His voice was as calm and distant as ever. He stood by the gondola, holding the door open, his gaze fixed on me with that infuriating composure.

And I could not stand him. He always seemed so controlled, so certain, even as my life unraveled at his feet. He commanded respect and obedience, looking at me as if he knew exactly how much power he held.

But what I hated most was the simple, inescapable truth: no matter how I felt about him, our Destinies were now bound together.

CHAPTER 13

From Clara's Diary

The bitter taste of farewell still clung to me as I stepped outside, leaving behind the warmth of my home. The damp night air felt colder now, biting at my exposed skin. I did not look at King Arisen. I could feel him there, at the edge of my vision, but I knew I had no choice except to follow.

He climbed into the gondola first, the vessel rocking with his movement. I followed and sat opposite him, keeping my eyes low. I let myself have one last glance at my house: the soft glow through the windows, the shadow of Kent moving inside, the faint outline of Hale's toys near the door. It felt like a piece of me was still inside those walls, and I had to tear myself away.

The gondola glided through the dimly lit canal. Lanternlight rippled across the water, warping the reflections of stone bridges and storefronts. The Royal Gardens came into view, quieter than before, stripped of their earlier music and laughter. What had once felt like a celebration now seemed hollow.

"What are we doing back here?" I asked.

"This is where the nearest Destiny gate is," he replied.

A Destiny gate. Here. So close to where I lived, hidden in a place I had walked past for years without knowing.

"How many gates are there? And why does no one know about them?" The sharpness in my tone slipped out before I could stop it.

He lifted a hand and pointed ahead. At first I saw nothing unusual. Then my eyes adjusted, and I noticed it: a narrow door, almost swallowed by vines and moss. It leaned into a stone wall near the waterline, plain and weathered, the kind of thing anyone could overlook.

The gondola stopped. King Arisen stepped out first. He turned and held out his hand to help me.

I hesitated, wanting to refuse out of sheer stubbornness, but the gondola bobbed unsteadily beneath my feet. I placed my hand in his.

Warmth surged up my arm, swift and startling. It spread across my chest, settling low in my stomach. My breath caught. For a heartbeat, I forgot to pull away. His grip was firm and sure, his skin warmer than it should have been in the night air. The mark on my arm pulsed in answer.

I snatched my hand back and rubbed it against my dress, as if I could erase the sensation. If he noticed, he gave no sign.

The door loomed ahead of us, ordinary and completely wrong at the same time.

"Destiny gates are crafted from the same magic that powers the Gaul Forest," he said. His gaze met mine briefly, steady and unreadable. "They are kept hidden because only the Destined can use them. The magic that sustains them is potent. Anyone else would not survive it."

My throat tightened. Lorraine's death flashed through my mind. If gates like this had been accessible to her, if she had been able to escape when Pagos turned on her… maybe things would have been different.

"There is one gate in Pagos, one in Polent, and one here in Ebony," he continued. "They connect the major cities and some smaller towns. We also share one gate by the Gaul Forest. It is the only one all three nations can access equally."

"Oh." It was all I could manage. The idea that this power had been hidden in plain sight my entire life was difficult to grasp.

"To enter, you simply walk through the door," King Arisen said.

He pushed it open. The hinges gave a low creak that echoed strangely in the quiet garden. He shifted my heavy bag onto his shoulder, kept his own at his side, and stepped through. In an instant, he was gone, swallowed by the darkness beyond the frame.

"Anything else I need to know? Will it hurt?" I asked, but the only answer was the rustle of leaves and the distant rush of water. He was already on the other side.

A chill wind brushed against my neck, slipping under the collar of my dress. It felt like a hand pushing me forward.

"I guess I'll just follow along," I muttered.

I drew in a deep breath and stepped through the doorway.

The world changed in a single heartbeat.

The temperature plummeted. A biting cold slammed into my body, stealing the air from my lungs. I gasped, my breath turning to white mist in front of my face. Goosebumps erupted across my skin, and the thin fabric of my dress did nothing to protect me as the chill sank deep, burrowing into my bones.

I wrapped my arms around myself, shuddering.
I was not prepared for this cold.

CHAPTER 14

From Clara's Diary

The bone-chilling cold seeped into my core as if I had been plunged into an icy abyss. The frigid air stripped the heat from my body, leaving me trembling.

I stumbled forward, my breath escaping in misty puffs as I tried to make sense of my surroundings. The air carried the damp scent of earth and pine, so different from the crisp, floral aroma of the Royal Gardens.

As my eyes adjusted to the dim light, I realized I was no longer in the gardens at all. I stood at the edge of a sprawling forest of towering pines. Frost blanketed the ground in a glittering sheet, and each hesitant step crunched softly beneath my feet.

Panic rose in my chest. King Arisen was nowhere in sight.

Had he left me here? Was I alone in this frozen wilderness?

My breathing grew shallow as the cold tightened its grip around my ribs.

"King Arisen?" I called, my voice trembling as it cut through the silent trees.

No response. Only the faint rustle of needles in the icy breeze.

I took a deep breath and forced myself to move forward. My teeth chattered uncontrollably. I cupped my hands and blew into them, but whatever warmth I managed vanished almost instantly.

Then a faint light glimmered in the distance.

I quickened my pace, stumbling over the uneven ground, drawn toward the glow.

King Arisen stood waiting for me, his tall figure silhouetted against the light. He appeared unaffected by the cold, his composure unshaken. As I reached him, he draped a thick wool blanket over my shoulders. I clutched it tightly, grateful for even a hint of warmth.

"Follow me," he said. "We must go two streets up to reach the city center, where we'll be staying."

I trailed behind him, the icy air stinging my cheeks. Even wrapped in the blanket, my fingers felt numb, the cold still seeping into my bones.

Pitores was unlike anything I had ever seen.

In Raster, the rain was constant, a damp companion that left the air heavy and cool. Here, snow ruled. The ground lay buried beneath thick layers of white, pristine and untouched in some places, packed down by footprints and wagon wheels in others. Every step felt clumsy as my feet sank into the snow.

Narrow streets wound between stone buildings huddled close together, as if they, too, were trying to keep warm. Icicles hung from the eaves, glittering like crystals under lanterns strung between the houses.

Warm, golden light spilled from the windows, casting gentle reflections across the snow-covered streets.

Elves moved quickly through the cold, their movements fluid and confident. One elvish woman stood barefoot at a market stall, her tunic thin and flowing as though the ice beneath her feet were no more bothersome than cool stone.

I must have looked pitiful by comparison—wrapped in an oversized blanket, shivering, shoulders hunched against the cold. As we passed, I caught snippets of whispered conversations, eyes flicking from me to King Arisen in recognition.

"He's finally outside that house and the forest," one elf murmured, their voice carrying easily through the still air.

The stars above were breathtaking. They appeared brighter and clearer than any I had seen in Raster. Without the persistent clouds that shrouded my home city, the sky felt vast and endless, a sea of sparkling lights bathing the town in a gentle blue glow.

We passed a small tavern with fogged windows. Laughter and the clinking of glasses spilled into the night, warm and inviting. I longed to step inside, to sit by a fire and forget, even briefly, the cold and the weight of Destiny.

But King Arisen pressed on, and I followed.

Soon, we stopped in front of a modest two-story house painted a deep forest green. Vines climbed up from the frozen garden, their tendrils wrapping around the façade. Only the upper windows remained clear of foliage, their frosted glass glowing faintly with candlelight.

King Arisen approached the door.

It swung open on its own. I jolted, jerking back. It was so different from my home in Raster, where my creaky door always needed a firm shove to open. "How did you do that?"

"Magic safeguards this place," he replied. "It only opens for the Destined."

As he spoke, the candles flared to life, illuminating what was easily the most beautiful home I had ever seen. Though much smaller and far more modest than the Royal Palace, its quaint charm made it feel infinitely more welcoming.

Inside, the air was warm and comforting. The earthy scent of burning wood wrapped around me, and a green fire crackled in the hearth. Bookshelves lined the walls, crammed with worn leather-bound volumes. Plush armchairs circled the fireplace, their cushions soft and inviting.

I let the blanket slide from my shoulders to my elbows, savoring the heat against my chilled skin. This house felt like a sanctuary, a reprieve I hadn't expected. For the first time since leaving home, my body began to relax.

King Arisen moved further inside, his tall frame outlined by the eerie green glow of the fire. His movements were unhurried, familiar, as though he had walked these halls countless times.

Reluctantly, I followed. My footsteps echoed faintly over the polished wooden floor. He didn't glance back, and for some reason, the silence between us felt heavier than the cold outside.

We walked through a kitchen where glass-front cabinets displayed neatly arranged shelves—apples, crackers, and items I did not recognize. A faint, sweet scent lingered in the air, like cinnamon and cloves but not quite, maybe herbs unique to Pitores.

He kept walking, and I kept pace, the only sound our footsteps.

We reached a landing where the stairs forked in two directions. I hesitated as he paused, his eyes flicking briefly between them before he gestured to the left.

"This way," he said quietly. "Your room is up here." After a brief pause, he added, "I'll take your bag."

I handed it to him. Our fingers brushed, just for a heartbeat. The contact sent a small jolt of awareness racing up my arm, and I gripped the blanket tighter, as if that could steady me.

He climbed the stairs, and I followed. By the time I reached the top, my bag was already inside a nearby room, resting at the foot of the bed.

"Get some rest," he said. "I'll meet you downstairs at sunrise to train."

"Already?" I asked. "We don't even know what Destiny we have yet."

He turned to face me, his eyes sharp in the dim light. "You'll find out soon enough. Training starts tomorrow."

A knot of anxiety tightened in my chest. Part of me wanted to challenge him, to demand answers he kept sidestepping. Another, more exhausted part wanted to believe he knew what he was doing—that there was some logic in all of this, even if I couldn't see it yet.

He lingered as if expecting me to speak. When I didn't, he gave a brief nod, then turned and descended the opposite staircase toward his own room.

For a moment, I stood alone at the top of the stairs, staring at the door to my room. Then I opened it and stepped inside.

The space was small but cozy, with a window overlooking the snow-covered streets of Pitores. A large four-poster bed dominated the room, its blankets thick and inviting. I sank onto the mattress with a grateful sigh. The exhaustion of the past few days washed over me in a single, heavy wave.

Even my busiest shifts at the healing ward felt tame compared to this.

I took in the pale blue walls and the delicate forest patterns etched into the woodwork. Above the bed hung a painting of a waterfall, its serene image pulling at my chest. It reminded me of the shattered waterfall painting at home, the one Hale loved so much.

Lying back, I tried to set down my worries: the uncertainty of my Destiny, leaving Kent and Hale behind, the looming task of discovering whatever powers I had been given. But sleep hovered just out of reach.

I spent the night tossing beneath the covers, my mind circling the same questions, the same fears.

Staring out the window at the darkened streets below, I made a silent promise.

Whatever lay ahead, I would find a way to face it.

For Kent. For Hale.

For me.

CHAPTER 15

How could King Arisen be so certain we would discover my powers soon? I studied the intricate symbols on my arm under the candlelight. They seemed to shine even more now that we were closer to the forest. Beyond the golden markings of the Gaul Forest, their meaning was a mystery to me.

I reached for my parestine in the nightstand drawer and walked to the desk. Quickly, I scribbled messages.

To Kent: *I have arrived safely in Pitores. Please let me know how you and Hale are doing in Polent. Is she okay?*

To Marcos: *I miss you already, friend. I hope everything is going well there. Please keep in touch.*

I folded the parestine neatly and placed it back in the drawer, hoping for replies soon.

The adjoining bathroom was small but welcoming, so I drew a hot bath. Steam rose as the tub filled, and I slipped in, letting the warmth soothe my body. For a few blissful moments, I considered staying there forever. Before long, however, the sound of footsteps downstairs reminded me of my obligations.

Reluctantly, I climbed out, dried off, and dressed. I laced up my brown knee-high boots and pulled on the black coat from the closet. The Destined symbol was embroidered in gold over the chest, and I wondered briefly how it had ended up there. Shaking off the thought, I tied my hair into a ponytail and glanced at my reflection. Dark circles smudged beneath my eyes, proof of a restless night.

Downstairs, I caught sight of King Arisen shutting the front door as he carried in a basket of fresh fruit and pastries. His coat mirrored mine, the gold embroidery catching the light as it stretched across his shoulders.

"You might like these," he said, setting the basket on the table. "They are made by elves here in Pitores."

I paused. Why was he being pleasant? "Thank you," I replied cautiously.

"You humans need more food than we do," he explained in a matter-of-fact tone, peeling an orange with practiced precision. "And you will need your energy for the training we will begin soon."

I picked an apple from the basket and took a bite. Flavor burst across my tongue, sweet and vivid, unlike anything I had tasted before. Soon I was reaching for grapes and a piece of fresh bread. King Arisen ate his orange in calm silence, his gaze steady on me as though he was studying every move I made.

"So," I asked between bites, trying to dispel the awkwardness, "what is the plan for today?"

Without looking away, he peeled another slice of orange. "There are three stages of preparation for every Destined. The first stage is about harnessing your powers. We will go as close as possible to the Gaul Forest without stepping inside. Your magic is not strong enough to withstand the forest's influence yet."

The mention of the forest sent a spark through me. I had never seen it, but I knew enough to be wary. I finished my bread in silence, waiting for him to continue.

"Once your Destiny is revealed, we will enter the forest to train in using and controlling it. This stage is dangerous because there are creatures you must be wary of."

"I need to see my family before we reach that stage," I said firmly.

King Arisen paused, his eyes flickering. After a moment, he gave a slight nod, though his reluctance was obvious.

He finished his orange and leaned back in his chair. "The final stage involves the other Destined. You will train together, learn to communicate, and work as a team."

I nodded, though my mind was already racing. I needed to talk to Karlos, the other human Destined from Ebony, to understand his perspective. Eliza intrigued me as well. Her intelligence and confidence were qualities I admired, and I could see us working well together. Allies would be essential.

After a moment of thought, I asked, "Are you also getting a new Destiny?"

"Yes," he replied. After a pause, he added, "When I was Destined to Queen Alondra, my Destiny was knowledge. I learned everything there was to know about the Gaul Forest and its magic. I helped create the policies that sustain our nations and protect the forest."

Everyone knew about his previous Destiny. Queen Alondra had been known for calming wild, magical creatures, a gift that shaped Polent's reputation for training them. King Arisen's contribution, however, had always been described in vague, distant terms. Hearing him speak of it now, I realized how deeply the forest's power had shaped him.

For the first time, I saw a glimpse of the man behind the title. The moment passed quickly. As his eyes met mine again, the mask of the king slid back into place.

"Do you know what it is this time? Will we share the same Destiny?" I pressed, hoping for some reassurance.

His brow furrowed slightly. "Many Destined share similarities in their powers. We will not, which means our bond will be stronger." His tone was blunt, almost as if the idea of such a connection was something he preferred not to think about.

A disappointed sigh slipped out as I wiped my hands and mouth with a napkin. "All right," I said, trying to shake off the uneasy feeling. "I am ready."

We pulled our coats tighter and headed toward the door.

"We will walk several miles until we reach the outskirts of the Gaul Forest," he said, his voice calm and authoritative once more. "You must learn how to harness and control your powers quickly. Start by focusing on generating warmth from within, or you will not survive the cold long enough to even begin training."

"And how am I supposed to do that?" My voice betrayed my rising anxiety as I glanced out the window at the unforgiving snow.

He opened the door, and the frigid wind hit me at once. Instinctively, I shut my eyes and braced myself against the biting air. There was no way I could survive this for more than a few minutes, let alone walk miles through it. I had barely managed the short trip from the Destiny gate to the house yesterday, and that had left me drained.

"It is one of the easiest powers to manifest," he said. "Your arm feels warm when you are near me, does it not?"

"Yes," I admitted quietly.

"Good. Then follow me."

He stepped into the white expanse without another word. I hesitated at the threshold, the warmth of the house at my back and the ruthless cold ahead, then forced my feet to move. The world outside was frozen, and I was already trembling as we trudged into it, the contrast between the warmth I felt near him and the unforgiving cold around us jarring enough to steal my breath.

CHAPTER 16

As soon as we stepped outside, the cold overtook me, stealing my breath and making me shiver uncontrollably. The freezing air pierced my skin, slowing my movements until it felt like I was wading through ice.

King Arisen marched forward, his boots cutting through the deep snow. The fabric of his pants clung to his thighs, each step pushing him onward with effortless strength. I tried to keep up, but my legs struggled, and the wind hit my face, numbing my lips. My mind screamed at him for not teaching me how to summon this so-called warmth he had mentioned, but the words froze on my tongue.

We had made it two miles in. Six more to go? The deeper we ventured into the mountains, the more treacherous the terrain became. What had seemed like a quaint, snowy village now felt like a trap designed to keep outsiders like me from ever reaching the Gaul Forest.

I faltered. My knees buckled, and I collapsed into the snow.

I fell again.

And again.

And again.

The cold seemed to push me down each time, daring me to stay on the frozen ground.

Finally, I toppled backward, sinking into the thick blanket beneath me. My body refused to move. King Arisen was barely a shadow ahead, growing smaller with every step he took. The thought slid through my mind: maybe I was not meant for this. Perhaps this was how Destined met their end, alone in the cold, forgotten.

Hale's face flashed in my mind. Her laughter echoed faintly in my ears, a memory that forced me to keep breathing and stay awake.

A gentle tap on my forehead brought me back. I blinked, dazed, and found myself looking up into King Arisen's eyes, his hair falling like a dark green curtain around his face. He was closer than he had ever been, his features sharpened by the pale light. His fingers were warm against my frozen skin as he checked my pulse, his thumb lingering at my throat for a heartbeat longer than necessary.

"Take my coat," he said, his voice gruff but soft. He pulled me up with ease, his hands firm on my waist.

I wanted to argue, to tell him it would not help, that I needed a fire, not a coat, but the words would not come. All I could do was let him drape his jacket over my shoulders. It smelled faintly of pine and something darker, something that was just him. Even without the extra layer, he only trembled slightly in the cold. His kind's resilience seemed to shield him from it.

"I can't," I whispered, though part of me was clinging to the heat he left on my skin.

He cupped my cheeks, his palms searing compared to the air around us, wiping away the tear that had frozen against my face. The closeness made my pulse stutter.

"We are almost there, Ms. Lildar. You need to focus on your mark and sense the forest's magic," he said, guiding my hands to his neck.

My fingers brushed the edge of his marking, the warm skin beneath it, and a sharp awareness raced through me. I felt the steady rhythm of his pulse under my fingertips. He held my hands there, his own covering mine, his breath fanning across my face.

"Breathe," he murmured. "Feel the Destiny inside you. It is there; you have felt it before."

The air burned my lungs with every inhale, and each exhale cut through my chest like shards of glass. His hands stayed steady over mine, anchoring me. I squeezed my eyes shut, doing everything possible to block out the cold and the fatigue. The warmth from his body seeped into my fingers, up my arms, and I tried to pull that heat into myself, to claim it as my own.

Slowly, warmth trickled from my mark. It was not enough to over-power the cold, but it was there, faint and insistent. Hale's laugh rang in my ears again, her tiny hands reaching out to me in my mind, and I clung to that image.

The warmth spread further. It started from my fingertips, moved through my arms, and reached my chest. The shivers subsided. My teeth stopped chattering. My breathing grew steadier. My hands were still on his neck, the skin beneath my fingers hot and alive, our marks humming between us.

"Good," he murmured, his voice nearer than I expected. "Now focus on pushing that warmth outward. Protect yourself."

I imagined the heat expanding from my core, forming a shield around me. The air shifted, and the sting of the cold retreated, if only a little.

When I opened my eyes, a faint glow surrounded me, emanating from the mark beneath my clothes. The golden hue shimmered softly, light piercing through the fabric and illuminating the air around us. For a moment, the reflection glowed in his eyes, turning them almost molten.

King Arisen watched me closely, his gaze lingering, his eyes gleaming. "You are doing well, but this is only the beginning. It will take time to learn."

His hands on mine suddenly felt too much. I pulled my hands away from his neck, the break in contact leaving a strange emptiness in its wake. The closeness, the warmth, the awareness of every place our bodies had touched—it all felt far too intimate.

I took a step back, letting the cold nip at my fingers. It was uncomfortable, but now it was bearable. I handed his coat back, shoving my arms into my pockets.

"Why did you not teach me this sooner?" I asked, frustration sharpening my voice.

"Destiny reveals itself when you are at your limit," he replied. "That is when it can take root, when you are forced to call on it. It will always be there if it can survive inside you at your lowest."

"You could have at least warned me," I shot back. He did not understand. How could someone like him, an immortal elf, ever grasp the meaning of death the way I did?

"You made it farther without magic than any human I have ever known," he said, a hint of respect threading through his tone. "That was… impressive."

The word settled between us, heavier than it should have. I pushed past him, anger and stubbornness giving me the strength to move ahead. For the first time since we started walking, I was the one leading.

Going up the mountain felt less impossible now. The warmth inside me kept the worst of the cold at bay as I trudged forward. Eventually, the ground fell away beneath my feet, and I reached a precipice overlooking nothing but thick fog and darkness. Below, an endless emptiness stretched out, veiled in shadow.

I turned, and there was King Arisen, leaning casually against a tree. His silhouette blended with the shadows, but the faint glint of his golden markings caught the fading light. His arms were folded across his chest, his posture relaxed, as if he had all the time in the world.

"You have found the Urten Cliff," he remarked, kicking at the snow with the toe of his boot.

"The what?" I asked, squinting into the fog that obscured the horizon.

"It is the last point before we reach the Gaul Forest."

I narrowed my eyes and noticed a structure in the distance—a bridge. Its metal beams were barely visible, stretching far into the mist.

"We cross that bridge when you are ready," he said.

"How do we even get across that?"

"It takes a great deal of magic. The forest does not just let anyone in. But that is for later. First, we train here," he added, gesturing to the clearing around us.

Exhaustion began to creep back into my limbs, settling into my muscles like lead. I lowered myself onto a nearby boulder with a tired huff. "Fine. Let us get this over with."

King Arisen approached slowly. Snow caught in the green strands of his hair, standing out against the dark fabric of his Destined coat. His eyes locked onto mine, steady and unblinking.

"Take off your gloves," he said quietly. "I need to touch your marks."

Touch me… again?

My pulse quickened, and I swallowed, suddenly acutely aware of how isolated we were on that cliff. I met his eyes, searching for any sign of hesitation, but there was none—only that unwavering focus and the faint, dangerous pull of Destiny tightening between us.

CHAPTER 17

"**M**s. Lildar, will you not extend your hand?"

A cold shiver rippled through me at the realization of what he was asking. The idea of King Arisen touching my bare skin was unfamiliar, unsettling… and, if I was honest with myself, not entirely unwelcome. But there was no avoiding it. If I truly wanted to understand this Destiny that bound us, I had to let him in, even if it was only through a single touch.

With trembling fingers, I removed my gloves and carefully rolled up the sleeve of my coat, exposing the golden marks etched along my forearm. They pulsed faintly, reacting to the magic thick in the air. Feeling exposed under his gaze, I hesitated for a moment before slowly extending my hand.

He moved closer, his eyes never leaving mine as his fingers traced the patterns on my skin. His warm touch contrasted with the cold air, and the moment his hand covered mine, everything shifted between us.

It was more than just physical contact. Our Destiny marks seemed to recognize each other, reacting in a way that made the air hum. A gentle current moved through me, a pulsing heat that drove away the cold. His hand stayed, his fingers tracing the glowing lines with unexpected care. My breath caught in my chest, and the space between us suddenly felt dangerously small.

"What do you see?" I managed to ask.

King Arisen's eyes narrowed as he studied the markings more closely. The faint golden glow from my arm illuminated the space between us, and I watched his expression shift, first to curiosity, then his eyes darkened. His brow furrowed deeply, and he exhaled through his nose.

"Your Destiny mark," he began, his voice quieter now, "is unlike anything I have ever seen."

I felt his fingertips hover just above my skin, as if he were reluctant to break contact. "The outline of the Gaul Forest is unmistakable. But this," he continued, tracing the long, jagged line running from my wrist to my elbow, "this looks… forced. As if the magic was not given freely."

My breath hitched. "Forced?" I echoed, staring down at the designs on my arm.

King Arisen hesitated before speaking again. "I felt the same thing when I was marked," he admitted. "When I became Destined with you, the pain was not like before—smooth, natural. It was as though the magic of the Gaul Forest itself was resisting. My mark, yours…" He trailed off, shaking his head, as if putting it into words would make it too real.

I pulled my hand back, suddenly aware of how much his touch had steadied me. I stared at the design etched into my skin. "What could it mean?" I murmured, more to myself than to him.

"The others—Eliza, Karlos, and Rogers—knew their Destiny almost immediately upon seeing their marks," he said. "Their powers aligned seamlessly with their roles."

I thought of Eliza's green markings, spreading across her shoulders like vines, perfectly reflecting her command over plants and roots as an aldaron. Her magic made sense. So did the others'.

My gaze drifted up to King Arisen's markings, tracing the lines etched into his skin. They carved down his cheekbones and swept along his jawline. Their golden glow pulsed faintly in the dim light; the energy in them was more volatile than I had ever seen. Despite who he was, I couldn't help noticing how striking they were—beautiful, even.

"And what about you?" I asked quietly. "Do you know what your Destiny is?" I knew I had asked before, but he had never answered. If he knew, maybe it could help guide me.

The way his body responded told me the answer before his words did. His jaw tightened, and he looked away, his expression hardening. "That is not something we need to dwell on," he replied curtly.

"Not something we need to dwell on?" I repeated, disbelief sharpening my voice.

He turned and walked a few steps toward the edge of the cliff, facing the distant outline of the Gaul Forest. The wind whipped through his green hair, but he stood unmoving, carved out of shadow and gold.

His silence fed my frustration. "I am not asking for much," I pressed, my voice growing sharper. "Just honesty. I cannot keep standing here, in the middle of nowhere, bound to someone who will not answer a simple question."

Still, he did not turn.

When he finally spoke, his voice carried back to me on the cold breeze, low and even. "Some truths are not meant to be spoken yet."

His cryptic calm only made my irritation rise. "I deserve to know what is happening," I shot back. "What I am risking my life for."

King Arisen moved then, taking two long strides toward me. The space between us vanished in an instant, and I had to tilt my head up to meet his gaze. His nearness pulled at me, that invisible thread of Destiny tightening in my chest.

"You think I do not want to tell you?" he said, his voice low and rougher than before. "Do you think I have not struggled with this every moment since the wedding?" His eyes burned into mine. "Do you know what it was like to feel that pull—to feel Destiny itself ripping through me—and not be able to find you? It drove me mad, Ms. Lildar."

I blinked, thrown off by the intensity in his voice. My breath caught as he continued, softer now but edged with pain. "You disappeared. I searched all night. I scoured every corner of Raster, every possible place you might have gone. The pain…" His hand lifted toward his neck, fingers grazing his mark as if the memory itself ached. "It felt as though my very essence was being torn apart. And I knew you were going through the same. Likely worse. I could not bear that thought."

I swallowed hard, the raw vulnerability in his words making me unsteady. He was right. It had been terrible, and I wasn't sure I would have made it without Marcos by my side.

"Why was it so painful?" I asked quietly, my voice trembling. "It was… unbearable." I looked down at my hands, my fingers shaking at the memory. "That is not normal, is it?"

He hesitated, his jaw tightening as though choosing each word with care. "The Gaul Forest is tied to us. The magic there, what remains of it, is volatile and unstable. Being bound to that forest in this state…" He exhaled. "It is a death sentence."

I took a shaky breath, trying and failing to steady myself. "I do not know if I am strong enough for this," I admitted.

As the confession left my lips, a single snowflake drifted down, landing on the tip of my nose. I flinched at the cold touch and brushed it away, my breath emerging in a soft puff of mist. More flakes followed, tumbling gently from the sky, each one vanishing as it kissed the ground.

For a moment, everything around me faded. The storm, the cold, the ache in my chest—all of it blurred under the quiet fall of snow. My Destiny's warmth kept the chill from settling into my bones, but the stillness of the moment held me in place.

King Arisen's gaze was fixed on me, clear even through the swirling flakes. He stood tall and unmoving, a striking figure against the white backdrop. Frost clung to his hair, turning strands of green into silver.

When I looked back at him, his eyes caught me off guard. He was watching me—not with the usual cold detachment, but with a focused intensity that made my heart stumble. His gaze lingered, and my Destiny responded, heat blooming in my chest. I held my breath, unsure if I should look away—or step closer.

Without a word, he closed some of the distance between us. The snow fell steadily, softening the edges of everything but him. He lifted his hand as if to brush away the flakes caught in my hair, his fingers hovering just inches from my cheek. For a suspended moment, I thought he might actually touch me.

Then he pulled back, his hand curling loosely at his side.

His eyes did not leave mine as he broke the silence. "We should not stay out here much longer. The storm is going to intensify soon."

The pine trees swayed ominously as the wind picked up around us. King Arisen turned, leading the way back, and this time, we walked side by side. The distance between us had not vanished completely, but it was smaller now, filled with unspoken questions and the lingering echo of his touch.

This first day of training had been… a lot.

The descent from the Urten Cliff felt far shorter than the final few blocks leading to the house. Along the way, elves greeted King Arisen by his first name, which struck me as odd. In Raster, no one would dare address him so casually.

"Why do you spend most of your time here?" I asked when we finally found a moment of quiet between the greetings.

"The magic here is stronger. I need to stay close to the forest."

His answer made sense, but it felt incomplete. I glanced around at the elves passing by, offering him warm nods and friendly smiles. They were completely at ease around him, no royal titles, no rigid formality. It was the opposite of everything I had experienced in Raster.

I hesitated before asking, "Why do they call you just… Arisen?" The name felt strange without "King" in front of it.

He looked at me, a small trace of a smile touching his lips. "The people here are more accustomed to me as a member of their community rather than a ruler. Titles have their place, but not everywhere." He paused, his gaze steady on mine. "I would prefer it if you called me Arisen."

I blinked, trying to process the request. Addressing him so casually felt almost improper, given everything I knew about him as a ruler and an elf. "You want me to call you Arisen?" I repeated, my voice cautious.

"Yes."

I considered this for a moment and found myself nodding. We were not on friendly terms yet, but if he was offering even a small kindness,

I could meet him halfway. "All right, Arisen," I said, testing the name on my tongue.

He seemed pleased. A warmth flickered in his eyes, and I had to look away. "Thank you," he said, and the simplicity of his words made the moment feel surprisingly genuine.

After a beat, I added, a faint smile tugging at my lips, "Then you can just call me Clara."

"Clara it is, then."

A silence stretched between us, but it was no longer uncomfortable. His expression was thoughtful, as if he was considering what to say next.

"Is that the only reason you stay here?" I asked. "Because the magic is stronger?"

"No," he admitted. "I have spent the last two decades here with the Destined, studying the forest's decay."

"The last two decades?" I echoed, frowning. "You knew about the decay before there were any visible signs?"

"I could sense there was an issue long before the signs appeared. The Gaul Forest has always spoken to the Destined in ways others cannot hear. I have spent many days, sometimes weeks, inside it, trying to understand."

I hesitated. "What have you learned?"

He exhaled, his gaze drifting toward the distant tree line, where the mist of the forest loomed thick and heavy. "It feels still. Too still. There is little movement, even from the creatures that once thrived there. As if they are hiding."

A chill ran down my spine. "Hiding from what?"

He turned back to me, his eyes catching the moonlight. "That is what I have been trying to figure out. I have walked the forest with the other Destined, but the land is too vast for us to cover."

This was not just about the Gaul Forest losing its magic. Something was driving it into silence. And if the King of Ebony had spent two decades searching for answers, whatever it was, it was not easily fixed.

When we finally returned to the house, I kicked off my boots, grateful for the warmth under my feet. Arisen headed toward his room, and I slipped into the kitchen for a small meal before going to mine.

In the comforting stillness of my room, the warmth wrapped around me like a blanket. I sat on the edge of the bed, opened the nightstand drawer, and pulled out my neatly folded parestine, now filled with messages from Marcos and Kent.

Their words felt like a lifeline as I unfolded it, grounding me in the world I knew.

Clara,

I am well, although I already miss you. Everyone in Ebony is surprised by the news of our king being Destined for the second time. The word of who you are is getting out. The story is positive, but as you can imagine, some elves are questioning your integrity. I have been working with my networks here to ensure that as many people as possible are supportive. But to be honest, our attention has also shifted to the aqueducts.

Do you know why we keep getting flooded? I was only an inch away from having water inside my house.

Take care and write often.

My heart sank at Marcos's message. Before I could fully process it, new words from Kent appeared.

We have reached Polent and are being treated well. We have been given accommodations within the castle. This place is grander than Raster, and it is nice to be among humans. You would be surprised to see all the basilisks within the castle grounds. There are also other creatures I have never seen before. They call them sleipnirs. They look like eight-legged horses, apparently a newer species taken from the Gaul Forest. They are not fully trained yet, but King Llorent uses them often.

Hale is safe and doing well. There is a program for children her age, so she is learning and has met other kids. After her nap, she goes to the castle grounds every afternoon to play. Rijor has been around. He seems especially interested in helping Hale settle in. She misses you and often asks about you. I will let her know you wrote and that you are safe.

The only thing I find hard is the weather. It is different from the constant rainfall of Raster. I miss the rain. I miss the way it sounded against our windows, the rhythm it brought to the day. Somehow, the quiet here feels louder without it.

With much love,

Your brother Kent

The words faded, taking the brief smile from my lips. They were all right. Hale was more than all right; she sounded happy. Maybe, after all, this arrangement wasn't as bad as I had feared.

I folded the parestine again and returned it to the nightstand.

As I lay in bed, the day replayed in my mind: the Urten Cliff, the strange sharpness of our marks, the way Arisen had looked at me beneath the falling snow, and the messages from Marcos and Kent. They tangled together, leaving me feeling unsettled and oddly hopeful at the same time.

Outside, the snow kept falling, casting a gentle glow through the window and blanketing the town in white. It was a peaceful scene, one I wished reflected how I felt inside.

I shifted restlessly, searching for a comfortable position, but my thoughts would not quiet. With a sigh, I turned onto my side and stared out at the snowflakes drifting past the glass.

I knew there was one thing I had to do, although I suspected it wouldn't be easy. If I wanted to find my Destiny, I had to connect with Arisen—truly connect—in a way that went beyond just reluctant cooperation.

As the night stretched on, I drifted in and out of sleep, caught between dreams and waking. Images flickered through my mind: forests swallowing the horizon, waterfalls pouring from the sky, Hale's small hand in mine, Kent's tired smile.

Eventually, exhaustion won.

Outside, the snow kept falling.

And just like that, three and a half months slipped by.

CHAPTER 18

Three months and eighteen days, to be exact. Three months and eighteen days without Kent and Hale. Three months and eighteen days without making faster progress.

I woke up every day to the sound of Arisen's footsteps downstairs. It had become a familiar rhythm; one I had learned to anticipate. Even though I was an early riser, he always beat me to it, up well before dawn. My body ached, a dull soreness from the constant exertion, but Destiny flowing through me softened the worst of it. Without that, I was not sure I would even be able to get out of bed.

Our days had fallen into a predictable, almost mechanical routine.

He woke before me.

We shared breakfast, the only part I genuinely looked forward to.

We climbed a different path up the mountain.

We trained.

And trained.

And trained.

We returned, drained from the day's efforts.

I soaked in a bath, my muscles screaming for relief.

I wrote to Kent and Marcos.

I slept.

Then the cycle began again.

The training was intense. Mornings were spent meditating, remaining still for hours and focusing on the magic flowing through me. Arisen said this was crucial to unlocking my Destiny, but it often left me restless and frustrated. He guided me as I tried to quiet my thoughts and go inward. Some days, I sensed the faintest glimmer of connection, a pulse of energy deep inside. On other days, I sat for hours, battling impatience as my mind wandered.

Afternoons were for physical training. Arisen tested my endurance, pushing me to run through dense trails or climb steep, snow-filled inclines, my legs burning with every step. He showed no mercy and insisted that strength and resilience were as crucial as magic.

"Your body must match your mind," he would say.

Then came combat training. Arisen taught me how to wield a blade, his movements fluid as he demonstrated each technique. I was not naturally skilled, but his patience never wavered.

"Focus," he reminded me whenever I faltered, his eyes steady on mine.

We sparred endlessly. By the end of each session, my arms felt like lead, but even I could not deny the improvement in my stance and reflexes.

Some days, we trained together to harness my magic in combat. It was draining, both physically and mentally, but those brief moments when I could feel the magical energy surrounding me kept me going.

Evenings were quieter, but no less demanding. Arisen asked me to recount what I had learned, pressing me to reflect on my progress and identify weaknesses. His scrutiny was relentless, yet there were rare moments when his praise broke through, a small smile softening his usually stern features.

It was exhausting. It was also necessary.

The Gaul Forest remained out of reach. I had tried crossing the Urten Bridge last week, determined to push further, but the moment I reached the halfway point, a horrible pain shot through my head. It began as a dull throb and quickly escalated into a blinding ache that nearly dropped me to my knees. My vision blurred, and the world spun as the bridge swayed beneath my feet.

I collapsed, clutching my temples, gasping as I struggled to stay conscious. The sharp mountain wind whipped around me, but I barely felt it over the agony coursing through my mind. The pain grew so intense that I could not tell whether I was still awake or had already passed out.

"Clara!" Arisen's voice cut through the pressure behind my eyes. He was at my side in an instant, kneeling beside me, his hands brushing my shoulders.

"You should not have pushed yourself this far," he muttered.

I wanted to respond, but the words would not come. The world tilted as I fell forward.

He caught me without hesitation, his arms wrapping around me as he lifted me from the ground. He cradled me against his chest, my head resting against the warmth of his coat.

"I have you," he murmured, his voice softer now above the howling wind.

Through the haze, I caught glimpses of his face. Concern tightened his features; his eyes focused on the path ahead as he carried me back across the bridge. My body went limp in his arms, too weak to do anything but trust him.

Time blurred. The snowfall thickened, flakes landing on my face as I drifted in and out of awareness. Now and then, I felt him adjust his grip, his arms tightening as he navigated down the mountain.

When we reached the outskirts of Pitores, the familiar sight of snow-covered rooftops greeted us. The lights from the houses looked distant, like stars just out of reach.

He brought me into the house and laid me on the couch near the fireplace. The fire roared to life the moment we crossed the threshold, flooding the room with warmth and melting the cold that had settled into my bones.

My eyes grew heavy. The last thing I remembered was his gaze on me as he knelt at my side, his fingers brushing a strand of hair from my face.

"Rest. You will be all right."

Darkness claimed me, the pain fading as exhaustion finally took over.

The experience left me drained and frustrated. Three months and eighteen days had passed since I first stepped into Pitores, and I still had not set foot in the forest. Why was it taking so long? What was wrong with me?

At least I had my parestine. Writing long messages helped the time pass.

From the responses I received, I learned that the floods in Raster continued. They were not catastrophic, but they were damaging enough to displace families and stir tension between elves and humans. I had been told Rijor was handling it, but a part of me felt guilty, as if we should have been there helping.

Marcos mentioned that his work with the community had helped those most affected. He had organized a group of a few hundred humans to deliver supplies to the outskirts of the city.

Kent's messages were more personal, filled with reassurances. Hale was thriving in her new environment, attending school and making friends, while Rijor had taken a special interest in helping them settle into Polent. Hale had even grown attached to him. Being so far from the people I loved felt strange, and I was not used to trusting someone else to care for them.

I was pulled from my thoughts by the sound of footsteps below. Reluctantly, I crawled out from the warmth of my blankets and dressed, choosing dark trousers, lace-up boots, a long-sleeved white tunic, and my Destined coat. After months of hiking and training, my feet had swollen so much that I was grateful for boots with adjustable laces.

Heading downstairs, I half expected to find Arisen in his usual formal attire, ready for another long day. Instead, I stopped in the doorway.

He was seated at the kitchen table, dressed more casually than I had ever seen him. His long green hair was loose, falling past his shoulders. He wore a simple cream cross-knit tunic and fitted brown pants. Seeing him like that, relaxed and almost ordinary, felt new.

"Good morning," he said.

"Hello?" I replied, unsure how to respond to this version of him. "Are we not going out to train?"

He nodded toward the window. "Look outside. The weather has changed. We cannot go anywhere today. Not until it clears."

I moved closer and looked through the frost-covered vines that clung to the glass. Snow piled up against the window, a thick wall of white obscuring everything beyond it.

We were snowed in. Another delay.

I had not attempted to cross the Urten Bridge since that day, and now the snow would push us back further.

I opened the pantry, took out some fruit, and arranged a small platter. My movements were slow, weighed down by disappointment I did not want to name. I sat at the counter beside him and stirred my warm oatmeal. The scent of cinnamon filled the air, comforting and familiar. It reminded me of home.

"What are you doing?" I asked.

Arisen did not answer right away. His gaze stayed on the parestine in his hands. Finally, he said, "Sending directives to Rijor. The water levels must be controlled. If the aqueducts overflow, the inner city will flood."

"The inner city," I repeated quietly. "That is where most of the humans live."

His eyes shifted to me, something difficult to read flickering in the blue specks within his irises. "That is exactly why my focus is there," he replied. "The humans in Raster are my priority, Clara. I will not let them drown."

I nodded slowly, a part of me reassured, another part wary of needing that reassurance at all.

"Rijor has the directives," Arisen continued. "But I will need to double-check his execution. Some things are better overseen personally."

There was a subtle edge to his voice, as if he was not entirely confident that what was being done would be enough.

Silence grew between us, broken only by the soft click of our spoons against ceramic.

"Can you tell me more about Rijor?" I asked at last. "I have only met him once, but he seems close to you. And now he is close to my family."

For the past three months and eighteen days, Kent's messages had mentioned Rijor often. The only time I had seen him was that first day, and now he was an integral part of my family's new life. The thought unsettled me more than I wanted to admit.

"I chose him as my right-hand two years ago to help unite humans and elves. He is from Hertm."

"Hertm?" I echoed, surprised. "It is rare for someone from such a remote place to hold a position of power."

Arisen nodded, his expression thoughtful. "Hertm has always been overlooked in matters of governance. Its people, mostly humans, have long felt disconnected from decisions made in Raster. When I ascended the throne, I made it a priority to bring more diverse voices onto the council. Rijor seemed like the perfect choice."

He took a sip of tea. "From the beginning, he presented himself as an ally to both humans and elves. He is one of the rare few. An Elythian."

I tilted my head. "He is human and elf?"

"Yes. Such unions are incredibly uncommon, not only because of the physical and cultural differences between the races, but because they require a depth of trust that is seldom found. His existence alone stands as a symbol of unity."

"That must have made him different," I said quietly, still piecing things together. I had only encountered a few Elythians in my life, and they all seemed more reserved than even the elves.

"It did," Arisen agreed. "Rijor spoke passionately about coexistence. He wanted a future where humans and elves could live together without resentment or mistrust. It was refreshing, especially coming from someone rooted in Hertm, where such partnerships are rare and often misunderstood."

I frowned, trying to reconcile this image with the man at my doorway months ago. "Is he someone I can trust?" I asked, the question that mattered most.

Arisen's answer came slowly. "Trust is complicated with him," he said. "Rijor has a way of making himself invaluable in any relationship. He knows how to place himself where he is most needed, and that makes him difficult to overlook. When it comes to Kent and Hale, though, I am confident Llorent will keep them safe under his care."

The implication was clear, even if he did not say more. I nodded, uncertain, and followed him into the living room.

We settled there, the crackling green flames casting an emerald glow across the room. I took the sofa, and Arisen chose the chaise across from me, leaning back with a rare hint of ease.

"Maybe we can use this time to get to know each other better," I suggested, trying to make something useful of the enforced stillness.

His lips twitched slightly, the smallest hint of amusement. "I already know you better than you think."

I froze, my spoon hovering above my bowl. His words were casual, but there was a quiet certainty in them. How could he possibly claim that?

"What do you mean by that?" I asked, narrowing my eyes. As far as I knew, our understanding of each other was shallow at best. Three months and eighteen days, and I did not even know his favorite food, or whether he preferred silence to music. Not that those details truly mattered, but the thought stood.

He tilted his head, a faint smirk pulling at one corner of his mouth. "What do you want to know?" he asked, turning the question back on me.

"I… I am not sure," I admitted. The idea of interrogating the King of Ebony about his personal life felt ridiculous.

He leaned forward, resting his elbows on his knees. The shift in posture made him look less like a distant king and more like a man willing to talk. "Then I will start," he said. "What has been the most unexpected part of this Destiny for you so far?"

I considered the question. "The connection," I said finally. "I can feel you sometimes. Your presence. It is like a thread tying us together, even when you are not in the room. Have you felt that too?"

His gaze held mine, his expression guarded, but I caught a flicker of recognition. "Yes," he answered.

"What do you think it means?" I asked.

"It is the essence of Destiny," he said. "A bond that transcends everything. Magic. Time. Even understanding."

His answer only led to more questions. "What about your first Destiny?" I pressed. "What was it like?"

His expression shifted, a faint shadow crossing it. "It was during the war," he said quietly. "Every nation was exploiting magic, each desperate for more power. The Gaul Forest collapsed under the strain, and we were close to losing everything. That was when the pact of Destiny was forged."

He paused, his eyes distant. "Ebony, Pagos, and Polent had no choice but to come together. The forest's magic was the only thing holding our lands together. To restore balance, we created a pact, binding the strongest warriors, healers, and scholars from both elves and humans. We thought it was our design. We believed we were the ones in control."

His gaze returned to me, a deeper knowledge behind it. "But the moment the pact was sealed, the Gaul Forest took over."

"The forest chose?" I asked.

"Yes. It became more than an agreement between rulers. It decided who would be Destined, binding humans and elves in ways we could not predict. Queen Alondra was pivotal. She convinced Pagos and Polent to agree to the terms, but it was my role to shape those terms. I was Destined with knowledge, an understanding of how humans and elves impact the Gaul Forest and each other."

"And you used that knowledge to create the agreement," I said softly.

He nodded. "It was meant to ensure balance and cooperation, but time has eroded that unity. Resentment and mistrust have taken root again."

I thought about the floods in Raster, the tensions between humans and elves, and the fragile peace that chained the three nations together. I thought about how desperate I had been to discover my Destiny, as if solving that one piece would fix everything.

The conversation fell into a comfortable silence as we finished our tea. Morning light filtered through the window, illuminating the snow piled against it. It was a rare moment of calm, and I found myself grateful for it.

A question rose to the surface. "Do you still have your first Destiny mark?" I asked. "Do you feel anything from it?"

His expression grew somber. "No," he said. "I stopped feeling it after Queen Alondra passed. The mark is still there, but it has faded. I still have all the knowledge I gained from that magic, and the house and the Gaul Forest still welcome me as a past Destined."

I looked down at my covered arms. My marks felt alive, constantly humming beneath my skin, especially when Arisen was nearby. Part of me wanted to tell him that. The thought made my cheeks warm.

Instead, I stayed quiet, brushing the edge of my sleeve as if making sure everything remained hidden.

Out of the corner of my eye, I saw Arisen recline further, his green hair falling slightly into his face. It was rare to see him so unguarded. Faint lines etched his forehead, his jaw clenched as if he was wrestling with words unsaid.

"Everything all right?" I asked softly.

"I am fine. Just tired."

I studied him, searching for any crack in his mask. Whatever troubled him, he clearly was not ready to share it.

"Commander Vasa will be here tomorrow," he said suddenly, his tone clipped as he stood. Then, almost so quietly that I thought I imagined it, he added, *I do not want to see her.*

I paused. "Why do you not want to see her?"

"I did not say that," he replied sharply. His gaze flicked to me, then away, as he started toward the stairs.

I watched him go, confusion gnawing at me. Just before he disappeared from view, I could have sworn I heard him repeat the same words under his breath.

"I do not want to see her."

Silence settled around me, broken only by the distant hiss of snow against the window. I leaned back against the sofa and stared into the green fire.

Three months and eighteen days.

My life had become a blur of training, snow, and unanswered questions. One thing was clear. I needed answers. I was determined to uncover my Destiny, no matter how painful or complicated the path ahead might be.

And I knew it had to happen soon.

CHAPTER 19

Another day lost. Another day without training. The growing frustration wasn't just about the lack of progress but also about the overwhelming sensations that Destiny forced me to feel. Whenever I thought about it, or, worse, actually felt it, anxious energy surged through me. Hot waves spread over my marked arm, heating my skin in a way I could no longer ignore. And when Arisen was near, those waves didn't stop at my arm. They crept into my chest and clenched it.

The weather had finally cleared, and the air outside was crisp and biting. We would resume training tomorrow, but today we waited at the house for Vasa. Part of me wanted to go out. I already knew the way to the Gaul Forest. But Arisen was vigilant, and he was not one to let things slip by unnoticed.

It hadn't always been like this. About a month ago, during a rare moment of rebellion, I went out in the middle of the night. Restless and desperate for a taste of normalcy and elvish wine, I needed an escape, even if only for a little while.

My disguise was simple. A plain dark brown cloak with a hood that covered most of my face, obscuring my hair. Simple leather boots that blended in with the cobblestones. Bandages wrapped around my hands to hide the markings on my arms. It was enough to make me just another passerby.

No one in Pitores cared for details anyway. The town was busy but indifferent, and I moved unnoticed through the streets until I found a small bar near the town square. It was a cozy, dimly lit place buzzing with low conversation and the occasional clink of glasses. Locals filled the room, unaware of me. For the first time in weeks, I felt like I could breathe without Destiny hanging over me.

The bar smelled of wood smoke and ale. I slipped onto a stool at the far end of the counter, pulled my hood lower over my face, and ordered a glass of elvish wine. The warmth settled into my bones, momentarily dulling the ache in my nerves. I allowed myself a second glass, then a third, savoring the quiet anonymity.

And then he found me.

I did not hear him come in. I was mid-conversation with the bartender, laughing softly, when my arm grew warm. Too warm. Glancing over my shoulder, I froze. He stood just inside the doorway, his eyes scanning the room until they locked on mine.

Arisen's expression was not anger. It was concern. His brow furrowed, his jaw set, tension radiating from him even as he remained composed.

He did not speak at first, but his gaze made my skin prickle. The conversations around me faded. The realization of his presence drowned out everything else. I swallowed the rest of my drink, trying to appear unaffected, but the heat rising in my chest said otherwise.

"Clara."

I raised an eyebrow, feigning nonchalance despite the wine swirling in my system. "King Arisen," I replied, dragging out the title. "What brings you here?"

His gaze dropped to my empty glass, then returned to my face. "We are leaving."

I laughed too loudly. "I am enjoying myself. I am not ready to go."

He stepped closer, the muscles in his jaw tightening as he leaned in. "This is not up for discussion. We are leaving."

The way his eyes lingered on my flushed cheeks and wine-stained lips made me feel like there was more behind his insistence than duty.

I stood, swaying slightly as the alcohol made itself known. "Why do you care where I am?" I challenged, the wine giving me more courage than sense.

His eyes softened just a fraction. In one swift motion, he reached for my wrist, not harshly but firmly enough to command my attention. "I am responsible for you, Clara. You are my Destiny."

The bar had gone quiet. I barely noticed. All I felt was the warmth of his hand, the way his touch sent another wave of heat through me, one that had nothing to do with the wine.

"Fine," I muttered, pulling my arm free. I tossed a few coins onto the counter and gave the bartender a half-hearted nod before following Arisen outside.

The night air hit me like a cold slap. We walked back in silence, me keeping at least two steps ahead. By the time we reached the house, the door swung open quickly, as if sensing my mood. I stormed inside with him close behind.

He did not say anything. He did not have to. His steady, unrelenting gaze followed me, as if he could see through every layer I had built to protect myself.

That stare, that watchful, piercing look, had not left me since that night. It was not anger. It was something else, something that made me think he was being more protective than usual. If I left, I knew he would find me.

All of this began because I wanted to feel like myself again, to escape the reality of what my life had become, even if only for a few hours. Truthfully, Pitores had grown on me, and my relationship with Arisen had deepened, yet I still felt lonely. I wasn't used to this kind of isolation, having only one person to talk to day after day. Back home, I had Kent and Hale, and my work as a healer kept me surrounded by people. Here, that part of my life felt distant, like a piece of myself I no longer knew how to reach.

Just like yesterday, I prepared for another day. I chose more casual clothes this time, a jade green satin dress that fell just below my knees, soft and loose against my skin. I left my hair down, letting it cascade over my shoulders, hoping the small change might ease my restless mind.

But unlike other mornings, he felt off.

The pacing footsteps of Arisen, which had become my reliable morning rhythm, were absent.

I had not seen or heard from him since he went upstairs last night. After he left, I retreated to my room and spent the evening writing to Kent and Hale. Hale's brief scribbles made me smile, even though the parestine erased them quickly after I read them. I ran my fingers over the now-blank pages, wishing for more, but it was late in Polent and Raster, and they were probably asleep.

Sighing, I closed the parestine and went downstairs, taking my time with each step. There was no rush, no urgent training today. I had braced myself for another quiet morning, but as I neared the kitchen, familiar voices stopped me in my tracks.

Arisen. Eliza. Rogers.

Eliza and Rogers stood near the entrance; their black Destiny coats dusted with fresh snow. Damp strands of hair clung to their faces, and both of them looked exhausted, especially Eliza. Her eyes were a deeper red, like she had not slept in days.

"Morning," I greeted them, grateful for the company.

They replied with tired but genuine smiles. Relieved for the change in routine, I busied myself with tea. Rose leaf and honey filled the air as I stirred the cups. The simple act of making tea brought a small sense of calm.

I returned to the living room with the tray, the faint rattle of porcelain punctuating the quiet. Eliza and Rogers sat near the hearth while Arisen leaned against the wall, his eyes following me as I approached.

"Tea?" I offered, handing a cup to each of them. Eliza accepted hers with a grateful nod, and Rogers gave me a weary smile that barely touched his eyes.

Rogers wasted no time. "The imbalance of magic is affecting the plants and trees. What we saw out there is not written in any Destiny prophecy or documented in any library I have studied." His voice carried an edge of desperation. "Half of the Gaul Forest is dying, not just the trees but the animals. We just returned from the river. Dead animals are floating downstream, carried over the waterfall. The few creatures still alive are barely hanging on. At best, I think we have only a few months left."

Eliza's expression tightened, her exhaustion transforming into intense focus. "Where the waterfall ends, Clara, there is a mountain of corpses. Water creatures. Land creatures. It looks like the forest has become a graveyard. King Arisen, this is beyond anything we have seen," she said, her voice trembling as if she was barely holding back her horror.

Rogers stepped forward, his brow furrowed. "There are marks on the ground too. Long, thin gashes that cut across the soil, then suddenly vanish, only to reappear farther down. It is as if something is dragging itself through the forest."

I tried to ground myself in logic. "How do you know it is half the forest?" I asked, hoping they were exaggerating. Maybe it was some natural cycle, a phenomenon we had not yet understood.

"There is a line," Eliza said flatly. "A clean, visible boundary. On one side, the forest is alive. On the other, it is barren. We have been measuring it. The dead side is spreading." She hesitated, then added quietly, "It is growing. Every single day."

Her words hit me hard, but the look on Arisen's face said he felt it too. The Gaul Forest, known for its eternal spring and life-giving magic, was meant to flourish, not rot and kill everything within it. He had not been able to return in months because of me, and guilt settled heavy in my stomach.

Without a word, Eliza reached into her bag and pulled out what looked like a dead fish. Its front scales were coated in thick black mucus that oozed from every pore. She let it drop onto the floor. The wet splat reverberated through the room as the fish continued to leak, a viscous darkness pooling beneath it.

"There are thousands like this, and more waiting at the base of the waterfall. The stench, the sight, it is death incarnate," she said.

I stared at the dead creature, my stomach turning. The fish, nearly as long as my forearm, lay limp, its blackened eyes dull and unseeing. A foul smell filled the air, pungent and decaying, worse than any natural rot. It felt wrong, twisted, like it had been intentionally corrupted. In all my years as a healer, I had never seen anything like it.

I could not look away. The longer I stared, the more my mark burned, a scorching reminder of when Destiny had first claimed me. The pain was almost unbearable, like a warning pulsing through me that something was deeply wrong. My breathing grew shallow, and my legs weakened beneath me. I reached instinctively for my arm, as though touching the mark might ease the heat. It did not.

Arisen's jaw tightened. A vein pulsed at his temple as he tried to make sense of the scene. "No human or elf could cause this kind of devastation," he muttered, more to himself than to us. His hands clenched into fists. "This does not make any sense."

Eliza's voice was urgent. "We need you both to come to the Gaul Forest. This is critical, and we cannot wait any longer."

Arisen's gaze flicked to mine, his eyes dark with uncertainty. "We are not prepared. If we go now without fully understanding Clara's Destiny, we might be putting her, and everyone else, in greater danger. We already tried to cross the Urten Bridge."

Our eyes met, and I saw the same hesitation in him that I felt in myself. We both knew the stakes. I was far from ready, and stepping into the forest now could mean disaster. Still, the urgency in Eliza's voice made it clear we could not simply sit and wait.

"I would rather risk that than stay here doing nothing," I said, my voice trembling despite my effort to sound steady. "We do not have time to wait for my Destiny to make sense. If this…" I gestured to the fish. "If this is happening now, what will it look like in a week? Or a month?"

Arisen's eyes locked onto mine, his thoughts brushing against my own in that strange, tentative way they did when our marks connected. He did not need to speak for me to feel his worry.

Their discussion resumed, voices overlapping as they weighed possibilities, but their words grew distant as I focused on my arm. The burning refused to subside. I swallowed hard and looked back at the fish.

Its body lay limp in the slick pool of black muck. My stomach churned, but I forced myself to move closer.

The stench was overpowering as I crouched down. My hand trembled when I reached for the creature, wanting to get it out of the house, to throw it outside and slam the door on the smell and the sight.

Then it moved.

The fish twitched violently, its scales slick and cold against my fingers. I gasped and dropped it. It landed with a wet slap and convulsed.

Thick, oily mucus clung to my hands, slow and sticky, impossible to wipe away. Panic flooded through me as the fish's movements became more frantic. Its dull eyes rolled back, and for a moment, I swear they glowed, a faint sickly green that chilled me to my bones.

"Clara!" Arisen's voice cut through my panic, sharp and commanding.

I looked up at him, my breath coming in ragged gasps. His mark was blazing now, the golden light spilling from his skin like liquid fire. It illuminated his face, highlighting the rigid line of his jaw and the sheen of sweat on his brow.

"What does this mean?" I asked, my voice shaking as I looked around at them. Eliza's eyes were wide, Rogers's jaw was clenched, and Arisen's gaze felt like it saw straight through the moment and into me.

CHAPTER 20

Eliza reacted first. She grabbed a large pot, filled it with water, and rushed to my side, her red eyes wide.

"Here," she said, breathless.

Together, we plunged the fish into the pot.

The moment it touched the water, the once-clear surface turned murky, eddying with shades of gray and brown. Yet despite the clouded water, the fish shimmered faintly below, its scales catching the dim light in brief glimmers.

Gradually, it began to move, its sluggish twitches smoothing into slow, steady strokes. The decaying gills and rotting flesh knit back together, the rot fading as its body was restored. Its scales glowed beneath the surface, and soon it swam in lazy circles as if nothing had ever been wrong. The water, too, cleared, returning to a calm, glassy stillness.

Silence followed. We exchanged looks, all of us searching for words that would not come. The impossible had just unfolded in front of us.

Before we could process what had happened, a sharp knock sounded at the door.

Arisen crossed the hall and opened it. Vasa stood on the threshold, framed by the cold. Her dark hair fell neatly around her face, and her sharp eyes swept over the room with practiced precision. Dressed in a perfectly tailored green uniform, she carried the kind of authority that did not need announcing. Her gaze flicked briefly to me, then the fish, before settling on Arisen again.

"What is going on?" she asked as she stepped inside, her arm slipping possessively around his waist.

Arisen's eyes were locked on mine. "We've discovered Clara's Destined power."

Vasa's eyebrows lifted a fraction. "Oh," she murmured, her gaze moving between the pot and me.

Before I could speak, Rogers stepped in, his attention drawn to the golden light still pulsing faintly from Arisen's marks. "And yours, King Arisen?" he asked. "Have you discovered your Destiny yet?"

Arisen parted his lips to answer, but Vasa tightened her hold on him, her knuckles whitening against the dark fabric. "King Arisen, we need to discuss the latest reports," she said firmly.

He nodded, but his eyes lingered on me as if he were reluctant to pull away from whatever had just passed between us.

Then he sighed and turned to her. "All right. Let's go."

They disappeared down the corridor. The heat that had flared in the room cooled with his absence, leaving the space feeling oddly hollow. Discovering my Destined power should have been a moment of triumph, but instead it left me with more questions than answers.

What in the world had just happened? And how could reviving a dead fish possibly help us save the Gaul Forest?

Eliza's eyes lit up. "Well, this is fantastic!" she exclaimed, smiling brightly.

I tried to mirror her enthusiasm, but my smile felt thin. I could feel Destiny pressing deeper into every part of me, weaving through my very essence. It was an overwhelming force I could not push away.

Part of me was in awe. The power, the connection, the unmistakable feeling that I was linked to something greater. But another part of me recoiled, uneasy and resentful, as if every new discovery pulled me further from the life I had chosen. I didn't know how to accept this without losing myself, and that uncertainty gnawed at me, leaving my resolve as fragile as the smile on my lips.

Rogers leaned forward, wonder softening the exhaustion in his features. "No other Destined has ever had the power to connect with and revive animals," he said. "Queen Alondra controlled them, but this is entirely different. It's incredible, Clara."

Eliza tilted her head, studying me with quiet understanding. "It makes sense," she said, thoughtful and steady. "Your power goes beyond connection. It's restoration. It fits with your background as a healer. You don't just bond with them; you mend what's broken. You bring them back."

Their words only made the pressure in my chest tighten. Sensing my unease, Eliza gently took my arm and guided me to the kitchen stools. I sat, focusing on my breathing as the distant murmur of Arisen and Vasa's voices rose into a heated exchange somewhere down the hall. Their argument sounded muffled, like it was happening in another world entirely.

Eliza began outlining possible next steps, but my mind kept returning to the moment my hands had touched the fish—the rush of power, the burn of my mark, the feeling that the magic was using me just as much as I was using it. Beneath all of it, quietly pulsing, was the thread that connected me to Arisen.

"I need to be honest with you," I said, cutting across her explanation. My voice came out quieter than I intended. I did not know Eliza well, but I trusted her more than most. "Did you need time when you first received your powers? I feel… exhausted. Like I have too much energy inside me and no idea how to control it."

Eliza's expression softened, her gaze dropping briefly to my sleeves where my marks pulsed faintly beneath the fabric. "I did," she admitted. "And I had the full six months to process it. You've had none of that. It's unfair, Clara, and I'm sorry."

"I don't even know how to use my power," I whispered. "How do I begin to understand it?"

She reached across the table and took my hand. "I knew what my power was immediately, but it still took months to learn how to wield it properly," she said. "You just revived a creature that had been dead for a week. That's no small feat. Your power is extraordinary."

The room suddenly felt too small. Too warm. Too close.

"I need time," I said, my voice edging toward a plea. "Before we move forward, I need to see my family. Just for a few days. Matry and Reato won't even be here by the time I return, so it won't disrupt the plan."

Eliza frowned, uncertainty clouding her features. "Clara, we're running out of time—"

"Please." I met her gaze, forcing my voice to steady. "I need this."

She hesitated, lips pressing into a thin line, and her silence said enough. I could see the conflict in her eyes—duty wrestling with empathy. I forced a small smile anyway, pretending it didn't sting.

"Am I interrupting?"

We both turned. Commander Vasa stood in the doorway, her presence filling the space as easily as a shadow. Her gaze flicked between us before settling on me.

"I just heard about your Destiny, Ms. Lildar," she said. "Congratulations. I imagine it's been… an adjustment."

I managed a tight smile, resisting the urge to glance away. "That's one way to put it."

Her tone remained cool, clipped, all business. "I'm here to relay updates from Pagos and Polent. The situation is stable. But there are concerning signs. Decay in the land. Growing unrest among the people. Revolts have begun, though nothing alarming yet. Still, the unrest is spreading."

My breath hitched. Revolts. My mind jumped immediately to Kent and Hale. Were they safe? I looked to Eliza, whose furrowed brow mirrored my own anxiety.

"What is happening?" Eliza asked, her voice edged with concern.

Vasa's lips thinned. "There have been signs of the magic decaying," she replied. "Animals dying without cause. Trees withering before their time. Regions losing color, vitality. And now the people are reacting. Small pockets of revolt have broken out in both nations. They're unorganized, but they've begun."

"Revolts?" I echoed. Images of Polent in chaos flashed unbidden through my mind—crowded streets, frightened children, Hale's small hands reaching for Kent. A wave of dread settled over me. "Why was I not told this sooner?"

Vasa's eyes narrowed slightly. "Because the situation is being handled," she said, her tone sharpening. "People are losing faith in their rulers, yes, but we are addressing it. King Arisen is confident that order will be maintained. He believes there is no reason to worry, and neither should you."

Her dismissiveness only deepened my unease.

Eliza stepped forward, her tone cooling. "These are people's lives we're talking about, Commander. If the decay is causing this, then there is every reason to be concerned."

Vasa tilted her head, regarding Eliza with a detached calm. "And yet concern alone will not solve it," she replied. "King Arisen trusts the leadership of each region to manage their own people. King Llorent, in particular, is more than capable. Despite being human, he has proven his strength time and time again."

The way she emphasized "human" did not go unnoticed, but I pushed past it. "You're saying my family is safe because they're under King Llorent's protection?" I asked, struggling to keep my voice from shaking.

She met my gaze directly, her expression softening just enough to appear sincere. "Yes," she said. "Your family is under his rule, and his kingdom is well-guarded. Besides, Rijor is there with them."

Her reassurance rang hollow, and I glanced at Eliza, who still did not look convinced.

"If the revolts spread," Eliza said, her words measured but firm, "there will not be much of a kingdom left to protect."

Vasa raised one eyebrow, her composure unbroken. "Which is why we are doing everything in our power to prevent that outcome," she replied. "But the Destined have their roles to play. That includes you, Ms. Lildar."

Her words hit hard. In that moment, guilt, fear, and anger twisted into a sharp ache in my chest. I hated that she was right.

"Thank you for the update," Eliza said, her voice tight but controlled. She placed a reassuring hand on my arm, though her gaze stayed locked on Vasa.

Vasa gave a curt nod. "Ms. Lildar," she added, her tone cool but pointed, "this isn't just about you anymore. The sooner you embrace that, the better."

Without waiting for a response, she turned and left the room, her footsteps fading down the hall and leaving a heavier silence in their wake.

I sat there, frozen, the echoes of her words pressing against my ribs. My first real conversation with Vasa—if it could be called that—had been nothing like I imagined. Abrupt. Dry. Completely devoid of warmth. If this was what every interaction with her would be, I was not sure how many I could endure.

I let out a shaky breath. Eliza's grip on my arm tightened briefly before she let go. "Don't let her words get to you," she murmured. Her voice was steady, but her eyes were not. "We'll figure this out. Together."

I nodded, though my thoughts were far from settled. The idea of staying here, waiting, while my family faced potential danger was unbearable. The decision solidified in my chest before I even realized I'd made it.

I had to go to Polent.

Sitting idly while we waited for the other Destined was no longer an option. I needed to see Kent and Hale with my own eyes, to know they were safe. Only then could I muster the strength—physical and emotional—to face whatever Destiny demanded of me next.

Eliza must have sensed it. She squeezed my shoulder and said quietly, "I'll come for you when you're ready."

As soon as she left, I hurried to my room. I grabbed my parestine and scribbled messages to Kent and Marcos, my words spilling out in a rush—questions, reassurances, everything I hadn't had time to say. When I finished, I tucked the parestine into my backpack and began to pack, shoving clothes and essentials into a bag with shaking hands.

A firm knock at my door made me jump. My heart leaped as I opened it and found Eliza standing there.

"I'm ready," I said, slinging the bag over my shoulder.

She nodded once. "Let's go."

The cold night air bit at my cheeks as we stepped outside. I pulled my cloak tighter around me as we moved through the quiet streets. Fresh snow dusted the rooftops and muffled our footsteps. The marketplace, usually alive even at late hours, was strangely still. Dark windows. Empty alleys. Only a few elves passed us, their faces hidden in their hoods.

At last, we reached the Destiny gate. The stone archway loomed above us, its faint glow spilling across the snow. Eliza stepped forward first, her movements confident from practice.

I paused. The memory of my first time crossing tugged at me—cold, disorienting, the feeling of being pulled apart and put back together. I was not eager to repeat it.

But there was no turning back now.

Drawing in a steadying breath, I followed her, stepping beneath the arch. The air hummed with energy. Just as my foot crossed the threshold, a voice cut cleanly through my mind.

"Don't go."

I froze, my breath catching. It was Arisen's voice, clear and urgent, threaded with a concern I had not expected from him.

For a heartbeat, I hesitated, my heart pounding so hard it hurt. Should I step back? Should I listen?

But the gate's magic had already taken hold. It wrapped around me, pulling me forward. The sensation was all-consuming, swallowing sound and sight and thought.

Before I could make a choice, the world dissolved.

And then, I was gone.

CHAPTER 21

"What Commander Vasa said was unexpected. The moment I saw your expression, I knew you'd make a move. I'd rather have you with me than risk you facing the unknown alone."

I was surprised that Eliza, whom I barely knew, already understood me well enough to anticipate my actions. Her willingness to come with me was a relief. Despite how little time we had spent together, her support made this journey possible. It reminded me I wasn't completely alone; we were both driven to uncover the truth. Even though she was Pagostonian, she cared deeply about her people, and any threat to them would always push her to act.

We stepped out of the Destiny gate together, and the world around us shifted into darkness. The brief cold from the gate faded quickly, but what truly unsettled me was the overwhelming void that greeted us.

"Why is it so dark?"

I felt Eliza beside me, her arms slicing through the air. A gentle glow gathered at her fingertips, a tiny spark that slowly grew brighter. It flickered once, then expanded, casting long shadows over the jagged rocks.

Her silvery magic glow spread like cupped moonlight, lighting up the narrow patch of ground we could safely claim. Beyond her glow, the darkness stretched on, vast and unyielding, unwilling to give even a hint of what lay beyond.

"Stay close," Eliza murmured. Her light flickered with her words, as if warning us it could disappear at any moment.

I nodded and moved nearer.

"I can teach you how to use your power to harness light. We all possess this ability," she offered.

With that small circle of light around us, I finally saw where we were: a damp underground cave that smelled strongly of livestock. It was the kind of heavy, sour scent that only the dirtiest barns carried.

"We are in Polent now, at the gate inside the basilisk sleeping quarters," Eliza said quietly. She led the way down a rough-hewn corridor, stone walls weeping slow trickles of water through narrow cracks.

I stayed close, unwilling to lose sight of her light. The sound of our boots hitting shallow puddles echoed through the stillness of the underground chamber.

"We must be fast and careful. We do not want to wake the basilisk," she warned, pressing a finger to her lips. "From now on, no talking. We need to navigate these tunnels as quietly as possible. Fortunately, the exit is near."

I nodded and took her extended hand. She illuminated the path ahead with her free hand, and I placed each step with care, avoiding loose rocks and deeper puddles that might splash.

Concentrating was difficult with the smell of decay growing stronger. As we walked, the glow from Eliza's hand revealed the source: the corpses of small livestock hanging from the ceiling, their carcasses shriveled and dried. Beneath them lay bare bones and dark stains on the stone—old blood, long soaked into the rock—evidence of the basilisk's meals.

We moved, holding our breath, for what felt like an eternity until we saw the cave's exit. A large, round opening carved into the rock, with stalactites hanging like jagged teeth. Water dripped slowly from their points, each drop tapping softly against the ground.

At last, a sliver of night sky appeared ahead, filled with stars. The serene beauty of it tugged at my attention, but the faint rustling of scales snapped me back. We both froze.

Curled near the exit, the basilisk slept.

Its massive, serpentine body was tightly coiled, scales layered over one another in a pattern that seemed to shift with every slow breath. The rise and fall of its chest made a faint brushing sound against the stone. It wasn't wearing a blindfold. One wrong look into its eyes would be fatal.

There was only a narrow strip of space between the creature and the wall, just wide enough for us to squeeze past.

We exchanged a tense glance, our joined hands tightening. We stood there, frozen, each of us waiting for the other to decide what to do next.

Then Arisen's voice cut into my mind, sharp and clear.

"Basilisks have keen eyesight but poor hearing. Stay silent, and you can pass safely."

I flinched, the suddenness of it startling me. How could he sound so close when he was thousands of miles away?

"Keep calm. I'll guide you. Keep hold of Eliza's hand, motion for her to extinguish her light, and follow the path ahead," he continued.

My heart hammered against my ribs. I'd heard him before, but never this clearly, never with his words sliding so easily into my thoughts. How did he know where I was?

As if hearing the question I didn't voice, he said, *"Clara, you don't have much time before the creature wakes. I've been there many times; I know how to help you."*

I swallowed hard and motioned for Eliza to dim her light. Her eyes widened in confusion, but there was no room for argument. She closed her hand, and the glow vanished.

Darkness swallowed us.

I clung to her, my nails digging into her skin. All we could do was breathe—quietly, carefully. Each inhale felt too loud.

"Now walk to the farthest right of the cave. You'll feel a rope tied to the wall. Use it to guide you to the exit. And remember… make no sound."

I reached out with my free hand, fingers brushing rough, damp stone until they finally met coarse fibers. A rope. I grabbed it and guided Eliza's hand to it as well.

Without Eliza's magic, only the faintest outline of the exit's distant glow remained. We moved slowly, gripping the slick rope as we edged forward. It was wet from the constant seepage through the rock, and parts of it felt worn, as if it might give way under our hands.

Just a few steps from the exit, the basilisk stirred.

The sound of scales dragging across stone cut through the dark, sending a cold shiver down my spine. A low rumble vibrated through the cave as the creature shifted, uncoiling.

We froze, barely daring to breathe.

"Run."

The word rang through my mind with undeniable force.

Clutching Eliza's hand, I ran forward. Behind us, the basilisk screeched, its sound piercing the air and bouncing through the cave.

The ground shook beneath its movement, but I kept my focus on the expanding sliver of open sky ahead.

We were almost there when my foot caught on a jagged rock.

I crashed down onto my hands and knees. Pain tore through my legs, sharp and immediate, but there was no time to feel it fully.

"Easy there, girl!" a voice boomed, deep and commanding.

I turned my head just in time to see King Llorent emerge from the shadows near the cave's mouth. His tall frame radiated both power and control. His green eyes, shielded by lenses, were locked on the basilisk with a focus that held the entire space in a breathless pause.

He raised his hand toward the massive creature and spoke in a low, measured tone.

His voice softened into a melodic murmur, words indistinct but filled with undeniable authority. The basilisk's head recoiled slightly, its body tensing as if caught between attacking and obeying. Its scales rippled in agitation, but Llorent didn't waver.

Slowly, the creature lowered its head. The tension bled from its body as it curled back into the shadows, retreating with a reluctant hiss before finally going still.

Llorent remained motionless for a moment longer, his hand lowering only when the basilisk was fully subdued.

I scrambled to my feet, my knees protesting fiercely. Each step toward the exit tested my will, but I kept going until the cool night air hit my face. I staggered out of the cave and slumped against the outer rock wall, gasping for breath.

The open air irritated the scrapes on my knees and palms, but the pain was nothing compared to the fading adrenaline ringing in my ears. My vision blurred, then gradually cleared. When it did, I caught sight of my Destiny mark faintly glowing beneath my sleeve.

Llorent stepped into the open, his figure silhouetted against the moonlight. His long black braids, beaded with intricate red jewels, swayed gently as he walked toward me. The glow of his green eyes, softened by the lenses he wore, was matched only by the concern in his expression. His neatly trimmed beard framed his face, sharpening the angles of his jaw.

"You're safe now," he said quietly. He took a small step closer, his hand lifting as if to steady me. "Easy."

I nodded weakly, still too shaken to muster more than that. My chest heaved as I tried to catch my breath. Eliza leaned heavily against the wall beside me, her face pale, her eyes still wide with lingering shock.

"Thank you," I managed. "For… for coming to our aid."

Llorent inclined his head, the sharp lines of his features softening. "It was the least I could do. You are both welcome here in Polent, under my protection."

Eliza murmured her thanks, but her voice faded into the background as his gaze returned to me. When our eyes met, his expression changed— curiosity, recognition, and a hint of emotion I couldn't quite identify.

"I've seen you before," he said softly, stepping closer. His gaze studied my face with unnerving focus, as if he were trying to fit me into a half-remembered vision.

Heat crept up my neck, and I fought the flush threatening to climb into my cheeks. Even through the haze of exhaustion, I couldn't ignore the pull of his presence.

"You must rest," he said, his voice dropping into a gentler register. "We'll make sure you have everything you need to recover."

His words held both kindness and authority. In the wake of what we had just faced, I clung to them like an anchor. As he stepped back to give me space, I exhaled shakily, the tension easing just enough for me to feel the aching weight of my own body again.

For the first time since stepping through the gate, I let myself believe it: we were safe for now.

CHAPTER 22

"A *re you okay?"*

Arisen's voice reverberated through my mind, cutting through the pain. The words came through our Destiny link. But I was too overwhelmed to respond; all my effort went into simply staying upright and moving forward.

Somehow, I found myself leaning heavily on King Llorent. One arm was wrapped around his waist, the other gripping Eliza's shoulder as we made our way toward the Polentian castle. Every step sent sharp jolts through my knees, but Llorent's presence beside me was oddly steadying.

"I must apologize for Stace," Llorent said, his tone calm. "She's our protective basilisk, enchanted by the Destiny spell. If it's any consolation, I don't think she would have harmed you."

Eliza huffed beside me, her irritation clear. "Why put a basilisk at the cave mouth? It wasn't there the last time I came."

He chuckled softly, the sound rich and unbothered. "With everything happening in the Gaul Forest, I have to ensure Polent is protected. That includes the cave."

Eliza muttered words under her breath, frustration radiating off her. I stayed quiet, focusing on keeping the pain at bay. As much as I understood her irritation, I couldn't deny the logic in his actions.

"And how did you know we were coming?" Eliza demanded.

He glanced down at me briefly, the corner of his mouth curving in a faint smile. "King Arisen sent several urgent parestines."

Eliza and I exchanged a look. Her eyes were wide with surprise. I wasn't shocked.

"I'm glad you found us in time," I said, steering the conversation away from tension. Eliza shot me a sideways glance, clearly annoyed at my attempt to smooth things over, but kept her comments to herself.

Destiny was still new to me, but I could feel its magic working, knitting my wounds faster than they should have healed. The pain in my knees lingered, yet I knew it wouldn't last.

We reached the castle grounds just as the sky blushed with the soft orange of dawn. Polent's castle rose high above us, its crenelated ramparts gleaming in the early light, the stone almost alive with power.

Guards patrolled the grounds astride sleek, muscular sleipnirs. The creatures moved with fluid grace, their sharp blue eyes scanning the horizon as if nothing could escape their notice. Their riders were just as alert, leaving no doubt they were ready for anything. My gaze drifted further, landing on the basilisks my brother had once described—impossible to miss, even from a distance.

As we neared the main gate, my eyes found King Llorent again. The rising light traced the strong angles of his face and deepened the green of his eyes.

"You need to rest," he said softly, his tone threaded with genuine concern. "You'll have everything you need to recover here."

I nodded, grateful. As much as I wanted to unravel Destiny's complexities, all I really craved was to close my eyes and let the pain slip away.

The terrain shifted to grass, making each step more bearable. A paved road led toward the entrance, bordered with beds of roses. If my knees weren't scraped raw, I might have knelt to smell them.

"Are you all right, Your Majesty?" one of the guards called, riding toward us on a sleipnir.

"Yes, we're fine."

"Let us assist you, Your Majesty," another guard added, his gaze flicking between the king and me, clearly noting my limp.

"Take Eliza with you to the castle," Llorent instructed. "Show her to her room and ensure she has everything she needs."

The guards nodded. Eliza approached the nearest sleipnir. The creature bent one of its eight legs in offering, but she was already mounting, needing no help.

"Clara, come," Eliza said, patting the back of the sleipnir, waiting for me to join her.

I took a tentative step forward, my body still aching, but before I could reach her, I felt Llorent's arm wrap more firmly around my waist.

"That's all right, I've got her."

Eliza raised an eyebrow, her gaze darting between us. I felt the unspoken question in her eyes, but I gave her a small nod, silently assuring her I was fine.

Without further protest, she took off into the sky, leaving the king and me alone.

His arm remained around my waist as we walked to the sleipnir waiting for us. He matched my slow pace.

"Are you in much pain?"

"I've been better," I said, attempting a faint smile.

His expression tightened, lines deepening around his mouth. "You'll be looked after here. Polent is safe, and so are you."

"Thank you," I murmured.

With a quick wave, Llorent dismissed the remaining guards, though he kept the largest sleipnir at his side. The creature was breathtaking— sleek and powerful, its silvery-gray coat shimmering in the morning light. Its piercing blue eyes gleamed like polished gemstones.

It lowered itself with quiet grace, one of its eight legs bending to form a natural step.

"If I may," Llorent said gently.

Before I could answer, he lifted me easily onto the creature's back. The plush ruby-red saddle cradled my aching legs, its unexpected soft- ness a small mercy.

Without pause, he mounted behind me, his arms wrapping around my waist as he took the reins. The warmth of his body at my back helped cut through the lingering chill.

"Try not to move much. We're going to fly," he murmured, his breath brushing my ear.

My pulse jumped, but I forced my focus onto the horizon.

With a powerful sweep, the sleipnir's wings unfurled. In one fluid motion, we launched into the sky.

Wind rushed against my face, stealing my breath. I gripped the reins tightly, my knuckles whitening. As we climbed higher, the world below dropped away, and lightness flooded my stomach.

The pain in my legs melted into the background, replaced by the quiet, wild thrill of soaring.

Below, Polent unfolded like a painting brought to life. Rolling fields stretched in every direction, teeming with creatures that seemed to dance across the landscape. Rivers shimmered under the early sun, winding through the countryside like veins of silver. The castle shrank behind us, quickly becoming a distant shape on the horizon.

I couldn't help but marvel. The land felt so alive, so impossibly bright compared to the suffocating darkness of the cave we'd just escaped.

Without thinking, I glanced over my shoulder and caught a glimpse of Llorent. His green eyes were fixed on the horizon, his expression calm and focused. There was a quiet authority in the way he held himself, a steadiness I hadn't realized I needed until now.

Before I could stop myself, I leaned back slightly, letting my body rest against his solid chest. His breath rose and fell against my back, and his arms tightened, just barely, around my waist, holding me in place.

For a fleeting moment, I let myself relax. The anxiety that had wrapped itself around me since I became Destined loosened, just a little. My pulse quickened, but this time it wasn't because of the height.

It was him.

The quiet strength he carried, the way he anchored me without effort, was disarming in a way I hadn't expected.

Maybe it was the months of isolation, of speaking to only one person day after day. Maybe it was the relentless training that left no room for anything else. Or maybe it was simpler: I hadn't been this close to a man in longer than I cared to admit. And this man, this king, was undeniably handsome. That much was common knowledge. Even Marcos had mentioned it, teasingly.

But he was a king. And I was a Destined.

What was I doing?

Was I really entertaining the idea of feeling anything for him?

And yet, I couldn't deny it. For the first time since Destiny took hold of my life, I didn't feel completely alone. His presence, just for now, filled the hollow place inside me.

Just for this moment—maybe just for a few days—I would allow myself to feel. Not with the intention of doing something reckless, but because I needed to feel real, which reminded me of who I had been before my life was rewritten by magic.

As the sleipnir began to descend, the landscape sharpened, the rolling fields and glimmering rivers of Polent rising to meet us. I let out a slow breath and straightened, putting a small, careful space between us. Heat crept into my cheeks, and I quickly reminded myself why I was here.

Kent. Hale. Destiny.

Those were my priorities.

They had to be.

CHAPTER 23

From Clara's Diary

The sun crested over the horizon as we descended toward the castle. Light sifted through the trees, catching the soft morning mist in pale gold. The warmth touched my face, and for a moment, the exhaustion from the journey eased.

As we landed, I knew my priority was seeing Kent and Hale. But before I could take a step, a familiar figure strode toward us, cutting through the fragile calm I'd just found.

Rijor.

His short blond hair was as recognizable as the deep green suit he wore, accented by the golden tree pin on his chest.

"Good morning, Ms. Clara Lildar."

Behind me, Llorent dismounted the sleipnir with an ease that spoke of long practice. He extended a hand to me. The sleipnir lowered itself smoothly, but my legs still wobbled as my boots met the ground. Before I could stumble, Llorent's arm came around my waist, firm and steady, pulling me against his side.

Heat flared where his hand settled, fingers pressing through the fabric of my dress. For a heartbeat, my body leaned into his without thinking.

Rijor's sharp eyes flicked first to my scraped knees, then to that hand at my waist. His expression shifted, just slightly.

"I visit every few weeks to ensure your family is well," he said. Then, kneeling, he inspected the scrapes on my legs. "It seems you're the one who needs looking after this time."

"Thank you for checking on them," I replied, forcing my attention away from the solid warmth at my hip. "I've come to see them myself— and to understand what's happening with the revolts Commander Vasa mentioned."

My gaze slipped between Rijor and Llorent as I spoke. Llorent hadn't moved his arm.

Rijor straightened, his eyes narrowing thoughtfully as he took my hands in his. "There's much to discuss. And you'll need to be prepared for what you might hear."

His hands were warm. Too familiar for someone I barely knew. The contrast to Llorent's quiet, anchoring touch made my skin prickle. I gently slipped my hands from his, my voice firm but polite. "Thank you, but I'd like to see my family first."

He paused, then nodded. For the first time, his gaze shifted entirely to Llorent. His eyes lingered on the arm that still rested, unapologetically, around my waist.

Llorent didn't flinch. "I will take her to see Kent and Hale," he said evenly. Then, turning to me, his voice softened. "Come, I'll show you the way."

His hand slid from my waist to the small of my back, guiding me toward the castle entrance. Even through my coat, the contact sent a line of warmth straight up my spine.

"Your family is staying in a room at the end of the hall," he said as we walked. "I couldn't secure the room directly beside them, but one is available in my corridor if you need to be nearby."

"That's perfectly fine," I replied, meaning it. "Thank you."

His eyes flicked to mine with satisfaction flashing there before he looked ahead again.

When we reached the large wooden door at the end of the hall, I paused, listening to the soft, familiar sound of Hale's voice inside. My throat tightened. I knocked gently, and within moments the door swung open.

Kent pulled me into a tight embrace before I could speak. Hale latched onto my side, her little face glowing with excitement.

I let out a breath I didn't realize I'd been holding. She still remembered me.

As I stepped fully inside, I glanced back. Llorent was still in the hall, watching us with a small, private smile. When our eyes met, his softened even further—then he inclined his head and turned away, giving us privacy.

Hale's excitement was contagious. I could hardly believe how much she had grown. She was at least an inch taller, with her white-blonde hair bouncing in two playful ponytails, and her Polent-red dress swirling around her knees.

"Clara, you're back!" Kent exclaimed, hugging me again.

"I missed you both so much," I whispered, clinging to him.

I knelt to Hale's level and pulled her into my arms. A tear of joy escaped as she giggled, squeezing me tight.

Eventually, we all pulled back. Kent's expression sobered, his eyes searching mine. He knew this wasn't just a visit.

"Clara, what's been happening out there? We've been worried."

I sank into a chair. "There's been a lot," I admitted. I told him about Pitores, the rising tensions, my Destiny and the fish, and what Eliza and Rogers had seen in the Gaul Forest. With each detail, the concern in Kent's eyes deepened.

"You need to be careful. I don't like the sound of all this. It seems dangerous, Clara."

"I know. I'm worried too," I said. "But not as much for myself—more for what's happening with the Gaul Forest."

Hoping to ease his worry, I shifted the subject. "I ran into Rijor earlier. He said he's been checking on you. How have things been here?"

Kent relaxed slightly. "Yeah, Rijor's been around. He checks on us regularly. He's gotten close to Hale, and she really likes him. King Llorent… he's been great. He spends a lot of time training, but he's made sure Hale gets lessons with the other children here."

I smiled and glanced at Hale, who sat on the floor playing with a carved wooden basilisk. I lowered myself beside her and she immediately climbed into my lap. My heart swelled as I played with her, letting that simple, familiar rhythm steady me. This—Kent, Hale—was why I had to see everything through.

A knock at the door pulled our attention. The hinges creaked as it opened, revealing Llorent. His gaze swept the room until it landed on me.

"Clara," he said, his tone apologetic, "there are matters we need to discuss."

I gave Hale one last squeeze before setting her down. "All right," I said, standing and brushing my hands over my dress, suddenly aware of the way his eyes followed the movement. "I'll be right there."

He waited in the hall, then fell into step beside me as we walked. The brush of his shoulder against mine felt accidental… and not entirely.

We went to his office, a bright room despite its dark gray walls, with morning light flooding in through tall windows. A long table occupied the center, clearly meant for councils and war meetings.

"I know you're tired, Clara. We won't take long," he said. He pulled out a chair for me, one hand resting briefly on the back as I sat. His fingers brushed my shoulder for the slightest moment, a light touch, but enough to make me acutely aware of how close he stood.

"I appreciate that," I replied, forcing myself to focus.

The door opened again, and Eliza walked in, arms crossed, green markings shimmering faintly in the light. Her usual confidence seemed to on edge.

"I wanted to speak with both of you," Llorent began. "Eliza told me everything Commander Vasa said, and I believe it's important to clarify some of it."

My stomach tightened. "What is it?" I asked, looking between them.

He hesitated. "I have my reservations about Commander Vasa," he said. "Eliza does as well. And so does King Arisen."

I blinked. "Arisen? But… they're engaged. I just saw them together a few hours ago."

Eliza let out a humorless laugh. "A marriage of convenience isn't always convenient. Their engagement was never about love, or even trust. It's political. King Arisen knows that, and so does Commander Vasa."

I had suspected it, but hearing it so plainly still jarred me.

"Then why keep her so close? Why give her so much responsibility?"

Eliza's gaze hardened. "He doesn't trust her. He keeps her close so he can watch her—track her moves, her motives. It's not trust; it's strategy."

A chill slipped over my skin. Arisen, that calculated?

I turned to Llorent. He stood with his hands braced on the table, sleeves rolled to his forearms, veins and tendons visible beneath his skin. "Have there been revolts, like she claimed?" I asked.

Llorent shook his head. "No revolts. Polent is peaceful. However…" His brow creased. "It's been increasingly difficult to tame the creatures here. You saw it with Stace. She has never been that aggressive before."

The memory of the basilisk's hiss sent a shiver down my spine.

"What do I do about the Commander?" I asked, looking back at Eliza.

"Keep your distance," she said flatly.

My eyes widened. That tone wasn't just tactical. It was a warning.

Instinctively, I reached inward, testing the fragile link between Arisen and me. I didn't know what I expected—comfort, denial, anything.

Nothing came.

He wasn't answering, yet I could still sense him. Not gone. Just… held back. As if he were standing behind a closed door in my mind.

I pushed harder.

Arisen?

Silence.

Just as I started to pull away, something brushed the edge of my thoughts. Not quite a voice, more like a breath caught between words.

"Believe them."

The whisper moved through me like wind through leaves—soft, quick, and gone.

My heart hammered. I looked at Llorent, then at Eliza, and nodded.

"I will," I said. And I meant it.

We moved from his office to a smaller adjoining sitting room, where a fire already burned. The conversation stretched longer than any of us intended. We spoke of the decaying magic, the Gaul Forest, and how its slow death was rippling across every nation.

The fire's warmth wrapped the room, yet every so often a chill still crept over my skin.

"The Gaul Forest has always been more than a source of magic," Llorent said, leaning forward, elbows on his knees. The loose fall of his braids shifted with the motion. "It shapes how our nations survive. In Polent, we rely on its energy to train the creatures that roam our lands."

I knew pieces of this but not the details. "How do you do that?"

"The animals that pass through Polent carry fragments of the forest's magic," he explained. "Those fragments let us bond with them. Basilisks, falcons, even smaller creatures gain heightened instincts and become more attuned to our commands. That connection has strengthened our army and our defenses."

Eliza exhaled. "Ebony has always claimed the strongest tie to the Gaul Forest. Arisen's first Destiny cemented that. The forest is on his land, and he understands its power better than anyone. That's why Ebony shaped most of the policies."

I turned to her, hearing the strain in her voice. "And Pagos?"

"For us, the forest's magic is survival," she said. "It enriches our land, makes the desert bloom where it should be dead." Her jaw tightened. "But Queen Franes controls where that magic goes. For years we assumed it was shared. Now I see it isn't. Her loyalists thrive. The outskirts starve."

The words settled over us like a heavy cloak. The Gaul Forest's power wasn't just fading; it was being twisted.

"If the magic was meant for all of us," I said quietly, "then we have to find a way to take it back."

Eliza's eyes met mine, sharp and steady. "That's exactly what I intend to do."

We all sank back at once, a collective exhale. The pressure in the room eased, leaving only fatigue.

Llorent stood, smoothing the fabric of his tunic. "You should rest," he said, looking at me. "Both for your sake and for theirs." His gaze flicked briefly, almost instinctively, toward the window facing the direction of Kent and Hale's quarters.

When he motioned for me to follow, Eliza stayed behind, leaning in the doorway. Our eyes met. She gave me a single, meaningful nod. We were aligned now—whatever came next.

I followed Llorent through the narrow corridors, our footsteps echoing in the quiet. The castle was waking; distant voices and the clink of armor drifted faintly from other halls, but here, it was just us.

We stopped at a door carved from dark mahogany, the sinuous form of a basilisk coiling around the frame. Each scale was so intricately carved it looked like it might shiver to life. A polished brass handle gleamed beneath its gaze.

"This is your room," Llorent said, his voice low. He pushed the door open.

Warmth spilled out. The glow of the fireplace bathed everything in gold. Tall windows were draped in heavy velvet, and paintings of fantastical creatures lined the walls. A large bed sat at the center, piled high with linens and woven blankets in crimson and silver.

It was beautiful. It felt... safe.

I stepped inside, but something else caught my eye. Another door, half open, tucked to the side.

Curiosity pricked at me. I moved toward it and nudged it wider with my fingertips.

Another room lay beyond, similar in warmth and detail, but this one was clearly lived-in. A jacket folded over a chair. A book left open on the table. A carved sleipnir figurine resting by the bed.

Realization settled in my chest. I turned back to him.

"Our rooms are connected?"

"Yes."

"Why?"

"For your protection."

I narrowed my eyes. "You think I'm unsafe?"

He stepped just inside the doorway, closer than before. Firelight slid over the lines of his face, catching the green in his eyes. "I think you're in Polent," he said.

I lifted my chin. "That is not an answer."

One corner of his mouth twitched. "You're not just a visitor, Clara. You're Destined. That makes you a symbol, a source of power, and a target. Some will try to use you, control you… or worse." His jaw tightened. "As long as you're under my roof, I won't let that happen."

The conviction in his voice sent a strange, unwelcome warmth through me. It sounded less like a king speaking of his duty and more like a promise.

"You're very serious about this," I said, attempting lightness.

"You should be too." His gaze dipped briefly to my mouth before returning to my eyes, so quick I almost convinced myself I imagined it.

I studied him, aware of the scant distance between us, the closed door at my back, the open one to his room at my side. Dressed in deep

Polentian red, with his braids still loose from the flight and the faint scent of leather and smoke clinging to him, he looked every inch the king everyone whispered about.

And yet in this small space, with only the fire and our breath between us, he felt less like a distant ruler and more like a man I shouldn't want to lean toward.

"All right," I said at last, softer than I intended.

He nodded once and stepped back toward the threshold, though not far enough to break the pull of his presence. "Rest, Clara. We have much to do in the coming days."

The way he said my name made a flutter low in my chest. Too familiar. Too easy on his tongue.

"Goodnight, Llorent," I murmured.

"Goodnight."

The door clicked closed behind him, but the quiet that followed felt anything but empty. His scent still lingered in the room—clean, earthy, tinged with a hint of sharpness and wildness from the flight.

I turned toward the adjoining door. It remained half open.

For my protection.

Right.

I closed it just enough to stop seeing his bed, his books, his life, but not enough for the latch to catch. A sliver of space remained between the door and the frame, thin as a breath.

Just in case.

Because as much as I told myself I was here for Kent, for Hale, for Destiny, and the Gaul Forest… a small, traitorous part of me wondered what it would feel like to hear his footsteps cross that threshold in the middle of the night.

And that, I reminded myself sternly, was exactly why I needed the door.

CHAPTER 24

From Clara's Diary

For the first time in months, I slept undisturbed and well past noon. When Eliza's firm knocks echoed through my room, I stirred reluctantly, my body still craving more rest. I pushed myself out of bed and opened the door to find her standing there, dressed in dark clothing, the Destined symbol shining on her chest.

"How are you feeling today?"

I hesitated. Too many emotions churned inside me to fit neatly into a single word. "Fine" felt both true and a lie.

Eliza seemed to read my silence. "I know yesterday was a lot for both of us," she said. "But today we need to train. Now that we have clarity about your Destiny, we have to focus on honing it and exploring your other abilities."

Thankfully, my knees had mostly healed. I dressed in an outfit similar to hers but chose long black sleeves to cover my mark. When Eliza noticed, she raised an eyebrow in a quiet question but let it go. I was grateful for that small mercy.

We gathered our things and headed into the corridor. As we walked, Eliza outlined the plan. "Since your Destiny is similar to Queen Alondra's, we should see what other abilities might manifest, especially with the creatures here in Polent."

I nodded, but my mind drifted elsewhere.

Arisen's voice broke in without warning. *"I'm growing tired of you running away."*

I quickened my pace, irritation flaring hot beneath my skin. *"You said I could see my family before we entered the Gaul Forest,"* I shot back, sharper than I meant to. *"I've done exactly that."*

"I said you could," he replied. *"But only with me."*

"You were busy."

Silence. His sudden absence from the conversation was almost as frustrating as his intrusion.

Eliza must have seen my expression twist, because a knowing smirk curved her lips. "So," she said lightly, "I see you're starting to figure out how the link works."

"Not really," I muttered. "I said something, but he hasn't answered."

She laughed softly. "He's probably choosing not to respond."

I exhaled sharply, then asked, "How does the Destiny link even work, anyway?"

"It's like a thread," Eliza explained. "Always there, woven between you. Once you master it, you can hear your Destined's thoughts and communicate that way. The stronger the bond, the clearer the connection."

I frowned. "That seems incredibly invasive."

She shrugged, a small, knowing smile playing at her lips. "Destiny essentially makes you one person. While the link can feel invasive, you do get used to it. And… it seems like King Arisen already has a stronger hold on your link. Once you perfect yours, you'll be just as strongly on his mind."

I blinked, absorbing that. "Then why leave me waiting? He's infuriatingly cryptic."

Eliza stopped walking and caught my shoulders to halt me too. Her red eyes locked onto mine, expression softening.

"The Gaul Forest has been struggling for a long time," she said. "Now it's reaching a breaking point. King Arisen has tried everything to fix it. His relationship with Commander Vasa, and…" She paused, lips pressing into a thin line.

"And?" I prompted.

"And all thirty of his marriages," she finished quietly.

I stared at her, momentarily forgetting how to breathe.

"I've already said more than I should," she added. "If you want the truth, you need to ask him directly. The last thing I'll say is this: King Arisen's hand doesn't always have the best intentions. Remember that."

She released my shoulders and strode ahead, her black coat flowing behind her. I followed, a few steps back, letting her lead while my thoughts churned.

We reached the courtyard, where two sleipnirs waited. One of them—a sleek gray—immediately stepped toward me, nudging its head gently against my shoulder.

"King Llorent said his sleipnir has taken a liking to you," Eliza said. "He's letting you use it while you're here."

My hand slid along the creature's muscular flank. Its eight legs shifted with easy strength. Being near it felt strangely like standing near him—steady, grounded, and somehow… aware of me.

The sleipnir bent one leg to offer a step. As I placed my foot in the stirrup, I noticed a small piece of parchment tied delicately to the saddle. My heart gave a ridiculous little lurch.

Curious, I untied it and unfolded the note.

May today bring you strength and courage. I hope the morning light guides you.

—Llorent

His handwriting was elegant but firm, the ink pressed into the fibers as if he'd leaned his weight into every stroke. The simple words wrapped around me warmer than any cloak ever had.

A smile tugged at my lips before I could stop it. I folded the note carefully and tucked it into the inner pocket of my coat—close to where my mark pulsed beneath my sleeve.

"Ready?" Eliza called.

"Ready," I said, though a part of me stayed with the ink still ghosting my fingertips.

"We're going to the training grounds outside the city," she explained as I settled into the saddle. "For everyone's protection, that's where the creatures the royal handlers train are housed."

The sleipnir responded to the slightest pressure, as if it already understood me. Was that my Destiny… or the lingering trace of its king?

As we galloped across the fields and lifted into the air, Arisen's voice cut in again, startling me.

"You should train with the basilisk."

I gripped the reins tighter. "What do you mean?" I muttered under my breath, though the question was more for him than for Eliza.

The sleipnir's movements were so smooth that the flight felt effortless. Wind tore through my hair as we soared over a patchwork of wildflower fields and scattered houses. The air was cool and clean, carrying the scent of grass and bloom. For a moment, hovering above all of it, I felt almost free.

"It is the most powerful creature," Arisen said. *"If you can master the basilisk, you can handle almost anything."*

I tried to ignore the way my stomach knotted. I had revived a fish by accident… and now I was supposed to train with the deadliest animal in Polent?

No.

By the time we reached the training grounds, I dismounted the sleipnir with surprising ease. I hadn't realized how comfortable I'd become with it until my boots touched the ground and I already missed the steady rise and fall of its breath at my back.

Eliza led me into a sprawling area where at least six different species were housed. We moved from enclosure to enclosure, passing creatures unlike anything I had ever seen.

The first held a cluster of untrained sleipnirs. Their many legs shifted restlessly, some rearing, others stamping, their wild energy a stark contrast to the calm mount I had just ridden.

Farther along, we saw horses with spiraling horns and coats that shimmered like starlight. In another pen, a creature made of shifting shadow flickered in and out of sight. Some beasts had elongated limbs that moved with eerie grace. Others had eyes that glowed like fragments of the night sky. A few defied descriptions entirely. It was like they were more magic than flesh.

I was in awe. The power radiating from each enclosure left me breathless. Still, through it all, my Destiny remained quiet.

That changed when we reached the basilisk enclosure.

The enormous creature turned its head toward us, its deadly eyes concealed beneath a thick black cloth. Towering nearly ten stories tall, the basilisk's sinuous body coiled around rocky outcrops that dotted its domain.

The space itself mimicked the Gaul Forest. Towering trees stretched overhead, their canopies scattering light. Rocky ledges jutted out for the basilisk to rest upon, while a winding stream fed a crystalline pond that reflected the filtered glow. The air was cool and humid, tinged with the scent of wet earth. Thick, vine-covered stone walls ringed the enclosure, reinforced with magic. Above, an observation platform with shatterproof glass allowed handlers to watch safely.

Eliza handed me a pair of black lenses identical to the ones she now wore. My hands trembled as I took them.

"You look tense," she observed.

She laid a reassuring hand on my shoulder. "You've already shown incredible potential," she said. "Trust yourself and the connection you share with these creatures. You're stronger than you think."

"I've only managed to resurrect a dead fish," I protested. "This is a living, breathing creature. And the fish fit in my hand. This…" I glanced at the towering serpent. "This could crush me."

"Your Destiny connects you to animals, big or small," Eliza replied. "We need to know if your power extends to both the living and the dead. That's the only way to understand it."

Arisen's voice echoed in my mind again. *I am here, Clara. I can guide you. Trust me.*

"Guide me? You're not here," I shot back.

"This is the closest we've ever been," he said. *"Our bond is growing stronger. Let me help you."*

His words should have soothed me. Instead, my unease sharpened.

"You'll be fine," Eliza said, sensing my hesitation. "Remember—you are Destined. Your powers are manifesting. You need to harness them."

With that, she retreated to the safety of the observation tower.

I drew a deep breath, willing my heart to steady as I stepped toward the basilisk. I extended my hand, focusing on the creature.

I closed my eyes. Darkness swallowed everything. Only my heartbeat remained, pounding in my ears. Sweat beaded along my temple as I searched for… something.

Then I saw it: a faint glow, no larger than a distant star. It flickered, fragile yet potent, suspended in the void.

I knew instinctively it was the basilisk. The symbol of our bond.

I reached for it.

Slowly, I reached out my hand toward the light. It pulsed and moved closer until I felt it; the raw energy of the creature pressing against my consciousness. When my fingers touched it, everything changed.

A surge of magic coursed through me, lighting up every nerve. The darkness receded, replaced by a vivid connection between us. I sensed its thoughts, caution, old wounds, and strong loyalty. The wildness Queen Alondra once inspired into battle had been softened through years of training, resulting in something both formidable and calm.

It recognized me.

When I opened my eyes, I gasped for breath. The basilisk stood where it had been, massive and waiting. Though its eyes were still covered, our bond hummed with its desire.

It wanted to see me.

Compelled, I stepped closer, hand lifting toward the straps of the blindfold.

"What are you doing?" Eliza's voice rang out from above, edged with panic. She leaned over the railing, eyes wide. "The blindfold is there for a reason. Even with the lenses, its gaze is dangerous. Basilisks flying over the city are always blindfolded and guided by their masters."

"It wants the blindfold off," I said softly. The creature's urgency pulsed through me, almost painful.

Arisen's voice cut in, calm but insistent. *"If it wants the blindfold off, listen to it."*

"And what about what Eliza just said?" I argued.

"You know the creature better than anyone alive," he replied. *"Trust your instincts."*

My heart hammered. Eliza's warning, Arisen's coaxing, the basilisk's need—all pulled in different directions. My fingers tightened on the strap. Then I forced myself to let go and step back.

The basilisk's disappointment rippled through the bond. The ground trembled as it shifted, restless.

I couldn't stay. Not like this.

I signaled to Eliza, and she nodded, relief apparent even from a distance. We left the enclosure together.

She guided me to another section of the grounds where cattle grazed lazily. Among them, a goat lay lifeless, tied to a post, its neck sliced, dried blood staining the grass.

Eliza motioned toward it. "This goat was sacrificed to feed the basilisk. I want you to try bringing it back."

"Eliza… are you sure?" I asked, throat tight. "This feels… wrong."

Her gaze softened. "I understand," she said. "But you have to learn to wield your power. It's not about right or wrong right now—it's about understanding what you're capable of. This is your Destiny, and I'm here to guide you through it."

Reviving a fish without meaning to was one thing. Choosing to resurrect a larger creature—something clearly dead—was another. My stomach churned as I knelt beside the goat and pressed my hand near the wound. Its cold skin seeped into my palm.

Closing my eyes, I focused. Heat gathered in my mark and climbed my arm. I tried to recreate the connection from before… but nothing happened.

"Remove the gloves, Clara," Arisen's voice urged.

I looked down at my covered hands and hesitated. Deep down, I knew he was right. Slowly, I peeled off the gloves, revealing the shimmering golden patterns of my mark.

The glow intensified, like liquid fire racing beneath my skin. The symbols writhed softly, alive.

"Trust it, Clara."

I took a breath and placed my bare hand on the goat again. This time, I felt it—the connection. Warmth flowed from my mark into the animal. Beneath my palm, something shifted. A faint, staggering rise and fall.

"Feel it," Arisen murmured in my mind. *"Let the energy flow."*

Over my shoulder, Eliza's voice trembled with awe. "You did it."

The goat jerked, eyes snapping open. It scrambled to its feet, legs wobbling before it tottered toward the other animals, as if dragged back from the edge of a dream.

I stared, chest heaving, hand still tingling from the echo of the magic.

"You can bond with the dead and those that cause death," Arisen said, his voice resonating again, quiet and almost reverent. *"That makes you, Ms. Clara Lildar, something deadly."*

CHAPTER 25

From Clara's Diary

For the past few days, we trained until our bodies gave out, stumbling back to the castle long past midnight. Every muscle ached, my limbs heavy from the relentless routine Eliza had built for me. Yet beneath the strain, I could feel progress taking root not only in my abilities but in my understanding of what Destiny really meant.

Arisen lingered in my thoughts almost constantly, like a presence pacing just behind my shoulder. He never spoke of Vasa, never mentioned where she was or what he was doing, but in the long stretches of quiet in my mind, I knew he was with her. And still, whenever doubt crept in or frustration clawed at the edges of my resolve, he was there.

"You're stronger than you think," he would say, his voice low and steady in my mind.

He never let me disappear into self-doubt for long.

In those same days, I learned his name.

Kito.

The basilisk.

My connection to him had deepened in ways I hadn't anticipated. It wasn't just that I could sense him; I could *feel* him. His presence hovered at the edges of my awareness even when he was nowhere in sight.

Kito.

He had become more than a creature of Polent. More than a weapon. Somehow, I had grown close to him. Close to a creature so powerful and feared that entire kingdoms relied on his kind for protection.

I didn't just feel his nearness. I felt his emotions. During training, I caught flashes of his anticipation, a sharp curiosity whenever I stepped too close or faltered in my stance. Sometimes I sensed something stranger still, as if he always knew exactly where I was—when frustration tightened my chest or exhaustion made my legs shake, and he answered with a ripple of attention through our bond.

The first time I whispered his name, *Kito*, a soft pulse of recognition moved through me.

Almost like an answer.

Almost like acceptance.

That bond had become a quiet comfort. No matter how brutal the training, no matter how loud my doubts, I knew Kito was there. Watching. Waiting. Understanding.

The only other thing that came close to that feeling was Llorent.

Every night, without fail, he left something behind: a note, a small token, some quiet gesture that told me he had thought of me. I never expected them, but I started listening for the soft knock at my door, checking the saddle before each flight, glancing at my nightstand before sleep.

One night, after an especially brutal day, I sat on my bed, rubbing the soreness from my legs, when those soft knocks came.

"Come in," I called, trying to sound less exhausted than I felt.

The door opened, and there he was, leaning against the frame.

Moonlight poured through the window, cutting silver paths across the room. It caught the sharp angles of his face, tracing the strong line of his jaw and the high curve of his cheekbones. His green eyes gleamed in the dim light, almost luminescent, and for a moment I forgot about my aching muscles and could only see *him*.

He looked every bit like a king, and somehow, in my doorway, he seemed more.

His features were striking, almost carved in their precision. High cheekbones. A strong jaw shadowed by a neatly trimmed beard. Braids, threaded with red jewels, fell over his broad shoulders. He carried himself with the weight of his station, but here in the quiet of my room, the edges of that formality softened. He felt... closer. Less untouchable.

His gaze swept over me, lingering for a heartbeat, as if he could read every line of fatigue in my posture. Then his expression gentled, concern settling in his eyes.

"Are you all right?" he asked, closing the door behind him. His voice was low, careful, like he didn't want to startle me.

"I'm just tired," I admitted, managing a weak smile.

The room was mostly shadows, lit only by the moonlight slipping between the curtains, drawing pale ribbons across the deep green walls. He moved closer, every step deliberate, until he sat on the edge of the bed beside me. The mattress dipped under his weight, bringing us just a little nearer than was entirely proper.

His scent found me. It was a warm mix of spice and earth, like black pepper and thyme after rain. It surrounded the space between us, subtle and grounding.

What I thought would be a brief check-in stretched into hours.

He talked about Polent and its people, the castle's history, and the creatures that had made their home inside its borders. His voice was deep and steady, and I found myself watching his mouth as he spoke, tracing the way his lips formed each word. I forced my eyes back to his, hoping he hadn't noticed.

Then he shared information I hadn't known.

His connection to Destiny.

His fingers brushed the red jewels braided into his hair, a faint, almost self-conscious gesture. "Queen Alondra was my great-grand-mother," he said, pride and something softer tangled in his voice. "Even though I'm not Destined, I know what it is to carry a responsibility larger than myself."

I saw beyond the king in that moment. Beyond the polished armor and expectations. I saw the man bound by bloodlines and stories, by promises made before he was born. The weight of it sat in the small crease between his brows, the way his shoulders never quite relaxed, even here.

"I understand," I murmured. "At least… I'm starting to."

His eyes lifted to mine, searching. The space between us seemed to shrink, not physically, since we were still sitting where we had been, but in the quiet way understanding filled the air.

I felt the pull of him. Of this man who carried a kingdom and still made time to ensure I didn't fall apart under the pressure of my own role.

I listened, captivated. And for a fleeting, dangerous second, I wondered if the connection was mutual. His gaze lingered, just a breath too long. His knee brushed mine when he shifted, sending a small spark racing up my leg. He didn't pull away.

He stayed until the early morning hours, our voices hushed as we talked in the half-dark, sharing pieces of ourselves that didn't belong in council rooms or strategy meetings.

The next day, I woke to find a delicate pair of ruby earrings resting on my pillow, warm from the sunlight streaming in. Beside them lay a neatly folded note.

Queen Alondra wore these. They will match your necklace.

— Llorent

My heart stumbled. He had noticed my necklace—the one I had worn at the wedding, before any of this made sense. The thoughtfulness of the gift, the intimacy of knowing it had once belonged to his great-grandmother, left my cheeks burning and my fingers trembling as I traced their shape.

Gratitude didn't quite cover what I felt.

It was more than that.

With a new day underway, my focus returned to training.

For three days, Eliza and I worked with Kito, practicing resurrection on various animals. Every morning she met me at the training grounds where he waited, a towering silhouette against the Polentian sky. I still hadn't found the courage to remove his blindfold, but every time I approached, I felt his silent plea through our bond.

Today, on the fourth day, I was done hesitating.

When I dressed, I chose a simple and functional outfit: a sleeveless beige tunic falling just above my knees, dark fitted pants, and sturdy boots. I tied my hair back to keep it out of my face, though a few strands escaped, stubborn as ever.

Kito loomed before me, scales catching the light in muted glints. A low, raspy breath rolled from his chest. I closed my eyes for a moment, steadying myself. Beneath my nerves, Destiny thrummed, drawing me toward him.

I extended my hand.

Kito lowered his massive head until it hovered at my level. When his snout brushed against my palm, the contact was surprisingly gentle, almost cautious. The bond between us tightened, warm and sure.

I slipped the black lenses from my eyes. The world sharpened, the air cooler against my face. The blindfold still covered his gaze, but this felt like my first step toward seeing him as he wished to be seen.

Calm, not fear, flooded me.

"Put the lenses back on!" Eliza's voice rang from the observation tower above, sharp with panic.

I barely heard her.

My fingers slid along the intricate ridges of Kito's scales until they found the heavy chains securing the blindfold. The links were cold against my skin as I gripped them.

The training of the past days—all the doubt, all the pushing—had brought me to this exact moment. I refused to let hesitation claim it.

The metal clinked softly as I loosened the bindings. Kito remained still. No recoil. No flinch. Only a steady, powerful patience humming through the bond, as if he were holding his breath with me.

Trusting me.

A deep rumble vibrated through his chest, rolling up my arm and into my bones. Encouraging. Waiting.

With one final tug, I lifted the corner of the blindfold… just for a breath.

And in that breath, I met his gaze.

Gold. Blazing. Slit pupils pinned directly on me, brimming with the untamed power of the Gaul Forest. The sight hit me like a blow, sharp and blinding. It should have killed me. Turned my body to stone and left me as another warning on the training grounds.

But it didn't.

I was still breathing.

My heart thundered as I dragged the blindfold back down, fumbling to secure the chains before Eliza could reach me. My hands shook violently, but my mind raced faster.

He had let me see him.

And I had survived.

Eliza stormed toward me as soon as I stepped away, her face pale and furious. "What were you thinking?" she snapped, grabbing my arm. "You could have *died*."

Her words barely registered.

Somewhere deep inside, I knew an invisible boundary had shifted. Kito and I had crossed into a new realm. I wasn't just training with a basilisk anymore.

I was *bonded* to him.

Before I could untangle that realization, riders appeared at the far end of the field.

Victor and Karlos approached on midnight-colored sleipnirs, their silhouettes sharp against the open sky. Victor rode slightly ahead, his tall frame making the powerful creature beneath him seem small. His dark brown skin glowed under the afternoon light, his features sharp and resolute. A thick braid ran down his back, threaded with golden rings—the unmistakable mark of a Destined from Polent. His expression was serious but not unkind, his gaze sweeping over me as though assessing my condition before bothering with a greeting.

Karlos, in contrast, was leaner, his presence quieter but no less grounded. His dark hair was tied back, his fair skin carrying faint traces of sun. The golden ring along the edge of his irises caught the light as he glanced past me toward the basilisk enclosure.

Their sleipnirs slowed to a graceful halt, wings folding neatly along their flanks.

Victor dismounted first, boots landing with a dull thud. He strode toward us, his deep voice carrying easily across the field. "You look different, Clara," he said, tilting his head as he studied me. His gaze flicked briefly to Kito before returning to my face. "More at ease. Stronger."

Karlos slid from his mount with a softer step. He looked from me to the basilisk and back again. "I heard about your Destiny," he said. "And about your training."

I glanced over my shoulder at Kito. He remained still, but the bond between us thrummed with awareness. Pride stirred in my chest, unexpected and fierce.

"There's a lot to tell," I admitted. "But first, let's go back."

Victor nodded and swung into the saddle again. "Then let's ride."

I mounted my sleipnir, the reins familiar and comforting in my hands. Karlos and Eliza followed, and together we rode back toward the castle. The wind cooled the lingering heat on my face as we cut across the open fields, the mountains and towers of Polent rising to greet us.

We went straight to Llorent's office.

Inside, everyone gathered around the long table. As I stepped into the room, a familiar warmth tingled along my arm—Destiny stirring at the proximity of other marked souls.

Victor was the first to speak. "The Gaul Forest will answer our questions," he said, spreading a large map across the table. "Staying here isn't helping. We can't afford any more delays."

Karlos nodded. "We need to be prepared. Death awaits us in many forms."

The word *death* slid under my skin like ice. Even with the progress of the past week, the thought of stepping into the forest and facing what waited there tightened my throat. Having the power to revive dead creatures didn't make me comfortable with the concept. If anything, it made the fragility of life feel sharper, not duller.

Matry, quiet until now, leaned forward. "Now that you have your Destiny, you should be able to enter the Gaul Forest without issue," she said. "Before, the forest might have rejected you. Now, your connection is solidified. There's no reason you shouldn't be able to step inside freely."

A feeling in me eased. One of my worst fears—that the forest itself would still push me away—loosened its hold.

"Agreed," I said, forcing my voice to steadiness. "We'll leave tomorrow morning."

The moment the words left my lips, a wave of sadness followed.

I wanted to stay for Hale—to hear her laughter, answer her questions, and feel her small hand in mine. Leaving her was like leaving a piece of my heart behind.

I wanted to stay for Kent, who had always been my anchor. Walking away from him meant stepping into danger without the one person who had known every version of me.

And then there was Llorent.

That part was harder to name: the idea of staying a little longer, to get to know the man behind the crown, to see if the connection I felt was more than imagination. It pulled at me in ways I didn't want to examine too closely. We were little more than allies, maybe friends. Yet I couldn't deny how often my thoughts drifted to him. I wondered, foolishly, if his ever drifted in my direction.

Victor tapped the map, drawing my attention back. "We've identified several critical areas where the forest's death is spreading fastest," he said, indicating clusters of marked points. "These are our primary targets."

Karlos leaned in, expression grim. "We focus here first. If we can contain the spread, we might be able to reverse the damage."

Victor added, "The creatures inside the forest are becoming more aggressive as their environment deteriorates. Expect resistance—from the land itself."

"Our best approach," Karlos said, "is to use all our strengths together. If we can wield Destiny within the forest, we may be able to determine what's causing the decay and how to stop it."

Llorent stood at the head of the table, arms folded loosely across his chest. Even without a mark, his presence anchored the room. "Polent will provide whatever you need," he said. "Our Destiny gates will remain open to you as long as it takes."

We mapped every detail—supplies, transport, communication. Nothing was left to chance. Each of us had a role, and the mission depended on all of them fitting together.

My fingers drifted to the edge of the map, tracing the jagged line of the forest's border. The realization of what lay ahead pressed down harder now, becoming real. I would walk into that dying forest. I would face whatever waited inside.

And all the while, I felt him.

Arisen's presence stirred quietly in the back of my mind. He didn't speak. Didn't guide. He simply *listened*. He hovered at the edge of my thoughts, following every word as if he were seated at the table beside me.

When Victor and Karlos spoke, I could sense his silent approval—a subtle thread of agreement gliding through the link. He wasn't here in body.

But in every way that mattered, he was.

With us.

With me.

The room dimmed as the sun went down. The last rays of light slanted through the windows, painting everything in orange and gold. People began to drift out, voices dropping to low murmurs as they made their way toward dinner and rest.

There were still things I wanted to do before the day ended. One of them was speaking with the other human Destined from Ebony.

Karlos.

I waited until the room had nearly emptied. Llorent crossed to me first. He stopped directly in front of me, close enough that I had to tip my chin up to meet his gaze.

"You know," he said, voice low and warm, "I'm quite impressed with you, Clara. You've made an impact in the week you've been here. Not only with your Destiny, but with the creatures that roam my land."

The corners of his mouth lifted, slow and deliberate. His eyes lingered on my face, tracking from my eyes to my lips and back again. Heat crawled up my neck.

"I hope I keep surprising you," I replied, my voice softer than I intended, laced with a hint of challenge.

His smile grew wider, a clear pleasure flickering in his eyes. "I look forward to it," he murmured.

For a heartbeat too long, neither of us moved. I became acutely aware of the space between us—small, fragile, easily crossed. His hand brushed mine as he stepped back, the brief contact sending an unwelcome, thrilling jolt through me.

Then, with a final nod, he turned and walked toward the door.

I watched him go, a mix of nerves and an emotion dangerously close to excitement humming beneath my skin.

When the room was almost empty, I crossed to Karlos. "Karlos, could you stay for a moment?"

He looked up, our eyes meeting. "Of course."

We settled into two gray leather chairs in the corner, just far enough from the door to feel private.

"I've been wanting to talk to you," I began, shifting until the chair stopped creaking. "As the only two humans Destined from Ebony, I… wanted to get to know you better."

His posture relaxed, but his attention sharpened. He brushed a lock of hair from his forehead. "I've heard a lot about you, Clara," he said, a small smile tugging at his lips. "You've made quite an impression since you arrived."

"I'm just trying to do my part."

"You've done more than that," he replied. "Your abilities, your connection with the creatures—it's impressive. And it's good to have someone else from Ebony here. Makes this all feel a little more like home."

"I feel the same," I admitted. "It's been… a lot. Knowing someone else understands what it's like back home helps."

He nodded thoughtfully. "Ebony has its challenges, but there's strength there, too. I think we both carry that with us, no matter where we are."

"Absolutely," I said. "But how did you manage everything that came with Destiny? And how did you navigate your relationship with Victor?"

Karlos's gaze softened. He leaned forward, forearms resting on his knees. "You never truly get used to it," he said. "I've learned to appreciate the relationships I've formed with the elves and the responsibility of holding so much power. But it's easy to lose yourself in all of this. Don't let that happen."

"I have my family to keep me grounded," I said quietly, maybe more to convince myself than him.

"I draw strength from mine, too. Especially my son." His shoulders slumped slightly. "But I see them less and less as time goes on."

"What do you mean?"

"The responsibilities of being Destined keep you away from what matters most," he said. "Your family grows older; you don't. I've been Destined for forty years. I miss being a normal human. I still look like this." He gestured to himself. "My family does not. My son, Frederick, looks nearly as old as I do now. It's… difficult, not being able to visit Hertm as often as I wish."

Destiny had extended the lifespan of all humans, allowing us to live well beyond two hundred years. Those chosen as Destined could live even longer. I tried to imagine a world where Kent and Hale were gone and I remained. My chest tightened.

"Count yourself lucky you've seen your family within your first year as Destined," Karlos said. "It took me three."

His words sank heavily. "Where is your son now?" I asked.

"In Hertm," he replied. "He's still there, so I visit when I can."

I nodded, then hesitated. "I knew someone from Hertm. Someone very special to us. Did you ever meet Lorraine? She was my niece's mother, but she died during the storm."

"Lorraine…?" he repeated, brows knitting. "I know a few Lorraines, but I don't recall any storm."

"The storm that hit Hertm two years ago," I clarified, a little too quickly. "Many people died. She was one of them."

"I'm sorry for your loss," Karlos said. "But I don't remember hearing about any such storm."

"It was two—" I started, but the door opened.

Eliza stepped inside. "It's almost time for dinner," she said. "Would you both care to join us?"

"I'm having dinner with Kent and Hale," I replied. "But thank you."

"I'll join you, Eliza," Karlos said. "Just give me a moment."

She nodded. "Enjoy your evening, Clara." Then to Karlos: "I'll wait for you outside."

When the door closed again, I turned back to him. "I didn't mean to press you about Lorraine," I said. "It's just… Kent and Hale have so many questions. I hoped you might have known her."

Karlos's expression softened. "I understand," he said. "It's important to find those connections. If I remember anything, I'll let you know."

"Thank you. That means a lot."

We stood, and he took my offered hand, his grip warm and steady. After he left, I turned to the window. The sun had almost disappeared, leaving only a smear of pink at the horizon. The conversation sat uneasily in my chest.

As if sensing it, Arisen spoke.

"The storm you mentioned to Karlos… what were you referring to?"

"The one that took Lorraine from us," I said. *"The storm in Hertm two years ago. Don't tell me you haven't heard of it either."*

There was a pause—long enough to feel deliberate.

"There was no such storm," he said at last.

My stomach flipped. *"But Lorraine died in that storm."*

"I understand your pain," he replied gently. *"But I've checked the records. There's no mention of a storm in Hertm's recent history."*

I stared at the window, at the fading light, trying to force his words to make sense.

Lorraine's urn. The way people had spoken of it. The grief that had gutted Kent.

The storm *had* happened.

Hadn't it?

CHAPTER 26

Once I reached Hale and Kent's door, I paused before knocking. Pushing aside my swirling thoughts, I gently tapped the door, hoping not to disturb them. To my relief, Kent opened it with a warm smile.

"Hey there," he greeted me. "Come on in."

Stepping inside, I was met with the comforting sight of Hale playing with her toys on the floor. This time, she wasn't playing alone; Rijor sat beside her. The light streaming through the window illuminated both their blond hair, casting a nearly blinding glow that seemed to connect them in some intangible way.

Hale's bright eyes lit up as she saw me. She reached out eagerly, and I wasted no time scooping her into my arms.

"I missed you," I said softly, holding her close. Though it had only been a few hours since I last saw her, the conversation with Karlos had left me unsettled. Would Hale grow into adulthood while I remained unchanged? The thought twisted painfully in my chest. I couldn't imagine that kind of future for her… or for myself.

Kent chuckled. "She's been asking about you all afternoon."

I smiled, pressing a kiss to Hale's cheek as she giggled and wrapped her tiny arms around my neck. Her warmth and innocence reminded me of what truly mattered.

Rijor stood from where he'd been seated, his expression brightening as he approached. "Great to see you, Ms. Clara Lildar."

I turned toward him, still holding Hale. "I've heard how well you've looked after my family, and I thank you for it," I said sincerely, meeting his gaze.

Rijor inclined his head, his voice steady as he replied, "They are family to me as well."

We settled in for dinner, a roasted duck taking center stage on the table, surrounded by dishes of seasoned vegetables and golden-brown potatoes. The conversation was light, filled with pleasantries and warmth, but my eyes drifted to the silver box in the corner of the room.

The box gleamed in the dim light, its surface spotless, as though Kent had recently polished it. He always kept it clean, a gesture of love and remembrance for what it represented.

After dinner, Kent excused himself to clean up, and I took Hale to bed. I pressed three soft kisses to her cheeks, her sleepy giggles melting my heart. Her tiny fingers curled around mine as I smoothed back her hair, waiting until her breathing evened out and her lashes fluttered closed.

When I returned to the living room, Rijor was still there. Kent had gone, leaving us alone in the quiet space. I felt his gaze settle on me as I hesitated near the doorway.

I cleared my throat and sank into a chair across from him. "I've been thinking a lot about Hertm lately," I admitted. The words came out before I could overthink them.

Rijor's brow lifted slightly. "Have you?"

I nodded. "It's strange. I don't know why, but it's been on my mind more than usual." I hesitated, then asked, "You're from there, aren't you?"

"I am."

"Then maybe you can answer some of my questions."

He leaned forward, resting his elbows on his knees, his gaze sharp. "I'll do my best."

I considered where to start. "What kind of place is it?"

Rijor hummed, glancing around the room as if measuring his words. "Hertm is… unique," he said finally. "A place full of power and magic all on its own. It doesn't need to be woven into spells or channeled through Destiny. It simply is."

"That's why it's dangerous, isn't it?"

"Some might say that," he admitted. "But others would call it sacred."

I chewed on that before shifting the subject. "Do you know about Lorraine?"

At that, Rijor stood abruptly. The movement startled me, but not as much as what he did next. Without hesitation, he stepped toward the corner of the room and reached for the box.

I stiffened.

No one touched that box. No one but Kent.

My breath caught in my throat as Rijor ran a hand along its surface, his fingers tracing the edges as if he were reading something unseen. The room felt colder suddenly, or maybe it was just my imagination.

"One of the strongest."

I gripped the arms of my chair. "What do you mean?"

Rijor didn't answer. His fingers tightened briefly around the box before he set it back down with a careful precision that felt almost reverent. Then, as if nothing had happened, he turned back to me with an easy, unreadable expression.

"What about the storm?"

For the first time, Rijor hesitated. It was a fraction of a second, but I caught it. The way his jaw tensed, the way his fingers twitched before he folded them together.

"The storm. A curious thing, isn't it?"

Before I could question him further, he exhaled and straightened. "It's late," he said, his voice back to its usual smooth control. "I should let you rest."

That wasn't an answer.

But before I could press him, he was already moving toward the door.

"Good night, Clara," he said, pausing just long enough to glance at me over his shoulder.

I swallowed the unease rising in my throat. "Good night, Rijor."

He left without another word, and I sat there, staring at the silver box long after he was gone.

CHAPTER 27

From Clara's Diary

I left Kent and Hale's room confused. From the moment I became Destined, I had been overwhelmed by so many emotions that it felt suffocating.

Conversations were overwhelming. The Gaul Forest was overwhelming. Life was overwhelming. I would give up everything if it meant I could go back to Raster with Kent and Hale.

As I opened my door, I was momentarily surprised to see the one across from mine open, revealing Llorent.

"Clara, is everything all right?" he asked. He was wearing a casual outfit: a fitted red vest and loose trousers. He leaned on the doorframe, his arms across his chest.

"Yes. Why do you ask?" I replied, trying to muster a convincing smile.

"Your eyes seem… troubled."

I hadn't realized how much the day's conversations had affected me until he pointed it out.

Llorent's expression softened, and he pushed himself away from the doorframe. "Let's go for a walk," he suggested, closing the door behind him. He moved closer, his hand gently resting on my lower back. His touch was reassuring as he guided me toward the palace grounds.

As soon as we stepped outside, we were greeted by a familiar creature. His, or dare I say, our, sleipnir stood waiting, its glossy gray coat shining under the moonlight as if anticipating this moment.

"Care to go for a ride?" Llorent asked, a soft smile tugging at his lips. I paused momentarily, but before I responded, the sleipnir knelt, offering its back to me.

I smiled as I climbed onto the creature, letting my body settle into the saddle. It was strange how comforting it felt, this connection I had formed with the sleipnir. For a moment, the anxiety and tension slipped away.

Llorent mounted behind me, his arms braced on either side as he took the reins. The warmth of him so close made me feel safe in a way I hadn't felt in a long time.

"I think he likes you more than he likes me at this point," Llorent teased, his voice near my ear, sending a pleasant shiver down my spine.

I turned just enough to meet his gaze, a smile spreading across my lips. "Maybe he just knows how to appreciate good company," I replied, letting a hint of playfulness enter my tone.

He chuckled softly, his breath warm against my neck.

We rode through the palace grounds, the cool night air brushing against my face, and the moonlight painting the landscape silver. There was a serene silence, interrupted only by the rhythmic sound of the sleipnir's wings cutting through the wind.

After a while, Llorent spoke, his voice softer now, almost hesitant. "You seemed lost when I saw you earlier. Something happened, didn't it?"

I sighed, my eyes fixed on the dark horizon. "It's just… everything, really. It all feels like too much sometimes. There are so many questions, and I don't have answers for any of them."

His grip on the reins tightened as he leaned a little closer. "You were thrust into a choice you didn't make, with Destiny choosing you and a power never before given. That's not easy." He glanced at the moonlit path, his voice becoming more tender. "But you don't have to do this alone, Clara. There are people here, myself included, who care about you more than you realize."

I swallowed, the sincerity in his voice touching a feeling within me. "I've struggled with letting people in," I admitted. "But this experience has me questioning whether I even want to do this. And it feels horrible to say because I know I have to."

"I can see that," he said, a faint smile in his voice. "But you don't always have to be strong by yourself. Even the strongest of us need someone by their side." He hesitated, and I felt the warmth of his hand on my back. "You have me if you ever need someone."

I glanced back at him, our eyes locking. There was a hint of unguardedness in his face—a vulnerability that reflected my own—and I longed for it.

"Thank you," I said, my voice barely audible over the sound of the wind. "That means a lot."

Llorent's smile grew, and he looked away, his focus returning to the trail ahead. "You don't have to thank me," he said. "I mean it."

Feeling him behind me was comforting. There was a certain quality to how his arms felt around my waist, how he smelled, and how my body fit against his. He eased the tension that had built up, allowing me to breathe more freely. I took a deep breath of the cool air, feeling it refresh my lungs.

As we reached the gardens, Llorent brought the sleipnir to a halt in a secluded corner, away from prying eyes. With a gentle touch, he helped me dismount from the creature's back, his hand lingering against mine for a few seconds.

We walked the path in silence, and the closer we got, the harder it was to pretend I was unaffected. I kept catching myself in his eyes, in the quiet gravity of him beside me, like my body knew where it wanted to be before my mind could argue. By then, my thoughts weren't on the mission or the forest ahead. They were on him, on the pull that had been growing for days, sharpening into something I could no longer deny.

"I am going to miss this place," I murmured.

I doubted myself for feeling so attracted to a man I hadn't known long, even if, somehow, I already knew him well. In such a short time, he had offered me some of the most thoughtful, profound conversations I'd had in years, and that closeness made the pull between us feel both impossible and undeniable.

The silence was comfortable as we walked through the quiet, moonlit gardens. The soft leaves rustling in the night breeze added a soothing backdrop to our conversation.

"I want you to know that I appreciate the care you have provided for me and, most importantly, my family. We are forever in your debt."

Llorent paused, turning to face me, his expression serious. "You and your family are always welcome here," he replied, his voice husky from the cold air. "Polent is a place where we value community and support. Your family is part of that now."

"I appreciate that more than you know. When I leave tomorrow, I will keep in touch. Perhaps next time, I can come for a longer time," I replied, trying to keep the emotion out of my words.

Llorent smiled, a genuine warmth in his eyes. "You are always welcome here."

We continued to walk down the path, our footsteps crunching softly on the gravel. The conversation flowed effortlessly, moving from the mundane to the profound like it usually did.

As we reached the end of the garden path, I realized how much time had passed. Over an hour had gone by, yet it felt like only minutes. The conversation had been the most honest and open I had had in months, a refreshing change from the guarded interactions I had become used to.

Llorent stopped and turned to face me, his expression serious once again. "Clara, I want you to understand that whatever happens in the Gaul Forest, you have my full support."

"Thank you, King Llorent. Your support means more than I can say."

"We'll face this together."

We crossed a short bridge over a waterfall; the water was at least a hundred feet below us. I looked at the waterfall, its top adorned with stars and the night sky. I shifted on my feet, finding myself closer to him.

He closed the distance between us, his presence wrapping around me. The air between us was charged with a tension neither of us could ignore.

I shuddered as his breath brushed my skin, sending a ripple of anticipation through me. Slowly, I turned to face him, my eyes locking onto his. He was waiting—for permission, for a sign that I wanted this as much as he did.

But there was no hesitation left in me.

"You are exquisite, Clara."

And then his lips were on mine, stealing the breath from my lungs, unraveling me completely.

The kiss was urgent, heated, and filled with a hunger that had been simmering between us. A gasp escaped me as his desire crashed against mine, my body yielding to the fire that burned between us. My arms wrapped around his neck, fingers threading through his braids, tugging him closer. He groaned into my mouth, the sound vibrating through my entire body.

His beard was rough, grazing my skin in delicious contrast to the softness of his lips. Every stroke of his tongue, every press of his body against mine ignited a feral impulse inside me.

I ached for him.

The intensity of his kiss sent heat pooling low in my stomach. His hands roamed my body with a desperate reverence, memorizing, claiming, worshipping. When his fingers brushed over my thighs, lifting the hem of my dress, I gasped against his lips, my body arching instinctively into him.

He pulled his lips from mine, trailing kisses down my neck, each one sending a fresh wave of heat through me. His hands moved with purpose, caressing, exploring, making me tremble beneath his touch. When his fingers finally found the slickness between my legs, he groaned, his breathing ragged.

"You're already ready for me."

I could barely form a response, too lost in the way his fingers teased me, in the way my body responded so easily to him.

The throbbing between my legs was almost unbearable now, an aching emptiness only he could fill. My hands roamed over his chest, feeling the tense muscles beneath his clothes. I needed to touch him, to pull him impossibly closer.

Then, I felt him—*hard*, pressing against my stomach. A soft whimper escaped me at the realization of just how much he wanted me too. I reached for him, my fingers sliding beneath the waistband of his trousers, wrapping around his thick, pulsing length.

He let out a ragged moan, his grip on me tightening as his hips jerked involuntarily into my touch.

"Clara," he rasped, his voice strained.

He pulled away suddenly, his breath coming in heavy gasps. His hands captured mine, stilling my movements.

"Stop," he murmured, though the need in his voice betrayed him.

Confusion flashed through me, my cheeks flushed, my body humming with frustration. "Did I—?"

"I will please you first," he interrupted, his look dark with promise. "Do not move."

My breath caught as he slowly sank to his knees before me, lifting the fabric of my dress. His warm hands trailed from my knees to my thighs, sending shivers across my skin. With one swift motion, he bent me forward, his breath hot against my bare skin.

I gasped as his fingers traced along my entrance, teasing, exploring, making me writhe with need.

"Llorent—"

A strangled moan tore from my throat as he slid one finger inside me, then another, curling them just right, sending sparks of pleasure shooting through my veins. My hands gripped his shoulders, my body barely able to hold itself up as he worked me into a frenzy.

His lips found my breast, his tongue flicking over my hardened nipple before he bit down softly, drawing a sharp cry from me. The contrast of pain and pleasure sent my head spinning.

Instead of relief, the need inside me grew, an insatiable hunger that only he could satisfy.

I was trembling, on the verge of release, but before I could fall completely, he pulled his fingers away. My breath hitched as I watched him, mesmerized, as he brought his fingers to his lips.

He licked them slowly, savoring the taste of me, his eyes locked onto mine the entire time.

"Delicious."

A shudder ran through me. I couldn't take it anymore. I needed more of him, all of him.

I surged forward, capturing his lips in a heated kiss. My fingers tangled in his braids, pulling him closer, deepening the kiss until there was no space left between us.

I dropped to my knees, my fingers fumbling with the clasp of his pants, desperate to feel him in my hands, in my mouth, to return the pleasure he had given me.

But before I could free him, a strange heat spread through my arm—a sensation I recognized instantly.

A warning.

"We must go. Now."

Eliza's voice.

The moment shattered.

I jerked away, my breaths coming fast and uneven, my cheeks flushed with lingering heat and embarrassment.

Eliza stood just a few feet away, looking anywhere but directly at us. She held up two backpacks—hers and mine.

"King Arisen wrote," she said firmly, though I detected the awkwardness in her tone. "He insists we leave *now*."

I swallowed hard, my body still trembling from everything that had just happened.

Llorent adjusted his clothes, but his eyes never left mine, still dark with unfinished desire.

"I thought we were leaving in the morning," I muttered, my mind still trying to catch up with reality. "There are still a few hours left."

Eliza shook her head. "King Arisen insists."

Her words felt heavier than they should have.

Llorent stepped closer, his fingers brushing mine briefly as he leaned in. His voice was a husky whisper, meant for me alone.

"Go," he murmured, his lips grazing my ear. "We will have time again."

I met his gaze one last time before reluctantly turning away. As I took the backpack from Eliza and followed her into the night, I stole one last glance over my shoulder.

He was still watching me, his eyes burning with a longing I knew matched my own.

And as much as I hated leaving, I knew—*this* wasn't over. Not yet.

CHAPTER 28

We walked in silence for a while until Eliza finally broke the quiet. "So, what exactly did I just witness?"

I stayed silent, my mind still spinning as I processed everything. The moment with him, the abrupt end, the warmth of his body… none of it was easy to put into words.

Eliza sighed, glancing at me. "Look, it's wonderful you've found a connection, especially as a Destined. But in my experience… it doesn't always end well." There was a sadness in her voice that made me look at her more closely. "I do hope, for your sake, that it does."

"What happened?"

Eliza sighed again, her expression growing serious, her eyes distant, as though remembering something painful. "Being Destined is a heavy responsibility. It changes everything. Relationships, especially romantic ones, don't stay simple. They become… complicated. The responsibilities and sacrifices are a lot for anyone to bear."

I studied her, sensing a deeper story beneath her words. "Did something like that happen to you?" I asked gently.

She hesitated, her gaze dropping for a moment. When she looked back up, her red eyes were filled with a quiet sorrow that surprised me. "Yes," she said. "I loved someone once, before all of this. She was human." She paused, the words lingering in the still night air. "Relationships between elves and humans aren't forbidden, but they are rare. And for good reason."

She looked away, her eyes searching the darkness. "She was everything to me. But as an elf, I have immortality, and to me, our time together felt like it passed in the blink of an eye. It was fleeting, barely a breath in the vastness of my life. For her, it was everything. But for me, it was a beautiful dream that ended far too soon."

She swallowed, her voice revealing her emotions. "We tried to make it work, but the difference in our lives, in who we were, became too much. Loving a human when you have centuries ahead of you… it's like trying to hold onto a moment that's always slipping away. It broke us apart, and before I knew it, she was gone. And I was left with nothing but memories that felt like they'd barely lasted. Clara… as a Destined, you will outlive any humans you get too close to. You are now the closest to an elf a human can be."

I looked down at the path as I processed her words. I had always known why relationships between humans and elves were rare, but now, hearing Eliza's story, I truly understood it.

I had never been with an elf myself, and Llorent was a human… perhaps that made things different for us. Still, I knew that Eliza's story resonated with my Destiny in more ways than I cared to admit.

"I'm sorry. I can't imagine how hard that must have been."

"It was, but it taught me to be cautious. To understand that as a Destined, our paths are never entirely our own. You now have a responsibility that will pull you from your loved ones when you least expect it."

"Do you think it's possible to have both? To fulfill our duties and still find happiness with someone?"

Eliza gave me a small, sad smile. "I think it's possible, but it takes a lot of work and understanding. And sometimes, even that isn't enough. But I hope, for your sake, that you find a way."

We finally reached the entrance to the gate, and there was Stace, the basilisk, just where we had last seen her. Stace's massive, coiled body shimmered faintly in the dim light, her dark green scales glistening like polished stone. Despite her fearsome appearance, I felt my Destiny stirring, forging a bond with her almost immediately. I was surprised at how quickly and easily it happened this time—how natural it felt. This bond, though, made me miss Kito; I hadn't gotten to say goodbye to him.

"She will let us pass," I said confidently.

I grabbed Eliza's hand and led the way inside the cave, guiding us through the cold, narrow passages that we had navigated just a few nights before. The air was biting, and I saw my breath fogging before me as we moved deeper into the dark.

When we reached the Destiny gate, Karlos and Victor were standing watch. They looked exhausted, with dark circles under their eyes and drawn, pale faces. It was clear that they had been woken abruptly from their slumber. Despite that, they were dressed in the Destined coat, the heavy fabric meant to protect against the cold that waited beyond the gate.

"You made it," Karlos said, his voice filled with relief as he stepped forward. He reached out and placed his hand on my shoulder in a gesture of reassurance, a small smile tugging at his lips.

I smiled back and nodded, my eyes meeting his before moving to each person in turn. We all looked tired, but in that moment, I realized we shared an unspoken understanding. The pain wasn't something any of us were strangers to. As I looked at Karlos, Frederick came to mind—his son, whom he spoke of so fondly, the bright hope that kept him going. Whether human or elf, we all experienced love and craved it.

Eliza was the first to step forward. She gave us a slight nod before crossing the threshold of the gate, Victor right behind her. "I'll see you in Pitores," she said, and then, in the blink of an eye, she vanished, leaving no trace that she had ever been there.

Karlos and I exchanged glances. He extended his hand, and I took it, our fingers intertwining. Together, we stepped toward the gate. The familiar sensation of being pulled through time and space washed over me, disorienting and strange. When we emerged on the other side, the first thing that struck me was the heat.

It was unbearable, a scorching heat pressing against us from every side. My eyes widened in confusion as I looked around. Pitores was supposed to be cold, the kind of chill that made every breath feel sharp. But here, the air was thick, almost suffocating, and an intense, unexpected heat baked the ground beneath our feet.

Something was wrong. Very wrong.

CHAPTER 29

From Clara's Diary

I glanced around, my vision blurry and my thoughts disoriented. The landscape was unrecognizable and harsh, the ground beneath me burning with an unbearable intensity. Panic rose in my chest, but I forced myself to stay calm.

Taking a deep breath, I focused my energy and raised my hand to light up the space. At first, the glow was faint, but it gradually grew stronger, providing enough light to reveal our surroundings. It wasn't as powerful as the light Eliza produced, but it was just enough to guide me forward. And at this moment, I was so happy she took the time to teach me the skill.

Just a few feet away, Karlos lay on the red sand, unconscious. I rushed to his side, the heat of the sand enveloping my feet through my boots.

"Karlos!" I called out, trembling with fear. I knelt beside him, gently shaking his shoulder. "Karlos, wake up!"

His skin was pale, and beads of sweat covered his forehead. I checked his pulse, relieved to find it steady but weak. I had to get him out of here, but where were we? The red sand, the unbearable heat… none of it made sense.

I looked around frantically, the light from my fingertips creating shadows on the rocky terrain. In the distance, I saw jagged cliffs and strange, twisted rock formations. The sky above was a deep, unsettling shade of crimson.

Drawing on the strength that Eliza and Arisen had helped me cultivate, I hoisted Karlos into a sitting position, supporting his weight as best I could. "Come on, Karlos, you have to wake up," I urged, my words cracking with desperation. It seemed the gate's malfunction had taken a toll on his body. As we crossed, I saw a flash of light—brief but searing—hitting him square in the chest. Now, his breathing was shallow, his skin clammy, and his usually sharp eyes were unfocused. Whatever had struck him had drained him, leaving him weakened.

He stirred slightly, a low groan escaping his lips. His eyes fluttered open, and he looked at me, confused. "Clara? What… where are we?"

"I don't know," I admitted, trying to keep steady. "But we need to find a way out of here. Can you stand?"

With my help, Karlos stood, though he leaned heavily on me for support. "We need to find shelter," I said, scanning the horizon for any sign of refuge.

We stumbled forward, our breathing labored. The Destiny gate had vanished; there was no longer a door, no trace that it had ever existed, as if it had never been there.

In the distance, I spotted a dark opening in one of the rock formations. "There," I said, pointing toward it. "It looks like a cave. Maybe we can find water and figure out what's happening."

Karlos nodded, and we pressed on, driven by the hope of finding answers—or at least some relief from the unbearable heat.

When we finally reached the cave, I wasted no time. The suffocating heat had stripped away any sense of modesty. I quickly removed as many layers as possible, unbuttoning my coat until I was left with only silk undergarments.

I rushed over to Karlos, who was struggling to take off his coat. Without hesitation, I unbuttoned his jacket, shirt, and pants and helped him undress. With each layer I removed, his breathing grew uniform, and the heat eased its grip on him.

"We are in Pagos," Karlos said as he gathered his strength.

"What are we doing in Pagos?"

"An error must have occurred with the gate, and that has never happened unless dark magic is involved," he replied, wiping the sweat from his forehead with the shirt I had just taken off.

"Dark magic?"

I knew he was Destined with knowledge of dark magic, so this revelation shocked me. According to my understanding, wielders of dark magic did not exist, so how could someone use it?

"Our magic fuels the Destiny gates; when mistakes like these happen, something causes them. It almost seems purposeful…"

"What should we do? I have never been here, and this looks like a barren land."

There was no water in sight, and with the heat creeping over us, I knew we would need hydration soon. I opened the backpack Eliza had made for me, relieved to see the parestine folded inside. I took it out and found messages waiting for me to read.

I am back in Raster, Eliza wrote.

I am in Pitores, Victor wrote.

We are in… Pagos. Karlos and I, I wrote back.

The parestine's ink shimmered briefly, indicating that my message had been received. I glanced around at the dry, arid landscape.

The decay of magic is affecting the gates. You must get to the Gaul Forest by foot, Arisen's words appeared.

Out of all the Destined, we had the longest journey ahead. I was unfamiliar with Pagos and didn't know anyone.

Stay safe, all of you, I scribbled quickly, feeling a pang of worry for my fellow Destined scattered across different regions.

"We're going to have to continue on foot," I said to Karlos, who was now shirtless and leaning heavily against the rocky wall. His exhausted state had me deeply worried.

Karlos's chest rose and fell in ragged breaths, his skin glistening with sweat. A fresh wound marred his side, the dark bruising around it contrasting with the defined ridges of his muscles. His broad, muscular chest heaved with every inhale, the damp curls of hair clinging to his skin, darkened by sweat.

"What should I do?" I asked Arisen through our link, but I was met with silence.

I sense you are trying to communicate with me. I cannot reach you either. His words appeared on the parestine.

This wasn't good. This was really bad.

I clenched my jaw, feeling the strain of the unbearable heat. Neither of us could channel our Destiny, and it was evident that Karlos was struggling the most. I chose not to respond, as I was too preoccupied with our situation.

"We need to find water and shelter first. We can't survive in this heat much longer," I said, my voice sounding dry and cracked.

We ventured deeper into the cave, the darkness engulfing us as the air grew cooler. It was a stark contrast to the scorching sands outside; at least here, the ground no longer burned beneath our feet.

Our footsteps echoed in the stillness, the silence broken only by our labored breathing and the distant sound of dripping water. I strained my ears, hoping to locate the source, clinging to the hope that finding water would be our salvation.

After hours, we finally stumbled upon a small underground stream. I helped Karlos down to the water's edge, and we drank greedily. The cool water soothed our parched throats and restored some energy.

"We'll rest here for a while," I said, trying to sound confident. "Then we'll figure out our next steps."

CHAPTER 30

I woke up multiple times throughout the night. Karlos's body was burning with fever, and I spent hours walking back and forth between the stream and where we lay, dousing his body with water to cool him down. If I were back home, I would have access to an arsenal of medications and tools to help, but here, all I had was his wet shirt to squeeze water onto his skin. He remained still, barely moving, which only deepened my concern.

As the morning heat rose, I sat beside Karlos, who was still asleep. I took out my parestine and found two long messages waiting for me: one from Eliza and one from Arisen.

Clara, you are in my home country, and I can help you navigate it. I have written to a dear friend who can shelter you as you leave the country. You and Karlos are Ebonians; you know Pagostonians do not get along with your kind. Keep your head down and conceal yourself as much as possible until you reach my friend.

She also drew a map of where I needed to go in her message. From the looks of it, it was a library just a short distance from where I was. As quickly as I could, I drew the map in the sand to memorize it before it disappeared from my parestine. Shortly after, Arisen's words appeared.

I can sense that you are not well. I have begun my journey to get to you. If you head south, you will find softer terrain, eventually leading to the Sierra of mountains that marks the beginning of the Gaul Forest. Move with caution. I will find you. I need you.

I closed the parestine and looked down at the crude drawing of Eliza's map I had managed to sketch. Karlos let out a low grunt beside me, and I quickly fetched more water, placing his wet shirt on his forehead. I studied the map one last time, trying to commit every detail to memory.

Before leaving, I squeezed Karlos's hand reassuringly. Then I took the red scarf Eliza packed for the cold and wrapped it around my head, not only for sun protection but also to hide my face, leaving only my dark eyes showing.

With the scarf in place, I ventured out of the cave.

From the mouth of the cave, I could see we were close to a populated town. Homes made of sand and sun-bleached stone dotted the landscape, their edges crumbling from years of wind and heat. Many leaned precariously, their wooden beams warped, their roofs patched together with mismatched scraps. The narrow streets were nearly empty, save for a few elves moving in the distance, their steps graceful but brisk, as if lingering too long outside was a risk no one wanted to take.

I kept my head down, avoiding eye contact and any chance of interaction. The sand shifted beneath my feet with every step, dragging at my boots, but I forced myself forward with purpose. None of the elves around me seemed to struggle, and I refused to be the exception.

In my mind, I replayed Eliza's map, guiding myself toward the library she had marked. The trek felt endless, each step heavier than the last beneath the relentless sun. Heat wrapped around me like a second skin, and sand worked its way into everything: my clothes, my boots, even my mouth. But eventually, I saw it.

The library.

Unlike the crumbling homes around it, the building stood tall and solid, its stone walls still intact. Age showed in the weathered seams and softened edges, yet it had endured. The heavy wooden door was cracked along the frame, and the windows carried faint scars of old repairs, but compared to its surroundings, the structure looked almost untouched. It felt cared for, respected. Maybe because the knowledge inside still mattered to someone.

Relief loosened the knot in my chest, and I quickened my pace. When I reached the door, I knocked, the wood cool and dry beneath my fingers.

A moment passed before it creaked open.

An elvish woman stood in the doorway. She was young, with short mauve hair that stood out starkly against her otherwise dark attire. Her blood-red eyes were sharp as they scanned me, cautious and assessing.

She was tall, dressed in a long black robe cinched at the waist with a green rope. Her posture softened the moment our eyes met.

"Your eyes aren't red. You must be Clara."

"Yes, Eliza sent me."

"Come in quickly," she said, opening the door wider. "I've been expecting you."

Inside, the library was cool and dim. She led me to a small room lined with books, where comfortable chairs were scattered about. The place was empty, and I slowly unwrapped my scarf, letting the cool air brush against my overheated skin.

"My name is Margo Lear, but just call me Margo," she introduced herself, her eyes softening slightly. "Eliza told me you might need help. Where is your friend?"

"He's back in a cave, not too far from here. He's very ill. I need to get him to safety."

"I have some people who can help. We'll bring him here and do what we can."

She left briefly and returned with two elvish men, both tall with striking blood-red eyes. I took a deep breath, trying to comfort myself—trusting them was my last resort, but I had no choice. I needed their help, and so I led them back to where Karlos lay.

They carried a makeshift stretcher, gently lifting Karlos onto it. We moved along the narrow paths, each step careful to avoid jostling him, our progress slow but steady.

The path twisted and turned through the rugged terrain, with loose stones that shifted under my steps, causing me to slip more than once. Tall stone walls rose on either side, making the narrow passage feel even more cramped.

"How far are we?" Karlos rasped. His lips were cracked, dry, and flecked with blood from dehydration.

"Not too far, just beyond the clearing," one of the elves added.

Karlos groaned softly, stirring on the stretcher. I walked beside him, reaching out to take his hand. "Hang in there, Karlos. We're almost there," I murmured, trying to infuse my words with as much strength as I was able to muster. His fingers tightened weakly around mine, and I squeezed back, willing him to hold on.

The elves led us around a final bend, and I saw the faint glow of an opening ahead.

As we made our way to the library, I wrapped Karlos's scarf around his face, hoping to conceal his features as best I could. Despite our efforts to blend in, I felt eyes on us. We moved quickly, keeping our heads low, hoping that no one would follow.

Once we were safely inside the library, Margo and her helpers laid Karlos on a cot. I immediately fetched the cool water and herbs already laid out. My hands moved instinctively as I prepared the medicine, applying it to his feverish chest and forehead. The damp cloths soaked with herbal mixtures were our best attempt to reduce his dangerously high body temperature.

Karlos stirred slightly, his breathing ragged. His eyes fluttered open, unfocused. I leaned over him, squeezing his hand gently. "Karlos, it's me. You're safe now."

He blinked slowly, his dry lips parting. "Clara… did we make it?"

"We did. We're in a library."

He sighed, his eyes drifting closed again as if even keeping them open was too much. I fixed my gaze on him, watching every labored breath, hoping the medicine would take effect soon.

My body felt heavy as I sank into a nearby chair, muscles aching, but my mind refused to follow. I took in the dim library around me. The cool, shadowed air was both comforting and unsettling, like a place that remembered too much. Margo had locked the door behind us, securing the room against any intrusion.

For now, we were safe.

My eyes burned from exhaustion, but I couldn't bring myself to close them. I stayed alert, watching Karlos and willing my magic to be enough.

When his breathing finally calmed and the tension in his face eased,

I slipped into the narrow hallways. The shelves pressed close on both sides, packed with dust-softened spines that seemed older than the town itself. I looked for anything that might explain what was happening, anything that could help us survive what was coming.

I grabbed three books from the stacks, two on the Gaul Forest and one on magical creatures. If we were stuck here for a while, I needed every bit of knowledge I could get. I went back to Karlos's room, tucked into a corner, and opened the first volume, letting the words draw me in as he recovered.

As the hours passed, I occasionally looked up from the pages to glance out the window. The sky, once a bright crimson, had started to darken, with the rich colors deepening into a muted red as the day faded away. Outside, the dead trees looked like they were on fire, their twisted branches lit by the fading sunlight, creating the illusion of burning from within. The changing sky and shifting light made me sharply aware of the time passing—the many hours I had spent lost in the books, searching through every page for knowledge that could help us.

The room grew dimmer as the sun sank below the horizon. I shifted slightly in my seat, and the strain of sitting for hours settled into my muscles.

"How are you holding up?" Margo's voice broke the silence, making me jump.

I looked up, surprised to see her standing in the doorway. "I'm fine," I said, though a sigh slipped out as I spoke, betraying my exhaustion.

She squinted slightly, as if reading me with unnerving accuracy. "You read as if you're trying to erase everything happening around you."

"I…" My lips moved, but no words followed. She had seen right through me, and it left me momentarily speechless.

Margo stepped further into the room, her gaze steady, her honesty disarming. "I became a librarian because it's the only place in this country where a woman can truly be alone. No one expects anything of me outside of my work here. Reading is my escape from the harsh realities beyond these walls. I met Eliza before she became Destined. She was always different. I loved listening to her plans, the way she spoke about changing everything, making this place better."

I paused, taking in her words, feeling an unexpected kinship. "I did not choose this life, and yet, here I am, scared for Karlos, scared to lose him. Before all of this, all I knew about Destiny were the stories shared, and the uplifting news we always received. The reality is much different," I said, showing a vulnerable part of me.

We looked at Karlos, who still lay there, deep in sleep.

"Destiny runs deep in Karlos; his body is slowly healing. He'd be long gone if it wasn't for that," Margo said as she walked over and placed the back of her hand against his forehead.

"Back in Raster, we were told stories of the Destined who changed humanity, but so little is ever written about the experiences of those who are Destined," I said, almost to myself.

Margo smiled softly. "It's amazing how the stories we once saw as mere tales take on new meanings when we live through them. It inspires me. One day, I want to become a writer. Serve not only as a keeper of books, but also as someone who shares the voices that have never been heard. The stories of people who've lived through what others can only imagine."

Knocks on the door interrupted us, signaling that Margo was needed elsewhere. She glanced back at me, her expression thoughtful, before bending down to retrieve something from the bag at her feet.

"This book might be more useful to you," she said, handing me a heavy tome.

"Thank you." I opened the book, my eyes skimming over the pages. I had thought basilisks were intimidating, but some of these creatures appeared equally dangerous, if not more so—each one more fearsome than the last.

"Eliza wrote to me about your Destiny," Margo said, watching me closely. "I think these books might give you some ideas on using Pagos's local creatures for traveling to Pitores." She gathered her belongings, preparing to leave.

I nodded, still absorbed in the pages. "The creatures I worked with in Polent were all influenced by Destiny's magic. They responded well—happy, even, to follow my commands." As I scanned through the illustrations, I couldn't help but wonder how I was supposed to manage these beasts. One of them was quite literally breathing fire.

Margo, already by the door, chuckled at my comment. She paused, her gaze meeting mine. "I may not be Destined, but I know enough about your kind to hope that one day, I can write about each of you. Any good writer is a good observer and listener, and in the short time I've spent with you, Clara, I've seen a strength that goes beyond what most humans or elves are capable of under these circumstances. You have within you a resilience that can command any creature—including that dragon," she added, nodding toward the illustration of the fire-breathing beast.

I looked into her blood-red eyes, and in them, I saw why Eliza trusted this woman. She was kind. She was observant and trustworthy.

"Thank you," I murmured, putting the other books to the side and opening hers.

I spent the night reading it, absorbing every word. And she was right; this book was helpful.

But dragons?

No, thank you.

CHAPTER 31

From Clara's Diary

I didn't realize I had fallen asleep until I found myself wiping drool from the corner of my mouth. Thankfully, Karlos didn't stir from the thud of the book hitting the floor.

The book lay open to a page I hadn't reached yet. At the top, the name *Amphisbaena* was written in gold lettering, accompanied by a drawing of a serpent with a head at each end. According to the text, this creature was fast, could fly, and was endemic to Pagos. I stared at the illustration, examining every detail of its serpentine body.

It flew using wing-like scales and could see in all directions. Both heads had venomous fangs with no known antidote, and the creature regenerated lost body parts. How was I supposed to bond with something like this?

I was lost in thought until sunlight filtered through the window, casting a deep orange glow across Karlos's hollowed features. He stirred. I rushed to his side, gently grasping the hand that rested limp beside him. His skin felt warm… normal.

Thank goodness.

His eyes fluttered open, and he shifted to sit upright. I moved to support him, gently easing him into a comfortable position.

"I feel like I just got run over by a sleipnir," he said with a hoarse chuckle. "Clara, this is the most human I've felt in a long time."

"The decay in magic is impacting us in ways we didn't expect," I replied, trying to sound encouraging. "But you'll be back to your usual self soon. You have to."

"I normally heal much faster. I can feel Destiny's power within me, but it's like a faint memory compared to before."

"I think you'll start feeling better once we get closer to the Gaul Forest." I placed a reassuring hand on his arm, hoping my touch conveyed the strength I wanted him to feel.

I picked up the book I'd been reading and flipped to the page on the amphisbaena. "I have an idea that might get us back more quickly," I said, trying to sound optimistic. The detailed drawing of the creature filled the page—two heads, their bodies intertwined, with wings sprouting from its sides.

Karlos's eyes widened as he took in the image. "Are you serious, Clara?" he asked, his tone hesitant. He studied the drawing for a long moment, his brow furrowing. "That thing looks… dangerous. How do you plan to control it?"

I met his gaze, forcing confidence into my expression. "I know it won't be easy, but if we can convince it, this might be the fastest way to Pitores. We're running out of options."

Karlos exhaled deeply, his eyes flicking between the page and me. "If anyone can pull this off, it's you, Clara. Just… be careful. You know how unpredictable these creatures can be."

At that moment, Margo entered, balancing a few books in one hand and a basket of food in the other. The aroma of freshly baked muffins and glistening apples filled the room, making my stomach rumble.

I eagerly grabbed an apple and a muffin, handing one to Karlos. He took it but seemed too distracted by the amphisbaena illustration to eat.

"Thank you," I muttered, focusing on the food in an attempt to settle my nerves.

"You're welcome," Margo replied warmly before turning to leave.

"Margo," I called, following her to the doorway.

She turned back. "Yes, Clara?"

"There was a drawing of a creature called the amphisbaena in one of your books. Can you tell me more about it?"

A smile tugged at her lips, her eyes sparking with interest. "The amphisbaena is a rare and powerful creature," she began. "Known for its speed and ability to fly, but it is not exactly kind. You must convince both heads to follow your command, and one is always in a foul mood. It's a challenge, to say the least. Why do you ask?"

"It might be our best chance to travel quickly and safely. Do you know where we might find one?"

Her smile widened, admiration or amusement flickering in her gaze. "You're bold, Clara. I know of a place, but getting there and convincing the creature will take everything you've got. They're kept at Queen Franes's castle to protect the grounds."

My stomach sank. I'd hoped they lived in the wild, or at least somewhere far from the queen. The thought of sneaking into the castle, knowing her hatred for Ebonians and humans alike, made my skin prickle.

The risk felt enormous, and the margin for error felt nonexistent.

"Thank you, Margo. I appreciate your help," I said, forcing my voice to stay steady and my face to hide the disappointment.

She studied me for a moment, her eyes narrowing in thought. "You know someone with the queen's ear. Perhaps they could help."

I nodded slowly, her suggestion kindling a small, cautious spark of hope.

When I returned to the room, Karlos had managed to eat a few bites of his apple. It was a good sign. He looked better, but he was still fragile, like one hard breath could undo the progress we'd made.

I pulled out my parestine, meaning to write Eliza. As I unfolded it, two messages waited for me. The first was unmistakably from Llorent.

Dear Clara,

Though you have only been gone for two days, it feels longer. Your presence is deeply missed, and I find myself thinking of our last moments together.

Your family is well, and they remind me of you in many ways. Word has arrived about the struggle with the gates. I have secured Stace and sleipnirs at the gate, although they are becoming increasingly difficult to tame.

I look forward to the day when we can continue our journey together.

I quickly wrote a response, updating him on our situation.

Your words bring me joy, and you have no idea how much I needed them right now. Keeping the gates secure is a wise choice. Karlos and I are in Pagos, where magic's decay is already visible. Please, keep yourself, your people, and my family safe.

With much appreciation,

Clara

As my message disappeared, another one appeared.

I have made it out of Pitores and am a five-day ride from you. Stay safe.

It wasn't signed, but I knew it was from Arisen. I couldn't afford to wait five days. Karlos's condition was too precarious.

I wrote to Eliza:

Eliza,

I know you're in Raster, facing your own challenges. However, Karlos and I are in a dire situation. We must travel quickly and safely, and the amphisbaena is our best chance. As you know, they reside in Queen Franes's castle.

Can you help us gain access? I trust in our shared Destiny to convince the queen to reconsider her position toward us.

Yours in Destiny,

Clara

Setting the parestine aside, I turned to Karlos and explained my plan. To my surprise, he agreed. From the corner of my eye, bold words appeared on the parestine. I hadn't read them yet, but I knew they were from Arisen.

CHAPTER 32

Brave was the simplest word for it, even if I didn't feel it in that moment. What kind of person comes up with a plan to walk into Queen Franes's court and ask to borrow an amphisbaena? The creature was dangerous, one of her most prized possessions, and approaching her at all felt like stepping into a furnace on purpose.

As a Destined from Pagos, Queen Franes was bound to protect me and every other Destined. But she was also an elf who carried a deep hatred for humans, a hatred that, at times, seemed to burn hotter than her disdain for King Arisen and the Ebonians. I knew what lived behind her smile, and I knew I was walking straight toward it.

That hatred had roots older than any of us. It went back to the origins of Destiny, to the era when Pagos fought for every ounce of magic we now share. Our country has never been easy to survive in. The relentless heat turns living into labor, and the remnants of our past still linger in the blood-red eyes of our people. For years I resented my own eyes, a mark of the greed that once defined Pagos.

Before Destiny, we exploited the Gaul Forest without restraint, draining it to transform our desert into an oasis. We had everything: riches, comfort, power. Polent and Ebony had nothing. And our greed was our downfall. When Destiny was forged, Pagos was forced to share its wealth and resources. We lost it all in a single sweep, and what remained was only a shadow of what we once were.

This history fueled animosity toward other nations and, especially, toward humans. Many Pagostonians argued there was no reason to share our wealth with what they considered an inferior race. They were wrong, of course.

Destiny was working, but only as a patch to a larger issue, one that needed more than temporary solutions. It needed a new leader in Pagos, someone willing to reevaluate our policies and history.

As a Destined, I had the privilege of asking questions that many Pagostonians refused to ask themselves. Were the distribution policies fair? No. But were they the best we could manage for now? Possibly, although there was room for improvement. Only a few shared my views—those who took the time to understand others' perspectives. That's how I became close to Margo Lear.

Working alongside King Arisen, I knew he had dedicated his life to ensuring Destiny's success, even enduring thirty arranged marriages to strengthen alliances. However, Queen Franes's hatred for him was rooted in politics, and her disdain extended to everything he represented.

Few knew the truth: these marriages weren't King Arisen's idea. They were his council's. It didn't help that when Rijor joined, they became more common.

King Arisen was convinced that political marriages were the most effective way to maintain peace and reinforce the power of Destiny. So, he complied, wedding countless times in a relentless pursuit of alliances that rarely held firm. Each marriage was a sacrifice of personal freedom for the sake of his kingdom. Yet, no matter how many unions he forged, the fractures within the realm remained.

He was a ruler who would do whatever was necessary, no matter the personal cost. But in that same determination lay an unsettling truth. His strength became his burden. By constantly bending to the demands of diplomacy, he allowed others to dictate the course of his reign, trapping himself in a strategy that yielded diminishing returns. His rule was defined not just by authority, but by concession, by an unspoken resignation to a fate he could never fully control.

Destiny thrived on connections, or so his council claimed. The truth was far more complicated, and political machinations often overshadowed King Arisen's genuine intentions. His marriage to Vasa was the most insincere of all.

King Arisen never loved any of his wives. He didn't even share chambers with them. The lack of an heir made that clear. He provided them with comfortable lives, but the absence of affection wore on them over time. Most left out of boredom or loneliness.

Who would want to spend endless nights alone in Raster while King Arisen remained in Pitores? Not one of his thirty wives.

I considered King Arisen a friend, and it pained me to see him bury his grief under layers of duty. Over time, he had become a man devoid of emotion. That was until Clara.

She awakened him. I first noticed it during the wedding in the atrium at Raster. I passed Clara and brushed her arm by accident, and for a heartbeat I wondered what a human with that kind of beauty and presence was doing there. Access to the atrium was no small thing. It meant connections, influence, a door someone had opened for her.

Then I saw King Arisen's gaze catch on hers. Wide-eyed. Stunned. Maybe even captivated. In that brief moment, a crack showed in him, a vulnerability I had never witnessed before.

When Clara later entered Raster Castle as a Destined, Arisen was furious. But beneath the anger was an entirely different feeling, something he was trying to bury so deep I almost missed it.

In Pitores, it became impossible to ignore. I watched the way he looked at her, the way he restrained himself, fighting the instinct to reach for her when she learned the truth of her Destiny. It was clear to anyone paying attention. Yet Clara, tangled in worry for her family, remained oblivious to the man in front of her, silently yearning for a glance that lasted longer than a second.

But as the golden light of his mark intertwined with hers, flickering in perfect synchrony, I couldn't help but notice that their Destinies were bound in ways deeper than any before them. It wasn't just Destiny… it was something far more profound, something neither of them had fully understood yet.

Later that evening, Vasa relayed troubling news about Pagos and Polent, but I suspected she wasn't being entirely truthful. King Arisen had always been transparent with me, and hearing details from her that he hadn't shared felt unsettling. However, the hurt in Clara's eyes was unmistakable. Feeling betrayed, she left to be with her family.

I found it strange when King Arisen sent me the urgent request to return to Pitores. We still had hours to rest, but I complied.

Upon arrival, I saw Clara with King Llorent. She stood close to him, laughing softly at a remark he had made. The tension that so often lined her features was absent, replaced by an ease I rarely saw in her. She looked happy, relaxed—more *human*. The way she leaned toward him, the way his hand lingered at the small of her back, suggested a familiarity that had been growing in my absence.

Part of me suspected I had been sent there to interrupt the moment.

I stepped closer, my gaze narrowing as I took in the scene before me. Clara's fingers brushed against King Llorent's chest, tentative yet deliberate, and he responded by tucking a stray strand of her hair behind her ear.

And then I realized, this was not just a conversation.

Her breath hitched as his lips hovered near hers, his hand gently trailing down her arm with a slow, confident touch. Clara didn't pull away. If anything, she leaned in closer, her fingers tightening around the fabric of his shirt.

I froze.

I had walked in on Clara on the verge of giving herself to King Llorent. I wanted to turn around and leave, to give her the time to release what she had been holding for so long, but I was under direct orders.

A mix of emotions roiled within me: discomfort, surprise, and a lingering sadness as the scene reminded me of the woman I once loved. I had grown close to Clara. She had become a friend, someone I deeply cared about. But now, she and Karlos needed my help, and I was determined to assist her in reaching her goal.

If anyone could bond with an amphisbaena, it was Clara.

And so, I responded to her request:

Clara,

I will contact Queen Franes immediately. Remember, as a Destined, she owes you safety. Convincing her to lend you an amphisbaena will require an offering, one that may cost you more than you're comfortable giving.

Please stay safe. I am in Raster, where the rain continues. The aqueducts are full and holding, but the situation is precarious. I must find someone trustworthy to prepare the inner city for evacuation if necessary.

Take care, Clara. I will help in any way I can.

Yours in Destiny,

Eliza

And as I signed my parestine, I knew that only the ultimate sacrifice would convince that evil queen.

CHAPTER 33

From Clara's Diary

An offering. What offering would someone like Queen Franes want? What could I possibly give to someone I had never met?

Eliza,

I appreciate your help. I will come up with an offering valuable to Queen Franes. Please connect with my friend Marcos. He is well-known in the city, and his partner, Jastop, is well-connected as well. They can help. I will let them know to expect you.

Yours in Destiny,

Clara

After sending the message, I wrote to Marcos. He read my note immediately and replied, *I will do anything.* I knew Eliza could count on him.

Closing my parestine, I paced, trying to find something valuable enough to offer the queen. She was known for her vast wealth and extensive collection of rare artifacts. What would catch her interest?

I rummaged through my belongings, hoping for inspiration. As I sifted through my backpack, my fingers brushed against the smooth surface of the ruby necklace. But was it enough?

Karlos stirred, his movements drawing my attention. He was watching me with a curious expression, his brow furrowed.

"What's on your mind, Clara?" he asked, his voice still raspy from sleep.

I need to make an offering to Queen Franes. An item valuable enough to convince her to lend us an amphisbaena.

I touched my ears, considering the ruby earrings Llorent had given me. Their immense value seemed appropriate for such an offering. But Karlos seemed to read my thoughts, shaking his head slightly as he sat up, wincing.

"She already has enough riches. Queen Franes values power and influence. Perhaps it's not just an object you need to offer but something representing a significant alliance or a promise of future cooperation."

That wouldn't be easy, but Eliza did warn me. "Perhaps I can offer my assistance as a Destined. She could be enticed by the influence and power that come with having a Destined owe her a favor."

"It's a bold move, Clara, but it might just work. Queen Franes is known for her strategic mind. If she sees the potential benefits of having a Destined ally, she might be willing to agree. But are you sure you want to offer yourself—your worth—to her?"

No, I wasn't sure. But I had no other option unless she would take the earrings.

I prepared for the meeting with Queen Franes, going over what I would say and how I would present my offer. It was crucial to convey confidence and strength, to show her that I was a valuable asset worth her consideration.

With a plan in place, I felt more at ease.

Did I want to offer myself to her? No.

Did I want to get out of here and save the Gaul Forest? Yes.

The next step was to arrange a meeting with Queen Franes and present my offer. I supposed she would concede to a visit if I showed up unannounced; after all, as a Destined, that was the least she owed me.

As the sun rose higher in the sky, Karlos and I prepared for the journey to Queen Franes's castle. The heat of Pagos was relentless, but it only fueled my determination.

"We'll get through this, Karlos," I said, offering him a reassuring smile.

He returned the smile, but his eyes looked tired. "I believe in you, Clara. Let's do this."

We said our goodbyes to Margo, an elvish woman to whom I would be indebted for a lifetime. Then, with our bags on our shoulders, we set off.

CHAPTER 34

From Clara's Diary

The trip to the castle should have taken less than half a day. I could see it from the library window, yet the hike was exhausting. The relentless heat pressed down on us, and we had to stay alert. Scarves covered our heads, leaving only our eyes visible, but our shorter height still made us stand out from the tall Pagostonians. Our cover story, that we were merchants, would only work for so long.

We stopped often for Karlos's sake. My body had begun to adjust to the sweltering air, but he struggled, though he refused to admit it. I saw the strain in his posture and felt it through our Destiny. My arm, which should have been warm with his presence, felt almost normal, and that was a troubling sign.

The city was a maze of stacked, crumbling homes, many barely standing. The streets reeked of dust and decay, and the farther we went, the more unmistakable the desperation became. Hollow-eyed Pagostonians slumped against walls, ribs stark beneath tattered garments. Hunger had carved the strength from them. My heart clenched at the sight, but I forced myself to keep moving.

Navigating the alleyways meant weaving around people sleeping outside, stepping over uneven cobblestones, and dodging merchants pushing their wares. The constant clamor made it hard to focus on anything except putting one foot in front of the other.

Ahead, the castle loomed, carved into a massive stone cliff that rose from the desert like a monument. Its towering walls stood in cruel contrast to the squalor below, a world of luxury sealed off from the suffering at its feet.

Above the castle, two amphisbaenas circled slowly, their long, twisting bodies weaving through the darkening sky. Each creature had two heads, each one scanning the land below with sharp, unrelenting focus. Even from a distance, their screeches pierced the air, shrill and haunting. Occasionally, one let out a guttural hiss. It was a deep, vibrating sound that sent a tremor through my chest.

The wind carried their cries across the desert, a chilling reminder that no matter how far the shadows reached, the Pagostonians were never beyond their watch.

Karlos stumbled beside me, his pace faltering.

"We need to find a place to stay," I said, steadying him with a hand.

"Clara, no place in this city will welcome two Ebonians."

I sighed, the reality of his words pressing down on me. We were outsiders here; unwelcome, and as humans, even more conspicuous.

The city sprawled around us, a maze of narrow streets and collapsing markets. The air throbbed with noise, merchants shouting over each other, children laughing and crying out in the same breath, carts rattling over uneven stone.

As we pushed forward, I spotted a quieter alley tucked between tall, crumbling buildings. It was thinner, darker, and blessedly empty, far from curious eyes.

"This way," I murmured, guiding him toward it, hoping the shadows would buy us a moment to breathe.

I motioned to Karlos, and we slipped into the alley, finding a small alcove between two buildings. It wasn't much, but it would do for now.

"We'll rest here," I said, helping him lower himself onto the ground. "But we need a plan."

He leaned back against the wall. "We can't stay too long. Someone will notice us."

I nodded. Pulling out my parestine, I quickly wrote to Eliza, detailing our situation and asking for advice.

While I waited for her response, I rummaged through my bag and handed Karlos a bottle of water. He drank it in slow, measured sips, though his hands trembled slightly.

"We need to reach the castle by tomorrow," I said. "Eliza is trying to convince Queen Franes to help us. We just have to hold on a little longer."

Karlos managed a tired smile. "We've come this far. We'll make it."

We were deep in hostile territory, but at least we had each other and a plan. Huddled in the shadows, we tried to rest. The city's noise faded into a dull hum, and for a moment I let myself believe we might be okay.

Until we weren't.

I woke up to a sharp pain in my ribs, only to find a long glaive with its blade pressed against my side. The slightest movement drove the blade deeper, causing my ribs to throb painfully under the pressure. Beside me, Karlos was tightly bound by thick ropes. My heart raced, knowing that one wrong move could end me instantly.

Our captors were elvish men with dark, blood-red eyes and expressions carved from cold disdain. They wore Pagos's white uniforms, lightweight fabric that shimmered in the sunlight, paired with gleaming silver armor over their chests and legs. Their stares felt like knives, slicing over me with an unsettling intensity, as if they were measuring what I was worth.

"We request a meeting with Queen Franes," I forced out through gritted teeth.

"Ebonians don't make requests. You have no right to speak in this country," one of them spat, his voice sharp with contempt.

Karlos stirred beside me, rigid with discomfort, but he couldn't answer. A wad of fabric was stuffed into his mouth, gagging him into silence.

I unraveled my scarf, letting the hot, dry air wash my face. "We are Destined. Put your weapons down now," I demanded, forcing a confidence I didn't feel.

The elf holding the glaive hesitated, narrowing his eyes as he studied me. The others exchanged uneasy glances. Even here, the title "Destined" still carried some importance.

"Destined or not, you are in Pagos without permission," the leader growled, though uncertainty crept into his tone.

"We seek an audience with Queen Franes," I repeated firmly, despite the searing pain in my ribs. "As Destined, we have the right to speak with her."

The soldier's grip on the glaive loosened slightly. Glancing at his comrades, he responded, "Queen Franes does not take kindly to intruders."

"Then let her decide our fate."

After a tense moment, the glaive was withdrawn, and I let out a breath I hadn't realized I'd been holding. The leader motioned to his men, who reluctantly untied Karlos and pulled the gag from his mouth. He coughed hard, rubbing at his raw wrists as he glared at our captors.

"You will come with us," the leader said. His tone was still wary, but the outright hostility had dulled. "Try to escape, and you will be dealt with."

We nodded silently as they confiscated our belongings, including my parestine, which was the only way I had to reach the other Destined. They herded us through the winding streets, their uniforms catching the sparse light filtering down from above. Karlos stayed close to my side, but I could sense him slipping away. His condition was worsening, and it was more than dehydration. Something deeper was wrong—something I couldn't name or treat—and the helplessness of it scraped at my nerves.

When we reached the castle, the massive iron gates creaked open. Beyond them, a courtyard bustled with activity. Guards stood at attention along the walls and walkways, their blood-red eyes fixed on us as we were led inside.

Inside the courtyard, the scene was nothing short of grotesque. Chaos reigned as elves engaged in violent brawls, the sickening sound of fists meeting flesh reverberating through the air. Pained grunts and ragged breathing punctuated the brutality, and the ground was streaked with fresh blood. But what made my stomach churn wasn't just the violence, but the unsettling contrast unfolding before me.

In other corners of the courtyard, pairs and groups were tangled together in raw, unrestrained passion, their cries of pleasure rising and falling alongside the sounds of combat. The contrast was jarring, ecstasy and agony pressed side by side, as if both belonged to the same frenzied ritual.

My breath hitched, and I fought the urge to look away. I had never witnessed such uninhibited behavior. Yet here it was on full display, violence and lust braided into a spectacle that defied reason.

I had known this place was dangerous. I just hadn't expected this.

Clinging to Karlos, I followed our captors deeper into the castle. The grand hall was no less disturbing. Tapestries depicting Pagos's violent history lined the walls, their vivid details almost too much to bear. Decapitations, battlefields strewn with bodies, the scenes were hauntingly lifelike, as though the dead were reaching out from the fabric.

At the far end of the hall, on a raised dais, sat Queen Franes. She was smaller than I had expected, and her stature was unusual for someone from Pagos. Yet her presence was powerful, and her blood-red eyes were filled with curiosity and disdain.

"What are two Destined Ebonians doing in my country?" She pushed her tangled, dark hair back, revealing a face that was both striking and unkempt. Bits of debris were caught in her lengthy, matted waves, adding to her disheveled appearance.

I stepped forward, bowing as deeply as my injured side allowed. "Queen Franes, we are Destined Clara and Karlos of Ebony. We come seeking your aid."

She leaned forward, her gaze sharp. "And why should I, who has no regard for Ebonians, offer you my assistance?" Her greasy hair draped forward, partially covering her face.

I took a deep breath, choosing my words carefully. "Because, Your Majesty, the fate of Destiny and the balance of magic depend on our safe return to the Gaul Forest. We need your help to reach it, and the amphisbaena could get us there quickly. If we don't make it in time, the decay of magic will worsen, affecting us all…including you."

The queen's expression remained inscrutable, but she waved a hand, signaling us to approach. "Speak, then, Destined. Convince me why I should grant your request."

I stepped closer, my heart pounding as I prepared to offer everything in this one moment.

CHAPTER 35

From Clara's Diary

"I offer you my services as a Destined in exchange for an amphisbaena. The fate of Destiny is at stake. Magic is decaying, and we need to reach the Gaul Forest to uncover what is happening."

My voice echoed through the throne room and was swallowed by silence.

Queen Franes regarded me with cold amusement, her crimson eyes gleaming beneath the gold of her crown. "And why," she drawled, "would I care about that?"

I forced myself not to look away. "Because it will not only affect Ebony; the decay will reach Polent and Pagos as well. Your people. Your land."

She scoffed, the sound sharp as a slap. "You truly don't understand, do you, Destined?" Her lips curled. "You took most of our magic, and we are barely surviving here. Perhaps it is time for Ebony to struggle."

"That was never our intention," I insisted, stepping forward even as the guards tightened their grip on my arms. "But if the Gaul Forest dies, the magic that remains will disappear. None of us will survive that. Not Ebony. Not Polent." I swallowed. "Not you."

Queen Franes leaned forward on her throne, eyes narrowing with disdain. "Your king doesn't care about Pagos. He cares for his frivolous wives and his precious agenda. Nothing you offer will make me want to help you."

The words hit harder than I expected. I tried to keep my expression neutral, but the flicker of hurt must have shown because her smirk widened.

"You think I care about your feelings?" she sneered. "You think I care about *any* Destined?" Her gaze slid to my arms, as if she could see the marks hidden beneath my sleeves. "I don't kill you because I am obligated to keep you alive. That is all. Obligation. Not mercy." Her voice cooled even more. "But that doesn't mean I cannot keep you locked away with your dying companion."

A broken gasp sounded beside me.

"Karlos," I breathed.

He was struggling to stay upright, his breath coming in shallow, ragged pulls. Sweat poured down his face, turning the dust of our journey into muddy streaks. His legs shook beneath him.

"I-I will also offer myself," he rasped, forcing the words out. "A Destined… in service to Pagos… in exchange for—"

Queen Franes laughed, a harsh, ugly sound that bounced off the stone walls. "You?" she scoffed, tilting her head as if she'd misheard. "Offering yourself to me in *that* state?" She rose from her throne, descending the steps with deliberate leisure, her emerald gown whispering over the floor. "A Destined who can barely stand, let alone serve?"

Karlos tried to push himself taller, but his knees buckled. He stumbled and fell, catching himself at the last second on shaking hands.

"The very idea is an insult," she said flatly.

"Let me go! He needs me!" I shouted, jerking against the guards' hold. Their fingers dug into my arms like iron bands.

Queen Franes stopped in front of Karlos, looking down at him with bored curiosity, as though inspecting a cracked ornament she'd already decided to discard.

"Please, Your Majesty," I tried again, my voice raw. "We need your help. I will do anything you ask. We *must* reach the Gaul Forest. Without your assistance, all of this—" I gestured to the hall, to her throne, to the country beyond it "—could be gone."

For a heartbeat, she simply studied me, her expression unreadable. I held my breath.

Then she leaned back slightly... and spat.

The glob landed at my feet, thick and shining against the cracked stone.

"Lock them in the dungeons," she said, her tone turning lazy, dismissive. "Let them rot for a while. Perhaps then they will understand how much we do *not* care."

The guards moved at once. Karlos was barely conscious as they hauled him up. My heart pounded, a frantic drumbeat in my ears. I knew this would be difficult. I hadn't understood how cruel she truly was.

They dragged us out of the throne room and down a narrow, spiraling staircase. With each step, the air grew colder and damper, until it clung to my lungs like a second skin. The torchlight dimmed, shrinking to small, flickering circles of orange on the slick stone walls.

A heavy iron door creaked open at the bottom, releasing a breath of stale, sour air. Our cell was small and low, barely more than a carved-out pocket of rock. Rusted chains hung from the walls. A thin trickle of water dripped steadily from the ceiling, counting the seconds we were losing.

They shoved us inside.

The impact of the stone floor jarred my bones. I scrambled toward Karlos as the door slammed shut behind us, iron clanging against iron. His breathing was shallow, each inhale a struggle.

"Karlos," I whispered, easing him to sit against the wall. His skin was clammy and far too pale. The mark on his arm, once bright with Destiny, looked weak and faded around the edges. Panic clawed at my chest. "What's happening to you? Why isn't your Destiny helping?"

His eyes fluttered open, focusing on me with effort. "It's…not your fault, Clara," he managed. "We'll…find a way out of this."

I reached out, fumbling in the dimness until I found his hand. It was cold. I twined my fingers with his and squeezed, trying to give him something—warmth, strength, anything.

Time blurred. Minutes—or hours—bled together in the dark. My legs cramped from sitting on the unforgiving stone, but I didn't move. The cell was damp and bitterly cold, the air thick with the scent of mold and old blood. Drops of water echoed somewhere in the distance, a slow, maddening rhythm.

My mind kept circling back to the audience hall. To Franes's eyes. The hatred in them. Not just for Arisen or Destiny, but for *everyone* who wasn't Pagostonian, and perhaps even for those who were.

I drew my knees to my chest and pressed my forehead against them, trying to keep my breathing steady. We were trapped. I had no parestine to contact Eliza. The Destiny link with Arisen felt…wrong. Muted.

I reached for him anyway.

"Arisen?"

Nothing.

Just an empty, cold stretch of silence where his presence should have been.

I pushed harder, focusing on the bond, on the thread I'd felt again and again from Pitores to Polent. This time, the thread felt thin and distant, like a frayed string lost in a storm.

No voice. No warmth. Just the oppressive weight of the stone around us.

I clenched my fists, nails biting into my palms. I couldn't break here. Not in this cell. Not in front of Karlos.

I thought of Kent's tired smile. Of Hale's laughter as she played with her carved wooden basilisk. Of Eliza's stubborn determination. Of Victor and Matry and Kito.

Of Llorent, standing at the head of his table, promising us support. Of how his eyes softened when he looked at me, as if I were worth standing beside.

CHAPTER 36

From Clara's Diary

I started counting the meals they slid to us to track the days. According to my account, we had been here for three days. They slid a bowl of porridge for us to share, and I left almost all of it for Karlos. He was getting worse. He barely moved from his cot, but still had enough strength to eat. He needed it more than I did.

Karlos stirred on his cot, his eyes half-open. He blinked slowly, looking up at me as I knelt beside him. There were moments when he seemed lucid, aware of where we were—this was one of those rare times.

"Clara."

"I'm here," I replied softly, taking his hand. His skin felt cold beneath my palm.

He gave me a faint smile, though the effort seemed almost too much.

"I keep thinking about Frederick," he said, his eyes distant, his voice trembling. "I wonder what my little boy is doing."

I nodded, squeezing his hand gently. Frederick wasn't a child anymore; he was a grown man, perhaps as old as I am, but Karlos seemed lost in his memories. "You'll see him again," I assured him, though my heart ached at how fragile he seemed.

Karlos's gaze shifted to meet mine, his clouded eyes momentarily clearing. "He's good with dragons, you know," he said softly. "He was always running in the Hertm Mountains ever since he was a child. I can still see him coming down from the hills, his hair full of snow, but his eyes were always clear."

He paused, a faint smile tugging at his lips.

"He has my eyes; did you know that?"

I leaned in slightly, studying Karlos's eyes. They were a deep, rich brown, but what caught my attention was the delicate ring of gold that encircled his irises. Despite his current condition, the faint glimmer of gold still held on.

A silence settled between us as I absorbed his words. His eyes drifted shut again, exhaustion overtaking him. But before he fell completely back into his haze, he murmured softly, "You'd like him, Clara. He has your kind of strength."

My throat tightened, but I forced myself to smile at him. "Then I can't wait to meet him."

He slipped back into a restless sleep, his breathing uneven. I stayed by his side, watching over him closely.

I spent the days in the dungeon lost in thought, my eyes often drifting to the small window high above. Through it, I could barely glimpse the open sky. The animals that sometimes passed brought small offerings. Sparrows, wrens, and once, even a butterfly. They couldn't carry much, but they tried. Pins. Needles. Once or twice, a bit of fruit. Their tiny efforts kept me going.

When I wasn't staring at that window, I was consumed by thoughts of Karlos, of all the ways I could help him if I only had the tools. I ran through every healing method I knew, every poultice I could have made, every herb that might ease his pain. But down here, with no supplies, no salves, no medicines, my knowledge as a healer felt useless.

On the third day, a crow arrived. Larger than the other birds, it brought something different: a small kitchen knife. I took it in my hands, the cold metal catching the faint light that filtered through the window. The blade was barely longer than my palm, and it wouldn't do much against a soldier in full armor. But it was something. I slipped it under my bra, the pressure of my chest keeping it hidden and secure. Even the smallest weapon gave me a sense of power I hadn't felt in days.

Now, on the fourth day, I looked over at Karlos. He lay on his cot, breathing shallowly, his body still fighting. The knife against my skin felt like my only chance, a slim, desperate chance to protect him, to protect both of us. My heart pounded as I listened, ears straining for any sound beyond the walls.

I heard it then, the creak of the door above us.

My breath caught. I swallowed hard, my hand instinctively tightening over the hidden knife.

Whatever happened next, I knew one thing with certainty: I had to protect Karlos. No matter what it took, I would not let them separate us without a fight.

It had to be noon... at least, that's what I guessed from the rays of sunlight illuminating one corner of our cell. I hated this part of the day, especially because it was when I could see our surroundings most clearly.

"Queen Franes requests your presence," one soldier said, peeking through the narrow crack of the door.

"Hurry up and get him moving," another guard barked, gesturing toward Karlos, who was still weak but managing to sit up.

I helped Karlos to his feet. The soldiers watched us closely but did not offer any help. We had no choice but to comply, so we moved quickly.

As we ascended the steep, narrow staircase, the moving torchlight dimly lit our path. Each step was worn smooth by countless feet over the centuries. The air carried the scent of mildew and feces from the dungeon below.

Karlos stirred and struggled with each step. I put my arm behind his back, helping him move. He leaned heavily on me as we exited the last few steps of the dungeon. The sudden shift from the dim, enclosed space to the bright, open corridor above us took a few minutes to get used to. I was disoriented, but I did not let any sign of it show.

Queen Franes sat on her throne, looking down at us. "You look worse than when I last saw you," she commented, her words dripping with sarcasm.

I held my ground, keeping Karlos close to me. "You requested our presence?" I said, keeping steady.

"An offering has been made. You are free to continue with your quest. I will aid you with two amphisbaenas. I hope this serves as a warning: Destined are not welcome in this country."

Her words took me by surprise. Who possessed enough power to convince this cruel woman to free us?

Then I felt him, the recognizable warmth, and from the corner of my eye, I saw him. My heart dropped to the floor again, and a knot formed in my throat. Arisen stood there, as always, hiding his emotions well.

The deep blue flecks in his golden eyes had darkened, his gaze sharp and unreadable as he surveyed the room, revealing nothing. His green hair was neatly pulled back, emphasizing the strong, angular lines of his face. He wore the embroidered robes of the Destined, the hilt of a sword visible at his belt. The only hint of his anger was the faint shadow along his jawline.

The golden crown with elvish ears rested on his brow and glinted in the torchlight, reminding this court of his position as Ebony's king. What had he bargained for? What had he done?

"Arisen?" I murmured, struggling to form a sentence. The shock of seeing him here left me nearly speechless, but the warmth emanating from my mark was answer enough.

He stepped forward, his expression obscure. "It's time to leave."

His gaze cataloged the bumps and scars covering parts of my body. One of his eyebrows arched slightly as he took in the state of my dirty clothes, which hung loosely from me due to the lack of food.

Still leaning heavily on me, Karlos tried to stand straighter, but his feet trembled under the effort. Sensing the power shift, the guards reluctantly released their hold on us, stepping back to allow Arisen to take control.

Queen Franes watched us from her throne. "Do not think this changes anything," she warned, her voice cold. "Ebonians cannot enter Pagos."

"We understand. Thank you for your… assistance."

With those words, he took three long strides toward us, his boots echoing loudly in the silent hall. The room was utterly still, every gaze fixed on him. Even the guards held their breath as Arisen reached Karlos and grabbed him by the shoulder to help him move. As Arisen adjusted his grip, the stench of soiled clothes wafted around us. Karlos had lost control, and it was painfully clear he was at the end of his strength.

Arisen, however, didn't react. His face remained still, his focus only on keeping Karlos upright.

The castle's heavy iron doors groaned open, and Arisen immediately took charge of Karlos, carefully supporting him. At times, when Karlos's legs gave out entirely, Arisen carried him. The courtyard stretched before us, dimly illuminated by the soft flicker of torchlight despite the hard daylight beyond the walls. Unlike before, it was eerily quiet; what I had witnessed just days ago was now a memory etched into my nerves.

Arisen's Destined cloak swayed slightly with each step, its folds catching the torchlight. His focus remained entirely on Karlos. Not once did he glance back at me, as though I were an afterthought in his calculated movements.

I stayed close behind them, my chest tightening as I watched Karlos lean heavily on Arisen. The desert heat hit us as we passed through the outer gates. My cracked lips stung as I mustered the courage to ask, "What did you do?"

Arisen's eyes flicked toward me briefly. "I did what had to be done. We have no time left. The other Destined are waiting for us inside the Gaul Forest."

As he spoke, he removed the crown from his head, as if it had grown too heavy to bear, and tucked it carefully into the pack slung over his shoulder.

What did he mean by that? I wasn't sure, but I wanted to know what he had bargained with Queen Franes for our release. Even so, there was no denying the urgency in his voice, the thin veneer of control barely containing the gravity of the situation.

We continued down a narrow, uneven path riddled with potholes. The low, guttural roars and hisses of the amphisbaenas reached us before the creatures came into view, and my heart began to race as the ground beneath my feet trembled with their presence.

When we rounded the final corner, I froze. Their massive forms radiated raw power, each scale gleaming like polished armor in the low light. Four heads twisted and snapped in different directions, forked tongues flicking as they tasted the air. Their eyes, piercing and impossibly bright, seemed to lock onto me.

The first creature hissed, its heads snapping toward me. My breath caught as I realized I had to face and connect with them. We had all sacrificed so much for this moment. My palms grew clammy, and I wiped them against my worn clothes, steeling myself for what was to come.

Arisen's voice cut through my rising fear. "You can do this."

I stepped forward, my marked hand faintly glowing. With its twin heads, the smaller amphisbaena watched me warily, its massive body moving restlessly. I extended my hand, palm outward, feeling the pull of Destiny. As I reached out, the first head lunged, stopping inches from my face. Its warm breath, heavy with musk and raw earth, washed over me. My body trembled, but I refused to move.

At first, the connection was faint, like a whisper in the back of my mind. The creature's wariness acted as a barrier I had to break down. I closed my eyes and focused, projecting calm and trust with every ounce of my being. The warmth of my mark grew stronger, and I sensed the bond beginning to form.

The second head was less cooperative, its hisses growing louder as it twisted away. I clenched my teeth, pouring all my remaining energy into the connection. My vision blurred from exhaustion, and my knees threatened to give out, but I couldn't afford to falter.

Then, a surge of power rushed through me. Arisen's voice echoed in the bond: *"Breathe, Clara."* I took a deep breath, exhaled slowly, and tried again. In. Out. In. Out.

The first head nudged my hand, its scales rasping beneath my fingers. Encouraged, I reached for the second and repeated the motion. It hesitated, then slowly leaned into my touch. The bond took root. Relief surged through me, but I knew the hardest part still waited.

The larger amphisbaena loomed nearby, its twin heads snapping at one another in constant agitation. I approached carefully, wary of their combined power. These two were different, stronger, more volatile. My body ached, every limb begging for rest, but I forced myself forward.

The third head lunged without warning, stopping just short of my mark. Its forked tongue flicked out, tasting the magic pulsing from my palm. Heat flared along my arm. I focused on the connection, steadying my breath, willing calm into the space between us. Slowly, the head lowered. The aggression ebbed, shifting into curiosity.

Then came the fourth.

It was the most resistant, its eyes burning with defiance. A piercing squeal tore from its throat, loud enough to echo down the corridor and, for a heartbeat, I was sure it carried all the way back to the city. It thrashed wildly, refusing to yield, each violent jerk a test of my will and my control.

Sweat dripped down my forehead as I poured everything I had left into the bond. My vision blurred, darkening at the edges, but I didn't back down.

Finally, the last head stilled. Its eyes met mine, no longer defiant, but watchful and accepting. The bond clicked into place.

Relief swept through me, and I dropped to my knees, trembling with exhaustion. The amphisbaenas began to circle slowly around me, their movements synchronized now, their connection to me sealed.

When I looked up, Arisen stood a few paces away, watching in silence. He stepped forward and offered his hand.

"You did it," he said, pulling me gently to my feet.

Though weak, Karlos managed a small smile. Arisen assisted him, gripping his arm firmly to help him stand. Together, they approached the smallest of the amphisbaenas, its twin heads watching them intently. Karlos's breath came in shallow gasps, his fingers trembling as he clung to King Arisen for support.

Arisen guided Karlos to the creature's side and helped him mount. The amphisbaena shifted slightly, adjusting to the new weight on its back. Karlos winced but settled into the saddle. The creature's heads turned to look at him, and I sensed through the bond that it understood the urgency of the task ahead.

Satisfied, Arisen stepped back, his eyes scanning Karlos's face for any sign of strain.

"He needs to ride this one," he said, nodding toward the smaller amphisbaena. "It's the fastest. It'll get him to the Gaul Forest a full day ahead of us. The forest's magic will heal him."

I nodded and stepped toward the creature, reaching out to strengthen the bond. Its twin heads dipped low in silent acknowledgment, a shared understanding passing between us. I rested my hand on its scaled body, willing every ounce of magic I had into one simple request.

"Please," I whispered. "Protect him."

With a powerful stretch, the amphisbaena unfurled its wings. Karlos glanced back at us, his pale face illuminated by the soft glow of the creature's aura. Then, with a few strong beats of its wings, the amphisbaena lifted into the sky, its twin heads stretched forward in unison. They rose quickly, becoming a silhouette against the darkening horizon.

A pang of longing tugged at my chest. I wanted to be with him.

When he finally vanished from sight, I turned my attention to the larger amphisbaena. Both of its heads shifted toward me, their intelligent, piercing eyes locking onto mine. I stepped forward carefully, extending a hand. The scales beneath my touch were rough and cool, but as I ran my fingers along the creature's body, I noticed patches of dried blood crusted between the ridges.

Their gazes didn't waver. They studied me, measured me, not with malice but with quiet judgment.

"They're ready," I said.

I climbed onto the front of the amphisbaena, settling into place as King Arisen mounted behind me. I felt the press of his legs on either side, his arms reaching around to grasp the reins resting lightly across my lap. The closeness was unexpected, not the same nearness that had once unsettled me. This felt different. Steadying. Familiar in a way I couldn't name.

As the creature rose into the air, I let out a slow breath. The desert fell away beneath us, the landscape reshaping into a maze of jagged cliffs and shadowed peaks. The terrain was harsh and unforgiving, a wild expanse that stretched on without end.

I turned my head slightly, my voice barely audible over the rush of wind. "What is all of this?"

Arisen shifted closer, his breath brushing against my ear as he spoke. "That, Clara, is what used to be the Gaul Forest before the war hundreds of years ago. Its magic once stretched to these lands, but it has shrunk to what remains today."

I gazed out at the miles of desolation, the charred remains of what was once a thriving forest. It was haunting, a reminder of the cost of greed and war. "We need to stop soon," Arisen said, his voice cutting through my thoughts. "Flying in this darkness is too dangerous."

I scanned the ground below, spotting a clearing amidst the burned landscape. "There," I pointed. "We can land there and set up camp for the night."

Arisen nodded, and I directed the amphisbaenas toward the clearing. The descent was smooth, the creatures landing with practiced ease. Once on the ground, they coiled their bodies, their heads resting on the scorched earth as though understanding our need for rest.

The fire crackled softly, its glow flickering across the darkened clearing. Warmth brushed against my skin, but it did nothing to thaw the chill between us. The only other movement came from the amphisbaena curled nearby, its twin heads watching us in eerie silence. Their rectangular pupils reflected the firelight, unblinking, unreadable.

I should have been afraid of it. But not anymore.

The stillness between us stretched, until finally, Arisen spoke.

"Not knowing how you were doing these past five days… I could not bear it, Clara. I need to know how you are…what you're doing."

I let out a dry laugh, still watching the creature.

"Interesting," I said, voice low. "Coming from someone who uses our link whenever it suits him."

I turned to him, raising a brow.

"You decide when to answer, when to invade my thoughts, and when to leave me in silence. That silence? It wasn't my choice. But you… You've made that choice more than once. I can feel you in my mind, Arisen. I know when you're there."

His jaw tightened.

"You wouldn't understand."

I tilted my head, holding his gaze.

"Try me."

He stood abruptly, crossing the clearing in sharp, restless strides.

I didn't move. I only watched him.

"See?" I said, after a beat. "You're doing it again."

He froze mid-step. Then, with a swift turn, he faced me. His cape flared around him like a shadow, the firelight sharpening the lines of tension in his face. A quiet war raged behind his eyes.

"Clara," he said, his voice rough and strained, "I can't do both."

I frowned.

"Do both?"

He stepped closer.

"I can't lead a kingdom when you're in the room. When you're near, I can't think of anything else."

My breath caught.

I searched his face, expecting that usual mask of detachment. But it was gone. In its place was raw honesty, bared and burning under the firelight.

He hesitated for a breath, then exhaled and ran a hand through his green hair. When he looked at me again, something in him had shifted. The gold mark on his neck pulsed softly.

"I need you to understand," he said. "If I ever go silent, it's not because I've chosen to ignore you. Not unless answering would cost you your life."

I blinked.

"What?"

"If staying quiet keeps you safe, if answering would put you at risk, then I'll choose silence. But otherwise…" His eyes held mine, steady and unflinching. "You will always get an answer."

His gaze softened, just slightly.

"You asked why I can't focus when you're around." He paused. "Do you really not know?"

My heart pounded.

"I do," I whispered.

A humorless chuckle escaped him, and he shook his head.

"It's because I feel you, Clara. Every thought. Every feeling. Whether I want to or not."

He tapped his temple.

"You're always here."

Then he placed a hand over his chest.

"And here."

I stared at him, stunned.

For the first time, I wondered if I had misjudged him, if the man I thought I knew was only a fragment of who he really was.

Behind us, the amphisbaena shifted in the dirt, its coils stirring, but neither of us looked away.

Arisen let out a breath, as though those words had cost him more than he wanted to admit. Then, without a word, he picked up the only blanket we had and handed it to me.

I took it silently, eyes still on him.

He hesitated for a moment, then turned and lay down a few feet away, his back to me.

And just as exhaustion began to pull me under, I thought I heard him whisper, so softly it could have been the wind.

"You are my Destiny, Clara."

The words clung to me as sleep took hold, settling somewhere between dream and truth, and refusing to let go.

CHAPTER 37

The night had been cold, and I woke to find my head nestled against Arisen's chest, his arm draped loosely around the back of my neck. His cloak had fallen open, exposing the smooth, bare skin of his chest, where my cheek had rested.

His other hand lay gently on my shoulder, fingers splayed as if to shield me from the chill. The intimacy of the position sent a jolt through me, and my heart pounded as I registered the firmness of his muscles against me. His slightly tousled green hair framed his face, softening his usually sharp features. For the first time, he looked relaxed.

I quickly moved away, my cheeks burning with embarrassment. As I disentangled myself, his arm slid away slowly and almost reluctantly. A slight crease formed on his forehead, and his eyes fluttered open. His confusion gave way to understanding as he realized our proximity.

"I'm sorry," I murmured, heat rushing to my cheeks.

He nodded silently and gathered his belongings. I focused on my own packing, hands trembling slightly as I stuffed my things together. To my relief, I found my parestine at the bottom of my bag. I pulled it out and shook it open.

Kent's notes were reassuring. Polent was unchanged, and he remained blissfully unaware of what had happened to me. I meant to keep it that way.

Marcos's updates confirmed he had met with Eliza and begun preparations for the evacuation. I urged him to move immediately. It was better to act now than regret waiting.

Eliza's messages burned with fury. She had made it to the Gaul Forest and was livid when she learned of my imprisonment. Her anger spilled through every line.

Karlos's message, though, brought a smile to my face. He had reached the forest and was already recovering. The closeness of its magic had strengthened him.

Llorent's words were reassuring. He believed in me, and that belief lit a quiet determination inside my chest. A smile tugged at my lips as I read, letting his confidence lift me.

Lastly, there was Arisen. His messages were short, precise, and to the point. His decision to come himself said more than any letter could. He had been eager to reach Pagos, and he had strongly urged me to stay with Margo Lear.

While Arisen finished packing and securing his gear to the amphisbaena, I took a few minutes to respond. "I've informed everyone of our progress," I said, looking up at him. "Hopefully, they read it soon and know we're on our way."

"Good," he replied curtly. "We need to keep moving. The Gaul Forest is still a day's journey from here."

The crisp morning air bit at my cheeks as we mounted the creature. I was eager to leave this desolate place behind.

"We need to be cautious," Arisen warned as the amphisbaena took flight. "The terrain will become treacherous the closer we get."

I nodded, feeling the bond with the amphisbaena strengthen as its wings beat powerfully against the air. The wind rushed past us, carrying the foul stench of charred earth. Arisen rode behind me, our occasional eye contact wordless.

"We're getting closer," he said, his voice breaking through the wind. "The forest is just beyond those mountains."

I squinted into the haze, barely making out the faint outline of greenery. As I urged the amphisbaena forward, my body ached from the hours of flight, but the promise of our destination pushed me on.

As we approached, there was a thin veil of mist, and the air shifted. I soon realized it wasn't mist at all, but water vapor rising from below. The temperature rose sharply, and the heat blasted into our skin like fire.

Arisen reacted first. "Higher!" he shouted, his voice sharp. "We need to fly higher!"

I pulled at the reins, urging the amphisbaena upward. Its wings beat harder, straining as we climbed.

The air grew suffocatingly hot, and each breath seared my lungs. Below us, fissures in the earth spewed thick clouds of steam, shimmering like molten waves. Sweat poured down my face, and my hands trembled on the reins as I fought to keep control. No wonder Pagos was so hot, with these these lands as its neighbor.

Finally, the temperature dropped as we ascended above the steam. Fresh, cool air filled my lungs, and I exhaled in relief. Looking back, I met Arisen's gaze. His face was flushed, but his nod of acknowledgment let me know he was okay.

"That came out of nowhere," I muttered.

"This land was damaged centuries ago. Magic takes time to heal."

The sun dipped lower, and in the distance, the Gaul Forest finally appeared. Lush greenery stretched endlessly, providing a vivid contrast to the barren landscape we had left behind. As we descended, the air cooled further, and the forest's magic wrapped around us like a welcoming embrace.

"Can you sense the others?" I asked, preparing to dismount.

"No."

I took a deep breath. Sensing my hesitation, Arisen moved closer. His hand found my waist as he guided me down.

With his help, I slid slowly off the amphisbaena's back. His grip lingered briefly before he stepped away. I nodded in thanks, trying to ignore the warmth his touch left behind.

The amphisbaena shifted, its twin heads turning to look at me. Running my hand along its cool scales, I felt the creature's power and intelligence. With a low hiss, it unfurled its wings and took off into the sky. Just before the bond severed, it sent a final warning through our connection: *Get out*.

I watched it vanish into the clouds, its message ringing in my mind.

CHAPTER 38

"**I**s everything all right?"

"I… I can't see or sense our group. Can you?"

"No. We need to find them."

I scanned the area again, trying to ground myself.

"They were supposed to meet us here," I said, my voice tight. "But there's nothing. I can't feel their presence at all."

Just then, my mark pulsed with a faint glow, and across from me, Arisen's answered in kind, flickering like a signal between us.

"The amphisbaena…" I murmured. "It warned us to get out."

Arisen's expression sharpened. He straightened, his eyes sweeping over the forest.

"A warning from it can't be ignored," he said, his voice low. "We could be in real danger. We have to move, now."

The seriousness in his tone snapped me into motion. I reached for my parestine and flipped it open, hoping for a message, anything, but the page remained blank. No updates. No reassurance. Only silence.

I stared at it for a heartbeat, willing words to appear. When nothing did, I let out a frustrated breath and slid it back into my pack. There was no time to dwell.

We needed to find the others quickly.

"We cannot continue waiting for their response. Let's make our way to the Urten Bridge. We'll sense them if they're nearby. We're too far from them right now, and our connection to Destiny is weak."

The Gaul Forest was disorienting. Its towering trees formed an unbroken canopy that allowed only slivers of sunlight to pierce through. Everything looked the same, making it easy to feel lost. I had seen countless illustrations and read extensively about this place, but the reality was far different. It was breathtakingly beautiful yet deeply unsettling.

As we ventured deeper, the forest's magic seemed to amplify my powers, unlocking an awareness I hadn't experienced before. I felt the presence of every life I had ever resurrected and each animal I had bonded with. The sensation was like a thousand threads pulling at me all at once.

I felt the amphisbaenas through our bond. Their vision showed me the scorched remains of the forest as they flew back to Pagos. They were fleeing the forest. I also sensed Kito back in Polent, his connection strong despite the loose blindfold that muted its sight. The creature was calm, its feral instincts subdued by the power of Destiny. I was glad to feel this bond, having developed such a strong connection to him.

The glow from our marks grew brighter as we moved further, lighting the path ahead. But the forest changed. The vibrant green of the trees gave way to decay, their leaves withered, their trunks stained a sickly dark brown.

I stopped to glance back at the lush greenery we had left behind. A clear contrast with the barren, lifeless trees ahead. Even the sky seemed to shift, taking on a gray, overcast hue reminiscent of Raster during rainstorms. Yet, here, the dry, cracked ground told the story of a land untouched by water for a long time.

Arisen and I moved cautiously, our shoulders brushing as we walked. Suddenly, he stopped and extended his arm, his hand brushing across my chest to halt me. His ears twitched slightly, a subtle sign of his heightened senses tuning into the faint rustling of leaves.

"There!" I whispered urgently, pointing toward a shadowy figure moving in the distance.

"I see them. Let's go."

We quickened our pace, adrenaline spiking as we closed the gap. The figure's erratic, jagged movements made it look as though it were convulsing. Something was wrong.

But then, as we drew closer, the movements stopped, and the figure came into focus.

It was Karlos.

He turned, his face lighting up with recognition. "Clara! Arisen! You made it!"

As we approached his side, my smile faded. Karlos looked pale, with faint black veins visible near his temples. He shivered, and his skin felt cold when I touched his arm. He had a sword tucked inside his coat, a new one he must have gotten while here.

I took his hand, worry seeping into my voice. "Karlos, are you all right? You looked like you were having a seizure, and you're freezing." My eyes lingered on the dark veins. "And these… what are they?"

He shook his head, attempting to wave off my concern. "It's nothing, Clara. Just the aftereffects of the journey," he said, his voice sounding louder than before.

I frowned, unconvinced. "Karlos, this doesn't seem like nothing."

He forced a smile. "I'll be fine. The moment I arrived, I could feel my Destiny strengthening me. It's already working."

I glanced at Arisen, catching the concern in his eyes. We didn't need words to share what we were both thinking. Still, I chose not to push—for now.

"Well, you do look better than before," I said, trying to reassure both of us.

Karlos nodded, smiling again. "Yes, just like you said. I feel much better now that we're all together."

"That's wonderful." I pulled him into a hug. Despite how cold his skin felt, I was simply relieved he was here…alive, with us.

I reached into my pack and pulled out a Destined coat. "I brought an extra."

"Thank you," he said, accepting it with a small nod.

Arisen stepped forward, eyes studying Karlos closely. He extended a hand.

"I'm glad to see you're all right."

Karlos shook it. "Thank you."

"Where's everyone else?" I asked.

"They're setting up camp nearby," Karlos replied. "I left to find you both. Come on, I'll lead the way."

He turned toward a narrow dirt path. I exchanged one last glance with Arisen before following. The worry in his expression mirrored my own.

Footprints dotted the trail—fresh, headed in the same direction. And yet… the silence around us was unsettling. No birds, no rustling of small animals. Just stillness. It was as if one of my senses had gone missing.

"Karlos, I can't tell you how relieved I am to see you. How are the others?"

"They're fine," he said. "Eager to see you."

I slipped my arm around his, grounding myself in his presence. We had been through so much together, and I loved him deeply as a friend.

"Have the others found any reason for the magic's deterioration?"

"No."

Just one word, and still, it was frustrating.

"Once this is over, we should visit our families," I said gently. "I'll go to Polent, and you can see your son in Hertm."

Karlos didn't respond. He kept walking, his expression distant. I studied him for a moment.

"Are you okay?"

"Yes, of course," he said after a beat. "I just miss Devon. And Hertm."

Before I could say more, Arisen caught up with us.

"Let's set up camp here," he said.

I hesitated. I didn't want to stop. The amphisbaena had warned us to leave, and yet we were venturing deeper into the forest's shadows.

"We're very close, Your Majesty," Karlos said quietly.

"We'll camp here," Arisen repeated, his tone firmer this time.

I looked around. The clearing was small, enclosed by dense under-brush and overshadowed by twisted, decaying branches. The ground was uneven, scattered with moss and brittle limbs. It didn't feel safe.

Karlos looked uneasy too, but he said nothing.

Arisen began unpacking, and I joined him.

"Keep the fire small," he said under his breath. "We don't want to draw attention."

I nodded and gathered a few dry twigs. The fire came to life quickly, its glow a welcome relief against the encroaching chill.

We sat close together, the flames flickering across our faces. The faint glow of our marks lit the space between us.

"Do you think we'll find the others soon?" I asked, breaking the silence.

"We will," Karlos replied with quiet certainty.

I nodded, clinging to that hope. He leaned against me, clearly exhausted. I wrapped an arm around him, offering what little comfort I could.

Night settled in, deep and suffocating.

Arisen stood and moved a few steps away, never taking his eyes off the clearing. When Karlos's breathing evened out and sleep claimed him fully, I rose and went to Arisen's side. He was watching closely, intently, the kind of focus that made the hairs on my arms lift.

"What is it?" I asked.

He didn't look at me when he answered.

"Clara... that's not Karlos."

CHAPTER 39

From Clara's Diary

"Clara, do you remember Karlos's son's name?"

I looked at him, puzzled. "He said it's Devon," I replied. And in that moment, I realized it was Frederick, not Devon.

"Perhaps he misspoke," I whispered defensively. "He has gone through a lot."

"Perhaps, but would you ever forget or confuse Hale's name?"

No. There was no way. Never.

"That is not my only concern. He has never called me 'Your Majesty.' I broke that tradition centuries ago; I am no one's master."

"That is an easy mistake to make," I said defensively. But something in me told me he was right. I had not sensed Karlos's Destiny in my mark, but I refused to believe that it was not him. Karlos was my friend;

that had to be him.

Arisen fell silent, his eyes locked on mine.

I turned to check Karlos, but the spot was empty.

Panicked, I scanned the area. The forest was silent, the only sound the crackling of the low fire. "Where did he go?"

Suddenly, a sound broke the silence, a low, guttural growl. We froze, our eyes scanning the surroundings for the source of the noise. I made out a shadowy figure moving toward us in the dim light.

"Stay close," Arisen whispered, his hand moving to the hilt of his sword.

The figure stepped into the light, revealing its twisted form. It was Karlos, but his eyes glowed green, and his movements were jerky and unnatural.

"Karlos?" I called out tentatively.

The figure snarled, its voice a twisted mockery of Karlos's. "Karlos is no more. I am a creation of the Queen of Dark Magic who rules this forest."

Arisen stepped forward, his sword drawn. "What do you want?"

The creature suddenly turned its head to make eye contact with Arisen. It laughed—the sound crackled, sending a chill through my bones. "I want what you seek to save—to destroy Destiny and subjugate the elves and humans under a new ruler."

"Where is Karlos?"

My question made the creature burst into a shrill laugh. He snapped its head toward me and quickly approached with large, quick steps. He was so close I could feel his breath on my face.

"You foolish human girl, we became this because of people like you. I was a human just like you, but now we are much more powerful than any human or elf and certainly any Destined," he snarled, the black gums in his mouth shining through his wicked smile.

"You did not respond to my question. Where is Karlos?"

"He made it to the Gaul Forest half-dead; did you think he was going to survive? He was almost back to being his old human self by the time he arrived here. Destiny left him. He was so weak, drinking his blood was easy."

My heart dropped. I looked over at Arisen, who had tightened his grip on the sword he held.

This creature had to be lying. My friend was not dead. There was no way. I refused to believe so.

At that moment, the creature lunged at Arisen, moving so fast that I instantly lost sight of it. Arisen managed to block its attack, and the clash of steel echoed through the space. I watched in horror as the scene unfolded almost too quickly for my eyes to follow.

The creature twisted, its grotesque face turning toward me even as it battled Arisen. "We have wagers on who will take over your body first," it snarled, grinning wickedly as it pressed its sword to Arisen's neck. Its eyes met mine, and it smiled, a dark, twisted expression revealing its black gums. "You look as easy, if not easier than Karlos was. His screams of pain were the best part of it all. Who knew a Destined could howl like that?"

Fear flooded me, and I felt my body betray me. Warmth spread down my leg, and I knew I had lost all control. I was paralyzed by terror, unable to move or even speak.

"But don't worry, Clara," the creature hissed, its voice dripping with malice. "You are being saved for our Queen." It released Arisen for a moment, stepping toward me with its grotesque form. Arisen swung at it, but it dodged and hovered closer until I smelled its rancid breath on my face. "However, you, King Arisen, will die by my hands," it finished, placing its cold, clawed hands on my cheeks.

The chill from its touch spread through me like ice. The creature's eyes stared into mine, and I felt a tear escape my eye. My heart clenched painfully as I realized to whom those eyes belonged. Those were Karlos's eyes. The eyes of my friend, the man who had been my ally and my companion through our darkest days. The man who had comforted me when we were prisoners together. The man I had grown to love.

"Karlos…" I whispered, my voice breaking as more tears followed, sliding down my cheeks.

The creature sneered at my vulnerability, its blackened gums parting in a vile grin. But suddenly, its eyes widened in shock, and the green light dimmed. Its mouth fell open, and a ragged, strangled sound escaped its lips. It stared at me with such hatred that I didn't immediately understand what had happened.

The tip of a sword was suddenly visible, protruding from the creature's chest, the cold steel grazing my own chest. I barely had time to react before the beast let out a final, guttural scream, its twisted form convulsing violently. A tremor ran through my body as I watched its mouth gape open, black murk oozing from between its teeth, staining its lips and pooling at its throat.

Then, with a heavy, final shudder, it collapsed at my feet.

For a second, all I could hear was the pounding of my heart. The world around me blurred, every sound distant and distorted, like I was under the pouring rain of Raster.

"Karlos."

I fell to my knees beside him, my hands trembling as I reached out. His body was unnaturally still. The gash across his side was deep, and his clothes were soaked with blood. But it wasn't just the wound that troubled me; it was the emptiness. His body was just a shell.

"No," I whispered, my voice breaking. "No, no, no, Karlos, stay with me."

I pressed my hands firmly over his chest, willing my Destiny to rise. My vision blurred as I fought to summon it, to find that golden thread of power that could stitch life back together. My breath came in frantic bursts, my fingers curling into his tunic as if holding him here by sheer willpower alone.

Nothing.

The air around me was silent, empty of the familiar hum of magic.

I closed my eyes, reaching deep within myself, searching for anything—any flicker of light, any thread of Destiny that I could grasp and pull forward.

I found only darkness.

A sob wrenched from my chest. "Come on, Karlos. Please."

I tilted his face toward me, my tears dripping onto his blood-streaked skin. "I can do this," I whispered against his forehead, my fingers gripping his shoulders. "Just hold on. Just—"

A hand rested gently on my shoulder.

I flinched at the touch, but I didn't look away from Karlos.

"Clara," Arisen said softly.

"No," I snapped, shaking him off. "I can bring him back!" My voice cracked, raw with desperation. I pressed harder against Karlos's chest, channeling every ounce of energy I had, forcing it toward him like I could shove life back into his body.

Nothing.

No warmth, no spark, no breath.

Arisen crouched beside me. "Bringing back a human is not in your Destiny. That is the kind of magic we cannot wield."

"Who says we can't?" My voice rose with a feverish desperation. "I won't let him die! I won't—"

Arisen's grip on my shoulder tightened. "Clara."

I shook my head wildly, gasping as if I could steal breath for him, give it back. My hands hovered above his heart, shaking violently. "I won't lose him," I whispered.

Arisen's gaze softened, but his hold remained firm. "You have to let go."

I let out a choked sob.

"I can't," I admitted brokenly. "He was my friend. He was…" My throat tightened around the words.

"I know. But holding onto the impossible will only cause you more pain."

I wanted to scream. To fight. To tear apart the world until I found a way to fix this. But there was no fixing it.

Karlos was gone.

I leaned forward, my forehead pressing against his, and let the sobs come. "I'm so sorry," I whispered. "I promise I'll visit your son in Hertm. I'll tell him everything about you."

Arisen helped me to my feet, steadying me. My fingers curled into fists at my sides, my nails biting into my palms.

"We need to keep moving. I'm worried about the others."

I wiped at my tear-streaked face, forcing myself to swallow the grief clawing at my throat. My hands still tingled with the remnants of magic, with the failure of what I could not change.

I nodded, my heart heavy with grief. I wished there was something in this damned forest I could use to cover him—maybe a flower or something to symbolize his burial. But as I looked around, there were only rotten, dead trees. I took the Destined coat I had given him earlier and covered his face with it. At least, this recognized him for what he was.

With one last look at his body, I turned away.

"What… what was that?" I asked between sobs.

Whatever it was, it was neither a human nor an elf. This explained why I haven't been able to sense anything in this forest. This creature is unfamiliar to me.

If Arisen, whose first Destiny was all the knowledge of the Gaul Forest, did not know what this creature was… we were in trouble.

A shiver ran down my arms as Karlos's words echoed in my mind. *The Queen of Dark Magic.*

If this thing—this nightmare—was her doing, then we weren't just dealing with an unknown creature. We were confronting something born from the darkest, most corrupt magic the world had ever witnessed. And worse, it meant she had the power to create more like it.

I took a deep breath, the first in the past few hours. I was so mad at myself, so angry at my lack of response when it first attacked. I was paralyzed with fear, and it almost cost me my life and my Destiny. I would not let myself feel so powerless again.

I would not need saving. Never again.

I changed into a clean set of dark leather pants and a red shirt before heading deeper into the forest.

CHAPTER 40

From Clara's Diary

The sun filtered through the canopy of the destroyed forest, its rays revealing the devastation around us. Trees were snapped, roots ripped from the ground, soil scorched. Whatever overtook Karlos couldn't have caused this alone. This level of destruction indicated an organized force.

"I agree with you."

I turned to Arisen, startled. We were walking side by side, but I hadn't said anything aloud.

"Our Destiny link has been fully restored," he said, a small smirk playing on his lips.

Despite everything, I smiled. Hearing his voice in my thoughts was reassuring. A sign, maybe, that our magic was finally aligning.

"Let's communicate this way," he added. *"No sound. I'm not convinced we're alone. We may be watched."*

I nodded, falling into step beside him as we moved forward. Each step sank into the uneven dirt beneath my boots. Through the dead trees and dense fog, a familiar shape began to emerge: the Urten Bridge.

We paused at its edge. Even shrouded in mist, it loomed, enormous and surreal. The metal beams caught the light in places, and the decorative patterns, swirls of leaves, flowers, and carved woodland creatures, seemed to whisper of a forest that once thrived. Now it stood like a tombstone for everything that had been lost.

"I sense the others. Do you?"

Warmth bloomed through my chest in answer. Confirmation.

"Yes," I answered silently, meeting his eyes.

As we drew closer, the details of the bridge became clearer. Vines and moss wrapped around its frame, blocking walkways and sneaking into joints. It was overgrown and too dense for Arisen's blade alone to cut through.

At the base of the bridge, evidence of recent movement caught my eye: broken branches, scattered belongings, disturbed earth. I bent down, heart sinking, and picked up a wrinkled, dirt-streaked coat.

"This is Eliza's."

"Leave it," Arisen said, voice low. *"They're close."*

I hesitated but obeyed, placing the coat gently back where I found it.

Fog thickened as we stepped onto the bridge. The wind howled through the steelwork, and the structure groaned under its own weight, as if warning us back. The damp air clung to my skin, and unease rooted itself in my gut.

"Something feels wrong," I whispered through the link.

"Stay close. Whatever is here—it's looking for us."

He slipped an arm around my waist just as a shadow broke through the mist.

My pulse spiked.

Then another. And another.

Figures emerged, silent and deliberate. The scent of rot and decay followed them, thick and suffocating. Their numbers grew until they surrounded us.

"Prepare yourself," Arisen said tightly. *"These are not the Destined."*

I froze as the first creature stepped into view. It bore only the faintest resemblance to a person. Pale skin, black veins, elongated claws that scraped the ground as it moved. Its eyes glowed an unnatural green. It was twisted, hollowed out, barely human.

Five creatures came into focus, draped in tattered tunics. Four wore shades of gray and blue, but the one in the center wore white. Its matted hair clung to its face. When it spoke, its voice rasped like shattered glass.

"It is you, Clara."

I went still. It knew my name.

Arisen tensed beside me, every muscle locked. His grip on his sword turned his knuckles white.

"I must say," the white-cloaked creature drawled, stepping forward, "I didn't expect you to make it this far. You weren't supposed to."

A laugh rippled through the others, jagged and metallic, cruel.

"You really thought your Destiny was fate?" it hissed. "That the Gaul Forest simply chose you? No, Clara. It was never fate. It was design. My design."

Arisen's voice cut through the tension. "What are you saying?"

The creature laughed again. "Oh, Destined King. So clueless. Neither of you were chosen by the forest. I chose you. I bent the forest's magic to my will."

My stomach twisted.

"That's impossible," I breathed.

"Is it?" It smiled. "The forest's magic can be twisted, repurposed. I made you Destined not to help you succeed, but to ensure your failure. With you both gone, the balance would collapse. Your death is my freedom."

Arisen stepped forward, rage boiling in his eyes. "You don't need Clara. Take me instead."

The creature grinned. "That's the tragedy. This dark version of Destiny should have destroyed you. It should have hollowed you both. But you survived, and that was never the plan."

I thought back to the night I was chosen, to the pain, the overwhelming heat, the feeling that something inside me had been torn apart. Now I understood.

"Why me?" I asked. "Why go to such lengths?"

Its expression darkened. "Because of your love for Kent and Hale."

My blood ran cold.

It knew their names.

A roar of anger surged through me. I stepped forward, fists clenched.

"Say their names again, and I will rip the words from your throat."

The creature only laughed. "Such fire. We'll see how long it lasts."

Arisen stepped closer, his sword halfway drawn.

"What are you?" he growled.

The leader's smile twisted. "We were the forgotten. The discarded. Humans who grew tired of waiting for change. So we took it. The magic of Destiny will no longer be hoarded. It will be ours."

My breath caught.

They were once human.

"And what do you want from us?" Arisen asked, voice sharp.

"The final piece. The spark of magic still bound to you. Once we take it, we can leave the forest—and conquer the rest."

"You'll never get it," I said.

"Oh, but we already have some of it." Another figure stepped forward, eyes gleaming. "Karlos was screaming Frederick's name when Iones ripped the power from him."

I staggered back, horror sweeping through me.

"He was a good experiment," another creature sneered. "Sorry for your loss."

My anger surged. I lifted my chin, voice steady.

"Thank you for naming the creature we killed. Iones is dead. And the rest of you? You're next."

The smug look on the leader's face faltered.

They hadn't known.

It struck without warning. A kick to the legs knocked me to the ground. Pain flared up my spine.

The leader crouched beside me, sneering. "This is how I like you—on your knees. Get used to it. You'll be begging for mercy soon."

It spat black sludge across my face, and I screamed. The acid-like burn seared my skin.

Arisen moved to strike, but another creature tackled him, pinning him down.

"Shut up, both of you," it growled. "I'll enjoy carving that mark off your neck, Destined King."

Rough ropes yanked our wrists behind our backs. Arisen's sword was ripped from him, my bag torn away.

The leader leaned in, voice low.

"Don't worry. Your group is still alive… barely."

CHAPTER 41

From Clara's Diary

We were led through the forest along an unfamiliar path, following the river's edge. The murky water flowed sluggishly, revealing dead fish drifting just beneath the surface.

It was hard to focus with the creatures surrounding us, especially with their eyes locked onto us.

The group was so large that we had to stop multiple times. On this stop, the creatures halted to feed. I stayed close to Arisen as we watched them descend to the riverbank.

They stood motionless as fish swam around their feet. Then, in a single quick motion, one plunged its hand into the water, grabbing a flailing fish. With a swipe of its long, jagged nails, it sliced into the fish's side and drank deeply from the wound. When it finished, it tossed the lifeless body back into the water, letting it drift among the others.

"*What was that?*" I asked.

"*They feed on blood. They drain their prey entirely, leaving behind a corpse filled with that black poison.*"

The smell of decay was disgusting, embedded in their clothes and their very skin. And these were the beings who had twisted the magic of the Gaul Forest—who had *made us Destined.*

"*Do not let them touch you with their nails. They're poisonous.*"

I swallowed hard and nodded, forcing myself to remain calm as we were pushed forward once more. We moved too quickly for me to form a meaningful bond with the animals we passed, but even so, aside from the fish and the occasional squirrel, there were no creatures near us.

"*We are in the Gaul Forest,*" Arisen reminded me. "*Let the creatures find you—they will seek you out soon enough.*"

I only hoped one of them could tell me where the other Destined were.

Just as I finished that thought, one of the creatures walking beside me shoved me. I staggered forward and crashed onto the jagged rocks below.

"I want to see you crawl to your deathbed," it sneered. "We're almost there, Destined."

A sharp cry escaped me as pain shot through my knees. Warm blood trickled down my legs.

Instantly, I was surrounded. At least thirty of them loomed over me, their glowing green eyes sharpening. The way they inched closer sent a pulse of alarm through me. I tried to push myself up, but pain flared through my legs, keeping me pinned to the ground.

Then, Arisen was there. He dropped to one knee beside me, his tied hands useless, yet still managing to drive his elbow into the closest creature's face. It stumbled back with a hiss, dark mucus dripping from its nose.

The creatures snarled and shoved each other. A fight was about to start. And *we* were their prey.

"Enough!" The leader in white stepped forward, glaring at the others. The moment it spoke, the others fell silent, though their eyes remained on us with seething hatred.

"You are all brutes. Now she must be carried. You *idiots* nearly broke her leg."

There was no true concern in its voice, only the need for control. A twisted form of mercy.

It turned, pointing at Arisen. "Untie him. He will carry her. I don't trust any of you in this state."

One of the creatures approached, slicing through Arisen's bindings with a sharp nail. "We'll be watching you," it growled.

I lay curled on the ground, my arms wrapped around my bloodied knees, trying to keep my breathing controlled.

Arisen flexed his bruised wrists briefly before moving toward me. He knelt, his voice soft in my mind. "*I have you.*"

He slipped his arms beneath my knees and around my back, lifting me effortlessly.

I wrapped my arms around his neck as we resumed the journey. The creatures' eyes never left us, their low, raspy breathing filling the silence. Even the stench of decay seemed stronger now, clinging to my hair and my skin.

"*The others are near.*"

I felt it before Arisen even confirmed it—*the mark on my arm burned where it pressed against his skin.*

We reached the crest of a hill, and the leader turned, pointing ahead with one clawed finger.

"There," it hissed. "The others are just beyond that hill."

I squinted through the dense mist. A faint glow shimmered in the distance.

Arisen carried me forward, and as we descended the hill, I saw them.

A large clearing stretched before us, lined with thick, ancient tree trunks. The ground was uneven, covered in patches of mud and trampled grass, evidence of frequent movement. Rough-looking tents, hastily assembled from mismatched fabrics and weathered tarps, were scattered throughout the space, their edges frayed and sagging as if they had been standing for far too long. Smoke curled lazily from makeshift fire pits, mixing with the dense fog that clung to the air, making it hard to tell where the clearing ended and the darkness of the forest began.

The other Destined were there, bound and kneeling in the dirt, their figures barely visible through the shifting fog. Surrounding them were more of the creatures, their gaunt figures and glowing eyes peering out from the shadows of the trees. They did not move, did not speak. They only watched—waiting.

"You will join the others," the leader declared coldly. "But know this. You are all destined for death. There is no escape from this forest."

Eliza was the first to react. Her face was pale and drawn, but the instant she saw us, relief broke through her exhaustion.

"Clara! King Arisen! You're alive!"

My throat tightened. "We're here."

We were shoved toward the others, where they sat tied to thick trees. Rough hands yanked my arms back, binding my wrists, and they lashed Arisen to the trunk beside me. I searched their faces: Eliza, Rogers, Matry, Reato. My heart sank when I realized someone was missing.

"Where is Victor?"

The Destined exchanged uneasy glances before Rogers finally answered. "He… he was being disruptive. They tied him inside a tent alone."

Before I could react, the leader of the creatures stepped forward, a cruel, grating laugh ripping from its throat.

"What a sight," it sneered. "Six Destined, bound before me, six Destined who will die. With your deaths, any hope of unity between humans and elves will crumble. Your existence means nothing, except for the power you carry."

Its words dripped with venom, and the surrounding creatures hissed in agreement. Jagged nails scraped against the earth in a slow, deliberate rhythm that made my skin crawl.

Rogers lifted his chin. "A sanguivora will never win this war."

The leader's grin widened, satisfaction flashing in its glowing eyes.

"We are closer than you think. You speak with confidence for someone bound, starved, weakened. A mere human whose Destiny will fade into dust by nightfall."

It raised a clawed finger and pointed directly at me.

"And you still don't understand, do you?" it purred, savoring every syllable. "Destiny isn't sacred. It's magic. And like all magic, it can be bent, reshaped. It relies on balance, a balance we intend to break."

The creature's voice lowered into something more personal, more ominous.

"I made you Destined, Clara. I made the king a Destined. This wasn't the forest's will. It was mine. And now, with all of you here, I will twist the power of Destiny into something I can wield… and use it to break free."

A sharp inhale from Eliza sliced through the heavy air. Her red eyes locked onto mine, wide with horror.

"What does that mean? They chose you?"

Silence fell.

Arisen's jaw clenched, his golden eyes blazing.

"They may have forced Destiny on us, but they couldn't control what kind we received." He turned to me, his voice steady and certain. "My Destiny won't allow anything to happen to Clara. And Clara's Destiny holds a power they can't begin to comprehend."

A growl cut through the air, low and furious.

"Enough," one of the creatures snapped. "Time to separate them."

Two figures leapt forward, skeletal hands clamping down on Rogers's arms. He fought them, muscles straining, fury etched across his face.

"No!" I lunged, but something slammed into my chest, knocking the breath from my lungs and sending me sprawling to the ground.

"Get your hands off me!" Rogers roared, thrashing against their grip. But he was outnumbered.

"Eliza!" His voice cracked through the clearing.

Her scream shattered the air. "Let him go!" She fought wildly against her restraints, her eyes glowing with crimson rage. "Please, don't take him!"

The leader laughed again, cold and sharp, unrelenting.

"Oh, but you will all share his fate soon enough."

With one final yank, they dragged Rogers into the shadows.

Eliza sobbed, a raw, broken sound. Her whole body shook as she cried out again. "No! Please! Please!"

The leader turned back to us; its face twisted with glee.

"Struggle all you want," it said, voice low and steady. "The Gaul Forest no longer obeys you. I've bent its magic to my will. Your bond, your Destiny, it will be taken from you. And once it's gone, my fellow sanguivoras and I will claim the power we're owed."

It crouched beside me, its green eyes narrowing as it whispered, "The portals are twisted. The pathways sealed. There is no escape. You, your king, your Destined allies... You belong to us now."

My stomach knotted. This wasn't just a trap. It was a prison.

The leader stood, tilting its head in mock sympathy.

"You should be grateful," it mused. "You won't have to hear the screams when a Destiny is ripped away. Stripping it hurts far more than receiving it."

Then, with a casual flick of its wrist, the forest swallowed Rogers whole.

And in that moment, I had never felt more powerless.

CHAPTER 42

Eliza was drenched in sweat, her crimson eyes clouded with panic. Her breath came in quick, shallow gasps, and her brows knotted tight, as though she were physically holding herself back from rushing into the shadows after Rogers. A desperate impulse we all knew would end in ruin.

Arisen had been silent until now. Then he spoke.

"We'll get him back."

The words hung between us, hopeful and fragile. None of us knew how.

I reached for him through our link. "Have you heard of a sanguivora before?"

"Only in old stories," he replied. *"They were believed to be extinct long before I was born. The only records left are buried in ancient texts, books*

thousands of years old."

If these creatures had been erased from history, what were they doing here now?

I turned to Eliza. "What exactly is a sanguivora?"

She exhaled sharply, her eyes flicking to the green-eyed monsters circling us.

"Rogers spoke to Victor before he was taken. Victor said they survive by feeding on blood—human or elvish. Drinking it allows them to mimic the form of their prey temporarily. But if they kill the host…" Her voice caught. "The transformation becomes permanent."

A sick twist knotted in my stomach.

"That explains what happened to Karlos," Arisen added grimly. *"And why they need our magic. They're not just trying to kill us—they're trapped here. Their own magic has bound them to this forest, and they believe our power is the key to escaping it."*

I struggled to understand. *"But they said they were once human. How is that even possible?"*

"Dark magic," Arisen said, his tone flat. *"It corrupts life itself. The Gaul Forest hasn't produced magic that powerful in centuries, but traces of it remain. Someone must have found it and used it."*

A horrifying thought took shape.

"So… they did this to themselves?"

He nodded. *"A group of humans, desperate for power, probably turned to that magic. But it came at a cost. It stripped away what made them human, reshaping them into monsters. This is what happens when magic is taken without balance. When the natural order is broken."*

Cold dread settled in my chest. These creatures, these terrifying beings, had once been like us.

Reato, the magic harvester, broke the silence. "Only those who are

Destined, human or elf, can truly wield the magic of the Gaul Forest. Anyone else who tries changes."

His gaze found mine and held. "That's what the sanguivoras are. They reached for power not meant for them, and the forest punished them. It bound them to its land and twisted their bodies. Look at the Pagostonians. When they tried to use magic they didn't understand, the forest marked them. Red eyes. A warning. But these creatures didn't stop. They let it consume them."

Everything clicked into place.

"If they were once human," I whispered, "and they need us… they think our Destiny can help them leave."

Reato's face darkened. "Yes. That's why they took Rogers. Why they've kept Victor alive. They believe stealing our magic will open a path out of the forest. And if they throw the balance of magic into chaos, they might succeed."

Eliza's fingers dug into the dirt. "Then we have to find them," she growled. "Victor knows dark magic better than any of us. If anyone can stop them, it's him."

Arisen nodded. "That's exactly why they've separated him. He's vulnerable, but his knowledge—and his Destiny—make him a threat." His jaw clenched. "They took Karlos at his weakest. We won't let them take Victor or Rogers too."

Eliza shifted, her panic rising again. The movement caught the creatures' attention. Their glowing eyes snapped toward her, slitted pupils narrowing like blades.

I turned to her quickly, keeping my voice steady. "Eliza, I have a plan. I just need time. Do you know where Victor is?"

She blinked rapidly, trying to push back the tears that spilled over anyway. "They blindfolded him," she choked. "He can't see anything. Not even through our link."

Her voice shattered me.

We had already lost too much. We couldn't lose more.

I inhaled deeply, forcing myself to shut out the monsters around us. I needed to connect with the Gaul Forest, to find anything small that could slip through the shadows unnoticed.

I closed my eyes and reached into the magic beneath us, stretching my awareness like fine threads across the forest floor.

For a moment, there was nothing.

Then tiny sparks appeared, faint glimmers in the dark.

Birds. Insects. Skittish creatures with fast-beating hearts. Most flitted away, afraid.

But one came closer. Curious. Brave.

When I opened my eyes, a rat sat on my lap.

Its dark eyes shimmered faintly, and its small hands twitched near its chest. It sniffed the air, sensing the bond between us.

I was still bound, but it crawled up my arm, brushing against my skin.

It understood.

The connection sparked to life.

The rat twitched its whiskers once, then turned and vanished into the underbrush.

To my left, I felt Arisen's gaze. I met his eyes, and he nodded.

We weren't powerless.

The sanguivoras thought they held control.

But they had no idea what was coming.

CHAPTER 43

From Clara's Diary

Matry, Reato, Eliza, Arisen, and I huddled by the fire. The flames' warmth provided comfort against the night. Matry and Reato leaned against each other, still drowsy from the little sleep they had managed to get. Eliza sat silently, her gaze fixed on the fire, her mind undoubtedly occupied with worry for Rogers. Meanwhile, Arisen and I communicated through our link, discussing a strategy for escape.

"Any news from your rat friend?" Arisen teased, attempting to lighten the mood.

A faint smile tugged at my lips. I closed my eyes, strengthening the bond with the rat, and soon, a dim vision emerged in my mind. Through its eyes, I saw Rogers first—he was tied to a pole in a nearby tent. Besides the straw bag covering his face and the ropes binding him, he was unharmed. Rescuing him would only take a few minutes if we could create the proper diversion.

Victor, however, was farther away. He was being kept in the tent at the edge of the compound. His condition was far worse; his hands were tied, his eyes swollen shut, and his face bruised. But he was alive.

Through our link, I relayed everything I had seen to Arisen. It was clear we would need a plan to rescue them both. However, with the sanguivoras always watching, passing information to Eliza, Matry, and Reato without speaking would be challenging.

The sanguivoras guarding the campground were mostly asleep, sprawled around dying campfires or slumped against makeshift tents. Only a few remained alert, their eyes lazily scanning the darkness, but even they seemed uninterested in their surroundings.

I waited until the leaves above us rustled with the wind, their whispers blending with the night, to speak. The natural noise would help mute my voice and ensure the sanguivoras wouldn't catch wind of our plans.

Using one of my boots, I gently nudged Eliza, the movement sending a sharp jolt of pain up my injured leg. It was healing, but I wasn't in any condition to run or stand for long. Eliza turned her attention to me.

"Eliza, I know where Rogers is. He's not far. If you follow this rat, it'll lead you to him," I said, nodding toward the small creature that had returned to me. Its tiny, bright eyes gleamed, and its trembling body was ready to act.

Blinking in understanding, she whispered, "How will we distract these sanguivoras?"

Matry and Reato, still asleep, needed to wake up and use their Destiny to create a distraction.

"Eliza," I whispered, "tell Matry and Reato they must find something to harvest energy from—rocks, twigs, leaves. Even a small amount of magic will work. They need to make it appear larger than it is."

Eliza subtly nudged them awake with her boot. Startled, the two groggily opened their eyes but quickly focused as she explained the plan.

"They'll need their hands free," Eliza murmured.

"I can handle that," I assured her.

The rat climbed up my leg and torso, wriggling beneath my clothing before settling near my wrists. I pictured the intricate knots binding our hands, directing the rat through the mental image. Its sharp teeth worked swiftly, the ropes loosening as it gnawed through them.

My plan was working.

Once freed, I discreetly retrieved the small knife hidden in my undergarments and passed it to Eliza. "Once your hands are loose, use this to free Matry and Reato," I whispered. The rat made its way over to Arisen and worked at breaking his bonds.

The camp was quiet. Most of the sanguivoras had retreated to their tents, the few remaining lurking in the shadows, appearing relaxed and unaware of our intentions.

"Eliza, move slowly and don't draw attention," I instructed.

Minutes dragged on like hours, but everyone's hands were eventually freed, and the knife made its way back to me. I kept the ropes loosely tied around my wrists to maintain the illusion of captivity.

"Small but powerful," I reminded Matry and Reato. They nodded, closing their eyes as though returning to sleep.

Matry and Reato drew energy from the forest's objects, rocks, leaves, twigs. The magic they gathered was minuscule, but they amplified its presence, shaping it into a force larger than life.

The air vibrated faintly as the leaves above us rustled. Then a distant scream tore through the night. It was so full of raw, genuine agony that the hairs on my arms stood on end.

The sanguivoras nearest to us stirred awake, their attention snapping toward the sound. One by one they rose and slipped into the darkness, vanishing from view as they moved to investigate.

Taking her chance, Eliza followed the rat as it led her through the safest path toward Rogers. Disappearing into the darkness, her silhouette melted into the shadows.

Arisen and I exchanged one final look before he rose, making his way toward Victor's tent.

The second scream cut through the night, louder and more desperate. The leaves above us rustled violently, the sound muting our words even more.

This was our moment.

We would rescue everyone. We would fight. And we would reclaim the Gaul Forest.

CHAPTER 44

From the edge of one of the tents, I spotted the rat scurrying toward me. It climbed up my leg with practiced ease, burrowing into a hidden pocket beneath my clothes. Moments later, Eliza and Rogers emerged from the shadows behind it, sprinting toward us. As they reached the camp, relief flooded Eliza's face, her breathless smile a stark contrast to the fear that had gripped us all.

Matry and Reato now sat together, their foreheads touching, their energy entwined. Pebbles floated around them in a rhythmic orbit, and their long white hair billowed as though caught in a mystical wind. Their Destiny was growing; another powerful distraction was brewing.

Eliza and Rogers helped me to my feet, each grabbing me under an arm. I wrapped my arms around their necks for support and hurried toward the corner of the encampment. I discreetly pressed the knife into Rogers's hand. The three of us stood together, silently watching Matry and Reato. They remained focused, their connection unbreakable. None of us dared disturb them.

Then, a sudden flash of light appeared in the distance, followed by the deafening roar of an explosion about a mile away. The ground trembled beneath our feet as the sound reverberated through the camp. Even though we had anticipated it, the blast startled all of us.

Matry and Reato separated, their faces pale from exhaustion. They nodded to signal they were fine, then rose unsteadily and joined us in the corner.

The camp was now in chaos. The explosion had stirred the entire encampment, and sanguivoras poured out of their tents like a flood. Their guttural growls echoed in the night as they scrambled to locate the source of the disturbance. Some snarled at each other, clearly irritated, while others sniffed the air, their glowing green eyes scanning the surroundings.

One sanguivora, larger than the others, barked commands, its voice grating and harsh. "Find the intruders! Spread out and guard the camp!" it hissed, gesturing wildly.

The sanguivoras moved with frantic energy, darting from tent to tent, their clawed feet scratching the earth as they made their way to the distraction.

Despite the commotion, three sanguivoras stayed behind, their gazes fixed on us. They were more intelligent than the others, unwilling to leave their prizes unattended. We were unarmed, and we knew they'd be a difficult threat to overcome.

"There is no way out of here, Destined," the three hissed in unison, advancing slowly. Their eyes glinted with malice, their poisonous nails dragging ominously against the ground.

Rogers stepped forward, clutching the small knife tightly. "Stay back," he warned.

One of the sanguivoras lunged at him with terrifying speed, its long, dark nails slicing through the air. Rogers dodged the initial attack with quick reflexes, but the creature was relentless. It knocked him to the ground, the force of the blow sending the knife skidding across the dirt. The sanguivora stood over him, its claws raised.

"Rogers!" Eliza screamed. Without hesitation, she grabbed a large rock and hurled it at the back of the creature's head. The impact drew a shriek of pain, and the sanguivora turned its attention to her, licking its lips hungrily as it prowled forward.

I closed my eyes and summoned every ounce of energy I had left, reaching outward with my mind. I felt wildlife nearby, a flock of birds perched high in the trees, watching. Their connection to me was faint, like a thread stretched thin across distance, but it was there. I called to them anyway, pouring urgency into the link and willing them to come to our aid.

Suddenly, the air erupted with the flurry of wings as the birds descended, their sharp beaks targeting the sanguivoras' eyes. The creatures shrieked in rage, flailing wildly as the birds attacked.

Rogers took advantage of the distraction, grabbing the knife and stabbing the sanguivora several times. Its shrieks grew weaker until it collapsed in a lifeless heap.

The remaining two, now blinded and disoriented by the birds, stumbled and flailed. Matry and Reato mustered the last of their strength to hurl large rocks at the creatures, knocking them further off balance.

"You need to move now!" Arisen's warning rang loudly in my mind.

"Let's go!" I shouted. Reato grabbed his cane, and together with Eliza and Rogers, we bolted through the forest. The blinded sanguivoras were left writhing, the birds still pecking at them.

The sanguivoras were a mess, their shrieks fading into the distance. My bond with the birds quivered, and I knew the flock's help was nearly over.

"We have to keep moving. I can't control the birds much longer," I urged. "We must find Victor and Arisen."

I sensed the delicate bond with the birds unraveling, and I knew that if we didn't move quickly, we would be their next target.

"We are trapped in this forest. The sanguivoras have blocked the Urten Bridge, but there's a section by the waterfall unknown to many," Rogers informed us. "King Arisen knows of it. Ask him to meet us there."

"I have Victor with me," Arisen responded through our link. *"We'll meet you at the waterfall's edge."*

The forest grew denser as we ventured deeper, its dark canopies blocking what little moonlight remained. Despite my injury, I pushed forward, unwilling to slow us down.

The sound of rushing water grew louder ahead, a steady, roaring pulse guiding us forward. The promise of the waterfall spurred us on, though my body ached with exhaustion.

Finally, we emerged into a clearing. The waterfall stood before us, a magnificent cascade tumbling into a shimmering pool. Mist clung to the air, cooling the sweat on my skin, but I barely noticed. My breath caught as a movement in the shadows drew my attention.

From the trees, Arisen appeared, supporting Victor.

The feeling of ease hit me so fast it almost knocked the air from my lungs. He was alive.

Victor barely seemed conscious, his face pallid and his eyes distant, as if he was caught somewhere between reality and grief. His body sagged against Arisen, entirely reliant on him for support. It was a stark contrast—Victor, the warrior I had known, reduced to a shell of himself.

His Destined was gone, and without that bond, he looked as if a vital part had been ripped from him.

Arisen shared words with Matry and Reato before gently handing Victor over to them. His movements were careful, as if he knew just how fragile Victor had become.

And then his gaze found mine.

He was bruised, his shirt torn, dried blood streaking one cheek. His eyes burned with focus—but they softened the moment they landed on me. He had his sword back, the familiar blade resting in his grip, likely recovered during their escape.

My chest tightened.

Not his blood. Please, not his blood.

The thought repeated in my head like a mantra. I couldn't look away from the crimson smeared across his face, couldn't shake the dread curling in my stomach.

Without thinking, I reached for the bond between us, grasping for it like a lifeline, needing to feel him. Needing to know he was truly there. Whole. Alive.

"It's not my blood." His voice curled around my thoughts.

I didn't realize how much I needed him standing here, in front of me, until I felt my own relief.

I swallowed, gripping my arms to keep them from shaking. *"You look awful,"* I said, trying to summon some semblance of lightness.

"And you look like you're about to collapse."

"Wouldn't be the first time."

His gaze darkened slightly, his jaw tensing. *"I should have been there sooner."*

I shook my head. *"You were where you needed to be."*

We were only a few feet apart. He was watching me, his eyes searching, and I had the unsettling feeling that he could see straight through the exhaustion, the forced steadiness, the tangled mess of emotions I was barely holding together.

I wasn't sure if it was Destiny, or something more, but I felt *him*—a presence so steady, so familiar, that it quieted the storm.

His fingers twitched at his side, like he was resisting the urge to reach for me. I felt it too.

Instead, he exhaled slowly, breaking the moment. *"Rest. We'll talk later."*

He turned, walking toward the others, but the warmth of him lingered.

And despite everything, despite the danger, the exhaustion, and the grief hanging in the air—I felt *safe*.

Because he was still here.

CHAPTER 45

From Clara's Diary

For the first time since leaving Polent, a wave of relief washed over me. The rat scurried out of my pocket, searching for a cozy spot as we sat together, watching the sunrise from the edge of the waterfall. For a brief moment, it almost felt like everything was okay. Mist rose from the falls, catching the golden light and creating a shimmering veil that made the world around us seem almost otherworldly.

And yet, the destruction around us was undeniable.

Victor sat quietly among us, his gaze distant and filled with sorrow. Eliza and Rogers leaned against each other, their exhaustion clear but softened by the relief of being reunited. Matry and Reato ate slowly, trying to regain their strength. A few feet away, Arisen rested against a rock by the waterfall's edge.

I sat beside him, cleaning the wound on my leg. The worst of it had begun to heal, though the pain lingered. Dirt and dried blood clung stubbornly to my skin, and I scrubbed at it with my nails, desperate to feel somewhat clean.

Arisen moved beside me, his eyes fixed on my leg. Without a word, he reached out and gently grasped it. He examined the wound carefully; his fingers, still stained from the fight, were surprisingly gentle as he wiped away the grime I hadn't been able to remove.

"Let me help you."

I nodded, watching him. His fingers lightly brushed my skin, hesitant for a brief moment before moving on. When he finished, he wrapped the wound with a clean strip of cloth, his hands lingering a second longer than necessary before he finally pulled away.

"That should hold for now," he said through our link, his voice quieter, almost subdued.

For a short while, the pain and exhaustion seemed to fade, replaced by an unfamiliar solace in his presence. Eventually, we all drifted into restless sleep.

When I woke up, my head had somehow ended up resting against Arisen's shoulder again. The second time in just a few days. My thoughts were still foggy from sleep when I noticed the others staring. I felt my cheeks flush.

Standing a few feet away, Rogers was the first to speak. "This is a good hiding spot, but we can't stay here forever. We need a plan."

Arisen shifted slightly beside me, his shoulder brushing mine as he straightened. "We should start by reviewing everything we know about the sanguivoras."

Victor, who had remained silent for most of the morning, surprised us by speaking. "I know more than most."

We turned toward him, waiting.

"Karlos and I studied dark magic," Victor began, his voice hoarse. "Karlos understood it more deeply. He was born in Hertm, the town where dark magic was first harvested over a thousand years ago."

At the mention of the town, Arisen's eyes darkened. "Hertm."

Victor nodded. "Dark magic is created by corrupting natural magic. It takes years to develop, and only the most skilled can wield it without harming themselves. The magic of the Gaul Forest was never meant to be changed. Only the Destined are meant to wield it. But recently, a new magic source was found in Hertm. It was small at first, not strong enough to attract much attention, but powerful enough to tempt those who wanted more."

"There are humans in Hertm," Arisen said, his voice grim.

Victor met his gaze. "That's where the first sanguivoras were created. The magic there wasn't enough to sustain them, so they vanished… or so we thought. Any records of them were erased or lost. But dark magic was revived, and enough was harvested to transform an entire group of humans. They found their way to the Gaul Forest, searching for more."

"And now they're trapped here," I said, piecing it together. "The forest won't let them leave."

Victor exhaled. "Not unless they use our Destiny to complete their transformation. If they cause an imbalance, they will break free. If they take what we have, they can use that power to open the gates." He hesitated. "If they succeed, they won't just leave. They'll spread."

A cold silence fell over us.

"The sanguivoras are using dark magic to unravel Destiny itself," Victor continued. "King Arisen and Clara should not have survived the process. Karlos believed it was a sign from Destiny itself, but… Karlos always tried to see the good in things."

Eliza furrowed her brows. "How do they even know this much about Destiny? How could they have twisted the Gaul Forest's magic?"

Victor hesitated before answering. "They've been studying us for a long time, decades, maybe centuries. Remember, they were human once. They understood the importance of the Gaul Forest better than most, and they knew how to manipulate it."

Arisen, who had been listening quietly, finally spoke. "They may have only revealed themselves in the last two years, but the damage to the Gaul Forest started long before that." His eyes darkened as he looked up into the canopy. "The forest has been decaying for decades. I sensed it long before the signs became visible. The magic that once pulsed through it, through its roots and its creatures, grew weak. And it wasn't just fading. It was being consumed."

He exhaled slowly. "At first, we thought it was a natural shift. The balance of magic in the world fluctuates from time to time, but it always corrects itself. This was different. The forest resisted, but a power was draining it. By the time I realized what was happening, it had already begun to rot from the inside."

Victor nodded. "That's because dark magic was being used in Hertm, pulling energy from the Gaul Forest. That's what allowed the sanguivoras to be created. But it was unstable—their existence was short-lived. That's why they came here. They needed more magic to sustain their transformation."

Arisen's gaze hardened. "And they found it. They found ways to take from the forest itself, accelerating its decay. The creatures, the plants, even the air in some parts of the forest felt different, as if the magic itself were suffocating."

My stomach twisted at his words. I had always known the Gaul Forest was dying, but hearing it laid out like this, understanding what had truly caused it, made the loss feel frighteningly irreversible.

"The sanguivoras didn't just drain the forest's magic," Arisen continued. "They warped it. They used dark magic to sever its natural flow. They didn't want power alone. They wanted control. And now, with their transformation incomplete, they need us, the Destined, to finish what they started."

Their existence, their purpose, were proof of how deep the divide between humans and elves had become. If we didn't find a way to bridge that gap, it wouldn't be the sanguivoras that destroyed us. It would be our own refusal to change.

Pagos needed a ruler who could unite its people. Polent, the only nation still ruled by a human, needed to guide the others, and King Llorent was the only one positioned to secure lasting peace. Ebony needed Arisen to focus on restoring the Gaul Forest's magic without the constant drag of council politics. No one else had his knowledge or his connection to Destiny. No one else could repair what had been broken.

For too long, our people had clung to a false story: that elves were superior, that humans were powerless, that division was inevitable. But the truth was simpler.

If we didn't stand together, we would fall.

Arisen's voice broke through my thoughts, his words slipping through the bond between us.

"Clara, how do you think the sanguivoras knew who you were? Do you know anyone from Hertm?"

The question hit me like a sudden gust of wind. My thoughts turned, unbidden, to a memory I had buried.

"Lorraine," my mind whispered back.

Arisen's response was immediate. *"That storm never happened."*

A sinking feeling twisted in my stomach.

He reached for my hand, the warmth of his touch grounding me. His eyes held mine, filled with a rare mix of sympathy and understanding.

I closed my eyes and thought back. I remembered Lorraine's insistence on traveling to Hertm. How eager she was. How she left just after giving birth. It hadn't made sense at the time.

But now, the pieces fell into place.

My eyes flew open. *"We need to contact Kent,"* I whispered, my voice shaking. *"He and King Llorent need to know."*

Arisen's expression hardened. *"Without a parestine, the only way to reach him is through the gate,"* he said. *"And the gate is near the sanguivoras' camp."*

"That's too dangerous," I said immediately.

Arisen met my gaze. *"We need to try."*

And I knew he was right.

I didn't know how I was going to tell the others.

The thought churned inside me. Lorraine's words, and the implications of what she had done, were too much to carry in my chest. I had no idea how to shape it into language, how to even begin.

I stared into the dark trees, listening to the wind stir the leaves in the distance. The others were finally resting, their exhaustion having overtaken them. Even Arisen was quiet next to me, his expression unreadable in the dim firelight.

"You're thinking too much."

I turned sharply. He was watching me, the faint blue in his golden eyes catching the flame's glow.

"Hard not to," I muttered. "I don't know how to tell them."

Arisen exhaled through his nose, shifting slightly. "Then don't," he said simply. "Not until you're ready."

I scoffed. "We don't have time for 'ready.'"

He was quiet for a moment before leaning forward, forearms resting on his knees. "Clara, whatever happens next, this isn't your fault."

I bit my lip, shaking my head. "I should've seen it sooner. I should've realized what Lorraine was—what she was becoming. If I had put the pieces together earlier, maybe—"

But how could I? She was Hale's mother. There had never been any signs before. Her trips to Hertm had seemed reasonable, expected even, for someone who claimed to have family there.

"No. You are not responsible for this. For her. For any of it."

Arisen sighed, his shoulders dipping as he dragged a hand through his damp green hair. Then he glanced back at me. "If we're talking about regrets, I have plenty of my own."

I raised an eyebrow. "Oh?"

His lips twitched. "Clara, I've made… questionable decisions. Ones I thought were for the greater good." He leaned back against the rock, tilting his head as if considering something. "I've been married thirty times, and you almost witnessed my thirty-first."

I blinked. This was the first time he had ever addressed it outright.

His smirk deepened. "I was married to a Pagostonian once."

I gaped at him. "You—what?"

He let out a low chuckle, shaking his head. "Not one of my better choices. It was a political alliance, a last-ditch effort to prevent a war. She was the niece of Queen Franes. Ambrely, I think?" He frowned as if trying to recall. "It lasted about three months before she tried to stab me."

My eyes widened. "She tried to—"

"Poison, technically," he corrected. "But the attempt was pathetic, and she got bored when it didn't work. Ran back to Pagos."

I stared at him, completely at a loss for words. "And you're telling me this now?"

He shrugged. "Seemed relevant."

I opened my mouth, then closed it, unsure of what to even say. After a sigh, I groaned, rubbing my hands over my face. "Why do I feel like that isn't even the worst one?"

"It's not," he said without hesitation.

I dropped my hands and gave him a look. "Arisen."

His smirk remained, but he didn't elaborate.

I let out a slow breath, shaking my head. "So, what was the reason? For all the marriages?"

His smirk faded slightly, with a more serious flicker in his gaze. "I thought it would save the nations. Fix relations with Pagos. Protect the forest." His jaw tightened. "I believed that if I did everything right, if I sacrificed enough, the Gaul Forest would heal. That the balance would be restored."

He exhaled, rubbing a hand over his face. "It wasn't just me. My council suggested it—pushed for it, really. They believed strategic marriages would strengthen alliances, prevent wars, and stabilize the magic that was already beginning to wane." His eyes darkened, his voice quieter now. "And I believed them."

"And?"

His gaze darkened. "And I was wrong. I was Destined with all the knowledge of this forest, yet every attempt I made seemed futile."

A silence stretched between us. He had given so much of himself to the world, believing he was doing the right thing. And yet, here we were.

"I don't regret trying," he said after a moment, his voice quieter. "But I regret believing that I could do it alone."

I swallowed, glancing toward the others. "I should tell them," I murmured. "About Lorraine. About what she might've done."

Arisen nodded, his eyes steady. "You should. But when you do, remember... this is not on you."

He watched me closely, and after a moment, he lifted his hand. His fingers brushed against my cheek, barely a touch, as he tucked a loose strand of hair behind my ear. I stilled, my breath catching as his touch lingered.

My eyes drifted down, tracing the faint glow of the golden mark on his neck, pulsing like the heartbeat of Destiny itself. The light extended toward his jaw, its lines stark against his skin. When I finally met his gaze, I could not stop the tears from swelling in my eyes.

"You're carrying too much," he murmured.

I exhaled shakily, struggling to keep my voice steady. "It doesn't seem like I have a choice. Like you said the day we met, Destiny isn't a choice."

His thumb brushed my cheek for a heartbeat before he pulled his hand away.

A single tear slipped free, tracing a hot line down my face. I barely had time to register it before his fingers returned, catching it with the pad of his thumb and wiping it away as if it mattered to him.

I looked up at him, searching his face for something I hadn't seen in days. Reassurance. Certainty. Anything that could make the weight in my chest feel lighter.

And for the first time in a long while, I found it.

CHAPTER 46

Returning to the camp was the last thing any of us wanted, but we were stuck between hiding and being found.

"I… I know who the leader of the sanguivoras is."

All eyes snapped to me. My heart pounded under their expectant stares.

"It's Lorraine. Hale's mother." The words felt unreal even as I said them. "She's the only person I know from Hertm, and I recognized her voice when the creature confronted me."

Eliza and Rogers exchanged uncertain glances, caught off guard. They had heard me mention Lorraine sporadically, but this revelation clearly unsettled them.

"But why?" Rogers asked. "Why would she do this? Why would anyone?"

I shook my head. "I don't know. But we have to tell King Llorent and Queen Franes if she's behind this. These creatures are already trying to get through the gates. Their armies need to be ready."

"The only way out of this is through a Destiny gate," Arisen added cautiously, breaking through my thoughts, "but we risk ending up somewhere else."

Victor, who had been silent until now, finally spoke. "We may have one chance. If we reach the gate, I might be able to use my knowledge of dark magic to open it, even if the sanguivoras have tampered with it."

A silence followed until Eliza broke it. "Then we move quickly. They could be closing in on us right now."

We moved swiftly through the forest, careful to make as little noise as possible. Daylight filtered weakly through the thick canopy, but even that small amount of light gave us hope. Every step was a risk; dead leaves and twigs made it impossible to move without drawing attention. Still, we pressed on until we spotted the gleaming lanterns of the camp in the distance.

"Victor and I will go to the gate," Arisen said. "We'll send a signal when we're ready."

"What will be the signal?" Reato asked.

I looked at the rat who was now perched on my shoulder, with its hands firmly grasping some of my hair. "It will go with you," I replied.

I softly placed the rat at my feet, feeling the coarse bristles of its fur against my fingers. Its small, fragile body was warm, alive, trusting. I strengthened our bond one last time and ran my thumb gently over its tiny head in farewell.

Be careful.

The rat twitched its whiskers, its tiny claws gripping the earth beneath it as though it understood. Then, without hesitation, it scurried off into the darkness.

Victor, Arisen, and the rat disappeared into the dense forest. I exhaled slowly, leaning against the rough bark of a tree, trying to find a position that would let me focus.

Eliza, Rogers, Matry, and Reato stood beside me, their bodies tense. If anything, or anyone, came near, we would fight.

I closed my eyes and let the bond guide me, slipping into the small, skittering perspective of the rat. Through its eyes, I caught glimpses of Victor and Arisen moving swiftly through the underbrush, their forms weaving between towering trees. Each step brought them closer to the campground.

The sanguivoras were nowhere to be seen.

For the first time, hope bloomed in my chest. Maybe this would be easier than I had feared.

The gate was in sight now. Unlike the others I had encountered, this one was woven between two massive trees, their trunks entwined by thick vines. Victor pressed his hands against the bark, and the twisted patterns of the vines pulsed as glowing letters appeared in ancient Elvish. I only recognized a single word: *Enter*.

We were so close.

Victor knelt, lowering his head. The black fog of his magic unfurled around him, curling through the air like living shadows. His mouth moved quickly, chanting words I couldn't hear, weaving the conjuration that would bring the gate to life. The magic rippled outward, and I watched in awe as the vines twisted and reformed, revealing the beginnings of an opening.

Almost there.

And then—

A sharp, searing pain stabbed through my chest, knocking the air from my lungs.

I gasped, my fingers clutching at my heart as an invisible cord snapped inside me. My vision blurred into nothingness—dark, absolute nothingness.

The bond was gone.

Not severed gently. Not weakened.

Gone.

I yanked my head up, my breath coming in ragged, desperate gulps. No, no, no—

The rat was dead.

I had felt it die.

"What happened?" Rogers's voice cut through my panic.

"I…I lost the bond." My own voice barely made it out, strangled by the dread crashing over me. My body felt hollow, like a part had been torn away.

Eliza took a step toward me, her red eyes scanning my face. "Do you think they were caught?"

I couldn't answer. My hands closed into fists as I forced myself to stay upright.

The rat had been my eyes. My tether to Victor and Arisen.

And now, something had crushed it.

My stomach twisted as the terrifying realization settled in.

They knew.

The sanguivoras had been watching.

And now, they were waiting.

"Yes," I said, standing despite the lingering pain in my leg.

We walked quickly through the forest, our steps barely touching the ground, until we reached a vantage point from which we saw the gate in the distance. Through the dark fog, I saw Victor lying motionless on the ground and Arisen struggling against a group of sanguivoras.

We sprang into action. Rogers led the charge, the knife gleaming in the dim light. Eliza and Reato followed him, their movements quick. Matry and I hung back, ready to support them with whatever magic we were able to muster.

I felt Lorraine's eyes on me. She knew I was here, but like me, she stayed back, looking at how the other sanguivoras attacked the Destined. Part of me was still doubting whether this was Lorraine. But the other part of me was so confident, especially seeing her now from a distance. I recognized that once-lustrous blonde hair… just like Hale's.

A slow smile spread across Lorraine's lips as she mouthed the words, *Took you long enough*, from a distance.

I turned to Matry, who stood beside me, taking in everything. In that instant, we both realized the truth—no matter how hard we fought, we were always outnumbered. The sanguivoras had orchestrated this moment perfectly. They had anticipated our return.

I squeezed Matry's hand, and together, we stepped toward the gate, where dozens of sanguivoras surrounded our captured friends. With each step, Lorraine mirrored us, closing the distance.

The fighting came to an abrupt halt as we faced off.

"Clara, oh, Clara," Lorraine cooed, her voice almost lilting with mock affection. "Your love for Kent and Hale has led all of you straight to this moment."

Hearing Hale's mother's voice come from the lips of this creature was more jarring than anything I could have prepared for. Nothing about this creature resembled her, except the voice.

"Why are you doing this?" I asked, doing my best to stay steady.

"Why?" she sneered. "Because I despise elves. They've overrun Hertm… destroyed it, and I've had enough." Her fingernails scraped the earth. "But more than that, I crave power. With it, I'll control all three nations."

"But why do you want this power?"

Her grin widened, and her eyes gleamed with madness. "Power is everything," she said slowly, as if savoring each word. "With power, I can reshape the world. I can restore Hertm to its former glory, free from the influence of elves and anyone else who stands in my way." She paused, her gaze piercing into mine. "And with control over all three nations, I can ensure that no one will ever challenge me again. I will be the ultimate authority."

I saw the fervor in her eyes, the unyielding desire for domination that drove her every action. It was a desire born not just from hatred, but from a deep-seated need to assert her dominance over the world.

"And what about the people? What about their lives and their freedom?" I pressed, hoping to find a trace of humanity in her.

She laughed, a cold, mirthless sound. "Freedom is an illusion. People need guidance, someone to show them the right way. I will be that leader. I will bring order out of chaos." She leaned back, her smile never fading. "In the end, they will thank me for it."

It would take everything we had to stop her.

"You all get chosen by Destiny and experience the most power any human or elf can ever have. And yet, so little is done with your abilities. We don't need more progress for the nations; we need more power for the people."

Suddenly, the shouts of the sanguivoras echoed through the trees, their voices a chilling chorus that made my blood run cold. My heart pounded as the sheer number of them became clear, forming a wall of shifting shadows in the mist. Lorraine smiled smugly, reveling in our growing fear.

I tried to steady my breath, but the oppressive sound made it difficult to think clearly. I glanced at Arisen—his face was grim, his jaw locked as he scanned the darkness for any sign of their advance.

"And the best part?" Lorraine mused, tilting her head. "Victor has done most of the hard work for us. He harvested enough of his magic to open the gate. Now, all I need to do is send a few of my men to the other side and cause an imbalance. You will lose your Destiny soon." Her eyes gleamed as she stepped toward the gate.

A low, rasping voice rose from one of the sanguivoras at her side. "We no longer need your blood to complete our transformation," it hissed. "That was a temporary solution. The real key was never in your veins. It was in the balance of the Gaul Forest's magic."

Lorraine nodded, dragging a sharp nail along the rough surface of the gate. "For two years we tried to take your magic directly, but the forest resisted. It fought back." Her lips curled into a sneer. "So we adapted. We don't need to extract Destiny from your bodies anymore. All we need is this." She gestured toward the swirling darkness within the gate. "A single fracture in the balance. If we cross over, the disruption alone will be enough to sever your ties to Destiny."

The Gaul Forest's magic maintained the balance between humans, elves, and Destiny itself. If that balance broke, if dark magic disrupted the natural order, our connection to Destiny would be severed. Not drained. Not stolen. Simply erased. The mere presence of these creatures beyond the gate would unravel everything we were bound to protect.

She placed her hands on the gate, her nails scraping the surface until the handle appeared once more. With a triumphant grin, she pulled it open, the ancient door groaning in protest as a swirling darkness pulsed on the other side.

"You will all learn what a world ruled by dark magic looks like," she declared, her white tunic flowing in the wind.

The sanguivoras erupted into another deafening cheer, sending a wave of dread through me. Three of them immediately stepped forward, crossing into the gate. The moment they did, a violent burst of energy exploded outward, sending a ripple of dark magic through the clearing.

I gasped as a piercing jolt of pain tore through me, followed by an icy numbness that spread like poison. The vibrant magic that usually surrounded us dimmed, thinning into an almost lifeless form.

I felt it slipping.

My connection to Destiny.

My link to Arisen.

I dropped to my knees, clutching my chest as the bond wavered. Across the clearing, the others reacted in kind—Eliza stumbled, Rogers groaned as he gripped his head, and Matry and Reato collapsed onto their hands, their bodies convulsing as though an essential part was being ripped from them.

"What's happening?" Rogers called, his voice barely a whisper over the pulsing magic.

"They're disrupting the balance," Victor groaned, still on the ground, fighting to stand. "If they succeed, we'll lose our connection to our Destinies entirely."

Eliza moved to support him, struggling under her own weight. "We need to close the gate," she rasped, "before it's too late."

Lorraine laughed. "It is too late for you. The process has already begun. Soon, all your powers will be destroyed, and I will have my daughter back."

I forced myself to look up, the edges of my vision blurring. "Your creatures won't survive outside of this forest," Victor managed through gritted teeth.

Lorraine's smile widened. "They won't need to. We only need enough time to retrieve three objects from beyond the gate, objects that will grant us true freedom."

Arisen, Victor, and Eliza were holding on, but barely. Matry and Reato hunched over, faces pale and drenched in sweat, retching onto the ground.

I could hardly move. The crushing force pinned me where I lay, leaving me curled in on myself, muscles trembling, skin slick with sweat.

Before she left, Lorraine knelt beside me, her expression eerily calm. One of her long, blackened nails traced a slow, mocking circle around my face.

"You think you're the only one with eyes beyond these walls?" she murmured, her voice almost pitying. Her hand drifted to the silver box at her hip, fingers sliding over its intricate surface. "This lets me see, to witness what happens beyond the gate."

My breath hitched. It was an identical box to the one Kent kept.

She sighed, feigning disappointment. "And you know what I saw?"

I tightened my fists, rage boiling beneath my skin, but my body refused to obey me.

"Too bad for Kent," she said, her mock sympathy twisting into cruelty.

Then she walked away, leaving me paralyzed, trapped in my own failing body.

I tried to rise, but the darkness swallowed me whole.

CHAPTER 47

From Clara's Diary

How long had I been out? By the looks of it, only a few hours, though it felt like days. My body ached, but I realized someone had tended to me. A coat was folded beneath my head as a makeshift pillow, the familiar scent of cedarwood clinging to it. Arisen's. His warmth lingered beside me, his hand resting lightly over mine.

I turned my head slowly, taking in his sharp features, softened now by exhaustion. His other hand rested on his knee, fingers curled as if they had been wrapped around mine not long ago and had only recently let go.

"What is going on?" I asked, my voice hoarse as I pushed myself upright.

"All of us, were dumped in a corner of the camp and left to die," Victor said. His voice was hollow, stripped of its usual steadiness. "Lorraine took our Destiny, our power, leaving us with nothing but our bodies. Our blood is no longer needed for their transformation. By the end of the day, the magic of this forest will consume us unless we find a way out. And without our Destined power, there is no way out."

We had failed millions of elves and humans who had no idea what was happening inside this forest. The secret buried for so long had led to this moment. I wanted to cry, but I was too drained. Even grief demanded energy, and I had none left to give.

"Let's go back to the waterfall," Eliza said, stepping closer. She extended her hand, her expression unreadable.

The remaining creatures didn't bother stopping us. To them, we were already dead, walking corpses no different from what they were. I hesitated before taking Eliza's hand, then forced my shaking legs to hold me as I stood.

Beside me, Arisen exhaled sharply and shifted as if to steady me, but I had already caught myself. It was strange how distant he seemed despite standing right next to me. I had gotten used to his voice in my head, so the silence between us now felt deafening.

The question trailed after me as we left the camp. What was he thinking? What did he think of us now?

As we trudged forward, the forest seemed to darken. Only the faintest glimmers of light slipped through the canopy overhead. We moved slowly, our strength spent. Each step felt heavier than the last. And still, Arisen was there, always there, and yet just out of reach.

We kept the same sluggish pace toward our hiding place by the falls. The forest's energy felt wrong, thin and sour, and along the path we passed more dead animals than before. How could creatures born of magic survive when the magic that sustained them was failing?

No one spoke. Heads remained bowed, as if we had already accepted what awaited us. Victor and Arisen led the way, their faces grim with determination. I longed for this nightmare to end, for the comfort of home, for Kent and Hale. The thought of never seeing them again made me feel hollow. Was this truly how the Destined ended, the legend I'd heard about my whole life and had only recently become part of? The idea of it made me shudder, not just for myself but for all of us, and for what kind of ending the forest might still hold.

As we neared the waterfall, we neared a hole in the ground that looked like a crater, its sheer size staggering. This hadn't been there before, so… what was it?

In the middle of the crater lay a colossal, serpentine creature, motionless and lifeless. Its once vibrant scales were dull and cracked, as if it had fallen from great heights and crashed into the earth, leaving debris scattered everywhere.

"A basilisk," Eliza pointed out, her tone low. The basilisks back at Polent, though formidable, were smaller; this one was much larger. The creature's coiled body filled the crater, looking lifeless.

If I had struggled to mount Kito back in Polent, there was no way I could even consider riding this behemoth. The memory of my training sessions flashed through my mind; each challenge, each near miss. This basilisk was on a completely different level, a living embodiment of the forest's magic.

We gathered around the creature, and I knelt beside it. My hand was only a fourth of the size of one of its eyes. This was my first time seeing one without its mask on, and I could only fathom how dangerous and beautiful its eyes must be.

Its scales were a deep, iridescent green, and they were surprisingly soft when I touched its head. Despite its enormous size, the creature had a peaceful appearance, almost as if it were simply sleeping. The sanguivoras had not infected this basilisk. Instead, it had succumbed to the lack of magic needed to sustain it. The larger creatures would perish first, their greater need for magic making them more vulnerable, while the smaller ones would take longer to be affected.

As I lay beside it, warmth spread through my body, starting from my fingertips and moving up my arm. It was as if the basilisk's remaining magic was flowing into me, rekindling the spark of my power that had been so cruelly snuffed out.

"I can feel the basilisk breathing!"

Arisen stepped closer, watching intently as the creature moved. The color of my cheeks returned, along with the strength of my limbs. The magic wove through my veins, giving life to the basilisk and me.

"What is happening?" Eliza asked.

"The magic of the forest… It's transferring," Arisen whispered, his eyes wide.

As the basilisk's breath grew stronger, a powerful surge of energy rose inside me, a thread reaching directly into the heart of the Gaul Forest. I closed my eyes and focused, allowing the link between us to deepen. Its magic flowed through me, and in that flow, I felt my old connections awaken. The creatures I had bonded with before stirred at the edges of my awareness, not gone, only waiting.

"The basilisk's lingering magic is merging with Clara's," Arisen said. "It's reviving her Destiny, and itself."

When I opened my eyes, the creature had risen. It towered over us and the trees, vast and unmistakably alive.

The others took cautious steps back, reminded that even being bonded to me, a basilisk was still a weapon of nature.

"Cover your eyes!" Matry shouted. Everyone lifted their arms to shield their faces. I didn't move. I knew the basilisk posed no threat to me.

Slowly, I looked up, meeting its gaze. Two massive red eyes held mine, orange swirls turning in their centers like living fire. The basilisk blinked once, unhurried, and something in me went still. I felt no fear. Only awe.

It stepped forward and nudged me gently, a clear invitation. I placed my hand on its warm scales, and the world tipped open. Memories rushed through me, not mine alone, but the echoes of every bond I had ever formed: the amphisbaena in Pagos, Kito in Polent, the birds that had guided us through this forest, even the fish that had first revealed my Destiny.

And with that renewed bond, my sight slipped beyond my own.

I saw through their eyes.

And what I saw destroyed me.

CHAPTER 48

Flashing images flooded my head, visions of what was unfolding across the nations. The first came from the amphisbaena. Through our restored bond, I saw a riot igniting outside Queen Franes's castle. Thousands of elves surged toward the gates, a tide of bodies and fury, and the soldiers stationed there were nowhere near enough to stop the stampede.

A group of elves had tied the amphisbaena to the outer wall of the castle, its massive form secured with thick ropes. Surrounding the amphisbaena lay hundreds of bodies of elves, fallen in the pursuit of binding it.

The amphisbaena stood motionless, its multiple heads surveying the scene. The castle grounds were in disarray, with fires burning in various places and the sounds of battle echoing through the air.

The devastation brought me to my knees. I gripped my hair, trying to remove the visions. The chaos, both outside and inside the castle, paused momentarily as the last image appeared. Commander Vasa entered the castle grounds, ready to protect Queen Franes. Her scream of "Long live the Queen!" as she entered with her army roared across the grounds.

Since when were they allies?

As the vision from the amphisbaena receded, another slammed into me, this one carried on Kito's bond in Polent. I saw him with his blindfold gone, his red-orange eyes burning bright. Around him, the creatures Polent had trained with the forest's magic were unraveling. Basilisks, falcons, beasts I couldn't name, all of them shaking free of their learned restraint as if a tether had been cut. Their instincts surged back, wild and hungry, and the order that had held them in check was crumbling in real time.

The basilisks guarding the castle grounds moved erratically, their hulking bodies crashing through walls, splintering furniture, and tearing through the grand halls in blind confusion. Their massive tails left destruction in their wake, their claws scraping against stone, their hissing filling the corridors like a warning.

Through Kito's eyes, I saw him moving closer to the courtyard, his instincts leading him toward the chaos.

Panic gripped the people. Some shrieked in terror and fled, while others froze, desperately shielding their eyes to avoid the creatures' lethal gaze. The air was filled with screams, footsteps pounding against the marble floors as soldiers and civilians scrambled for safety.

I felt Kito's confusion pulse through our bond—sharp, disoriented.

He was no longer controlled, yet he still moved, as if drawn toward something he couldn't understand. A force greater than himself pulled at him, twisting his instincts, overriding his will.

And beneath the confusion, I sensed something else.

Regret.

He hadn't wanted this. He hadn't wanted any of this. He had been a guardian, a protector of the castle and the people within it. And now, he was a monster spiraling toward devastation, leaving destruction in his wake.

He had lost control, his body moving without him, betraying everything he was.

He was a prisoner in his own body, forced to watch as his own actions led to ruin.

His grief was suffocating.

And there was no stopping it now.

And then I saw where he was heading.

My heart dropped.

A new vision tore through my mind, slamming into me like a physical force. I shuddered violently and screamed as it took hold.

Kent was kneeling on the ground next to the silver box with his arms wrapped tightly around Hale, pressing her tiny head against his chest. His voice was gentle but filled with desperate urgency as he whispered to her.

"It's going to be okay, Hale. Just keep your eyes closed. Don't look, no matter what."

Her small fingers clutched at his shirt, her whole body trembling. "Daddy," she whimpered, her voice low over the hissing of the approaching basilisk.

Kito slithered toward them, its shadow stretching across the floor like death itself.

Kent tried to move, tried to run, but as he turned, his eyes locked with Kito's.

His body stiffened instantly.

"No—" The word barely escaped his lips before his muscles froze, his breath halting in his chest.

I felt his fear, his anguish, even as the stone spread through him. He held onto Hale with everything he had left, shielding her within his arms, his last act of protection.

Hale sobbed against his chest, unaware of what was happening, unaware that the arms that held her would never move again.

Kent was turning to stone.

His face remained frozen in horror, his wide, unblinking eyes reflecting the red of the basilisk's gaze.

I couldn't breathe.

Then Rijor appeared in the doorway.

I barely registered his presence at first. Grief had me half blind, choking on itself, until I saw him move. He strode forward unharmed, untouched, as if he'd known exactly when to step in.

Protective glasses shielded his eyes from the basilisk's deadly gaze. Without a flicker of hesitation, he reached Kent, pried Hale from his petrified arms, and gathered her against his chest.

"You are safe with me, my niece," he murmured, his voice unnervingly calm.

My mind splintered.

Niece.

Hale's uncle.

Everything inside me twisted hard enough to hurt. Rijor was connected to Lorraine. He had known. He had known this would happen. He had played all of us, me, Arisen, Kent, pulling the strings so smoothly we never saw the trap until it snapped shut.

He had stood close, earned my trust, kept me in his confidence.

And now he held Hale.

I wanted to scream.

Kent was gone.

Kent was *dead*.

This—this was what true loss felt like.

A raw, gaping wound in my being, an agony that could never heal.

I hit my head with my fists, trying to force the visions away, trying to tear them from my mind. But they wouldn't stop. They wouldn't stop.

I fell to the ground, my hands clawing at my face as sobs racked through me.

It hurt. It hurt so much I thought I might break apart.

Kent was gone.

Rijor had betrayed us.

And Hale—Hale was in his arms.

A cold, terrible fury burned beneath my grief, rising like a fire in my chest.

I would not lose her too.

The basilisk in the Gaul Forest took a few steps back as it knew I needed space. It curled up in a corner farther from us and closed its eyes as if permitting the others to approach me.

Eliza and Rogers rushed to my side.

"Clara, what's happening? What did you see?" Eliza pressed urgently.

I struggled to find the words, my throat tightening as the images continued flashing through my mind. "It's Kent," I choked out. "He's gone. And…and… Polent and Pagos are under attack."

Rogers's eyes widened, and Eliza's face drained of color.

Arisen stepped forward, his breath sharp and unsteady, as if my pain had reached him. His hand found my shoulder—not just a gesture of comfort but a lifeline, grounding me in the moment. When I looked up, I saw the storm raging in his eyes—the quiet devastation, the fury barely restrained beneath the surface.

Without a word, he knelt in front of me, his forehead pressing briefly against mine. "You are not alone in this."

Our bond flared to life again. I reached through our link, pushing the visions into his mind, letting him see what I had seen.

The devastation. The betrayal. The looming war.

He saw it all—Vasa and Rijor's treachery, the castle in chaos, the amphisbaena restrained, the lifeless bodies of fallen elves. The basilisks tearing through Polent, the terror on the faces of those who had once trusted in the safety of their city.

I felt his body tense as he absorbed every image, every detail. And when he met my gaze again, the fury in his expression was no longer restrained.

Now, he understood.

"We must stop them," I whispered, trembling. "Commander Vasa and Rijor are behind this. They have orchestrated this, and they won't stop until they've destroyed everything."

There was nothing more I wanted to do than to try to make it to Polent to revive Kent, but deep down, I knew it wouldn't work. It almost seemed like a cruel joke; I could revive the deadliest creatures, but not who I loved the most.

"There's a reason this basilisk shared these visions with you. Clara, Destiny chose you—twice now. You've survived where others have not. The magic of this forest is weak, but it has gathered itself around you, and your bond with this basilisk is proof of that. Your heart, your family, and your Destiny will save our nations."

The basilisk ruffled its scales, almost as if acknowledging Arisen's words.

"Clara, I do not know what you saw, but Destiny has chosen you for a second time to see this through, and we will be here throughout the journey. We will help you, and we will fight alongside you," Eliza added.

The visions showed me what I needed to do—bring Hale back and settle the score with Rijor. He had no idea what was coming. I approached the basilisk, which had stayed curled up in a massive dome, and touched its head. This was the strongest bond I had ever felt with any creature, and somehow, I knew it would let me ride it. It nudged my hand gently, offering reassurance.

I shared with the group all the visions I had seen, including the betrayals and deaths that had happened because of them. The only place I hadn't connected with an animal or seen visions from was my hometown, the city of Raster.

"Eliza, you were the last person in Raster. How do you think they are doing without Destiny?" I asked.

"Without magic flowing through the walls of Ebony, the city wouldn't survive, and by now, the inner sectors are likely underwater. However, Raster is the least of your worries; you were right to bring us to Marcos. Arisen and I were able to plan an escape route with him that would get all the citizens to safety. Marcos knew what signs to watch for. Everyone in Raster will be safe, and we can rebuild the city once we return," Eliza explained.

Arisen walked closer to me. He stood between the head of the basilisk and me. "I never trusted Commander Vasa, so I left clear mandates to our army that if Marcos contacted them, they were to evacuate the city."

I took a deep breath at the news. Raster was fine, but Polent and Pagos were not. I had not seen Llorent in my visions, which worried me. The elves and humans from all three nations needed us.

Now, I just needed to figure out how to ride this enormous creature.

CHAPTER 49

From Clara's Diary

I approached the basilisk's side, running my hand along its rough, textured scales. Power pulsed beneath its skin, raw and untamed, connecting with my magic. The basilisk turned its head, watching me with those red, unblinking eyes, and then it lowered its body slightly, offering me a way to climb up.

After one final glance at the group, I grabbed a large scale and hoisted myself onto the basilisk's back. It remained perfectly still, its calm presence steadying me as it deliberately adjusted its body to help me climb. I scrambled upward, the texture beneath my hands rough and warm, every shift of muscle beneath its skin a reminder of the immense power coiled beneath me.

Reaching the top, I settled just behind the creature's head, gripping the thick ridges of its scales for balance. The basilisk shifted subtly to give me a steadier seat, and for a moment I marveled at the bond between us, how effortlessly we moved in sync.

Then we were off.

The basilisk glided across the clearing, its massive body undulating with surprising grace. I leaned forward, tightening my grip to match its rhythm as it surged through the forest. The ground blurred beneath us in streaks of green and brown. Though it had wings, they were tightly folded, still healing from the fall. They fluttered faintly, lifting only inches at a time. I reached down and ran my fingers gently along its injured sides.

"Soon," I whispered, the promise soft on my breath. "When the magic is restored, you'll heal. You'll fly again."

A few times, I nearly slipped, but each time the basilisk adjusted instinctively, keeping me steady. The wind whipped through my hair, the cold sting of speed biting into my skin as we tore through the woods.

Then the forest opened up.

The basilisk slowed, gliding to a stop at the edge of the sanguivoras' camp. It lowered its head, allowing me to slide to the ground with ease. I landed softly, crouching low.

The camp was still. For a moment, it seemed deserted, just the soft flicker of lanterns inside the tents and the occasional figure moving by the fire. But then I saw it: faint movement within the shadows. Figures, lying still but not asleep. Watching. Waiting.

Moments later, the sanguivoras began to stir. They gathered around the Destiny gate, forming a tight circle, their bodies tense, movements quick and focused. They were expecting something.

Even Lorraine was among them, standing in the center.

The basilisk trembled behind me, its body shivering from head to tail.

I felt it too, an invisible shift in the air, the pressure that comes before a storm breaks.

Behind me, soft footsteps signaled the arrival of the other Destined. They fanned out without a word, crouching low in the brush at my sides. We waited together, every muscle drawn tight with anticipation.

The Destiny gate began to hum, low at first, then louder, a pulse of dark magic vibrating through the ground. A dull blue light flared at its core, flickering like lightning trapped beneath water.

Three figures emerged.

Then two more.

My heart slammed against my ribs.

Llorent. Rijor. Hale.

Llorent struggled fiercely against two sanguivoras, his arms marked with raw, bleeding scratches. But Rijor… he walked freely. And in his arms was Hale.

Her terrified eyes scanned the crowd, her tiny body trembling.

I bit down on my tongue so hard I tasted blood. Every instinct in me screamed to run, to fight, to tear her from his arms. My muscles coiled, my body already half-poised to move. I could see nothing but Hale's face, wide-eyed and afraid, and the impossible truth that she was held by someone I once trusted. Rage surged up my throat, wild and choking. In that second, I didn't care who was watching, what plan we had, or what the consequences might be. I needed her safe. I needed her with me.

Arisen's hand clamped around my arm, firm and steady, stopping me before I could leap. He didn't look at me; he didn't have to. He could feel it through the bond. He knew I was seconds from ruining everything.

I forced myself to breathe.

Rijor. Elvish. Lorraine. Human.

They were siblings.

And they had Hale.

Lorraine stepped forward, eyes glittering with twisted triumph.

"Welcome, King Llorent," she purred, her voice a poisoned sweetness. "I hope your journey wasn't too unpleasant."

Llorent didn't flinch. His voice cut through the clearing, sharp and unwavering.

"Are you the one responsible for the destruction of my kingdom?" His eyes narrowed. "This madness ends now."

Lorraine laughed, a cold, hollow sound that echoed through the trees. "Oh, but it's already done. The Destined are dying in this forest. With them gone, there's nothing you, or anyone, can do to stop us."

Llorent's nostrils flared, his jaw tightening. "Where is Clara? Where are the others?"

Lorraine's smile curled into a mocking grin. "Ah, that's right. I heard there was something between you two. If you must know, she scurried off with her little group. Likely dead by now."

Llorent's gaze dropped to the ground, his long black hair falling forward to shadow his face.

Lorraine's tone turned sweetly vicious. "You care for her, don't you? Love her, maybe?" She laughed again, sharp and cruel. "I wish you could've seen her in pain. It was delightful."

Every fiber of me wanted to scream. I'm here. I'm alive. I wanted to bolt from the brush and throw myself into his arms, to feel again the safety I'd known in Polent. But I stayed hidden, teeth clenched, heart hammering against my ribs.

Then Rijor stepped forward, still holding Hale tight against his chest. She clung to him, trembling.

"We have everything we need," he said calmly, his voice steady and assured. "The balance of power is shifting. Soon, it will be ours."

Lorraine drifted toward Hale, her long, curved nails tracing the child's cheek. Hale's eyes widened in pure terror, her small body going still. She didn't cry. She was too afraid to make a sound. She was surrounded by monsters, and one of them was Rijor, a man who had stood beside us, only to betray everything.

"Now," Lorraine said, turning to the gathered sanguivoras, her voice thick with anticipation, "let us begin."

They moved in perfect, unnatural unison. Eyes glowing, bodies swaying, they lifted their voices in a chant that chilled my blood—low, guttural, like a creature dragged from the depths of the forest.

The air around the Destiny gate shimmered violently. Dark magic rippled out in waves, thick and suffocating, coiling through the clearing like smoke. The carvings on the gate pulsed wildly, light bursting from the stone in flashes that stung the eyes.

The energy spiked, raw and chaotic, as if the forest itself were recoiling.

"It's time," I whispered. "We have to stop them."

Eliza nodded, her crimson eyes blazing with fury, her jaw clenched tight enough to show the strain.

Arisen stepped forward. His voice cut through the rising chant. "This ends now."

His fists tightened at his sides, and the air shifted around him, thickening with a pressure that made my skin prickle.

The chanting faltered.

The sanguivoras paused. Some twitched. Others tilted their heads in eerie unison, as if pulled by the same string.

Lorraine turned slowly, deliberately, like a queen acknowledging a gnat. Her gaze locked onto Arisen's, cold and venomous.

"Oh, does it?" she sneered.

CHAPTER 50

From Clara's Diary

Led by Arisen, the group stepped out of the trees and into the wide circle where the sanguivoras stood waiting. From my vantage point, hidden alongside the basilisk, I watched everything unfold.

The sanguivoras moved, forming a perfect ring around the group. Their hollow, black eyes were fixed intently on the Destined, their pale, vein-covered faces twisted into faint smirks. Some tapped their long, blade-like nails against the ground in a slow, rhythmic taunt, while others stood unnervingly still. Despite their stance, they didn't attack. It was clear that Lorraine's orders held them back.

At the center of the circle stood Lorraine, her white tunic standing out against the darkness around her. Her presence demanded complete obedience from the creatures. She watched the Destined with a calm yet patronizing expression, as if savoring the moment.

Arisen led the Destined, his eyes betraying no fear. Eliza and Rogers flanked him; their faces set with determination. Matry and Reato followed closely behind, their fingers fidgeting as if ready to harness any trace of magic that might linger in the forest. Despite losing their Destined powers, their determination had not faltered—they were prepared to fight.

Lorraine's voice sliced through the silence. "I am surprised to see you all here," she said mockingly. "After all, why would a few powerless elves and humans dare to challenge us again?"

A low, guttural chuckle rose from the sanguivoras, their movements synchronized as they shifted slightly closer, yet still refraining from attacking.

Arisen ignored Lorraine's taunts, focusing solely on Rijor, who stood just behind her. Arisen approached him and yanked the gold pin from Rijor's chest.

"The betrayal you have brought upon me and Ebony is unforgivable."

Rijor sneered, showing no remorse. "Unforgivable? You speak of betrayal, Arisen, but you've always been ignorant in your naive desire to unite two groups. Dark magic is the only power strong enough to rule over all nations. Our people need strength, not your idealistic fantasies."

"You were my right-hand, Rijor. My trusted advisor for two years," Arisen replied, his voice rumbling with suppressed rage. "And yet you conspired, seeking power for yourself."

I stood next to the basilisk's tail, my heart pounding as I watched Lorraine closely. Her gaze wavered briefly in my direction as though sensing my presence. But she gave no indication of acknowledgment, her focus remaining on the confrontation before her. Her lips curled into a cold, knowing smile.

Through my link with Arisen, I sensed his inner turmoil. The only thing holding him back from beheading Rijor right then was Hale, still trapped in Rijor's arms, her face tear-streaked and trembling. Arisen would not risk her safety, even if it meant delaying his revenge.

Rijor laughed bitterly. "Your plans were doomed from the start. You and Queen Alondra cared too much about humans and their fragile alliances. Only dark magic can bridge the divide between our people. Only power can create unity."

"You are deluded," Arisen countered, stepping closer. "Your vision is one of tyranny, not unity. You seek to manipulate, not unite. This ends here, Rijor."

"You think you can stop us?" Rijor sneered. "Even if you still wielded your Destiny, you are no match for the power we now possess. Your time is over."

Eliza, Rogers, Matry, and Reato shifted into strategic positions, eyes sweeping the sanguivoras for any sign of movement. Outnumbered, they stayed ready.

The sanguivoras stirred, black eyes flicking between the Destined and Lorraine, waiting for her command.

"Your time is over," Lorraine said coldly. "This magic belongs to us now."

As Rijor tightened his grip on Hale, Arisen moved. In one swift, practiced motion, he wrenched Rijor's arm back, breaking his hold. Hale stumbled free, and Eliza caught her instantly, cradling her close. With shaking hands, Eliza tied a makeshift blindfold over Hale's eyes, shielding her from what was about to unfold.

My moment.

I swung onto the basilisk's back, its magic thrumming through me like a second heartbeat. Beneath me, the creature growled, a deep, guttural sound that trembled through the earth. Unease rippled through the sanguivoras. Their perfect unity faltered. Claws twitched. Feet shifted. The bravado they carried cracked, just enough.

Lorraine snapped her hand into the air, demanding silence. Her cold, calculating gaze didn't lift to meet mine. It fixed on the ground, as if she refused to grant me even that.

"Do not meet its eyes!" she barked.

Immediately, the sanguivoras obeyed. One by one, they turned away, shielding their faces with clawed hands, their eyes clamped shut. Even in their twisted forms, they knew better than to look into the basilisk's gaze.

I leaned forward and gave a single command. The basilisk surged ahead, gliding into the circle.

Lorraine's bitter smile didn't waver, but her jaw tightened. "You think this changes anything?" she hissed, her voice a venomous whisper that barely masked her frustration.

I didn't respond. My eyes stayed fixed on Hale and Eliza, blocking out the noise, the fear, and even Lorraine's taunts. With every step, the basilisk created a path, its deadly presence clearing the way. I slid off its back, landing firmly on the ground.

"Hale!" I called. The basilisk let out another growl, a warning that rolled across the clearing. I was going to get Hale back, no matter the cost.

Lorraine's voice cut through the air. "Give me back my daughter," she hissed, stepping forward.

"No," I said firmly, not even sparing her a glance. I rushed to Hale and took her from Eliza's arms. Her screams softened as I eased the blindfold away. "It's me," I whispered, my voice cracking as I pulled her tight against my chest. "I've got you. I love you so much."

Her sobs quieted, though her small body still trembled. I held her close, stroking her hair, murmuring whatever comfort I could find. I refused to let her go.

From the corner of my eye, I spotted Llorent. He was on the ground with his arms bound, his face pale and streaked with blood. My gut twisted, but I forced myself to focus. I couldn't fail him, or Hale.

"Stay with me," I whispered to Hale as I set her down gently and tied the blindfold back over her wet eyes. The basilisk moved closer, its glowing, unblinking stare pressing the sanguivoras into a wary retreat.

My heart pounded, but I forced myself to remain steady. I darted toward Llorent, my fingers trembling as I worked frantically to untie the ropes cutting into his wrists. His scratches were swollen and looked painfully infected, yet he didn't flinch, focusing entirely on me.

"Clara." His deep green eyes locked onto mine, shimmering with pain and profound relief.

"I've got you," I said softly. As the ropes fell free, I slipped my arm around his uninjured side and helped him to his feet. He winced in pain, his arm hanging awkwardly at his side, but his gaze never wavered from mine.

"You need to take Hale out of here," I urged. "Get her to safety. Please."

He nodded, lifting Hale into his arms despite his injuries. She clung to him, her tiny hands clutching his armor as if holding on for dear life. I stepped closer, placing my hands on both of them and pulling them into a fierce hug. The warmth of their presence grounded me for a brief, precious moment.

"Do you know where to go?" I asked, my voice cracking despite my best efforts to stay composed.

"We have a safe place. I'll get her there."

I nodded, swallowing the lump in my throat. "I'll see you there," I promised, though every fiber of my being ached at the thought of letting them go.

Llorent reached out, his fingers brushing a tear from my cheek. The tenderness of the gesture caught me off guard, and I froze as his emerald eyes searched mine. "We protect those we love. And I will always protect you and Hale."

As he moved toward the glowing portal in the distance, I couldn't tear my eyes away. My heart ached as I watched them leave, every step pulling them further from the danger that still surrounded us. I wanted to follow and ensure they were safe, but I knew my fight wasn't over. This was the only way to protect them.

Lorraine's furious scream echoed behind me, sharp and grating, but I didn't flinch. My focus sharpened as I returned to the circle, the basilisk at my side. I'd gotten Hale out.

"You took my daughter from me."

"You lost the privilege to call her that long ago."

Her lips curled into a bitter smile. "I am not the one who killed her father."

"No, you only killed her mother."

As if frustrated by our words, she moved closer with her eyes closed, her grin widening as though she could already taste victory. She stopped a few feet away, checked by the basilisk's low, menacing growl.

"Interesting to know you're riding a basilisk," Lorraine said coldly. "The one you left in Polent, with its blindfold loose, was responsible for Kent's death."

"Keep his name out of your mouth!" I screamed, the force of my anger trembling in my voice.

"Oh, Clara," she purred mockingly, her tone dripping with condescension. "How naïve you are. Do you think you're blameless? You brought him into this mess. His blood is on your hands."

"No, you brought all of us into this mess. It's on you. He died protecting his daughter. He died loving you."

"He was just as naïve as you," she said cruelly. "He saw all the signs of my plan, yet he refused to believe them, thinking I would stay and raise a family with him. I was already decades into this plan, leading this group from the magic of Hertm, and I finished the transformation as soon as I left. I will find Hale again. I'm not worried about that. Her mother will raise her."

The basilisk sensed my distress and let out a deep, guttural growl, its glowing eyes fixed on Lorraine. I took a deep breath, steadying myself. I couldn't let Lorraine's venomous words break me. I couldn't let her win.

"Do not believe a word she says. You had nothing to do with his death," Arisen said.

"You will never have Hale. This ends here."

With those words, the basilisk slithered closer to her. Lorraine's confidence faltered, her eyes flicking nervously from the ground.

I yearned to witness Lorraine's downfall firsthand. I wanted to see her fear, to experience her defeat. She needed to feel the same terror that Kent and the people of Polent had endured.

The basilisk's eyes locked onto Lorraine's, and instantly, the color drained from her face, her malicious grin frozen. She let out a strangled gasp, her body rigid and trembling. Her eyes turned a lifeless gray, her features contorting in a final, silent scream. Her strange body stiffened, then crumbled to the ground, a lifeless, stone-like husk.

The sight of Lorraine's death sent the sanguivoras into a rage. Their leader's defeat was more than just a tactical loss; it was a blow to their hive mind, their purpose, to what they had been planning for years. Their guttural growls and snarls traveled through the space, letting us know they were ready for war.

Their claws slashed through the air, and the once-ordered assembly became a chaotic battleground. Many of them tried to reach the gate, hoping they could escape as it remained open.

This was not a fair fight, and it was not intended to be. A basilisk would take all of this army down. And quick.

With a simple glance at the basilisk, it followed my command to stop all those attempting to reach the gate. The creature surged forward with astonishing speed, trampling dozens of sanguivoras in its path. Its massive body undulated as it moved, destroying tents and leveling the campgrounds.

Matry, Reato, and Eliza fought alongside the basilisk, their strength and training evident in every precise movement.

Reato stayed close to me, his cane transforming into a weapon. Though his movements were slower than the others, they were still devastating. Each swing of his cane struck a lethal blow, incapacitating many sanguivoras.

Eliza had positioned herself with a clear view of the battlefield, allowing her to target enemies from a distance. Every rock she hurled struck with incredible force, breaking through the creatures and disrupting their ranks.

With a mighty swipe of its injured wings, the basilisk sent a group of sanguivoras hurtling into the dead trees.

Suddenly, warmth surged through my marked arm, a familiar sensation that brought a renewed energy coursing through my veins. Destiny's bond was restoring itself, connecting us once again. The balance was shifting; as more sanguivoras fell, the forest regained its magic, empowering us.

Matry reacted first, her eyes glowing as she raised a protective barrier around us. "I can feel it," she whispered, her voice trembling with awe. "My Destiny is back."

Reato straightened, the cane in his hands crackling with newfound energy. He swung it with ease, its power amplifying his strikes.

Eliza moved with vigor. The boulders she lifted seemed almost weightless, her red eyes blazing. "This is it!" she shouted. "We can end this!"

The bond between me and the basilisk deepened, and its strength reflected our shared magic. I silently commanded it to continue its assault, and it obeyed, its glowing eyes scanning the battlefield for threats.

In mere minutes, the ground was littered with the lifeless bodies of the sanguivoras. The basilisk, now unchallenged, stood tall, its gaze surveying the aftermath.

Exhaustion washed over me, and I collapsed to my knees, overwhelmed by the magnitude of our accomplishments. I looked up at the creature and allowed our bond to break. The severance was like losing a part of myself, leaving behind a deep sadness. The basilisk let out a low, mournful growl before turning away, retreating into the forest's shadows.

As I regained my breath, my eyes found Rijor. He was frantically working to reopen the gate, desperation written across his face.

Arisen was the first to move. The glow of his mark pulsed rhythmically, mirroring the energy flowing through us all.

Arisen stopped just a few feet from Rijor, his hands empty, his breath controlled despite the rage simmering beneath his skin. He had never trusted Rijor completely—something about him had always felt *off*. He had shared this with me…back in Pitores, although neither of us could imagine this was what he was hiding.

But *this*—this level of treason—was beyond what even he had imagined.

"You have betrayed our people, Rijor," Arisen said, his voice steady despite the fury behind it. "You've twisted magic, manipulated lives, and condemned innocent people to suffering. Your hands are stained with the blood of those who trusted you."

Rijor's gaze glinted, calculating, searching for an escape. But there was none.

The confidence he had always worn like armor cracked, revealing his true feelings. *Fear.*

Arisen stepped closer. "Surrender now, and perhaps there will be mercy for you."

Rijor's face hardened. Whatever hesitation had flickered there vanished, replaced by something sharp and absolute. With a sneer, he drew his blade, a dark, unnatural thing whose enchanted surface seemed to drink in what little light survived in the clearing.

"I will not kneel to you," Rijor spat. "Not now. Not ever."

"So be it."

Rijor lunged first, his blade cutting a deadly arc through the air. Arisen dodged by instinct alone, twisting aside at the last moment. Unarmed, he had no choice but to evade, his body moving with ruthless precision as his mind tracked every angle, every opening, every mistake Rijor might make.

Rijor struck again, this time driving for Arisen's ribs. Arisen turned just enough for the blade to skim past him, and in that brief instant of imbalance, he saw it. An opening. A single beat where Rijor's guard faltered.

He moved fast, *too* fast for Rijor to react. With a sharp pivot, he grabbed Rijor's wrist, twisting it violently. Rijor let out a strangled gasp as his fingers spasmed, his grip loosening.

Arisen wrenched the blade from Rijor's grasp.

Rijor staggered back, shock flashing across his face, his hand clenching the empty space where his weapon had been.

Arisen didn't hesitate.

He surged forward, the dark blade now his own, slashing downward.

Rijor barely dodged, stumbling, his confidence crumbling with each step backward.

This was no longer a fight.

It was an execution.

Arisen advanced with the cold certainty of a king delivering justice. Rijor's desperation showed in every movement, erratic and frantic. He lunged wildly with his bare hands, but without his weapon, there was no precision, no control, only panic.

Arisen parried with ease, then drove the hilt of the sword into Rijor's gut. Rijor's breath burst out in a ragged gasp as he crumpled to his knees.

"It's over."

Rijor clutched his stomach, his breath ragged, but even as he knelt in defeat, his lips curled into a smirk. "You think you've won?" he rasped. "You can kill me, but the darkness I've set into motion will not die with me. It will spread."

Arisen didn't waver.

"The difference between us, Rijor," he said, gripping the hilt tightly, "is that you believe darkness is unstoppable. I know better."

With one swift motion, Arisen drove the sword up into Rijor's chest.

Rijor's breath hitched, his body jolting as the blade sank deep. His eyes went wide, not only with pain but with shock, as if even he hadn't truly believed this was how it would end.

His lips parted, but no words came.

Then, slowly, he slumped forward, his chest hitting the cold ground.

Silence fell over the forest.

Arisen stood over him, chest rising and falling, hands still locked around the weapon that had ended Rijor's life. His face was unreadable, his gaze fixed on the man who had once been an ally, someone who had walked among us, fought beside us, and lied to us all.

"It's done."

I swallowed the lump in my throat, my eyes shifting from Arisen to Rijor's lifeless body.

We had won.

But at what cost?

CHAPTER 51

With our Destiny restored, we approached the gate. It loomed before us, its frame tangled with vines, green and brown tendrils curling into every crevice.

We moved carefully, stepping around the lifeless bodies of the sanguivoras scattered across the clearing. Their corpses were pale and grotesque, dark blood sinking into the earth beneath them.

As we moved closer, the gate began to pulse softly but steadily, as if sensing the magic flowing through us. Arisen stepped forward first. His mark glowed with golden light, standing out against the shadowy clearing, and he pressed his palm to the stone.

At once, the gate stirred to life. The vines recoiled, sliding back as carvings emerged from the surface, interwoven leaves, celestial patterns, rivers etched in elegant arcs. The symbols lit with a soft, ethereal blue.

I stepped beside him, my hand trembling as I touched the gate. A low hum resonated from deep within the stone, growing louder as the others joined us one by one. The Elvish word *Enter* appeared.

Light burst from the symbols, spreading outward in radiant arcs. The remaining vines shriveled and fell away. The air crackled with energy as the glow intensified, nearly blinding.

Unlike before, when it had resisted the sanguivoras, the gate welcomed us. It opened without struggle, like an old friend recognizing its own.

Eliza was the first to step forward. "I am going to Pagos," she said firmly, her voice cutting through the gate's hum. "My country needs a new leader."

Standing beside her, Rogers gazed deeply into her eyes and nodded. "I will always support my Destined." They exchanged a brief, meaningful look before stepping through the gate together. The swirling light enveloped them, fading as they crossed the threshold.

Matry and Reato faced each other. "The mountains of Pitores always know how to heal us," Matry said with a gentle smile. Reato nodded, his hand briefly brushing hers as a sign of comfort and understanding. Without saying a word more, they left the forest, their silhouettes disappearing into the bright portal.

I turned to Victor, the last remaining Destined. He stood apart, and it struck me how solitary he appeared amidst the glowing remnants of magic. Losing Karlos had taken a heavy toll on him, and his grief was evident. Without his Destined, he would eventually lose the mark that served as a reminder of their bond.

As he watched everyone leave, his eyes were shadowed with sorrow. He took a deep breath and straightened his shoulders as he composed himself. "I am going to assist King Llorent and the people of Polent. This will help with my grief." With one final, lingering look at us, he stepped through the gate, leaving behind the forest and everything it had taken from him.

As the last of our companions left, I stood beside Arisen, the swirling portal casting its glow on us. The forest around us was quiet, except for the gentle rustling of leaves and the distant chirping of birds emerging after the battle. The air felt lighter, as if the land itself was beginning to recover.

"Looks like it's our turn," I said, attempting to step toward the gate, but a sharp pain shot through my back, halting me in my tracks.

"Are you okay?"

Before I could answer, I collapsed. The world dimmed as unconsciousness claimed me, but I wasn't entirely gone. I felt everything: Arisen's arms catching me, the panic in his voice as he whispered my name, the steady beat of his heart as he carried me.

Though I couldn't open my eyes or respond, I was aware of the days passing. At first, it felt like sinking deeper into a void, weighed down by the exhaustion that had overtaken me. My body had reached its limit, and Destiny had forced me into rest. Without the forest's intervention, I wouldn't have survived.

Time blurred. Even in that haze, I sensed Arisen's care, the way he stroked my hair, gave me water, and kept me warm. I felt his concern like a hand on my back, his quiet strength tethering me to the world.

With each passing day, Destiny worked within me. It repaired what was broken, weaving through my veins like threads of light. I could feel my strength returning, but it was more than just healing. It was transforming me, sharpening and expanding who I was. The magic reached into the depths of my Destiny and unlocked parts of me I hadn't known existed. My connection to the natural world deepened until it felt instinctive. I knew that when I woke, I would be able to communicate with animals in ways I'd never thought possible.

Images flickered through my mind: a dragon spitting fire, a hawk cutting across open sky. They weren't dreams. They were the final piece of my metamorphosis as a Destined settling into place.

When I finally opened my eyes, the sound of rushing water greeted me. My body felt different, stronger, clearer, more attuned to the magic around me. The forest pulsed with life, and its energy welcomed me back.

Arisen was nearby, relaxing under the waterfall. The sight of him took my breath away. His damp, glistening green hair clung to his chiseled jawline. Water cascaded down his muscular shoulders and chest, catching sunlight on his skin and illuminating every defined line. He moved with quiet strength, his eyes closed in a rare moment of tranquility.

When he opened his eyes, their vivid blue specks locked onto mine. My heart stirred, and for a moment, I was unsure if I had woken up.

"You're awake." He stepped closer. "How do you feel?"

"Stronger… thanks to you."

The sight of him, so raw and powerful, made my heart race. Arisen had always been handsome, but he looked different. The sunlight glistened off the golden mark on his neck as he emerged fully from the waterfall, water dripping from his toned body.

He smiled softly, closing the distance between us with slow steps. "You've been recuperating; your body needed more time. You overexerted your magic, Clara. It nearly took everything from you. It looks like you're ready to go back to Polent."

"Thank you for taking care of me."

"It was my honor, Clara. Our Destinies are intertwined after all. I will always be here for you."

"What do we do now?" I asked, leaning my back against the rocky wall for support.

Arisen sighed, looking away briefly before meeting my gaze again. "I must go to Pagos to pay my debt to Queen Franes, but you can return to Polent for Hale and King Llorent."

I had not considered that we would be separated. "You never told me what you offered Queen Franes."

"That is between the Queen of Pagos and me."

"You can't keep secrets from me, Arisen. We're Destined," I insisted.

"That is true," he said softly, "but my Destiny is to protect you, and what I offered will remain private, for your sake."

I stumbled as I moved closer to him. He reached out instinctively to steady me, but I brushed him off. "You don't get to help me if you won't let me know how I can help you."

"This is not something you need to worry about. I did it willingly for the well-being of all of us."

"That's not good enough," I snapped, my emotions spilling over. "You can't just make these decisions and expect me to follow. I have a right to know!"

He stepped closer, his eyes locking onto mine.

"And I have the right to protect you!" His voice was low, fierce. "It is my Destiny. You have no idea what I've sacrificed, what I've endured."

His words sent my heart racing. "What do you mean by that? You've never told me what your Destiny is."

He exhaled, his gaze never leaving mine. "I have," he said softly, "and I just did."

I stared at him, his words sinking in like ripples through me. He wasn't talking about duty. He wasn't talking about fate or obligation.

He was talking about *me*.

Arisen reached out, his fingers grazing mine, barely touching yet sending heat curling through my veins.

"Wasn't it obvious?" he murmured, his voice softer now, almost tender. "My Destiny has always been you, Clara. Protecting you, standing by your side, keeping you safe, even when you refused to let me." His thumb brushed over the back of my hand. "You are the light that guided me. The reason I could see an ending to all of this. Every moment, every choice, it was always you."

I swallowed hard. My lips parted, but no words came.

His hand traced upward, fingertips barely grazing my jaw. "Why do you think I offered my very essence to Queen Franes?" His eyes darkened, the gold in them burning like embers. "It was for you, Clara. Anything for you."

A sharp breath left me as my mind spun. I had spent so long questioning our connection, searching for meaning in the way our lives had tangled together, but he had known. He had always known.

"Arisen…"

He tilted my chin up, gentle but firm, forcing me to meet his gaze.

"You don't have to say anything," he murmured. "I will always stand by your side, Clara. That is my Destiny. The forest gave me this power because it knew we had a fighting chance."

My heart clenched at his words. This was more than duty, more than magic. This was a bond neither of us had chosen, yet one that had become inescapable.

My breath quickened, my pulse hammering beneath my skin. Arisen's chest rose and fell in time with mine, and for a second, we hovered on the edge of an irreversible moment.

His hands cupped my face, and before I could think, before I could breathe, his lips crashed against mine.

The kiss was fire and fury, desperation and relief all at once. My hands shot to his shoulders, clutching him as if he were the only solid thing left in my world. For a heartbeat I resisted, the remnants of my anger flickering between us, but it didn't last. His Destiny shattered every wall I had built, melted every protest on my lips. I kissed him back with everything I had, pouring into him all the frustration, the longing, the unspoken words that had hovered between us for too long.

His mouth moved against mine with a hunger that stole the air from my lungs. His hands slid to my waist, pulling me closer, and I felt the heat of him fold into me, anchoring me in the storm of emotions crashing through my chest.

Nothing else existed. Only the taste of him, the feel of him, the way our bodies fit together as if Destiny had woven us from the same thread.

Time lost its shape.

We finally pulled apart, our foreheads still touching, our breaths blending in the tight space between us. My fingers clung to his shoulders, reluctant to let go. His hands stayed on my waist, possessive and steadying, as if he could hold me still just by touching me.

The anger that had once burned between us had dissolved, replaced by something far more dangerous: need.

"What has Destiny done to us?" I whispered.

His lips brushed my forehead, lingering. "It's not what Destiny has done to us," he said softly. "It's what we've always been."

His arms tightened around me like a vow. "And I will protect you, Clara," he promised, voice low and rough. "No matter what it takes."

I knew, in that moment, that nothing would ever be the same.

CHAPTER 52

From Clara's Diary

The past year living in Polent had gone by quickly. Once on the brink of ruin, this country recovered in ways that astounded me and the court. Llorent's efforts brought unity and purpose to his people, and the castle, once a wreck from the basilisks, was now full of life and order.

Both Llorent and Hale warmly welcomed me. The first few months were spent caring for the injured, and with Destiny's help, I was able to help many Polentians heal more quickly. Over time, the markets regained their vibrancy, filled with merchants and laughter. Children played freely in the streets, and music filled the air.

When I walked among the people, they greeted me warmly, not just as a Destined but also as Llorent's partner. Hale often accompanied me, carrying books she had borrowed from the library. She had become braver, but the basilisk still haunted her nightmares. While she enjoyed watching me train with the creatures on the training grounds, the mere mention of the basilisk made her small hands clutch mine tightly. She refused to go anywhere near them.

The basilisk Kito vanished after the battle, retreating into the swamps of Polent. Some villagers said they saw him lurking around the marshes. As if he had chosen solitude over contact, as if he also needed to heal. That was a bond I refused to reopen, not wanting to see through his eyes again or feel his emotions.

After most of the restoration here was finished, Victor returned to Pitores with Matry and Reato. Together, they stayed in the Destined house, regaining their strength and recovering from the toll of the war. Although Victor had lost his mark with Karlos's death, his knowledge and remaining power made him a valuable ally. The gates of Destiny still recognized him, allowing him to keep a connection to the magic.

Eliza kept me informed about her plans with Rogers, though her updates were always shrouded in cryptic language. She had secluded herself somewhere in Pagos, waiting for the right moment to carry out a strategy she refused to disclose fully. Her answers were vague whenever I inquired about Arisen. She mentioned hearing that he was in Raster but admitted she knew little beyond that. A week ago, I received her final parestine. Without an explanation, she stopped responding and writing.

Polent thrived, its wounds healing as quickly as the land allowed, but something in me remained unsettled. The bond with Arisen had grown silent. I reached for him through our connection, only to be met with emptiness.

I sought information where I could. Marcos had been working closely with Arisen to rebuild Raster and assured me that Arisen had thrown himself into his work. "He doesn't talk about anything else,"

Marcos admitted when I pressed him. "He spends most of his time in Pagos."

Despite the peace around me, I still felt uneasy. What made Arisen retreat so completely? Why did he shut me out? Was he in Raster or Pagos? Hale and Llorent kept me here, and I wouldn't leave them, but part of me longed to understand what had gone wrong. I promised myself that no matter the answer, I wouldn't leave Hale again. I couldn't bear the thought of making her feel abandoned. She lost her father; she wouldn't lose me too.

On some evenings, Llorent and I would venture to the bridge. Suspended over the rushing river, the structure creaked gently underfoot, surrounded by the tranquil hum of the gardens. Countless nights were spent there, reliving memories and creating new ones.

One night, beneath the high-hanging moon, bathed in its pale silver glow, Llorent's arms came around me from behind. His chest pressed against my back, solid and warm, his breath a whisper against my ear. His touch should have grounded me, but instead, it sent my mind spiraling.

His lips found the curve of my neck, lingering, teasing, and I shivered beneath his touch. His hands moved to pin me against the railing, his fingers trailing downward. Like so many nights before, he knew exactly how to unravel me. His hands skimmed the fabric of my dress, lifting it inch by inch. The cool night air bit into my skin, making the heat that pooled between us all the more consuming.

When he finally entered me, my body tensed, overwhelmed by the rawness of it. I bit down on his shoulder, stifling the cry that nearly escaped, my nails digging into his arms as I tried to ground myself against the intensity of it all.

The bridge groaned beneath us as his pace accelerated, his grip tightening, each movement pulling me farther from thought, deeper into sensation. My breaths became ragged, my fingers clutching at him as pleasure built, relentless and consuming. His low, guttural moans echoed in my ears, merging with the rush of water below.

And yet—

Even as I lost myself in the moment, even as my body responded to his in ways I couldn't deny, my thoughts drifted.

As much as I wished I could let go completely, accept this, let it be enough.

Another part of me knew the truth. Knew that no matter how many nights I spent here, no matter how deeply Llorent touched me, no matter how much he claimed me—

Arisen's silence would always be louder. His lack of contact left me bereft.

I clenched my eyes shut and let Llorent's body steady me, let him chase away again the thoughts I wasn't ready to face. I would not leave this place. I would never leave Hale alone again, and that was more important than what my Destiny was telling me.

It had to be.

AUTHOR'S NOTE

Thank you, thank you, thank you for taking the time to read my first novel! Writing this book has been a lifelong dream… one that started when I was a Twilight-obsessed teenager, dreaming of being bitten by a vampire, seduced by a ghost, and loved by an elf like Legolas. I was utterly immersed in the world of romantasy back then, and I'm thrilled to be still just as enchanted twenty years later (wow, that feels like forever ago!).

I sincerely hope you enjoyed reading this novel as much as I enjoyed writing it. Since this is my debut, please forgive any lingering grammatical errors or typos. I did my best to catch everything, but I may have missed a few… so thank you for your patience!

This book wouldn't exist without a few key people in my life.

First, to my incredible husband. Thank you for taking care of our daughter while I was lost in this world. You also deserve credit for coming up with the name "Destiny Gates" … yes, that was all you!

Verónica, my daughter y mi vida. You rewired my brain the moment I became a mom, and now I get to experience a love like no other. Becoming your mother helped me write Hale with the tenderness, strength, and fierce protection that only a parent knows.

But please wait until you're 18 to read this book. Seriously. Love you endlessly.

To my besties who read countless drafts:

Rachel, your feedback was invaluable. This book wouldn't be half as strong without your insight. Love you friend <3.

Shabnam, your encouragement gave me the confidence to keep going. Fun fact: the sanguivoras were *absolutely* inspired by your nails. Shab is the best work bestie…the one who's more like a sibling and somehow always knows when you need a reality check or a coffee.

Monica, you bring so much magic into my life. Your love for the moon shone through these pages. Reader, if you ever want to add a little magic to your own life, follow her page @baringpetalslv to see her incredible work. Her magical candles are the very definition of enchantment.

Huge thanks to my talented cover designer, @ashtonmsmithdesigns—it was an absolute pleasure working with you.

And finally, thank you, dear reader. You chose to spend your time with this story, and that means everything to me. Time is precious, and I am deeply grateful that you gave some of yours to this world I created.

If you'd like to connect, you can reach me via Instagram at @vanessa.mari22. I would love to connect with you, so please send me a DM!

With gratitude and magic,

Vanessa Mari

Vanessa Mari is a mom to an amazing 4-year-old, a wife to a pretty great man, and an unapologetic lover of all things romantasy. Originally from Puerto Rico, she brings her cultural roots and imagination into everything she writes. Vanessa has previously published academic research in education, but this marks her debut into the world of fiction. She's thrilled to share her first book with readers who believe in magic, love, and a little bit of destiny.